PRAISE FOR
The Mark of the Vampire Queen

"Superb . . . This is erotica at its best with lots of sizzle and a love that is truly sacrificial. Joey W. Hill continues to grow as a stunning story-teller."
—*A Romance Review*

"Joey W. Hill never ceases to amazes us . . . She keeps you riveted to your seat and leaves you longing for more with each sentence."
—*Night Owl Romance*

"Dark and richly romantic. There are scenes that will make you laugh and cry, and those that will be a feast for your libido and your most lascivious fantasies. The ending will surprise and leave you clamoring for more."
—*Romantic Times*

"Fans of erotic romantic fantasy will relish *The Mark of the Vampire Queen*."
—*The Best Reviews*

PRAISE FOR
The Vampire Queen's Servant

"This book should come with a warning: intensely sexy, sensual story that will hold you hostage until the final word is read. The story line is fresh and unique, complete with a twist."
—*Romantic Times*

"Hot, kinky, sweating, hard-pounding, oh-my-god-is-it-hot-in-here-or-is-it-just-me sex . . . so compelling it just grabs you deep inside. If you can keep an open mind, you will be tr[. . .] your heartstrings."
—[. . .]*views*

continued . . .

Berkley Heat Titles by Joey W. Hill

THE VAMPIRE QUEEN'S SERVANT

THE MARK OF THE VAMPIRE QUEEN

A VAMPIRE'S CLAIM

BELOVED VAMPIRE

Berkley Sensation Titles by Joey W. Hill

A MERMAID'S KISS

A WITCH'S BEAUTY

Anthologies

UNLACED

(with Jaci Burton, Jasmine Haynes, and Denise Rossetti)

BELOVED VAMPIRE

Joey W. Hill

HEAT
New York

THE BERKLEY PUBLISHING GROUP
Published by the Penguin Group
Penguin Group (USA) Inc.
375 Hudson Street, New York, New York 10014, USA
Penguin Group (Canada), 90 Eglinton Avenue East, Suite 700, Toronto, Ontario M4P 2Y3, Canada
(a division of Pearson Penguin Canada Inc.)
Penguin Books Ltd., 80 Strand, London WC2R 0RL, England
Penguin Group Ireland, 25 St. Stephen's Green, Dublin 2, Ireland (a division of Penguin Books Ltd.)
Penguin Group (Australia), 250 Camberwell Road, Camberwell, Victoria 3124, Australia
(a division of Pearson Australia Group Pty. Ltd.)
Penguin Books India Pvt. Ltd., 11 Community Centre, Panchsheel Park, New Delhi—110 017, India
Penguin Group (NZ), 67 Apollo Drive, Rosedale, North Shore 0632, New Zealand
(a division of Pearson New Zealand Ltd.)
Penguin Books (South Africa) (Pty.) Ltd., 24 Sturdee Avenue, Rosebank, Johannesburg 2196,
South Africa

Penguin Books Ltd., Registered Offices: 80 Strand, London WC2R 0RL, England

This is an original publication of The Berkley Publishing Group.

Copyright © 2009 by Joey W. Hill.
Cover art by Don Sipley.
Cover design by George Long.
Text design by Tiffany Estreicher.

PRINTING HISTORY
Heat trade paperback edition / August 2009

Library of Congress Cataloging-in-Publication Data

Hill, Joey W.
  Beloved vampire / Joey W. Hill.—1st ed.
    p. cm.
  ISBN 978-0-425-22795-4
  1. Vampires.—Fiction. I. Title.
  PS3608.I4343B45 2009
  813'.6—dc22

                              2009001066

PRINTED IN THE UNITED STATES OF AMERICA

10 9 8 7 6 5 4 3 2 1

BELOVED VAMPIRE

1

THE Sahara had once been green. Lush, a verdant land support-ing civilizations. Then the Earth's orbit changed, the sun came a little closer, and the land altered, becoming a desert that swallowed armies. It had happened three or four thousand years ago, barely a blink in the nine-billion-year life of Earth, but in that blink, Heaven and Hell had switched places. Had it been cosmic boredom? A need for a different perspective? Life giver, life taker.

Jessica wondered which face the Sahara preferred. Since she'd come here to die, it was a point of interest. Barely two years ago, her body had been vigorous and fertile. Now it, too, was a barren skele-ton that repelled most sensible life forms. She felt almost at home here.

As the largest desert in the world, this was a place where one could walk for days—if one had the constitution of a camel—and see no other human life. But the history of the area was still mapped on this wasteland, if one had trained eyes. Though she'd had to learn about it primarily from within the walls of her prison, she'd done little else of importance during the past several years but study this, her final destination.

She didn't count killing Lord Raithe, her vampire master, as im-portant. The reason she was dying now was a mere dot in the overall scheme of things, as was the dead vampire who'd caused her wasting illness. Creatures lived, creatures died, and their bones became sand like this. At least Raithe would never torment anyone again. *That* mattered, though in truth, she'd been sick for so long, she couldn't even recall why that was as important as it had once seemed.

In contrast, Farida had remained significant to her. In the midst of a life so horrible Jess often thought she'd already died and somehow deserved Hell—though she couldn't recall her crime—Farida had given her a spark of light. The body's desire to live was stronger than anything, even despair. Maybe that was why she'd connected with a woman who had chosen love and then lost everything.

From the very first moment Jess opened the ancient binding and discovered the written memories of the sheikh's daughter who had lived more than three hundred years ago, a bond had formed between them. As a former archaeology student, Jess knew how unlikely it was that the journal truly belonged to a Bedouin woman, for precious few *men* of those tribes knew how to read or write then, let alone in English. Yet Farida had spoken in her memoir passionately, vibrantly, of a love worth any torment, and Jessica had been pulled into her story despite her skepticism.

Between being on the run as a fugitive and hoping she had the strength to keep going the next day, Jess had read Farida's words. Hiding in dank places that only society's forgotten frequented, there was nothing else to break her thoughts except the trickling background of an internal hourglass, the sands of her life running out. Her cells were being subsumed in that flow of sand, as if she were becoming part of a place like Farida's Sahara. But she was okay with that. There were those who believed that the Sahara would return to greenness, that the cycles of climate change would evolve again, the sun getting less hot and the rains increasing. A different way of life would return.

After Jess had killed Raithe, Farida's journal and the diamonds were the only things worth risking her life to slip back into his mansion to retrieve. Maybe even then, in her subconscious, she'd realized where she was going and what she was going to do with the short remainder of her life. It was no more fantastic than what her life had been for the past five years. And no one would look for her in Africa.

When she'd arrived in the Sahara, she realized that those who wrote of it as a desolate place, devoid of life, didn't know it. There *was* life here. Not just in the few peoples and creatures that called it home, but in the ghosts that whispered, finding voice through the movement of the sand, a haunting noise like blowing across the top of a soda bottle. She knew what that sounded like, for she'd done it as a teenager, clustered with her friends on the curb outside the Quik-Stop with soda and Cheetos, eyeing the boys that came in after school. Boys who eyed them right back.

God, that was a long time ago. She held those memories to her occasionally like a favorite doll, even as she knew the act was closer to that of a mother holding a dead baby.

The three men she'd hired thought her a madwoman, of course. Take a dying woman out to a remote part of the desert that wasn't on any map and help her find the marker for a dead woman's grave. But they were willing to indulge her because they were going to be rich men. She'd shown them the jewels, told them they'd be theirs if they helped her. She thanked whatever capricious deity watched over fools that she'd had the foresight to steal those diamonds. Raithe had had a hoard to rival a dragon's, so they'd never be missed.

Now, as she rolled the comfort of familiar thoughts through her head, a reminder of where she'd been, where she was going, she looked over the endless stretch of dunes. The breathtaking artistry of the wind upon them rivaled the greatest sculptors of the ages, and the sun collaborated, providing a different view with each degree it descended. But even that beauty couldn't distract her from the fact night was drawing close. God, she hated darkness. But the stars would help her find Farida tonight at last.

Reading the words of that diary made her feel as if she were in Farida's tent, where they cuddled on the pillows as girlfriends, pressed forehead to forehead. In the darkest time of night, Farida whispered in her ear. While everything in life could be taken away by uncontrollable forces, there was always a choice left. Something overlooked, if one didn't let fear overwhelm desire.

Farida's choice had been an incomparable man. Jessica's would be where she wanted to die.

Killing Raithe had seemed impossible, of course. Since he'd been able to read her mind as easily as she read Farida's pages, he'd

delighted in punishing her every time she'd thought of murder . . .
or of running. Eventually, she'd learned to make her mind blank,
a dumb, self-lobotomized creature who could endure anything,
her life merely a muddy haze of images and obstacles to avoid.
But that hadn't been sufficient. Raithe wanted her full attention and
enthusiasm.

Vampires were not only brutal and ruthless. They knew humans
so well that they could use kindness, cunning and desire to bait a
captive into awareness, no matter how often their subsequent cruelty
sent her scrambling back into the deepest cell of her mind. Once or
twice, she made the mistake of believing he could do no worse to her,
but evil was bottomless.

Oh, Jesus. Was she destined to follow him to Hell? Some said
vampire servants followed their Masters into the afterlife. Another
good reason not to die any sooner than she had to. She'd already
proven the will was far stronger than X-rays and blood tests. Though
Death wouldn't wait forever, she'd faced down the Grim Reaper and
made him blink, made him back the hell off, at least until she accomplished this one thing.

"So we wait here until dark, then?" Harry, one of her trio of op-
portunists, stood at her side.

While she needed the three men for passage and protection, for
their knowledge of the language and the Sahara, she would have preferred to do this alone. However, there were things she couldn't do
by herself anymore. Harry had put her before him on his camel a
couple of times when she fainted into one of her hours-long stupors.
She'd warned him of it, instructed him to keep moving no matter
what. Time was too short for her. She'd given him the compass heading and some landmarks, but not all of them. They thought they
were seeking only a grave marker, not the tomb, her true goal.

When they found the obelisk, she'd have them leave her there.
She wasn't sure she could make the final leg of the journey on her
own, but she certainly wasn't going to dishonor Farida by exposing
her secret resting place to others. She owed that not only to her, but
to the brokenhearted spirit of the man who'd loved her enough to
place her there.

"So are we in the right place?" Harry repeated patiently. They'd gotten used to her silences, her slow response time.

"I think so." She considered the lay of the dunes, checked her compass and then shuffled through her sheaf of notes, checked the GPS. They'd made camp a couple hours before and her camel's resting body was warm and solid at her back, a rhythmic vibration as the creature chewed her cud.

Harry sat down and leaned against his pack, considering her. "You know, you remind me of crazy Daisy Bates. She lived in the Outback for years among the blacks. Was as at home there as a baked lizard."

She glanced up at him. Harry was an expatriate Australian, one who'd lived in and around the Sahara for the past twenty years, a swagman gone walkabout far from home. He boasted he'd come here because he'd heard tell it was even hotter than Oz. He'd stayed merely to test it out. In reality, he'd left because he was wanted for killing a man in Queensland, a cuckolded husband who'd come after him with a knife.

Still, he wasn't a bad sort. Thieves and cutthroats with some type of moral code were the best partners for a fugitive, and she'd done well in that, for the most part. He could have been the type to take her out into the desert and leave her during one of her unconscious spells, going back to try for the jewels she'd promised.

Of course, she'd also made it clear that the bank would be expecting a specific code word from each of them before they'd release the jewels. She was too weak to do anything but die under torture, so any temptation Harry or Mel might have to beat it out of her before they got her to her destination was obviously futile.

Mel was far more unscrupulous, but Harry kept him in line. Despite her aversion to being touched, she worried little about traveling alone with them, and not because Harry's tastes didn't run to forcing women. She was skin stretched over bone. Her hair was brittle, lackluster. If she brushed it, it came out. She was as likely to vomit up a meal as digest it, and her hacking cough kept the clothes she wore flecked with blood and sputum so that sometimes she was too tired to wipe it away. The odor coming from her body was noxious, that of a sick and dying animal. The men tended to sit upwind, though Harry and Dawud were more courteous and discreet about it.

Though her flesh was desirable only to buzzards at this point, Dawud, her third man and native guide, often gently reminded her to keep her head and face covered. At one time, his kindly meant reproof would have rankled. Now she didn't mind wearing the head covering. Before they had left the known routes, it saved her questions from passing caravans. It also provided an unspoken barrier. She'd come from a modern world, full of the ideals of equal rights and independence for women. Yet in this culture a woman who demonstrated modesty, who respectfully kept herself covered, sent out a signal that she was deserving of respect. Didn't always work, of course, because the world was also full of those who did as they pleased, took what they wanted. But to survive to her final goal she'd utilize any protections the world offered, no matter how flimsy.

She liked young Dawud very much, besides. He hoped to use the funds to bring irrigation and education to his village, and she wanted him to have that. For him specifically, she made it clear to the other two that the bank would *not* be giving Dawud the jewels directly upon successful completion of their task, but handling the liquidation and management of funds for the village in trust. Mel and Harry could plan to rob and kill each other as they saw fit after they got their share, but she wasn't risking an innocent.

In fact, she could have done with just Dawud, except he was a guide and interpreter, not hired muscle. Plus, it would take two strong men to shift the obelisk. Dawud might not be willing to touch it, because of carved warnings on the stone: another way Farida's lover had protected her body, though he'd been unable to save her life.

The sun was setting now, the stars starting to appear, one by one. She watched them like beads on a rosary, a mantra of hope said over each one. She was so tired. Of course, she didn't remember what *not* being tired was, or sick. But it was almost over.

Would Jack, her murdered fiancé, have understood why this had become so important to her? If so, he'd have known her better than she knew herself back then. Until all this had happened, she'd had a laughable understanding of what sacrifice and true determination meant.

The two of them had been given so little time to know each other, but he'd been willing to die for her. When not a split-second instinct, such a premeditated sacrifice was too precious a gift to ever explain, a deep, soul-level treasure that she liked to think foretold what would have grown between them. Why Heaven dangled a precious gem like that and then took it away was anyone's guess—perhaps Heaven flip-flopped with Hell, like the Sahara, from giver to taker.

Harry was moving about now, helping Mel make their dinner. Jess picked up the bound diary, rubbed her hands over it. Though she knew the men thought her obsession with the book was odd, she needed the comfort of those words to stave off the unease the deepening night always brought. But when the full canopy of stars shone above this evening, she'd be able to locate the obelisk. Persephone's constellation would show her the way.

Opening the carefully preserved but well-read pages, she began to read her favorite passages. While she knew them by heart, enough to mumble them as she rocked along on top of her camel during the day, she liked to see the words, pass her fingers over the ink. Connect with Farida, as if that touch between paper and flesh could draw Jessica fully into her world, and out of this one.

Three centuries ago, Prince Haytham came to the aid of Farida's father against another warring faction. Riding at his side was a man who'd fought and adventured with the prince, a man he referred to as Lord Mason. Her information suggested he was British aristocracy, likely a second or third son who'd become a traveling soldier seeking his fortune, a common enough tale. Though according to Farida's words, there'd been nothing common about him at all.

If Jess could paint a picture of Heaven, that would be hers. A world where she could be Farida, their merged souls belonging to Lord Mason for all eternity. Closing her eyes, she let her fading mind take her to the one place she still had clarity, a place that existed only in her imagination . . .

2

The Sahara
Eighteenth Century

JOURNAL ENTRY 1, PAGE 1
Farida bint Asim

I was behind the screen when Prince Haytham entered the tent to speak with my father. My father valued my counsel and often allowed me to do this, perhaps because he knew how very restless I became in a woman's world. Why does Allah create dreams and appetites, the desire to live free and fierce as a man does, if those things are to be denied a woman's soul? I have often wondered this.

Then I saw the man with the prince. Those longings, banked always against my responsibilities as my father's daughter, exploded inside me like the brightness of stars, such that they couldn't be contained. I bit down so hard on my lip I drew blood, though I knew I must fly, sing, dance . . . all for him.

He had to be a djinn spun from the desert sand, for never has a man been so beautifully made. Face carved with the sculpted beauty of the dunes, but smooth as watered stone, as if a goddess had created him and then lovingly stroked him, over and over.

When they sat for coffee, he removed his robes, showing he wore the brown riding trousers and white shirt of a European. He lounged back on the pillows, a graceful animal. Though he smiled and listened in that relaxed way of men as coffee was prepared, he reminded me of a desert tiger, for his hair was burnished copper, an animal's pelt. He had it scraped back from his face, so every magnificent plane was emphasized. My fingers wanted to feel that fall of straight silk, tied back from his shoulders.

His eyes were true amber, like the tiger as well, an almost unnatural brilliance to them, as if he carried the fire of the desert within him. A djinn, as I have said. I heard Prince Haytham say later that he suspected Lord Mason was a British spy, for during the time he stayed with us, he was always gone by dawn, and returned at nightfall. He also spoke our language as well as a native, and his accent was not as precisely bitten off as other Englishmen who have met our camp.

The prince said Lord Mason's purpose was nothing that concerned us, though I imagined him stepping out of view of our camp and dissolving into a tornado of sand, a desert devil spinning across the dunes. He had too much energy to contain in the body of a mortal man. I imagined that he returned to us at night only when his need to exercise his powers was temporarily sated.

But I need to leave off my fancies and go back to that first time I saw him. As I bit down on my lip and tasted my blood, I must have made a sound despite my efforts, for he looked at me, found me behind the screen. Those tiger's eyes flickered. I saw his nostrils flare, as if he had my scent, knew every shameful thing I wanted. A passing moment, over in a blink. He shifted his attention away, not disrespecting my father by staring at a woman of his house.

But when he raised his hand to perform the salaam, I drew in another unsteady breath, thinking how those hands would feel on my flesh, compelling my surrender, my obedience, my devotion and love throughout eternity. I knew then. From that very first second, Fate tied a gentle but unbreakable tether around my throat and handed the lead to him. I would follow him, no matter what our end would be.

The Sahara
Present Day

Jessica knew that end had been tragic, horrific, but she didn't know how anyone could read about a young girl's hope, the surge of pure, passionate need, and not believe in it, not be moved by it. Of course, perhaps one had to be half insane, stripped to the level of survival, in order to slough off the veneer of cynicism and sophistication and hear that truth in Farida's words.

"Just another girl's romantic fantasy," Raithe had scoffed, taking a glance at what she'd found in the rare book library he maintained. She'd been a research assistant for the archaeology and history departments at one of Rome's universities before the vampire abducted her and faked her death, so one of her more mundane tasks for Raithe had been cataloging his library.

It was the binding he'd appreciated, which he told her was valuable for its age and condition. "The text was likely written by some aspiring author later that century, hoping a newspaper would run it as a ladies' serial. At one time, penning stories of the exotic East was a popular pastime, whether or not they were true."

Thank God Raithe didn't pay further attention to her absorption in the book. She took care not to be seen studying or researching it too often, or thinking about it in his presence. It had been an effort beyond description, not escaping to those memories when he'd required her blood, or satiation of his sexual needs, or those of his friends. To satisfy their need for pain, for her screams and tears.

To him it was a trite love story, fictional and typical. Two people had loved each other, wanted nothing more than a life together. They'd tried and failed. But whether it was her desperate need to believe in the woman's story, or intuitive scholarship, her desire to confirm what she suspected was a true story, whoever wrote it, became a carefully guarded obsession. Every scrap of information she discovered was another brick in the fortress holding what was left of her mind.

As with most histories, she found more when she focused on authority figures, namely Prince Haytham and Sheikh Asim. She confirmed the sheikh's eldest daughter was Farida, which didn't prove anything until she cross-referenced it with the annals of a Polo-esque adventurer who'd recorded a brief paragraph during his trip through the Sahara.

Encountered a hostile tribe today, the first that didn't offer me the sacred protections of a guest. There'd been a row related to the chief's daughter and a supposed British officer. The girl had finally been caught, after managing to run off with the fellow and evading capture for some time. She was killed in a ghastly way. The poor chap was buried alive in a pit of rock. Was able to placate them with my credentials and a hasty leave-taking.

A Romeo and Juliet tale, told a million ways, but with the same tragic ending.

After Raithe's death, and her flight to Africa, Jess hit dead ends seeking the remains of the couple, until she'd risked contacting the Egyptian consul. She claimed to be a retired American professor preparing a speculative article on authentic events that inspired Middle Eastern and African romantic poetry and prose. She met with him under a full-length abaya that covered her from head to feet.

"You are lucky," the consul told her, after making some inquiries on her behalf. "There is a descendant of Prince Haytham's who is a scholar of their family history. He will provide you some information that may be helpful to your article, as a courtesy from one academic to another."

Several days later, she'd been called back to the embassy to pick up a sheaf of papers, faxed over by the scholar. Returning to her hostel, burning to read the pages, she'd been frustrated by the weakness of her body, which made her stumble on the stairs and forced her to sit there until she regained her breath and could make it the rest of the way to her room to read the information in privacy.

But once there, she'd sunk down by the window, opened up the folder. The first thing had been a short series of letters from Prince Haytham to his father. The prince had been deeply grieved by the loss of his friend, but he'd been forced to condemn his rash actions as a dishonor to their friendship. Then her fingers had tightened on the page as she read his additional comments.

It is no surprise to me that he was harder to kill than expected, and escaped the pit. At least I believe it to be so, for I have heard that the girl's body, left to feed the desert scavengers, was gone within a day of her death. The family swore a blood oath to find and kill him, and reclaim her. But when the sheikh sent his oldest son on this mission, he returned two days later, his body dragging behind his frightened camel, his head mounted on the pommel. The rest of his escort never returned.

Lord Mason cannot be found when he does not wish to be. Which means he is seeking their blood as much as they are seeking his. I expect they will not be dissuaded from this now, but from my experience, they would be wise to leave him alone and let the desert absorb his rage and grief. They will not find her grave—it will be only where a desert tiger can find it.

Or one sick and dying woman who'd persisted, who'd put together a few hundred clues and discarded a hundred more, as if shuffling pieces of many different puzzles, until she'd at last found all the pieces to the one she sought. She was sure of it.

~

Jess glanced up at the stars. Using the accommodating body of her camel, she levered herself to her feet, hobbled twenty paces, checked her notes again, her detailed calculations using GPS and historical data of shifts in the night sky.

"Harry."

She'd stopped resenting the need to ask for help. Mostly. In the past twenty-four hours, as they'd drawn closer, the overwhelming desire to do this in profound isolation had returned. She was visiting a temple that should only be seen by those who understood the type of sacrifices made on its altar.

"Yeah, darling." He didn't have to be asked, sliding a hand under her elbow, another around her waist to steady her, taking her the next fifty paces. Jess was used to the casual endearments, which seemed to be his way of referring to any woman, but the first time he'd touched her like this she'd turned on him like a savage animal. When she'd yanked the knife from under her robes, she would have skewered him if he hadn't been far more agile. After she calmed down, she made herself bear his touch, because she knew it wouldn't be the last time she'd need help to move, as fast as she was declining.

Dying or not, though, she wouldn't tolerate Mel anywhere near her. Harry had either warned him, or she repulsed the other Aussie, because he never drew close. And of course Dawud would never touch her.

Sand and more sand. In the distance, to the left and right, were more dunes. One's steep slope escalated to two hundred feet. They'd traveled past even higher dunes, ones that would equal a fifty-story building. But this one held her attention because of her certainty about the stars and what had been here three hundred years ago.

It was ironic that the constellation named for the woman confined to Hades half of the year, shut away from the light, had marked the right location. Had Lord Mason thought of that when he did it, or had it merely been astounding coincidence, after he'd created the tomb?

Squeezing Harry's arm, she stopped about sixty feet away from the foot of that dune. "This is the place. Get the shovels."

She could be brusque without offending him, she knew. Talking drained her energy, and she'd conserved as much as possible toward this end.

"Right-o. You're okay here?"

She nodded.

As he left her, she settled next to the spot where they were going to dig. Though she was grateful for the consideration when Harry brought her a folded chair and helped her into it, the burning warmth of the sand had felt good. The night always closed in too fast. Even before she shivered, he was wrapping her up in the blanket he'd brought.

"Thank you, Harry."

He nodded, touched her chin briefly, giving her a thorough look. "Woman of your age and condition is a pretty tough bird to be here, Miss Anna. You sit tight. We'll have it dug up in no time."

She'd not told them her real name, of course. To the bank, the embassy, and all her fake papers, she was Anna Wyatt, not Jessica Tyson, and she'd been able to believably record her age as fifty-two. There was no better disguise for a twenty-nine-year-old fugitive than a wasting illness.

"If it's there," Mel observed dryly.

"If it's there," she agreed before Harry could quell him. "But it will be. If nothing else, I'm a smart crazy person, Mel."

His lips twisted at that. Even Dawud gave an uncertain smile, standing a few feet away from this unlikely group of infidels. She hoped they did find it tonight. The young man wanted to go home and missed his family. He also was wary, rightly so, of the two Australians. She missed her family, too, but of course she'd never see them again. In her worst moments, she feared they were already dead. After what she'd done, there was no way she would have returned home, but that didn't mean the vampires hunting her knew that. They might have tortured and killed her mother, father or siblings to try to find her. God rot her, she was too weary and sick to give the guilt any energy. It was just another thing she couldn't control. Another person she couldn't protect.

While they dug, she closed her eyes and went back to Farida, her words pressed against her heart beneath the robe.

As Farida's feelings grew, so too did Lord Mason's. In an environment where every action was under the scrutiny of others, subtle gestures took on the significance of passionate embraces . . .

JOURNAL ENTRY 17, PAGE 8
Farida bint Asim

Allah must forgive my weakness, for I am merely a woman, but when he rides, he entrances me. His strong, beautiful hands are gentle but firm on his horse's mouth, his seat so comfortable, as if he and the animal are one creation. Sometimes I think the fact they are separate is as much a surprise to him as to us, when he comes in past dusk and finds he can dismount.

He always strips off his robes and shirt in the shadows in front of his tent to wash off. I watch him out the slit of my tent. The tattoo of a tiger high on the back of his shoulder surprised me when I first saw it. It is not only inked but scarred into his flesh in a fascinating way, the image raised as if the creature is seeking to leap free. I think of passing my fingers over that, down the line of his broad back, where light perspiration runs down the narrow channel of his spine and darkens his waistband.

I have sought a way to approach him, and I know I will surely be punished for thinking that Allah provided me the way. Last night, he was on a raiding party with my brother and father, and I was told Lord Mason saved my brother's life from a sand trap. As the head-woman of the house, I knew I should make a gesture as my mother would have, out of gratitude for her son, for my brother.

So for that at least, I am not ashamed to say what I did. I did it before all that were within view of his tent, so I did not bring shame on myself or my father. But if they had known what stirred inside me as I did it, my father would have had me whipped until I bled.

I came and knelt before Lord Mason. He'd removed his boots and socks and was preparing to bathe his upper body as usual. I took the wet cloth from him and I bathed his feet. Oh, how I wanted so much to do the rest of him. I did not, of course. But I took great care over the arches and toes, the shape of his heel, the soles. And then, so his feet would not get recaked with sand, I dried his feet, my fingers stroking flesh and bone through the towel. I wanted to press my lips there, touch my forehead to the fine length of his calves.

His eyes were upon me the whole time, but as if he'd discerned my thoughts, I felt him grow ever more still, like a watchful desert tiger in truth. I had my face covered, but I dared the worst. I looked up and met his eyes.

Not as a wanton—Allah, no. I can't explain why he brings these feelings out in me, but I needed him to see, to let him know how I felt . . . and he did.

Later that same night, when he was eating dates after dinner, he placed one in his mouth and then, when no one was watching but me, behind my screen, he took it out again and put it on the plate, unmarked by his teeth. I came and collected the plates, and when I was back behind the screen, I lifted that date, placed it in my mouth. Thinking of the heat of his tongue, the press of his lips, I let our eyes meet again . . .

~

. . . Something amazing has happened tonight. Several hours before dawn, I awoke in my tent, restless, thinking thoughts of him. Somehow I became certain he was near, though I could not see him. I rose from my bed, and allowed my night garment to pool at my ankles. Stepping up to the back slit of the tent where no one could see, I let the moonlight come in and touch my flesh the way I wished for him to do.

And there he was. Barely moving against the hills of sand surrounding our camp. He held the reins of his horse, and though he was far away, I knew he could see me. So I parted the tent further, let him see me, my body that had never been seen this way by a man, and never would be except by him. I was sure of it. Though the coolness of the night air made me shiver, I held myself proudly, as the daughter of a sheikh should, and let him see what gifts Allah had bestowed upon me. His gaze moved over my skin like the hot wind, scorching me, and I wanted to be burned.

I thought if he came to me, I would not deny him, no matter the obedience I have always given my family. How is it I am so certain this is meant to be, that Allah has willed it so, even though it is against everything I have known?

When I raised my gaze again, he was gone. I thought he might have seen someone stirring, so I quickly stepped back into the tent. Djinn that he is, he was there, though my younger sisters slept only a few feet away. So I trembled for us both and said nothing as he reached out and touched my face for the very first time . . . only my face, while his clothed body stood so close to my yearning one. And then he was gone.

C LUNK. Jess opened her eyes as Harry let out a triumphant whistle and Mel a startled grunt. They'd dug down three feet, so when she bent to peer in, she was gazing at the sand-encrusted top of the stone obelisk.

She tried to school her face to a mask, but fortunately they were occupied with clearing the sides, using spacers to hold back the sand. Gripping the sides of the chair, she fought sudden light-headedness. It *was* real. Though she'd been afraid to believe otherwise, because of how little she could afford to lose at this point, the confirmation was staggering.

When they were done, the full four-foot height of the heavy marker was revealed. She had Harry brush off the seal and shone her flashlight on it. An orchid engraving, the flower least likely to live in the dry desert. It would be a miracle to find one here. The symbolism was strong, strong as a three-hundred-year-old heartbeat.

She pointed. "It needs to be shifted into that grooved circle to the right of the base. According to the legend, it announces to the spirit you have come to honor her, and mean no harm."

That was the truth, even if it had nothing to do with Farida's legend. Seeing Mel's irritated look, she added, "After that, your job will be done and you can go home."

Journal Entry 63, Page 32
Farida bint Asim

We have done it. We ran away together. Tonight was our first time truly alone with each other. I stood in the center of his cave, a place he explained he used when traveling the desert. It had as many caverns as an ancient kassar. I knew what I'd done, knew there was no going back. While he watched me look at his temporary home, I sensed he was also overwhelmed by the choice we'd made. It was right, though so momentous and destructive at once. But then all that died away when he came close, turned me toward him.

It was not the choice that made me tremble, but him, how he made me feel. A way that filled this small space, taking air from my lungs. I managed to tell him I could not breathe, and before I fell to my knees, he was there, holding me, his arms around my body, his hands upon me at last, blessed Allah. He gave me air, life, through his mouth and hands . . .

≈

Lord Mason had been an honorable man, Jessica knew. He'd married her in a handfasting, witnessed by the stars and God, before he bedded her. It had not been a modern relationship, a careful or even hopeful matching of likes and dislikes, quirks and habits. It had been a soul finding another soul, and the search for a life that would honor that bond.

They had almost a year together before it all ended, but the pages Farida wrote during that time had passages Jessica thought could compete with the most renowned love stories, steeped in innocent, sensual joy . . .

≈

He likes me to place grapes on my thighs. He eats them from my lap, one at a time, working his way to the fruit beneath, teasing me with his lips. And often, afterward, I bathe his feet as I did that day, only doing it as I wished to do it then, pressing my head to his knees in love and devotion . . .

~

He is stubborn, my lord Mason. Allah forgive me, but he can make me angry. A lifetime of never voicing my angers, and I could not stop myself from speaking sharply to him tonight. I feared I might be beaten, but he simply shouted back, and in time we were so amazed with ourselves, we laughed. When I asked him why he had not punished me, he told me that I would be, but he needed time to devise the proper rebuke. And Allah be merciful, he found one, such that I became determined to defy him at every possible opportunity . . .

~

As Jessica had expected, Dawud was nervous about the markings on the obelisk, warning of ancient curses and reprisals for disturbance. It was difficult to have more than two men maneuvering it in the hole anyway, so Harry and Mel had little complaint with the boy standing silently at her side to watch. It took rope, cursing and sweat, because the heavy stone had to be moved with care for its age and the preciseness of the relocation, but eventually it shifted to the right, fitting into the groove in a perfect lock. Another band of tension loosened around her churning gut.

If she had only a handful of months to live, how would she use her time? It had been an essay question in her high school English class. Dear Mrs. Tams, nearly seventy, had understood the importance of such a question, but to a shiny seventeen-year-old, it had been merely another dull exercise until the final bell. Jess wished she'd been insightful enough to tuck her answer away, to pull it back out and laugh or despair. She couldn't even remember what she'd written.

She did know that the true answer was elusive until it wasn't a hypothetical. Because what determined the answer were the circumstances of one's life when one found out death was imminent.

She had precious little time left. A couple days, maybe. Each time she lay down to sleep, the hold of oblivion grew stronger, more tantalizing. This effort might mean nothing to anyone but herself, but if every thread of the loom of the world was important, then she'd go out with hers strengthened by this one purpose. When some lucky archaeologist found the tomb a few centuries in the future, maybe they'd wonder about that second skeleton, curled up at the foot of Farida's. There might even be three, for Lord Mason certainly would have had his bones interred there when he died, if at all possible.

"Thank you," she said, coming out of her reverie to find the three men waiting out another of her far-too-frequent zoning trips. "You've earned your reward."

~

At dawn, they left, taking everything but one small packet of supplies. She was sorriest to see the camel go, for the white female had become a friend on the journey, her body giving Jess strength when her own failed her.

"Well, then." Harry held out a hand, and Jess took it, managing the shake. "It's been a most unusual journey, Miss Anna. I'm glad you found the marker from your story."

"Me, too." She nodded. "Travel safely. And please watch after Dawud."

"I'll look after the lad." Holding her hand a moment longer, as if he might say more, he nodded, released her at last and turned. She stood, swaying on unsteady legs, watching them mount up, hearing the camel's snort, the creak of gear and saddle adjustments. They'd left her a small tent shelter, which would be useful until night fell again and the stars returned, showing her the rest of the way.

As he approached, leading his camel, Dawud's gaze was upon her face, her trembling hands. "Perhaps, Miss Anna, we should stay—"

"No." She shook her head. "This is where I'll die, Dawud. There's no reason for you to stay. I'm not afraid to meet God alone. But thank you for your kindness."

He gave her a bow then, his expression again telling her he was uncertain what Allah had intended to teach him on this odd journey. However, a true believer, he also accepted things that were beyond human understanding.

Mel gave her an indifferent nod. She was sure his mind was already on spending his money and how to get more than his share. She prayed that Harry and Dawud kept one eye open on the return trip. Mel's greed was greater than his brains.

They were faces, just passing, soon gone in the shimmering heat. Preparing for her vigil to await nightfall, she settled back down, the memoir on her lap. If her information was correct, the shift of the obelisk would have pushed up a second, much smaller marker a quarter mile away, on the other side of the tall dune. It would be the lever to the tomb opening, an engineering feat worthy of the admiration of ancient Egyptians. As soon as dusk approached, when she was certain her escort was well gone from here, she would make her way to the place she believed that marker to be.

Farida and Mason had possessed the courage and strength to grasp their dream. She *would* make that quarter mile. Farida was exactly as she'd described herself, a responsible daughter, exceptionally intelligent and valued by her father. She'd run her father's household from a young age, after her mother's death while bearing one of Farida's siblings. It perhaps explained why Farida hadn't been married off as young as other Bedouin girls were. But if she'd been dreaming, longing for more, it was not evident until that first journal entry. Of course, in her world such dreams were not indulged, and perhaps never would have been if her soul mate hadn't stepped into her father's tent.

Jess didn't have the comfort of Dawud's faith. God, if such a being existed, had abandoned them all long ago, but she'd experienced a taste of an illusory paradise in stolen moments with Farida. Perhaps that was the only Heaven that truly existed, what love and imagination could create, explaining why she'd clung to belief in the story so firmly.

She wanted to step into Farida's body. She wanted not only to read about it, but to *feel* what she'd felt . . .

Journal Entry 102, Page 45
Farida bint Asim

He has a way of looking at me. I might be cooking my dinner, or using some precious water to wash. Though I rarely hear his approach, I know he is there. I close my eyes and smile as he takes the cloth from my hand and passes it over my skin, his male eyes watching it trickle down my breasts, my stomach.

"Bathing is a woman's job, my lord," I tease him. "A handmaid's task."

"I beg to differ. This is definitely a man's job. And in your case"— he moves my hair to the side and finds my throat, telling me of his hunger—"only mine."

"I missed you."

"I know. I felt it."

~

Jessica opened her eyes. *I felt it.* To be so close to another that such yearning emotion could be felt, even at a distance. It was the last entry, poignant and ironic at once. Ten days after that, just short of their leaving the Sahara to return to his family home, where they might have been safe for the duration of their lives, he was captured by the tribe, for they'd convinced the prince to help them with his resources. Farida disguised herself as a man and rode Lord Mason's stallion proudly into her father's camp. Then she pushed off her turban and requested the right to die with her husband.

She'd drifted off. Jess blinked. The moon was full and bright now, the stars sparkling, diamonds in a vast darkness, a promise of light in so much unexplained void.

During the day she'd managed to mostly re-cover the obelisk, pushing sand in with her feet, pacing herself. The desert winds would take care of the rest, as well as her shelter. She began to walk west. She had to stop several times, not only to check her direction, but to collapse, her bones quivering in the nighttime chill. Once she even slept, despite her best efforts to stay awake, but when she was roused by her own panic, it had been only a few minutes. Struggling back to her feet, she continued. Then she stopped to throw up bile and blood, and found she couldn't regain her feet.

"No," she rasped. Then, a harsher snarl. *"No."* She kept going, on her hands and knees. Since the moon and stars were bright, she didn't use her flashlight, but she was tempted. She might not fear meeting God alone, but darkness was an entirely different matter.

The last part of her journey took her up the back side of that tall dune. While less steep than the other side, it was still a challenge for her. Pushing back despair at her failing energy, she went, one struggling pace at a time, like a religious supplicant on a holy quest.

Seventy-five shuffling feet up, she stopped, gasping. Felt around. Sand would have shifted so much over this time, but she had to believe he'd allowed for that, figured out something. *Please let it be here. Please.* It was here. She knew it. She'd prayed for it, would have sacrificed her soul to find it, if the devil wouldn't have laughed at such a pathetic, battered offering. But maybe there was someone who could still find value in it.

Exhausted, she rolled onto her back to look at the position of the stars. Stared at Persephone and struggled to remain conscious.

Farida, name your price. Anything you want, anything in my power to give, is yours. Just let me find you. Let me know there was something that makes everything that's happened to me worth it. Dearest Jack...

She stretched her arms out to either side. From the sight of the heavens she hoped it was obvious she was offering herself up to whatever spirits were listening. The only fear she had left was of finding out darkness was all there was.

As she lay there for several minutes, she fought growing despair with a soft murmur, a vague lullaby of no words. She moved her twitching hands, passing them through the sand like the dip of a ladle, sifting in a soothing rhythm. She would find it. *She would.* In her frustration, she dug deeper, clutching the sand in a tighter fist... and her knuckles scraped something solid.

Struggling to her side, she found the tiny marker, no bigger than her palm. Pushed up by the movement of another stone a quarter mile away, just as she'd researched, though if she hadn't fallen in this exact spot, she never would have found it. While the top of the obelisk had been decorative, this one was unadorned, made to look like the sand itself, blending in unless one was on hands and knees like this, going by touch alone. A day's worth of sand had buried it a handful of inches back under the ground.

Digging down around it, she found it had a spring trigger that released easily, surprising and heartening her. She'd hidden a prybar from the men in her belongings in case, though she hadn't known if she'd have the strength to use it properly. The marker slipped from her grasp as the door beneath it ground open, letting sand tumble down into the narrow opening.

Clicking on her flashlight, she saw a small tunnel, barely big enough for a man's body to wriggle through on his stomach, leading into the dune at a downward incline. When she put her head inside, she inhaled, and her vitals tightened. An unmistakably fragrant smell. Did it linger from flowers or incense left down in the tomb all those years ago, the scent trapped and waiting to give the memory to the first person to visit?

She'd found it. *Hot damn*, she'd found it. The adrenaline got her into the shaft, struggling over the gritty layer of sand drifting in with her. She used her elbows, her toes, her hips, whatever it took to keep going, stopping when she had to do so. When she reached about eighty feet, she guessed from the increasingly steep grade and coolness that she was past the base of the dune and going even deeper into the earth. Thank God it was all downhill. The initial walls of the tunnel had been braced wood, remarkably undamaged by rot, perhaps because of the Sahara's lack of humidity. However, as she descended, the tunnel became rock. It widened after those first eighty feet, and she was able to lift from her belly and proceed on hands and knees again, keeping the flashlight beam in front of her until the tunnel dead-ended and emptied into a sudden hole. When she came to the edge of it, the light showed she'd found a large chamber.

She swept the beam over it slowly, for she didn't want to minimize anything about this moment. Her heart was thumping, even as ebullience paralyzed her. Safe. God, she hadn't felt safe in so long, and here she felt she was, at last. Even the darkness of the tunnel didn't bother her. She'd found it.

The drop into the chamber was about five feet. She managed it, landing in a clumsy heap that set off a paroxysm of coughing and jolting pain through her chest. She fumbled out her handkerchief to make sure she didn't spatter the chamber with blood or worse coming from her lungs. Here in the circular space, the wheezing of her breath was a harsh sound. Out in the desert, she'd been able to trick herself, lose it in the sound of the wind. It was okay, though. The end might be close, but she'd found her resting place.

When she at last struggled to her feet, she passed the flashlight over the chamber again at ground level. She started back, hitting the wall, sucking a painful gasp into her clogged throat. For long minutes she stood, staring at what was before her. Her mind whirled, denied it, tried to make sense of it. When she couldn't, she jerked the light away and passed it over the rest of the chamber, over the myriad objects scattered on the floor, the torch sconces embedded in the wall.

Sconces with fresh, unlit torches in them.

4

HER unsteady heart pounding, she hobbled to one of them, used her lighter to set it ablaze. Avoiding what was in the center of the room, she moved to the other sconce. The resulting light created an eerie hourglass-shaped set of shadows on the floor, reminding her of her earlier thoughts about her own internal hourglass. She switched off the flashlight with cold fingers.

Air currents carried the smoke away, indicating other hidden passages, or small fissures engineered to keep the chamber vented. Which meant her sudden cloying sense of being pressed on all sides must be coming from her mind, not the chamber.

Given the past five years of her life, she knew her mind wandered between reality and fantasy more than it should. To retune her brain fully to a reality station, she'd probably need an M&M bag full of prescription drugs. But Farida had brought fantasy together with reality, and Jessica had used all her training as a scholar to be certain, knowing she was anchoring all that she had left of herself to her belief that the story *was* real. Wasn't it?

She pushed away the grim specter of logic, which was trying to fight to the forefront of her mind and make her consider what was in the middle of the room. *No.* Nothing was going to ruin this place, a monument to enduring love, faith. Hope.

Turning her attention back to the rest of the tomb, she saw the floor was composed of hundreds of polished stones. Different types, sizes and colors, brought out by a glaze on the smoothed top of each. In that glaze, a dried flower had been pressed and preserved. She swallowed.

When I lie in his arms, he tells me we will travel everywhere. In every new place, he will pick the most beautiful stone, and the most beautiful flower. Each time we come home, he will add them to our bedroom floor, so that when I am an old, old woman, I will look over it and remember all the places we have been together . . .

She gripped her hands together, since there was no one else's to reach for, to give her courage, reinforcement. Taking a breath, she began to move, one slow, disbelieving step at a time, toward the sarcophagus in the center.

The immediate circle around the stone dais was ankle deep in fresh flower petals, the source of the exotic scent she'd smelled. Jess stopped outside of that boundary and removed her boots and socks. Lifting the lace scarf of her discarded hijab back over her head, only then did she move forward, for this was as sacred a place as any church she'd ever visited.

The dew-kissed silk of the petals brushed over her bare feet, their caress thickening the emotions in her throat. "No wonder he couldn't let you go," she murmured. "He never let you die." Her whisper echoed in the chamber, stirring the air, stirring spirits. But she wasn't afraid of spirits. She was too close to becoming one of them. As swept away as she'd been by the tale, even she had underestimated how much he loved her. This wasn't a tomb. It was an enchanted cave, holding a sleeping princess.

Farida's sarcophagus was embellished with floral engravings and Arabic. While she wasn't fluent, Jess caught "Beloved" and "Woman of Honor." Stepping onto the dais, she drew close to the open coffin, for there was no lid. She gazed down into the face of a woman dead three hundred years, who looked as if she had simply fallen asleep.

Turned on her side, with her folded hands tucked under her cheek, Farida wore a sheer white gown that bared her shoulder and showed the lines of her body. Her dark hair, spread across the pillow and down her back, was twined with ribbons. Imagining clumsy male hands weaving those ribbons brought the first tears to Jessica's eyes. Farida had liked ribbons, and he'd wanted her to have everything she liked. Stones and dried flowers from places she'd never go, ribbons in her hair. A gown she would have chosen when she lay down with him, as eager for his touch as he was for hers.

More rose petals had been scattered over the translucent white fabric, the flowers as tender a pink as her relaxed, almost smiling mouth. According to the stories, she'd been tortured to death. Burned, bones broken, stabbed, stoned, her face cut with pieces of glass. But there wasn't a mark on her. Her thick dark lashes fanned smooth, olive-complexioned cheeks. Slim, elegant fingers pressed together in folded prayer or repose.

Those muttering voices in Jess's subconscious, trying to process what was in this chamber with a rational mind, were bothering her. She shoved them away. She didn't need to be rational anymore. That had no place here.

Her gaze moved to a small pillar table next to the bed—for she couldn't think of this as a coffin now—and alighted on a crystal vase, with one snow-white orchid in it.

Some of the legends she'd uncovered had said that Lord Mason was so enraged in his grief he'd sold his soul to darkness and become a desert demon in truth, whirling across the sands of the Sahara and unleashing vengeance against her family. After which, he dedicated his damned eternal life to watching over her, hiding her grave and body from those who would harm her.

Another fanciful tale said that the week after she was killed, a fierce dust storm had buried her father's camp, no trace of it ever to be found. Sheikh Asim's brothers in other tribes renewed the blood oath to seek revenge, the ones Prince Haytham advised to stand down. She wondered if they ever heeded him.

Everything she saw here was beautiful, moving, a miracle. But she had to admit it was also discomfiting. She'd come prepared to see dry bones, maybe the unexpected—and highly unlikely—possibility of a dried flower husk, clutched in skeletal hands. A dusty tomb for the dead, a fitting place for her to fade into its tranquility, become part of the silence.

But unlike Jess's failing body, there was something vibrant and strong here, a love so eternal it may have taken a dark turn in its determination to endure. This was not just guilt and grief beyond comprehension, but dormant power that would wake and consume the whole world, if it would bring her back to him. What would a man become, if he didn't have the strength to let go, and possessed the power to hold on throughout all eternity?

That sense of uneasiness returned, a sly voice. *You know what he is.*

Shut. Up.

Sinking to her knees in the petals, she laid her temple against the sarcophagus. Along the walls Lord Mason had left his wife more gifts. Books, fantastic jewels, scarves. Horses carved of onyx. Clothing . . . a beautiful beaded wedding dress Farida would not have had when she made her own vows under the stars. All in all, there appeared to be several hundred gifts. One for every year she'd been dead.

Jess forced herself not to start counting. The way to open the tomb was an engineering trick, not magic. Perhaps Lord Mason had descendants. Perhaps he'd returned to England, eventually married, and his heirs came once a year . . .

Fate could not be so cruel as to bring her back full circle. Not after months of searching and hoping.

If vampires existed, so could other supernatural beings, right? Why not a desert djinn? But she'd been a researcher too long to ignore the possibility, in the laughing, mocking face of everything she now knew about the world.

The words of the memoir she'd treasured, memorized, as well as the documents she'd struggled to find, started to fire past her denial. Pinning her against the workings of her still too agile mind, they made her see the things she'd overlooked. Things that she, of all people, should have noticed. But she had read what she wanted and needed desperately to believe.

Sheikh Asim's correspondence to his brother: *This infidel is an unnatural being. Even the prince will shun him for what he is . . .*

Farida's own words: *As his lips closed on my throat, I knew his hunger . . . We are nighttime creatures now, for the comfort of my love, and avoidance of those who pursue us . . . I prepared my dinner . . .* A loving, submissive woman, speaking of preparing her dinner, not his . . . *He is always gone during the day . . .*

"No. No. *No!*" It was not possible. Lord Mason had become a djinn, like the stories suggested, a ghost visiting her grave throughout the centuries, a wizard able to preserve her body. Maybe even a fallen angel, defying God's will to be with her. Farida had loved him. It had bled from every pen stroke in that journal. This whole chamber said he'd loved her insensibly. A vampire did *not* love, and most certainly not *human* women. No woman could fall in love with a vampire to the depths that Farida had fallen in love with Lord Mason. It didn't happen. Vampires were savage, brutal creatures, obsessed only with power and control.

He is not as other men in his solitude. He ordered me not to bind my life to his, and yet I defied his will and insisted. At last he made me his, in a way deeper than any woman I know has experienced. He is inside me in all ways, in my mind and soul, the two of us linked together through all eternity.

Romantic, sweeping words she'd taken as romance, when she should have been reading other things.

No. No. No. What she was seeing before her was *not* the power of a vampire. They had no ability to preserve life this way, because this woman *was* dead.

"That's as tight a fit as a young girl's bum, that is."

Jessica stiffened and raised her head. Mel wriggled free and dropped into the chamber, giving her his ugly grin. "Well, darling, we didn't believe it was all about some dusty rock almost as big as my dick, and we were right, weren't we?"

Shoving aside her jumbled thoughts, she rose on trembling legs, bracing herself on the side of the sarcophagus. When Mel's gaze went to it, his eyes widened. "Hell's bells, look at that, Harry."

She wanted to shift in front of it, cover Farida from his sight. Then she realized he'd ignored the phenomenon in the center of the room for the treasures on the floor behind her. But as he started forward, Harry caught his arm, his self-preservation instinct greater. "What's going on here?" he asked sharply.

Her last act on this Earth was going to be bringing grave robbers to Farida's resting place. As if the horrific possibility whirling through her mind wasn't enough to handle.

"Your death," she rasped out. "This woman is guarded by the

spirit of the man who loved her. You touch one thing, and you won't leave this chamber alive."

"More of your fanciful rubbish. You're mad, old girl. We're about to be bloody rich beyond anything ever," Mel said. "That's all that's happening. And even dead, that girl's a lot prettier than your sick heap of bones. I say we wake her up and take her along."

One man might have sacrificed his heart and soul to ensure this place would remain pure in memory forever. She had to believe that, hope for it, no matter what other terrible alternative existed.

Jessica drew the knife from beneath her clothes, the one she'd almost gotten Harry with in their early travels. Perhaps because her movements were feeble, they didn't think to stop her, but they didn't know a Hell-based rage was burning deep in her breast, bolstered by her fear of betrayal and the threat of utter hopelessness. *Please, let me die before I learn the truth.*

"You don't belong here," she said, her voice rough and strange to her own ears. "You can't touch these things. These are his gifts to her. That he's still bringing her." How could they not see it? The fresh flower petals, the orchid, three hundred years of offerings? Or was she dreaming again, meshing the reality of their presence with the illusion of what she wanted this chamber to look like? No, she'd imagined dried bones, had even been comforted by that idea. Everything here was real, particularly their threat.

"Miss Anna," Harry said quietly, "none of us will keep you from staying here. Mel doesn't want anything to do with that woman. But you have no use for these treasures. What does it matter if we take a few?"

"Because they're *hers*. Because something has to matter enough that we don't take from it." From their startled looks, she suspected they could see that fire welling in her eyes, hear the raw, despairing fury in her hoarse voice. She was getting dizzy, a gray haze at the edges of her vision, but she defied it, brandishing the knife. "*Something* has to be sacred."

"Well, you go on and worship all you like, you crazy old witch," Mel growled. "I'm plundering to my heart's content."

"No, you are not." She swung the knife as he moved forward. Surprised, Mel leaped back as the tip snagged and ripped his sleeve.

"You will not touch anything here as long as I have breath to fight you."

"Fair enough," he retorted, and drew a knife of his own, the blade catching the torchlight.

"Mel," Harry snapped. "No call for that, now. We'll just knock her out. She couldn't fight off a baby."

"Why can't you leave her be? Why can't any of you . . ." As she choked on the pain of it, her head swam, the floor tilting. She wished Lord Mason had thought to bespell this chamber like they did in the movies, so that in the presence of grave robbers, cracks would run across the ceiling and the walls would crumble in, burying them all, preserving it forever. But then the chamber would disappear, as if it had never been, a figment of her imagination. No, it *was* here. She could see it, could see all of it. "You won't take from her, damn it."

"Jesus, Harry. She'll die here anyway. Might as well hasten the old bat along."

"I'm not old," she snarled. "I am twenty-nine years old."

That caught the men off guard, bought her a minute. Why not? She was tired of having it all bottled up inside of her. She'd endured months, years even, of trusting no one, talking little, even to Raithe, because most times speaking wasn't the primary use he had for her mouth. Even knowing they would think her crazy, she would confess it here and now, because it was all right. She could tell Farida, so she would hear it, before they killed her at the foot of her sarcophagus.

"I am Jessica Tyson, not Anna Wyatt. I was the servant of a vampire for five years. A vampire who killed my fiancé. That vampire did this to me"—she gestured at the wasted flesh of her face—"but I survived. To do this. To come to this woman's grave, to someone who understood . . . that life is the most horrible thing in the world, and the most marvelous."

Tears were running freely down her face now, though Jess was surprised her dried-up heart, pounding so erratically, had any left to give. "I beg you, if you have any scrap of decency, do *not* defile this place."

But she knew when it came to these men and decency, threats worked better. "If you refuse and kill me"—she pinned them both under her gaze—"I swear, no matter what deal I must make from the grave, I'll curse you for the rest of your days. You will know Hell on Earth, until you bang on the devil's door and beg him to let you in. She was Farida, daughter of Sheikh Asim, the lion, and wife and beloved of Lord Mason, the desert tiger. She chose to abandon everything for his love, and she died for him. You will *not* dishonor that."

"She's turned the corner, Harry," Mel muttered, though his face had lost some color. "A vampire. Jesus Christ."

Jess kept her eyes on Harry. His avarice warred with something that might be conscience, but unfortunately she suspected it was just fear. And fear wasn't enough.

Reluctantly, he drew his gun. "Best to end your suffering, darling," he said gruffly. "I'm sorry for it."

Mel chuckled, a harsh sound, recovering some of his brass. "If I was going to defile it, I'd take a piss on her, love," he said. "Which I'm likely to do, once I bag up some of these baubles, because it was quite a hike getting here. It's a goddamned miracle you made it, sick as you are."

"You will leave here," she retorted. "Or you will be eternally sorry."

When the air currents shifted behind her, she registered it a moment before the gazes of the two men did. In the space of one of her struggling heartbeats, the disbelief and lack of fear they had shown in the face of her meager threat transformed into something entirely different.

She didn't look behind her. Instead, her gaze strayed to the fresh orchid in the vase, clung to it. Before all this happened, she'd been a brilliant student, with an exceptional mind. Her professors had told her so, but she'd realized a person didn't know how brilliant she was until she endured things so horrible her mind was able to perform mitosis, splitting into two parts to survive. The academic side of her knew the psychology of that, just as her soul knew it wouldn't survive the impact of bringing reality and fantasy back together to face what was behind her.

It was the final insult, and would snap a mind frayed for so long it should have completely unraveled by now. Maybe it had, as Mel had implied. There was comfort in that. Perhaps she was in a dream, and could turn it in the direction she wanted. She could die right now, never knowing, and go into oblivion clinging to what she'd wanted this moment to be.

As Harry's eyes widened and Mel's face went satisfyingly pale, Jessica felt her body shudder, caught between terror and heartbreak. One inch at a time, she forced herself to turn her head, until she was looking at what had stepped from the shadows.

Though illness had shriveled her to a hunched state in comparison, he was still a tall man. Every bit as beautiful as Farida had described him. A man with the soul of a desert tiger, shining through his preternatural amber eyes, and copper hair that shimmered like the cat's hide in the firelight. Those eyes turned to her now. They made a thorough assessment of her expression, even the state of her body, in the space of a heartbeat. And she knew. Dear God, she knew.

He was a bloody, goddamned vampire.

5

"WHAT did you do to Dawud?" she rasped, turning back to Harry. The man was too busy assessing this new threat to answer, but Lord Mason did, in a velvet, dangerous voice that was a fluid blend of European and Arab accents, edged with an animal's growl.

"They slit the boy's throat when he tried to keep them from coming after you."

No. Oh God, no. Jessica's knees gave out on her then, and she fell into the petals. Oddly, the impact of bony kneecaps on stone didn't hurt, because he'd moved, putting his hand under her elbow to ease her down in a swift movement. The unexpected touch was gone before she could react to it. Mel rushed for the stranger. Harry was smarter, trying to scramble back up into the tunnel. It wouldn't help. A human couldn't escape a vampire.

Mel started firing, and the other torch dropped, dimming the chamber. Lord Mason leaped for him, but she was more concerned about the bullets. Lunging to her feet, she covered Farida, screamed in pain as one of the stray bullets punched into her. *Don't let her body be harmed. She's perfect . . . Let her stay perfect.*

~

Raithe had stolen her life, binding her to him with two marks. The first mark had allowed him to locate her wherever she was, and the second let him into her head, where he could read every thought she had, invade at any time to speak and command her there. Despite that, she'd tried to escape, again and again. Failed every time, been punished every time. Eventually, she'd realized he let her try only to give himself the pleasure of extinguishing her hope, indulging his fascination with whether she had the fortitude to strike it back to life again.

When she was befriended by two women in his household, she thought she was being offered comfort from fellow inmates. They asked about her life before, about Jack, her fiancé. It was the last time she made the mistake of trusting anyone. At first she wondered why he didn't lift the information from her mind, but later she realized it was more of his games, intended to underscore how alone she was now.

After her sixth escape attempt, Raithe told her she would not fully accept his ownership until she realized her old life was gone to her. So he found, captured and killed her fiancé in front of her. He broke Jack's spine, crushed his rib cage so it punctured his lungs, his heart, then wouldn't allow her to touch him as he wheezed his last. His uncomprehending eyes clung to her, his numb hand outstretched, trying to reach hers.

As Jack's body had been dragged away, Raithe told her if she tried to kill herself, he'd find her family and do the same to each one of them, only make it last longer. When he deemed her training complete, her mind malleable enough, he intended to give her the third mark. As she curled in a ball of grief on the floor at his feet, he explained in a gentle, even tone that this would be a gift. An honor. She'd be his fully bonded servant then, with the privilege of an enhanced mortal life span, perhaps as much as three hundred years, give or take a decade.

So life went on. It took a while for her to be as malleable as he demanded. Then, the night he finally decided to do it, vampire hunters attacked. Before he could complete her third mark, one hunter wounded him severely, but Raithe managed to get away, dragging her with him. When they reached a narrow dark alley, he'd stumbled, fallen, overcome by his wounds. Since he was still grasping her wrist, refusing to let go, it drove her to her knees. Her hand landed on a sharpened survey stake, discarded with construction trash.

For so long, she'd been numb, her mind beaten into complete submission, a cringing dog who had no thoughts other than what her Master would next inflict upon her and how to endure or avoid it. In hindsight, she knew that had been her best protection, because deep down where neither Raithe nor even she could go, the part of her that had waited for this one rare moment of vulnerability had hovered, beyond his reach. When the roaring compulsion came slamming back into her body, she reacted on instinct.

Now.

She seized his hair, yanked him off the ground and drove the stake into him. Wounded and dazed as he was, he didn't have a chance. There'd been countless times she'd huddled on the floor during his daylight sleep, chained to the foot of his bed, and felt her own ribs, figuring out exactly where the heart was located. Figuring out the angle she'd have to use, how strong she'd have to be. Whenever he heard such thoughts, the punishments were brutal, but that night, the knowledge came surging up, as if that unconscious part of her had been practicing, over and over. She did it as smoothly as a veteran vampire hunter, and his aborted third mark gave her the necessary surge of strength.

Divine intervention? Maybe. Or the luck of a dumb, savage animal who'd wanted to survive.

She'd stood in a frozen stupor for quite some time after, looking at his dead body. Only the sound of approaching feet stirred her. She knew hunters enough to know they'd consider her his ally, and kill her. Even if they didn't, they couldn't protect her from the retribution that would follow her, as soon as the vampire world knew she was still alive. Which she knew was going to happen, because when she glimpsed Raithe's second-marked servants coming to his aid, she was certain at least one of them saw her.

It was then she became aware something was happening to her, her strength deserting her, replaced by a flulike fever and aching that made it hard to stumble out of the alley and get away. The partially administered serum of his third mark had given her those few key moments to drive the stake in, but he hadn't finished the process. She hadn't drunk from his throat. If fully bonded, she would have died with him in the alley. Instead, she'd been given what she soon realized was a lingering, wasting death that transformed her physical appearance into that of a woman two decades older.

As if a human killing a vampire wasn't impossible enough, she'd managed to avoid the vampires hunting her for months afterward, and not just because of her altered appearance. No one expected her to disappear in the Sahara region, where few vampires lived in the sun-soaked environment. Farida had been her salvation, in more ways than one.

~

Whereas Lord Mason's true identity told her she was damned.

Farida's heart had been stolen by a bloody vampire. Maybe she *had* been a young, starry-eyed girl who'd been taken advantage of by a monster. But a year's worth of pages spoke of how Lord Mason cherished her, how he tried to protect her. Even the historical documents spoke of it.

And Farida *had* known. Jess knew it now. She'd known him for what he was, loved him anyway. The two women who'd tricked Jess had been committed to Raithe, too, an immoral devotion she hadn't understood, reminding her of some bizarre, pitiable Stockholm syndrome.

Her brain ached, her skull pounded and her breath came in shorter bursts. She slid back down the side of the sarcophagus to the floor, all of it churning inside of her. She prayed it would split open her heart and leave it bleeding out its last life fluid, but she knew it wouldn't happen until she was pushed far past the threshold of agony she was sure she could bear. Raithe had always preferred that, torturing her until she was mindlessly begging him for mercy, even knowing he'd have none for her until long after that point.

As Mel's screams resounded through the cavern and a dead woman slept with a half smile on her face, the laughter came, bubbling out of Jess's raw vocal cords like a witch's cackle. She saw Mel's startled glance, then his body thudded to the floor. Blood from his ripped throat pooled beneath him and began to ooze toward the circle of rocks, the petals scattered over them. She heard Harry's cry to her for help, for mercy, then he, too, was silent. Human death filled the chamber, ironically perhaps for the first time. But still she couldn't stop her terrible laughter.

Her heart was being compressed in a cruel god's fist, giving out at last, giving up. Mockery such as this could exist only in a universe devoid of a merciful god. She'd put her last shred of faith in this story, believing that no matter the horror she'd endured, hope and love and life still existed. Now she knew those were just the fantasy of six billion humans, looking for a manufactured reason for existence beyond eating, fucking, shitting.

She wasn't a crude person, but when one's body was breaking down in a variety of embarrassing ways, it was pointless to be anything else. Blessed lassitude swept over her, weighing down her limbs, and the laughter evaporated with what had been left of her soul. She imagined that same cruel god shredding it like a maniacal baby tearing paper, throwing it in the air with mindless glee in its destruction.

Somehow she was flat on the floor now, her cheek pressed to cold stone and petals, the smell of the roses filling her. She gathered them in her arms and rocked, self-comfort. When a shadow fell on her, she peered up into that perfect, despicable face.

Hell. I'm in Hell. As his eyes flickered, she knew she'd said it out loud. She'd survived the claim of one vampire, only to fall right into the hands of another. The story had been a fairy tale. Her mind had twisted it, another one of the coping mechanisms she'd developed, which had come back to haunt her, punish her again. Illusion and imagination had fled, and now there was only harsh, stinking reality. Was she holding petals, or dust? The cleanliness of the chamber seemed tarnished, as if there were dusty cobwebs layering all his gifts. If she managed to get to her feet, would she see a skeleton in a tattered white gown?

Farida had been seduced by him, and her death had likely been his fault. Yes, that was it. Jess wondered if she should be glad she was in her right mind at the end, rather than in fantasy. Or would it be better to exit this world in delusion, so she could see the desolation of what lay afterward in the same rosy glow? Because she would be going into darkness, and she was so afraid of the dark.

"I'm sorry. They weren't supposed to come with me." She owed him nothing, but she owed Farida the words. "I just wanted to die with her."

He studied her with those amber eyes. Rage was still close to the surface. Even if she didn't now know what he was, she would have believed every story about the revenge he'd taken on Farida's family. He had blood spattered on his white shirt. She also saw something in his face that wrenched her heart, because she didn't want to see it, feel it.

"So did I," he said. "But Allah decides when we die, *habiba*."

"What a bastard," she muttered. A glimmer of something passed through his gaze as her vision started to fade. Oddly, she thought it might have been bemused tenderness, a sad smile of agreement that eased the panicked stuttering of her heart. But that only meant her fantasies had kicked back in, for vampires didn't have compassion. Not the kind she imagined in his expression before she let oblivion take her.

6

*J*ESSICA *Tyson. Holy hell.* What in godforsaken, fucking hell was fucking Jessica Tyson doing here?

Every vampire knew about her, but she was hell and gone from Venice, where she'd supposedly participated in the slaying of her vampire Master and then made a run for it. The description circulated among all the vampire territories was that of a fresh-faced woman, twenty-nine years old, with curly, short brown hair and gray eyes, a sprinkle of freckles across her nose and a lean, athletic build. The face in the photograph had reminded him of a cheerleader, the body that of a gymnast.

Without his vampire senses, without the declaration she'd made in the tomb, she looked like a very unhealthy woman in her fifties. No wonder no one had been able to find her.

He cleaned up Farida's tomb first. In the bloody aftermath, he cared naught if the strange woman lived or died. She was as much a trespasser as the other two, though for now her words, her intent, had saved her life. She'd even taken a bullet to protect Farida's body. Why had Jessica Tyson come to Farida's tomb to die? *Why* was she dying?

After he finished the cleanup, he hesitated, squatting down next to her. She was unconscious, her breath shallow. The bullet had lodged in her lung, but since it was obvious she was hours away from dying, that hadn't altered her condition much. She should already be dead; her heartbeat was so faint and irregular. But still, he wrapped her in his robe, for she was shaking. Lifting a body that weighed no more than eighty or ninety pounds, he stepped on a lever and entered a tunnel doorway that led back to his caverns, the place he called home when he was in the Sahara.

He wouldn't have known about Jessica Tyson at all, but in the past couple years he'd had to be more involved in the vampire world than he wished. The abrupt abdication of Lady Lyssa due to the revelation of her Fey heritage and her forbidden attachment to her human servant Jacob had made her an outcast and left a power vacuum. Since she was one of his few friends, and she'd helped set up the Council, Mason had felt a cursed obligation to step in to balance things again, as he knew she wished him to do. Therefore, he'd seen firsthand some of the investigative reports that had come to the Council.

The night it happened, Lord Raithe's household servants claimed he'd been making preparations to turn Jessica to a full, third-marked servant. Then he'd been surprised by an attack of vampire hunters. He'd managed to kill most of them and escape. Two other house servants came to his aid, in time to see Jessica drop the bloody stake and flee the scene. They'd scoured the surrounding area, but assumed she must have been working with the network of hunters, who helped her escape.

Except since she was already second-marked, she couldn't have hidden such long-term plans from Raithe. Her staking of him had to have been spontaneous, a dangerous opportunity she took when he was wounded.

Further questions revealed she'd been forced to serve him, a lamentable state of affairs that most seasoned vamps knew was a tragedy waiting to happen. It usually ended in having to put the servant down like a rabid dog who couldn't serve the vampire's needs reliably. The younger vamps got drunk on their own power sometimes and foolishly thought they could bend a human's will to their own like a plastic straw. While a will could be broken, it could leave a sharp edge, like a stake. In Jessica's case, the analogy had been literal. Such forced servitude was a betrayal of everything the vampire-servant bond was supposed to be.

Sitting back on his heels in his cave now, he considered her. From her condition, the unpleasant aroma of her skin and the dull glazing of her eyes, he wondered if perhaps she'd contracted a disease after the event, some form of cancer, though it was unusual for a second-mark. While they were not as invincible as a third-marked servant, they did have a greater resilience to human disease and healed faster from wounds, with minimal or no scarring.

Stripping off her bloody, soiled clothes, he rewrapped her in a clean blanket, a wasted, skeletal creature needing the mercy of death. But she'd been unexpectedly fierce when she'd defended Farida's resting place.

Searching through the pack she'd been carrying, he withdrew a handbound journal of great age. Recognizing the cover, his hands trembled. *It couldn't be.* Farida had had two of them. He still had one in his possession, much more carefully preserved. He'd assumed the other was lost to the desert, destroyed by her family.

While he stroked the spine, he remembered Farida's hands holding it. The tilt of her head, her angel's smile as she wrote in it. She'd asked him not to read it. Teasing him, she'd claimed it was where she hid her thoughts about all his annoying habits, his rank and offensive odor, his great ugliness. In tender moments, she'd admitted it was where she spoke of her love in a woman's foolish, romantic way. *It would simply make you more unbearably arrogant than you already are, my lord,* she'd said, her eyes laughing, her mouth soft, kissable.

Lifting his gaze from the book, he found Jessica Tyson's eyes on him. On the way his hands held the memoir.

"Did you love her?" she whispered. "Or did I dream it all?"

Setting it aside, he pushed his own memories away. "I don't see how that's your business. Explain your presence here."

Her eyes drooped half closed, and the gurgle that came from her throat alarmed him, despite his desire to remain dispassionate. "Typical . . . vampire . . . asshole."

His brow lifted. "Jessica, I can ease your passage. But I will know why you're here. Should I expect others, like those two?"

"Nobody else. No one knew where we were going. If all dead . . ." Her brow furrowed. "Dawud. His village . . . I wanted to help his village. Now his mother will never know what happened. Like my mother." She raised her lids then, and Mason found himself confronting a pair of gray eyes that didn't match the gaunt face. They were determined and pleading at once. "If any part of it was true, if you have any mercy or love for her, as she believed you did—" A cough bucked her up from the ground, and her face contorted with pain, blood spewing from her lips.

Automatically, he moved to the side, sliding his arm behind her back to steady her. Despite how weak she was, she struck at him, twisting, making the coughing worse. The blanket fell open down the front, but she seemed unconcerned with her lack of clothes, or perhaps she didn't notice.

"Don't *touch* me." The panic and rage in her voice was startling, that of a trapped, wounded animal.

"Shhh," he said firmly, though he couldn't prevent another spear of compassion through his gut, damn the woman. "I intend you no harm. Steady. Try to relax. Easy."

As he stroked her shorn hair, which felt as stiff as straw under his hands, some of it came away with his touch. He wasn't repelled by it, only by what this young woman had become. *What the hell had happened?*

She'd gotten the coughing under control. Her body remained stiff under his hands, her revulsion at his touch obvious, but he sensed she needed the support as she gasped out the words. "Will you go to his village . . . tell his mother he died helping me? That he served God to . . . the end. In Cairo . . . there is an account. The contents should go to his village. I'll . . . tell you how to get it. You won't do it . . . likely take them yourself, but no one else will . . . so it doesn't matter, does it?"

Spittle drained out of the corner of her mouth, a green, foul substance. He wiped it away with a cloth. Her reflexes had dulled, because it wasn't until well after he'd finished that she swiped at a hand no longer there. "Don't touch me," she repeated. "Why . . . holding me? Stop."

"Why are you sick, Jessica? What happened?"

"Didn't . . . finish. He died in . . . middle of it. Third mark." Her lips pulled back in a discomfiting feral smile. "Drove it right into his chest. One gurgle . . . dead. So easy, that night, when it had always been . . . impossible. I wanted to laugh, but it hurt so badly . . . Jesus, it hurt. One thing. Just one thing left."

Allah, be merciful. That was it. She was only partially third-marked. He'd never heard of such a thing happening, but here it was before his eyes. It was a miracle she was alive at all. She'd been a fugitive for months, so it seemed that half-finished third mark had been waging a tug-of-war with the death of the Master who'd inflicted it, giving her strength and leeching it at once. Of course, what he saw in those snapping gray eyes reminded him that burning hatred could keep the body going far beyond where science said it could.

She spoke again, though the words were getting lost in the heavy wheezing. "Won't mean anything to you, won't understand, because you're the same as him. But will say . . . for her. I . . . She kept me alive, her story, her love for you . . . kept me going. And now, he can't hurt anyone else. That's got to be worth something. Even if nothing else means anything . . . that means something."

Mason stared at her a long moment. "Yes," he said at last. "It does mean something. I'm sorry that happened to you. What Lord Raithe did to you was wrong. He never should have forced you to serve him, Jessica. That's not the way it's supposed to work, for vampires and their servants."

That penetrated, such that those eyes came back up to him again, revealing shock. The distant smile of a woman in her grave crossed her face, startling in its sweetness, a haunting suggestion of the beauty she used to have. "You're kind. So now I know. None of this . . . real. 'S okay. I used to imagine I was her. Your arms . . . around me. I know she felt safe, so safe . . . and loved, with you. I wanted that. Never knew what it was to want that, until I was so afraid and alone, all the time. So alone . . . dark . . ."

"You're not alone now," he said. The remnants of the rage he'd felt in the tomb died away before the confusion in those dove gray irises. He wasn't a kind man, but he wasn't so hard-shelled he wouldn't offer comfort to a delusional woman, even as it twisted in him, brought back dark memories of his own. "I wish I could have kept her safe. It was a lie."

"No." She responded immediately, though he'd expected his words to escape her notice. Her voice dropped to a bare whisper that seemed to make it easier for her to talk, overlaid as it was by that death rattle. "On the floor beside his bed, his chain around my neck so tight I could hardly breathe, I'd imagine I was her. In a tent with you, on soft cushions. Your body wrapped around mine, your strong arms holding me close. The kind of possession a woman wants . . ." She smiled that wistful smile again, and her fingers curled around his, a weak grasp. "You gave us that, my lord. I don't want it to be a lie. I think she knew. You would have died to keep her safe. That was what mattered."

When Mason laid a hand against her face, she turned hers into it. He could tear her skin, it was so thin and dry. Her lips were chapped, teeth bloodstained from whatever she'd been coughing up. As a vampire, he had little firsthand knowledge of death and disease, but he'd seen it claim humans again and again, been appalled at what mortality could inflict, but this was beyond that. This was an affliction caused by mortality and immortality both, a limbo state that had let her live far longer than she would have as a mere human in the same condition. And yet, somewhere in the midst of what must have been agonizing pain, chronic fatigue and debilitating lethargy, she'd followed Farida's memoirs, stepped into her shoes.

"How did you find us, Jessica?" he asked, his voice quiet, more gentle now, letting her drift in her imaginings, since it seemed to comfort her.

"Book. Followed Farida's book. Found book, nobody wanted it. Raithe thought it was just a silly romance . . ." Her head moved, nestling into his hand. Her face was small and thin, cupped easily in his palm. "Studied. Used to be a researcher. Must sleep now. Time to go to sleep. Can we . . . Want to ride with you tonight, my lord. On your horse. Take me with you. That's what she wanted, that night . . . standing at the opening of her tent. Don't want to be alone. Not ever again."

"No, not ever again," he agreed, his throat constricted by her words, his memories, as she drifted off. Her heartbeat stuttered again, and his own stuttered with it. She'd be gone soon. Maybe even a few minutes. At least he'd ensured her last moments were relatively peaceful.

But was that all this young woman deserved? No one was ever

going to accuse him of being a humanitarian. Killing those two in Farida's tomb had been no more a blight on his conscience than wiping camel dung from his boots, and he'd disposed of them as distastefully. He had no care for who they were, or their circumstances. But this woman . . . she'd protected Farida's body. Stood over her, with no chance of defending herself, and he'd heard the raw emotion in her voice.

Something has to be sacred . . .

Though the third mark had not set, Raithe was pulling her into the grave with him in the end. However, Mason had known of two vampires third-marking the same servant. Rare situations, usually vampires who had married or bonded, and trusted one another enough to share that link. It was typically a mistake, for if either vampire died, the servant died, and the surviving vampire endured two losses. However, if Raithe had only partially done the mark, was it possible another vampire's third mark could heal her, keep her in the world?

He shook his head at himself. This woman was a fugitive. If the vampire world found her, she'd be executed summarily. Dealing with her, and them, would be excessively complicated. The best thing was to let her die.

Take me with you . . . Don't want to be alone.

Some vampires believed a third-marked servant was bound to them in the afterlife. If there was any truth to it, he might be sending her back to Raithe's keeping, in whatever Hell the vampire was in now.

What was the matter with him? He typically scoffed at such ridiculous ideas about vampire afterlife. She was too far gone, besides. It might not work, and if it did, but left her in this state, then he would have to kill her himself to end her suffering.

Her heartbeat was a scant thump every few seconds now. He thought of her gray eyes caressing his face, the brief flash of hope in her recollections. In that second, he'd seen a glimpse of who she'd once been. The laughing woman in the photo, which had been snapped before Raithe took her. Probably when he'd been stalking her, the bastard.

He also thought of that eerie laughter when she'd realized he was a vampire, and understood the desolate irony in it now. But her hand was still gripping his. Holding on.

She knew you would have died to keep her safe . . .

"This is the stupidest thing you've ever done," he informed himself, and then leaned over her. Turning her head to the side, he ran his knuckles down her cheek and jawline, soothing her. She murmured in her delirium, but when his breath touched her cheek, one weak arm slid up to his shoulder, as if welcoming him into her embrace. *I imagined myself with you in your tent . . .*

He bit as gently as he could. Fortunately it was merely one more discomfort among many, and it didn't stir her from wherever her mind now wandered. He could inject her with pheromones, ease the bite's pain with increased arousal, but at this point he didn't think any jolt to her blood pressure would be wise. When he tasted her blood, if there was any doubt left, he knew her words to be truth. He tasted her essence, her age, felt the imprint of Raithe's marks upon her.

At that distasteful impression, he started the first mark in her blood, overlaying Raithe's claim. He was much older than Raithe, so even if Raithe lived, Mason could have overwhelmed his mark and had a stronger hold on her. *If nothing else,* habiba, *I can keep you from being his in the afterlife, if such nonsense is true.*

Though she couldn't yet hear his thoughts, her fingers dropped, closed on his biceps. Her body lifted up to his incrementally, an unexpected offer of surrender that stirred his blood on instinct. But then she jerked, as if disturbed, fighting him at the same time.

"Shhh, *habiba*," he murmured, keeping her in her fantasy with the endearment, drawing her back from whatever dark place his bite had started to take her. "You are in my tent, here with me. Lying upon silk cushions. You inhale the scent of rich wine, for I have poured it upon your flesh, to drink from your skin . . ."

He heard her soft sigh, and kept going, releasing the second-mark serum, giving him the ability to speak in her mind and fully seal his mouth over the puncture mark.

I kiss your mouth, your breasts, worship every inch of you even as I declare you mine, the way my heart and soul and breath are mine . . .

I am yours, my lord. In all ways. I have no fear of it.

He closed his eyes, his hands tightening on her body despite himself. Farida's own words when he'd third-marked her, when she'd shown no fear of what he was. This woman's mind was broken, her thoughts echoing words in a memoir. This was a mistake. He was bringing back to life a creature who needed the healing only death could provide. He could see into her mind now, see how fractured it was between fantasy and reality. But her fingers slid into his hair, and with his eyes closed, he saw not the wasted body of a stranger, but remembered Farida, even as he felt something else, something new, a different person. Taking the plunge, he let the third-mark serum go, the ethereal blue color of it staining her skin on the outside as he injected the rest.

She arched up to him, her fingers clutching hard, a cry breaking from her throat. He cupped her skull, held her there, fought his own reaction. He should have expected it, for something primal tended to rise in a vampire when he claimed a human fully, but the strong surge of desire to possess startled him. Sliding his other arm behind her, he supported her waist, holding her to him as the serum raced through her bloodstream. He licked at her throat, closing the wound, letting it do what it was supposed to do. It wrenched him, the pain it caused, for she was crying, tears bathing the side of his face. While he continued to whisper to her in her mind, he kept his face pressed against her temple, for he couldn't bear to watch this woman suffer. It brought one particular woman's suffering back to him, as if it had happened yesterday.

I am here. It will pass, and all will be well. Hold on, habiba, *hold on. I will not let darkness take you. You are safe, now and always.*

Drawing a knife from his belt, still holding her, he nicked his artery and gently brought his wrist to her mouth, brushing her lips. Thank Allah her delirium let her respond on instinct, else he expected he would have had to force it down her throat.

Her esophagus worked, and when the blood pattered onto her lips, she closed the gap and drank. Not in thirsty gulps, but furtive, weak swallows, as if her body were tiptoeing around like a guilty child behind a strict parent, doing something of which the mind would heartily disapprove.

Trying to ease that tension, he spoke more soothing words to her. While he did, the brittle hair beneath his palm started to become softer, shinier, curling around his fingers. Loose, dry skin firmed, getting texture and moisture, creating a tantalizing smoothness where his thumb grazed her jaw.

He watched, amazed, as his third mark moved through Jessica Tyson, recalling her from death, from Raithe's poisonous mark. Flaccid breasts became rounder, still small but now high and firm, with delicate pink nipples. The belly transformed from a shallow pit beneath prominent ribs into a satin slope, drawing his eyes down to an appealing bare sex, telling him she must have had the hair there lasered away before she met Raithe, for it was an alteration his mark did not affect. The veins that had stood out in gnarled knots on her hands melted back, revealing slim, capable fingers and lovely wrists.

Because she was still too gaunt, something else the third mark couldn't remedy, he wasn't seeing the full force of the beauty displayed in her picture. But the potential was there, waiting to be nourished to full bloom again. Her dove-wing eyes had ebony lashes that fanned the slash of her cheekbones. Her touchable pink mouth drew a vampire's gaze to the graceful throat.

As delicate as she looked, she'd killed a vampire, fought through sickness and lived the life of a fugitive to come and die here. He'd made the same mistake with Farida, assuming she was fragile. She'd even teased him about his protectiveness.

Then, such tender games over forever, she'd ridden into the camp that day, her back straight and chin up, surely knowing what awaited her. But by Allah, she wasn't going to be without him, no matter who tried to tear them apart. He'd met few with that kind of courage, men or women. Ruefully, he acknowledged it hadn't made him less protective. If anything, it had reminded him, painfully, of the frailty of her mortal life.

Something about the information he'd received on Raithe and Jessica Tyson had bothered him, and the puzzle returned now, as he looked at her. Yes, she had some extraordinary qualities, but determination and a fierce resistance were typically not assets in a servant. So why had Raithe wanted her, badly enough to take her by force? Raithe had kept six second-marks in his household, all beautiful women, all willing.

As Jessica reached the proper dosage of blood, the power of the binding that came with the third mark rushed through him. It shimmered in his blood, caused an acceleration of his vital organs as they accommodated the meshing of souls. He closed his eyes, his hand sliding down to rest on the sweet curve between shoulder and neck, his thumb teasing the base of her throat, an instinctive proprietary response. The third mark would put her under his protection for the duration of her life.

Surprised at his strong reaction to the thought, struggling through the physical transition, he reminded himself she was going to present quite a challenge, what with the whole vampire world looking to kill her. But once he got that resolved, he would figure out a way to set her up in a situation where she could reclaim as much of the life she'd wanted for herself as possible. He didn't intend to keep her, after all.

He had a pair of third-marked servants who served him well. They were husband and wife, so they fulfilled each other, while his emotions were kept out of the equation. That was best, when it came to humans. If no other lesson had proven that to him, Farida's death had. He owed it to her, to honor her that way.

But those rational thoughts faltered when the third mark appeared, high on her inner thigh. After a third mark completed, there was always a visible reflection of it on the servant's body, something that looked like a cross between a scar and a tattoo. It was a mystical thing, for the vampire had no control over it. To date, none of them knew why it occurred. The husband and wife's marks had been a pair of mated wolves, appropriate to their relationship with their Master.

But Jessica's gave Mason pause, for it was a silhouette he knew far too well. It was a small replica of the decorative scarring that had been carved into his back, using his own blood, centuries ago. The mythical desert tiger. Only one servant had ever carried it for him. Farida, in exactly the same place.

He almost dropped her, recalling himself just in time to keep holding her. He supposed, as old as he was, perhaps the marks recycled themselves. He was not given to mystical fancy, and he was not going to imagine that the woman he'd lost three hundred years ago was sending him a message through this woman's flesh.

Fortunately, when he shifted Jess, something else caught his attention. Frowning, he drew her up to his chest, leaning her against his shoulder to see what his hand had touched on her back.

His mark would take away the sickness that Raithe's death had inflicted on her, and the gunshot damage. Wounds on a third-marked servant disappeared within days, hours or minutes, depending on the age of the servant, the severity of the wound and if the blood of the Master was available to the servant. A servant would heal from most everything except a heart staking with metal. But a third-marked servant *would* scar, if the wound was touched with the Master's own blood. Some vampires branded their servants, holding the brand with that blood. He knew Lady Lyssa had done that to Jacob, just above his hip bone.

What he was looking at took him a moment to digest, and then when he did, Jess stirred restlessly in his arms, probably feeling the wave of fury from him, even in her deep, unconscious state. Eleven scars, running from her shoulders to the rise of her buttocks, like the evenly spaced bars of a prison. Raithe had skinned her, and marked each strip with his blood to hold them there.

The number of scars broke something else loose in his memory. The background data on her said she'd run away from Raithe, unsuccessfully, eleven times. She stirred again, emitting a cry, and jerked. "Enough, *habiba*," he said, firm but gentle, and she settled.

Immediately. Her body became almost pliant. On top of the shock of the tiger mark, and the scars, something else clicked into place. He rolled the lingering taste of her blood in his mouth, thought about her attachment to Farida's memories. Her delusional murmurings. *The way a woman* wants *to be possessed.*

Oh, Allah. What if she'd been a natural submissive, but innocent to it when Raithe took her, the bastard? It was the kind of virgin that was almost irresistible to a vampire, a woman who intuitively sought to serve a man's love with her own, willing to trust the touch of the right Master. Seeing the abrupt, relaxed ease of her face, the idea even stirred his imaginings. He could see her sweetly on her knees, her total surrender tempting a male to never let her out of his sight.

It would explain why Raithe had to have her, though a wiser vampire would have exercised impulse control. *Son of a bitch.* Whether true or not, Mason wished he could reach through the veil of death, jerk Raithe through it and devise ways to make *him* scream.

Ah, hell. He needed to learn to control his emotions. "Easy," he whispered as she made a fearful whimper in her oblivion. He adjusted her, cradling her in his lap as she slept on. The press of her soft backside against his thighs hardened his restive cock, awakened by his unbidden thoughts. Good thing she wasn't awake.

If it was true, it was useful only as a key to getting her back on her feet again. If it wasn't true, it was all the same to him. The point was to help her.

He turned his mind to more practical matters. Usually a third mark invigorated a servant, but he expected she would be in restorative sleep for the next day or so as her body readjusted. He was glad for it, because it would give him time to get her away from here.

He would take her to his home in South America, a place where he would be better equipped to deal with her. Regardless of her sexual nature, when she woke and discovered she'd killed one Master only to be bound by another, her reaction was likely to be far from sweet *or* submissive.

7

$\mathbf{F}$OR so many months, Jess had fought her way out of sleep. When it took her down, it tried to keep her there, help her follow the natural order and slip into the waiting hands of Death. Though she recognized it as the one friend she had, she treated it as an enemy. She'd fall into the arms of forever slumber as soon as she slept by Farida's tomb.

Now, though, something was different. She was floating out of sleep, light, easy, becoming aware of sunlight on her face, a warmth that made her press her lips together as if holding the heat of a lover's mouth there. As she turned over on the soft mattress, her flexible limbs held her weight, shifted her, twined around pillows without protest. Her palm flattened, fingers spreading out.

No pain. She didn't hurt anywhere. She could be dead. Or it could all have been a dream. A horrible, horrible nightmare, and she'd open her eyes and be in her one-bedroom flat in Rome. On her way to the bathroom, she'd stumble over one of the stacks of books she kept piled up around her bed, watched by the mysterious yellow eyes of the many stray cats that she fed. They tended to wander in through open windows to perch themselves on the larger, heavier reference materials. She'd pull on her running clothes and head out for a quick five miles before getting ready for her workday at the university, dreaming of the day when she would go with the professors on the digs.

It was the only way to process it. It had to have been a nightmare, one of the most hideous in the history of all nightmares. It had seemed like five years, because one could live a lifetime in a five-minute slumber. Proof that bending time was possible, since it happened in dreams all the time.

Though the rest of her was light, supple, ready to shake off that dream and head out on her daily routine, her eyes were still caught in that other reality. Heavy, unwilling to open, as if they knew it was best to stay like this, in this suspended state of belief, where everything was still possible.

"It's okay," she murmured, reassuring them. "It was just a terrible nightmare. Wake up now."

Reluctantly, her lids opened. She saw a hazy, pale blur that didn't clear as she blinked, but then she realized she was in a canopy bed with gauzy curtains drawn around it. The covers were all white, but when she looked up, she found the canopy was open and she was staring at a painted blue sky, where a pair of swans flew, their bills and bright eyes glossy as they twined about each other in the surreal sky.

She swallowed. The curtains were moving, caressed by a gentle breeze coming through a pair of open French doors. The murmur of the ocean, the smell of salt, reached her senses.

Blood. Harry screaming. *Help me, Anna . . . for pity's sake.* Sheltering a dead woman with her body. A man's hands on her, lifting her. No, not a man.

Yes. A man, a man, a man, a man—not a vampire; vampires don't exist. It was a dream, it was a dream, it was a dream . . .

She closed her fists on the blanket, her breath shuddering in her chest, hyperventilating with a young woman's healthy lungs. But as she shifted, she felt the stiff pull of the scars on her back. Amber eyes had watched her die, his voice comforting her with romantic imaginings.

I kiss your mouth, your breasts, worship every inch of you even as I declare you mine, the way my heart and soul and breath are mine . . .

His mouth on her throat. Her head tipping back, surrendering . . .

Dropping the cover, she closed her hand on her neck. Two puncture wounds, not quite healed over, because a marking took longer to heal than a Master's simple feeding bite. Swallowing, she tried to ignore the yawning abyss opening in the base of her mind. But it was impossible to ignore a Hell pit, filled with writhing maggotlike bodies. She'd fall into them, and they'd squirm all over her flesh, feeding while she still lived, while she cried for mercy. Raithe would laugh at her, raise his wineglass and tell his house slave to bring him a different vintage. *Bordeaux goes so much better with her screams . . .*

A girl born in quiet, middle-class America hadn't been prepared for such casual cruelty, something she'd seen depicted only in the dramatic world of movies and books, or histories that happened then, not now. Not to her.

"Stop it." She made a strangled sound, grappling with her reeling mind. What . . . what had she been doing? The bite on her neck. She had to look, see if he'd done what she'd feared. She tore back the covers.

She was naked, and it was a distracting shock to see smooth skin, long limbs, straight and strong, ready to serve her. No, not her. A new Master.

For so long, her body had been a compendium of desecrations, scars, disease, putridity. Now, it took only seconds to find an aberration. She stared at the tiger mark high on the inside of her thigh, one paw resting with provocative intent on the crease next to her sex.

"Miss? Lord Mason said you were stirring. Can I draw you a bath?"

Jess raised her gaze to the slender form of a woman, standing on the other side of the sheer curtain. She had an impression of dark hair, beauty. Of course. Vampires didn't believe in ugliness. She'd learned to hate beauty. It was the strongest weapon evil had, for the fucking mind refused to believe something beautiful could be all bad, no matter how often predators used it.

A laugh croaked out of her throat. Jess scrambled to the side of the bed, stumbling off the high perch and tangling in the gauze like a shroud. She saw tall windows, beveled glass inlaid with gold and steel dividing lights. Beautiful. More beauty. She was surrounded by it. And she was beautiful again, which meant she had value.

"Miss?" The woman had circled the bed, was trying to help her as she spun in the veil. Instead, Jess ripped it down, took it with her. Her gaze swept the walls. *Ah, there. Perfect.*

Vampires were used to being on guard, rarely having a room where they didn't keep a weapon of some kind. It was too bad the human world didn't believe in vampires, because she'd become such a student of their sociology in the past five years she could have headed her own research department.

Lord Mason believed in subtlety, or multipurpose interior decorating. The weapon was a wall vase, holding a spray of fresh tropical flowers, lush fuchsia blooms. Ten inches long, made of beaten metal, the vase had a point at the base, perfect if a vampire needed to seize something from the wall to fend off an attack. But since it was metal and not wood, it couldn't be used against him. Fortunately, it could kill a servant.

The woman was moving more swiftly now, but not fast enough. Jessica lunged, snatching it off the wall. The blooms and water showered her as she plunged the lethal tip toward her own breast. It was sharp, and would plunge through the tangle of gauze, through flesh, to the wildly beating heart. So strong and healthy. She was laughing again, and she couldn't stop. She'd die with that laughter on her lips.

We will die the same way, Raithe. You should get some pleasure out of that, you sadistic bastard. If you're waiting in Hell, I'll consume myself in the fires before I will ever be bound to you, or the likes of you, again.

She was seized from behind, a large hand closing on her wrist just as the tip pinked her flesh. She howled, struggling, fighting. "No. You won't . . . do this to me . . . again. No!"

"Manacles," he barked, and her howl became frenzied screams. She spun, tearing at him with her fingers, striking at his face, kicking his shins, knowing her skills were too rusty. She'd taught herself to fight, but during her sickness she'd barely had energy to walk most days.

It didn't matter. At the height of health, she stood no chance toe-to-toe with a vampire. He took her to the ground, pinning her on her stomach, resting his hand on her nape, a knee in the small of her back.

Dignity abandoned, rationality gone, she kept screaming, the shrill, thin cries her only comfort. Saliva whipped into a froth on her lips. As metal cuffs clamped onto her wrists, her legs were parted enough to lock a thigh cuff on each leg, the wrist manacles then locked to them, keeping her arms immobile at her sides.

Her struggles increased, her mind willing to dislocate bones to get free. Those strong hands pressed her shoulders to the ground as he shifted his body to hold the rest of her still, preventing her from hurting herself. Her vocal cords burned; her eyes were blinded by tears. Her nose had begun to bleed, for she tasted it on her lips.

"Hurry." He spoke again, his voice, tense, clipped.

Another pair of cuffs was fastened onto her ankles. A short chain between them prohibited her from anything but the mincing steps of a slave. They were long enough to spread her to be fucked, though, whenever, and with whatever, he wanted. She kicked her legs violently. She wouldn't tolerate being trapped. The metal cut into her ankles, her movements jarring her knees and hip joints, but she embraced the pain.

The short chain was removed, her thrashing legs hooked together at the ankle cuffs. Realizing she'd been immobilized, the fight over, her mind crumbled. She couldn't bear any of it. His touch, the chains, where she was. Why wasn't she dead? Her bladder voided itself like a frightened animal's. The sickening warm wetness of it bathed her thighs, pooling beneath her.

"I won't go through this again." His face was a blur. She panted it, ten times, twenty, until her head was bobbing uncontrollably with the mantra. Emotions suppressed for months squeezed her chest so hard that she'd have been driven her to her knees if she were standing. Only she'd never kneel before a vampire again. He could cut off her legs first.

She'd loved him. Farida had loved him. Oh God oh God oh God, let me just go there. If I have to live through this again, let my mind shatter. Let me be there, in their world, not in this one.

Mason, alarmed, slid his hands up her arms as her breath strangled in her throat. Her heart was thundering, near explosion. Then her head dropped back, eyes rolling up as her body began to buck. She was having a seizure. *"Jessica."*

In the absence of anything suitable within reach, he forced the side of his own hand into her mouth. As her teeth sank down, his blood seeped out. Some of it would get on her tongue, down her throat. Despite Amara's gasp, he knew that would help.

It took only a minute or so, but it felt like infinity, watching her convulse, her jaw clench, the whites of her eyes roll and tears pour out of them. When she at last began to wind down physically, she was still careening through her mind, mumbling things he didn't want to hear.

When Amara had called for him, her urgent cry had only increased his pace, for he'd already been on his way. He'd been tuned to Jess's mind when she woke. Her meandering ribbon of thoughts intrigued him, until they'd turned toward darkness and he realized he needed to be there. Damn it, he'd thought she'd be calmer if she saw a human first. But now he knew the ripple of unease in his gut when he'd left her in the room before dawn had been a warning. He should have stayed with her, helped her come to grips with the reality with a firm hand. Not like this, chaotic confusion and mindless panic.

Enrique had been right on his heels and, thankfully, had closed the French doors while they struggled with her, so the tendrils of sunlight wouldn't turn him into a barbecue. Even in the shade, Mason felt the punishing reach of its heat. He'd thought she'd like a room full of sunshine, not thinking he might need to get into it before sundown.

Though Jess's body was bound, Amara still held her legs in reassuring hands to prevent further thrashing. His servant looked up at him, her eyes sheened with tears. "What did he do to the poor child, my lord?"

"If there's any justice, what's being done to him in Hell right now." Mason shook his head, preventing further conversation on the topic. Jessica still had his hand in her teeth, but instead of a deep bite, it was more of a spasmodic gnawing, like a distressed tiger cub might do. Her body continued to twitch.

"Shhh . . ." Drawing her away from Amara, he gathered her into his lap, heedless of her soiled state. She was shivering now, her skin cold. "*Habiba*, easy. I've got you. Amara, a blanket, quickly."

When he wrapped her up, she calmed further. Though part of it might be because he'd given her warmth and made her less vulnerable by covering her nakedness, she'd slipped below conscious thought, her vulnerable mind protecting itself from her untenable reality. He noted, as he had at the caves, that the deep aversion she bore toward his kind ebbed when her mind left her body in charge of determining who was a threat. She responded to his touch, to his voice.

As he stroked back her hair, he watched the lips slacken from their frightening rictus. Remembering his earlier suspicion, Mason tested the waters further. "You are being silly, *habiba*," he told her with gentle command. "You will stop this tantrum and listen."

Her tense expression eased another fraction. Slowly, her eyes opened to mere slits. She stared at him much as an infant might. Processing what and who he might be, this stranger holding her. But when recognition started to return, the revulsion came with it, and what she couldn't hide from him—soul-deep terror.

"Jessica." He spoke in the same resolute tone, before she could slide into hysteria again. "I need you to hear me. I swear you will not be harmed. Not by me, not by anyone here. Never. I swear it on my love for Farida, which is the one thing you want to believe is real and true."

Her fingers curled against her thighs, her wrists straining against the bindings. *Off, off, off.*

"Soon," he said. He wanted them off as soon as possible as well. They were only adding to her panic, her sense of being trapped in yet another situation she couldn't control. But in her swirl of emotions, he still saw the overriding demand for self-destruction. He willed her to listen, to understand.

"I gave you the third mark to save your life, nothing more. You will stay with me for your protection, but in time, as you regain your strength and your mind, you will be able to take advantage of your potential in whatever way I can help you achieve it. Do you understand? I will *not* hurt you."

"You're . . . lying." Tears leaked from the corners of her eyes. He caught them on his fingertips, brushed them against her temples. She shuddered, tried to draw her head away, though she felt a warring reluctance to do so, which only confused her further.

"Why would I lie?" He drew her attention back to him, engaged her mind to distract her from her instincts. "I have the upper hand. It serves no purpose."

"To torment me. To make me trust your words, and then betray me. To make me hope, and then take hope away. That's what you feed upon . . . despair." Her head dropped back, like a baby whose neck was too weak to hold it up. He caught it in the cup of his hand, but she was laughing now. Allah, he hated that demented laugh, the way it twisted her lips in an ugly scar, how it deadened her eyes. He wished he'd never seen the picture of her before, a laughing face and spirit as innocent as a child's recklessly bouncing ball.

Amara made another noise of shock, and Enrique's hand tightened on her, reassurance and forbearance at once.

"You're right," Mason said steadily. "That's what Raithe would do. But I'm not Raithe."

"It's not just Raithe. You all do it." She stared up at the ceiling, blood smeared on her lips and nose, her mouth. "I'm bound to you forever."

"Yes, you are. I can't change that. But that doesn't mean what it meant with Raithe. We are not all like him."

"You put me in chains, like he did."

Mason guided her chin back to him, allowing Amara to use a wet cloth on her face. When his servant drew back, he lowered his other hand to one of the wrist cuffs. He ignored Jess's flinch as he closed his fingers on her flesh over the cool metal. The position brushed his knuckles against her bare thigh, but again he kept his face impassive, not reacting to her jerk of aversion. "I put you in manacles to protect you. You tried to kill yourself. I have lived a long, long time, Jessica. Long enough to know that the one thing that endures is the will to live. This desire to take your own life will pass."

Lifting his hand back to her face, he cradled it, sweeping a thumb over her cheek, despite the fact she remained as rigid as a corpse in his arms. "While people do not essentially change, their needs and desires do. Frequently. What you feel today won't be what you feel tomorrow or the next day." He allowed himself a slight smile. "In fact, given that you're a woman, your desires change far more often than that."

Her body was trembling. She couldn't stop it. She could smell her own urine, and she hated that as well. She wanted the power to kill every fucking one of them, even if the conflagration took her down with them. She was tired and frightened, and tired of being frightened. She'd been so close to some kind of peace, even if it was just dust.

She'd always believed that being crazy meant not knowing one was crazy. Then she'd learned that she could know she was insane, and yet not be able to do a damn thing to change it. Now, as she wanted to hate his hand upon her, and she told herself she did, some twisted psychosis inside her wanted to lean into it, wanted to hope he wouldn't hurt her too badly, if she was good. If she pleased him.

His eyes darkened, and she saw a swirl of emotions there, torn between anger and tenderness. "You break my heart, *habiba*. If I could go to Hell and find him, I'd make him suffer for everything he did to you. You are a rare bloom, and Raithe's only desire was to tear apart the petals. He thought the prize was conquering and destroying something unique, rather than winning over your heart and cherishing it. But he didn't destroy it. You're still here."

She didn't want him saying these things to her, things someone who cared about her would say. She couldn't handle having her mind fucked with again.

"So now you can finish what he started."

"No." He shook his head. "You stood inside Farida's tomb and told two men who physically outmatched you that you would die defending her. You will not be harmed here."

She was too drained to think of a response to that. Physical exhaustion reduced her to a dull stare as he drew her attention to the two others, the woman kneeling at her feet, and the man who stood behind her. "These are my third-marked servants, Enrique and his wife, Amara."

Startling her then, he dropped a casual kiss on her shoulder, bared by the blanket. His lips were unexpectedly warm, not invasive, a passing brush. But his fingers whispered over the manacles, making her jerk with unease again. "These stay on, *habiba*," he said quietly. "You have too much rage and pain inside of you, and your mind is in a very fragile state right now. I won't allow you to harm yourself. When I sense that need is gone in you, and you are no longer a threat to your well-being, you will be released. Until then, Amara will watch over you."

She wanted to argue, but he could read her mind, couldn't he? He knew better than she did what she was feeling right now, and could use all of it against her. It was time to wrap her mind around her situation, determine what, if any, options she had. A vampire with *two* third-marked servants? Well, three, if she wanted to count herself, but he had a husband *and* wife? It confused her further, but then she noted Enrique's gaze on her bare shoulder.

It reminded her again she was naked beneath the blanket, and restrained. As if Mason had heard her thoughts, and of course he had, Enrique backed away and slipped from the room. Probably to give her a false sense of security. Of the two males, Mason was the one she should want gone, far, far away. But even now, her body was pulled between the desire to be held by him, without feeling fear, and a screaming need to get away.

Mason's amber gaze flickered, his mouth set. "I will be as near as your thoughts, Jessica. If you need me, call. Otherwise, Amara will let me know of your needs."

8

WHAT would it be like, to be born with no imagination? No ability to conceptualize beyond the reality right in front of her, behind her? She couldn't contemplate a future. She'd done that, and she'd rather die than do it again.

Twenty-four years old. She'd been twenty-four when Lord Raithe took her. Jack was a sailor who'd left college to take a job cruising a large sailboat around the world for a wealthy man. He'd never gone back, and when he and Jessica met in Rome, he'd been thirty, and owned a modest sloop himself. For all their travels, both were straightforward people when it came to love. They let themselves be swept up in the joy of it and each other. They planned to travel the world together, taking odd jobs in ports while she continued her studies. Simple, imperfect dreams.

She didn't know her joy had been noted by someone else. Jack told her she was beautiful, and while she'd never given much thought to it, she didn't know that a woman in love had a special radiance that could attract the interest of a predator.

Jack had to go on a short run to Turkey. When he returned, three weeks later, she'd been reported killed in a fiery car crash, the ultimate cliché. She wished to God he'd left Rome in his grief and been at sea somewhere, impossible to find.

When she learned Farida's story, Jess had foolishly believed she knew how Lord Mason had felt after they'd captured him. There he was, thinking things couldn't get worse, and then Farida had ridden into her father's camp. Fear for oneself was a terrible, frightened animal, but seeing the one you loved most of all, riding into the jaws of unspeakable horror, with no way to warn them or convince them to turn back . . . that was worse than any other torment Raithe had devised.

She'd killed Jack, as surely as if she'd done it herself. She'd wondered if Mason's grief had been wrapped in guilt, and that guilt had expanded into a feral creature's rage when he found out how they'd killed Farida.

But it had to be a lie, all of it. Raithe had been right. Someone had taken a few scraps of historic fact and turned it into a dramatic diary about an impossible love. Farida wouldn't have known how to write like that, just as Jess originally thought. No matter what she'd found out from the consulate, none of it made sense. Raithe had driven her to insanity. That was the beginning and end of it.

"Come now." The slender woman, Amara, reminded Jessica of the enhanced strength of three marks when she slid her arms beneath Jessica's back and knees and lifted her in her arms without effort, carrying her like a cradled child into the bathroom. The long dark hair beneath Jessica's cheek smelled of gardenias. "We'll get you cleaned up and then I'll show you around the grounds. We'll put those ankle cuffs back on a chain so you can walk on your own two feet."

Because she knew enough about vampire's servants, she told herself she wouldn't beg Amara to free her, though she wanted to do so. Mason was also probably lurking around in her mind right now, hearing every thought. Just thinking of it brought forward the best weapon she'd developed against Raithe, the mind-numbing blankness, though it had not been fail proof. It had simply challenged him to seek extraordinary methods to crack it. Killing Jack before her eyes, for example. The threat of tracking down her family and killing them, if she didn't participate with enthusiasm, was also often effective.

"Shhh . . . you're shaking again. You poor love." Amara had her in a wide tub and was running heated water into it, adding some calming scents. Scooping a handful of fresh flower petals from a basket, she dropped them with some bath beads into the water. "Here we are."

Jessica let her head be guided onto a bath pillow on the tub edge and stared off into space, tuning it all out, tuning everything out. She couldn't die, and they wouldn't let her take her own life. She didn't care anymore. There was nothing left to lose. Even if Mason used the same threat against her family to gain her compliance in whatever sick game he was playing, what did that matter? In a world overrun by evil like this, wouldn't they be better off dead? At strange, drifting times she'd even contemplated forcing Raithe's hand, making him do it, to end the shadow of an axe over their heads.

The blankness into which she descended now created walls of oppressive silence, leading to a visualization of steel, impregnable walls. A chamber with no noise, light, sound, a living death. The only place the dark wasn't frightening. She didn't see why she couldn't become catatonic and remain animated, no more than a puppet that Mason bent and moved as he wished, while her mind oscillated eternally in this dark, empty space.

But something was filtering in, an easy, knowledgeable touch, and the wisp of a song, drawing her attention reluctantly.

With Raithe, she'd been tense all the time, so her muscles cramped frequently. The sponge passing over her skin was followed by gentle, kneading fingers creaming soap over her flesh, bringing lavender to her nostrils. There were no lavender soaps or gentle touches in the steel room. Those things suggested a garden. A deserted garden of Eden, the best kind. There was stillness there, no animals, no humans, only her, amid bright tropical flowers. The trees were still, for there was no breeze. Movement attracted bad things.

So she stayed still in this unexpected garden, watching, listening, yearning to touch, move and feel, but far too afraid to do so. She knew that song, though. An Irish lullaby, a sleep song that hoped for angels to watch over her, keep her from all harm. If she'd been less weary, she would have drawn the blade of her cynicism, sneered at the words. Instead, she wanted to fall to her knees in the garden and weep. When the stanza repeated itself, she thought of Lord Mason in the tomb, his shirt covered with blood. He'd lifted her in his arms and held her close, against that evidence of his ability to savagely protect and defend what he considered his.

The breeze started to whisper through the garden, setting leaves and branches in motion, an elegant dance. A few birds joined the song. Preceded by rustling, a deer stepped out, staring at her with liquid brown eyes. She had a soft coat. Touch. She wanted to touch it, to connect.

Something was touching her. Jessica focused cautiously, and became aware of the tub, the heat of the water, though the garden stayed at the fringes of her consciousness. It unfurled behind Amara's feet where she knelt. Jess blinked at the trees, the bright eyes of a squirrel who paused on a branch to consider them. The doe stepped through blue flowers.

Setting aside the sponge, still humming, Amara soaped both her hands and glided down Jessica's shoulders, her arms, then back up to her neck. Over her sternum, over her breasts. As the woman's hands molded the curves, her touch was a caress, the thumbs making a light pass over the slick nipples, and then she'd moved onward, to the convex plane of Jessica's stomach and prominent ribs.

"We'll get you some food next. Small amounts at first, so you don't get sick, but you need nourishment, child."

Jess turned her blank gaze up to Amara's face, really looking at her for the first time. Along with the dark hair and eyes, she had unblemished olive skin, a remarkable, delicate beauty appropriate in the midst of Eden. She wore a wedding ring, another unexpected element. That hand passed over the flare of Jess's hip, and then her thighs. Coming up the narrow channel allowed by the ankle cuffs, Amara submerged the soapy sponge to rub between them. Clean her. Easy and gentle, just the two of them.

Jess swallowed. The garden started teeming with cautious life, things peering out of foliage, and her body wanted to move like the trees in the wind. Her gaze became full of Amara's intent eyes, her distracting mouth. She wore simple, elegant clothes, a halter over a pair of slacks, but her breasts, loose and unbound, drew the eye to the deep cleft, the tempting roundness of them beneath the cotton.

She was surprised by the direction of her thoughts, but she

supposed she shouldn't be. It had been so many months since she'd been touched by anyone. Men frightened her, and her sickly appearance repelled everyone else. Amara emanated gentle kindness and sensual beauty. While the woman was a vampire's slave, and therefore not to be trusted, Jessica thought she could be trusted for this, even if she was doing it for Mason's mental entertainment. Only it didn't feel like that. Amara's cosseting was easy, keeping the garden growing with life, not startling anyone back into the forest. The unfurling of desire, the needful response of a young, healthy woman's body, startled her, though. Her mind warred with her reaction, knowing how her arousal had been twisted, distorted in the past, by roads paved with good intentions.

Raithe had been good at this, too. When he didn't want her pain, he knew how to make his touch gentle, stirring, the way every woman wanted to be touched. Even against her will, he'd get her on the knife edge of climax, and then he'd bring the knife into it. He'd taken her over into orgasm with her mouth around the cock of a servant who'd been ordered to rub his genitalia with manure in order to suitably reinforce her degradation. She'd gagged, even as she'd screamed out her climax.

You're my little cunt, aren't you? Doesn't matter what's done to you; deep inside you want to please. It's awe inspiring. During the aftershocks of that particular orgasm, he'd replaced his fingers with a sharp kitchen utensil, and her cries became screams of pain. He'd made her bleed and refused to let her clean herself afterward, even prohibited her from brushing her teeth for several days. Then he punished her for being a filthy slut. While he was flogging her, he clamped a vibrator on her untouched clitoris so she came again and again, until she was reduced to tears, begging just for a bath.

A bath like this . . .

"No," she whimpered. The garden was drying up, blackening, and the animals were dead, rotting. She needed to withdraw, to go back into her steel room. Where was it? She turned, but her way was blocked. The angel that guarded the door to Eden with his multidirectional sword? *You're too filthy, too ruined to come back here.* The angel looked like Lord Mason, and she backpedaled, trying to run.

"Jessica."

Her name was being called, by a woman. Jessica blinked, and the bathroom swam into her consciousness. She looked down, wasn't surprised to see the blood, for he'd cut her, hadn't he? The water was swirling crimson. Then she saw her fingernails had dug into her thighs. Because she hadn't trimmed her nails in so long, they were rough and ugly. Amara's hand was cradling Jess's face. "Jessica," she repeated. "I would like you to kiss me. Will you kiss me?"

The wetness on her face wasn't all from the sponge. Awaiting her answer, Amara leaned forward and placed her lips on Jess's cheek, over the tear rolling down it, arresting its forward motion. So easy, so stimulating. Soft, sensual lips. Amara moved up the track, kissed Jess's eye as the lid closed, then moved over to the other. Up to her forehead, resting her lips on the place in the center above her brows, which seemed to bring a wary flood of peace. Jess's fingers curled again, only this time against her own palms.

She wanted to touch the woman. Male bodies, hard, unyielding— there was fear there, pain. But this . . . Raithe didn't allow the female humans in his household to touch. Jessica had been relatively inno- cent, but even she knew it was unusual for a heterosexual male not to want two women touching. Maybe he'd inadvertently given her a gift, one thing his presence hadn't soiled. She'd never been attracted to women, but this wasn't about sexual preference. It was a sudden need to touch a beautiful body, have it respond to her. God, how long had it been since she'd been touched like this, been invited to touch back, without pain or fear?

"Will you kiss me?" Amara lifted her head, asked again. "Please, Jess. I really want you to kiss my mouth. But it's your choice. It's all your choice."

~

Doesn't matter what's done to you; deep inside you want to please. It's awe inspiring . . .

Mason cursed and pivoted away from the wooden dummy, swip- ing the towel across his face. There were times he hated being right. This was one of them. Yes, it was a key to helping the girl. But thanks to Raithe, it was a key equally capable of destroying what was left of her mind, if it hadn't already.

The vast complex of underground rooms and corridors beneath his estate allowed him to set his own hours, for at his age, he did not need to find repose immediately upon sunrise. And too often his sleep did not bring rest. Like now.

Enrique was with him, but his servant had stood, silent and unobtrusive, as Mason used his bare fists until blood smeared his knuckles and the wood. Vampires were naturally dominant, demanding the submission and obedience of their human staff and servants. But what he saw in the depths of Jessica's mind, revealed by Amara's skilled touch, was sadistic cruelty.

When at last Mason paused, he kept his eyes on the post, his fists clenched. "What did you find out from the Council clerk?"

"The vampire world thinks she's still at large. No one even has a hint of where she might be. But once she is found, the Council expects her delivered to them immediately for justice."

"Justice." His jaw clenched, and this time when he hit the solid oak post, it splintered, a sharp crack before it toppled.

He'd seen the stirrings in her mind when Amara touched her, so when another panic attack loomed, he'd told Amara to suggest something unexpected, but nonthreatening. The sensuous touch of another woman. Though normally he would have enjoyed being on the mental sidelines, he had to pull out, close that link, because he was afraid his rage would spill out and frighten Jess.

There was no such thing as a civilized vampire. He scoffed at the Council members who pretended otherwise. However, there was a difference between the wild animal who accepted his natural savagery and one whose savagery twisted and became something evil.

Such evil had infiltrated Farida's family, for it was the only comprehensible explanation for their ability to take a beautiful, brave woman, one of their own blood, and stake her out in the desert sun, torment her and then let her broil there. She'd died in agony.

"My lord." He wondered if Enrique realized he'd just saved the support beam to the room with the quiet prodding. "Should I send word to the Council?"

"No." Mason uncurled his bloody fingers. Having been buried beneath a few tons of rock before, he didn't care to repeat the experience. "Not yet. First, we help her recover her mind. Then I will deal with the Council. But no one is ever hurting that girl again."

~

Raithe had taught her there were no absolutes. His will was everything, and he could bring things out in her she didn't even know were there. There were no definitions. She didn't prefer only men or women, or apple versus chocolate pie. Everything could become a pleasure or a torment, depending on the moment, the need, the desire.

That lesson had been so well learned she couldn't deny it. The twitchy need in her, the borderline panic about those restraints and her current situation, made it hard to breathe. But here was a distraction, a channel for the panicked energy.

She lifted her chin and straightened in the tub, awkwardly. "I want to kiss you," she said hoarsely.

"Then your command is my deepest wish, child." Amara settled her lips on Jess's, light, affectionate. But the platonic sensuality was fleeting, for Amara's clever mouth teased Jess's open to find her tongue, stroke and stimulate it so desire bloomed in her chest, warring with the panic constricting her chest. Jess made a strangled sound as Amara's fingers curled around the back of her neck, keeping Jess safely upright in the tub.

Closing her eyes, she let herself be taken over by it, with the tiniest tinge of despairing hope that it would not be followed by pain or horror. This did seem different. The garden was a transparent shadow, a ghostlike memory, but if she tried, she could imagine it in full, vibrant bloom around them. So many lush tropical flowers, the chatter of monkeys, birds with strange piercing cries. The shadow over her closed lids was a man's shadow, a man's hand cradling her face, tilting her head back to capture her lips. He pushed her back to the ground, demanding she surrender everything, give him herself, be his in all ways, and he would fill the aching emptiness inside of her. This was a magical place, the kiss spinning a spell that would keep away everything painful, real and ugly. She didn't have to be in the steel room. She could stay here instead, spinning in this fantasy vortex forever, her body lifting to his, wanting to surrender, give to him. Not be afraid of his touch.

Come for me, Jessica.

She imagined him saying those words, a voice inside her mind, male, urgent and yet calm, steady. If he said them, she could let go, could spin free and wild, because there was no choice. The thought swept every inch of her skin, rippling with heated water, his imagined touch, a woman's hands, the smell of lavender. Amara's hair curtained her face.

She strained against her bonds, wanting to wrap her arms around something, somebody. As if knowing her need, Amara's arms encircled her, arched her up against her voluptuous bosom, holding Jess as she shuddered, caught in yearning desolation and loneliness.

In the center of Eden, a serpent blinked at her with Raithe's eyes. But the arms held her closer, and she brought that male voice back into her head, gave it the words she needed to hear until it all spun away.

Fear no evil, for I am with you . . .

"There you are, sweet girl. We have you." Amara's voice. Jess reoriented herself as the woman eased her back into the water, stroking her hair. "You're so lovely. Thank you."

It took her a few seconds to realize why the woman was giving her thanks, but then Jess awkwardly managed a shrug, which reminded her of the manacles. "Please take these off."

"Only Lord Mason can take them off. It will be all right." Amara gave her a sympathetic but implacable look. "Let's finish getting you cleaned up, out of this tub, and we'll walk around the grounds. You need to know where everything is. And we'll feed you."

The shift from arousing lover to motherly nurse was smoothly done, Jess reflected. Too smoothly for her raw emotions and embarrassed, vibrating body. "Did he teach you to manipulate people like this? You're good at it."

Amara, removing a towel from a cabinet, stopped and turned. "Excuse me?"

The woman's tone was actually frosty. Intriguing. Raithe's servants had been like salespeople, handling negative reaction with sugarcoated words and blinding, fake smiles. "You heard me."

Amara tossed back a wave of sable tresses. Any man would want to bury his face in them. Long, beautiful hair, perfect face, unscarred body. Elegant and self-assured, reveling in a lifestyle Jessica had abhorred. *She hated her.*

"Yes, I did hear you," Amara said evenly. "My lord Mason has taught me a great deal about pleasuring myself and others, in ways that have enhanced my life, and my love for Enrique. But manipulation means twisting someone for your own benefit, not theirs. Everything done here will be for you, Jessica. For your benefit."

It's for your benefit Jack must die. It is a lesson you must learn. For your benefit, and that of those you love . . .

"Sure," Jess said, and turned her face away. *You lying bitch.*

Amara slid her hand under Jess's arm. "Let's find you something to wear."

Jess complied, using Amara's help to stand. The weakness she'd expected to be experiencing from the earlier seizure was already gone, an unsettling reminder that she, too, had a third-mark's strength, though it was likely somewhat less than Amara's, being newer and her body not properly nourished. After being near death for so long, going from one extreme of the spectrum to the other was jarring. But that center fulcrum, being a vampire's property, had remained the same, as if she were the hands of a clock, spinning around, thinking that time was passing, even as one end of those hands stayed anchored in the same place.

She wondered how often Amara had had to fight for her life. Had she ever been denied food for a week and then been shoved into a kennel with two starving Rottweilers as dinner party entertainment, the three of them in a fight to the death for a hunk of raw, rotted meat?

When Amara bent to retrieve the sponge and straightened, her face was inches from Jess's. Jess remembered the dog she'd pinned, how she'd hammered desperate fists into his windpipe until she crushed it, while he clawed skin from her naked body. As the life died out of his brown eyes, she'd known he was the lucky one. The other dog had cowered back, her dominance established, and waited for his share until she wolfed down her part of the meat. He'd been so hungry his eyes never left it. The blood dripping from her mouth was a contrast to the saliva dripping from his.

The brief glimmer of uncertainty in Amara's eyes was the only opening she needed. Slamming her forehead against the woman's temple, Jess forced her to stumble, and then threw her shoulder into hers. Amara's feet shot out from under her. She fell face forward into the tub, her rib cage striking the edge hard enough to break some bones.

Most accidents happen in the bathroom, after all . . .

Jess fell on top of the woman's upper body, forcing her head under the water. Bracing her feet at one end of the tub, Jess caught her fingers in one of the Jacuzzi's jet portals near her bound wrist to brace herself, hold Amara down. She used the woman's body to stay above the water. If she hadn't dazed the servant, she would have been thrown off, but as it was, Amara was still disoriented. Hitting someone in the head with her own made both opponents see stars, but Jessica had the upper hand. She fought through the dizziness to keep it.

When Amara went limp, unconscious from the blow and oxygen deprivation, Jess wallowed off her and struggled up to her knees, making it to her feet. If Mason wasn't tuned into them right now, she might have a window of opportunity to . . . what? Her ankles were locked together. She couldn't do more than hop. That didn't matter. The point wasn't escape; it was resistance.

Torture me, you bastard, but don't you dare try to trick me with kindness through one of your whores.

She sat down on the tub edge, used the fortunately placed wall behind it to lever her feet out of the tub. Amara was third-marked. Only a heart strike could kill her, so Jess was unconcerned about her drowning. Instead, she made it to her feet, wet, dripping, naked and impassive as Enrique burst into the room.

Though she tensed, prepared for attack, he ignored Jess. Lunging to the side of the tub, he lifted Amara out of the water, pushing her hair back from her face. It gave Jess a moment to study him. He was a complement to Amara's dark beauty, of course. Black hair, though cropped short, and a fine aquiline face and green eyes. Not quite as tall or broad as Mason, but he had a lean, elegant strength, like a ballet dancer, or an expert fencer. He displayed it now as he lifted his wife in his arms and bore her out of the room without a glance in Jess's direction.

She shivered a little from the damp cold. So what now? She hiccupped on a giggle. When there was nothing to lose, painting herself into impossible corners meant nothing. Then she glanced up, and he was standing in the doorway.

Despite the ferocity that had goaded her attack, a trickle of fear returned. Yet she forced herself to remain still while his gaze covered her, as if marking each bead of water rolling down her body, the thrust of breasts and point of sex. His look reminded her that Amara's kiss and her own imaginings had aroused her, mixing the cool wetness on her thighs with a warm and viscous reaction. When his eyes returned to rest on her mouth, she recalled the voice again.

Come for me, Jessica.

It had been his voice. *Jesus Christ and shit.*

"My intention is to have Amara tend to your needs until you are safe to release from your bonds. Bathe you, feed you, care for your more intimate requirements. You are in danger of having that option replaced by something you will like far less."

His hands on her, bathing her, feeding her. Touching her all the time, never a moment's peace. But there was no safety, no peace. Though her heart rate accelerated, she curled back a lip. "If you're going to fuck with my head and my body, do your own dirty work. Wipe my ass yourself."

Then he took a step into the room, filling it with his larger-than-life presence, his powerful body. The fury that had carried her through her attack on Amara drained away. No, it didn't drain away. She'd just reached the bottom of the barrel and hadn't realized it.

She'd learned to deal with Raithe, responding as he needed her to respond, holding that tiny kernel of herself somewhere else, but now that fortitude was . . . gone. Swirling away, like the water disappearing from the tub, because Enrique had opened the stopper when he recovered Amara.

She couldn't stop herself from flinching back against the wall, though she was glad it was there, else she would have fallen on her ass with her hobbled legs. Self-loathing flooded her. As he advanced, picking up a towel, she hated the fear that made her speak. "Please, don't."

"Easy, *habiba*. Easy." He didn't choose the cautious approach used on unpredictable animals, which would have made her more nervous. Instead he simply walked up to her. She couldn't strike out at him, but as she tried to twist away, he began drying her. Her hair, her shoulders and breasts, abdomen and stomach, down to her sex. When she made a whimper, he slid the towel in the narrow area between her legs, absorbing the moisture. His touch was familiar, recalling her imaginings when Amara was touching her.

Of course the bastard would have seen those visions, and had some way of making her feel his touch through his mind. Raithe thankfully hadn't been able to do that. His drying rhythm slowed, became something different, the terry cloth caressing her labia, her still-sensitive clit. Her body contracted, betraying her, but it meant nothing. Vampires knew how to make this dark part of her come forward, the part that would do anything to please him. She'd have it surgically removed if she could, and since she couldn't, all she wanted was death. Freedom from the shame of herself.

"Please don't touch me," she burst out. Her muscles spasmed, an involuntary resistance to the restraints. "If you mean it, about not hurting me, then don't touch me. It's agony."

He paused, considering her, that large body and distracting scent so close. Inclining his head a fraction, he wrapped the towel around her, tucked it over her breasts so she was covered, though she couldn't help how gooseflesh raised on the upper swells as his knuckles brushed her there.

"All right. Are you going to let Amara take care of you?"

She nodded, staring at his chest. *Go away go away go away.* Putting a fingertip under her chin, he made her lift it. "You will not try to hurt her again? Promise me this one thing, Jessica."

She closed her eyes. "Look at me," he commanded, with a sharpness she couldn't refuse. She stared up into those amber depths. He was a vampire. Vampire. Even his scent should repel her, and yet she'd relished the heat of his hands through the towel, and couldn't take her eyes off his mouth, the planes of his face. The man Farida had believed she loved.

She wondered if the brain could simply explode from the inability to reconcile nightmares and dreams come true. She felt like one of those supercomputers in a movie, given a problem it couldn't solve, therefore losing all ability to function. Only she wouldn't be that lucky.

"Jessica."

"I won't." Though in truth, she wasn't sure. She couldn't seem to control her reaction to him, part fear, part revolting need. The fury had taken her over, making it impossible for her not to hurt Amara. For the five years she'd been with Raithe, and the months on the run, she'd held herself on a tight leash, but she'd had a focus then. With Raithe, it had been to survive to protect her family. When she escaped, it was to find Farida. Now she had no focus, no understanding of this situation. No idea what she could hope to have here, only her certainty that hoping was futile around vampires.

"Good." His tone gentled. "She'll come back in a moment. I think you should consider an apology. She's not as placid as she appears. She may decide to hold your head under the water for a bit, and I won't come to your aid." Closing his hands on her shoulders, he lifted her off her feet and rotated her, pushing her down into a vanity chair. He arranged the towel to cover her thighs again when the movement parted the terry cloth to reveal her lower body almost to the juncture of her thighs. He did it all swiftly, but it didn't stop her from going rigid beneath his hands, and staying that way even after he withdrew. Her mind vacillated between *Don't hurt me, don't hurt me* and *Just close down, just close down*. She wanted to cry and rage. And she wanted the fucking restraints off.

"In time." He went to one knee next to her, curled a lock of hair around her ear, even as she tried to draw her head away from him. Vampires usually prohibited their servants from looking them in the eye, but he'd specifically asked her to look at him, a couple times now. However, right now, she stared at the terry cloth, not wanting to see his handsome face, feel the pull in her lower abdomen at the slope of jaw, high cheekbones, the firm lips and steady eyes.

"I meant what I said, Jessica. No harm will come to you here, but you cannot cause harm to others, either. Do something like that again, and I will keep you with me at all times." She noted from beneath her lashes that his glance strayed over her throat, then down to the tenuously tucked towel. "You know enough about vampires to realize that if I'm around you too much, I will not deny myself a taste of you, in several different ways."

"You said . . . I'd be safe." She swallowed as his brow lifted.

"You would be quite safe, Jessica. As safe as you were in Amara's arms. Keep that in mind before you decide to take out your anger on an innocent again. You need to fight with someone"—his gaze sparked in a way that inspired fear and yet heat again, low in her belly—"you call on me."

9

HER mixed reaction to that threat plagued her for the rest of the afternoon. Raithe had been able to get her body to respond to him, but her mind had always been repelled. Lord Mason seemed to have an additional weapon in his arsenal. He'd restored her health by binding her to him. He claimed when he deemed her ready, she would have options to live her life as she chose. Raithe certainly had never offered that. And since the whole vampire world was seeking her, Mason was risking some retribution by hiding her.

But more likely, it was all a ruse, exactly as she thought.

Thinking about it, flipping between confusion and suspicion, depleted her anew. Even a third-mark's strength couldn't compete with emotional exhaustion. When Amara returned, she had a swelling bruise on her forehead that matched Jess's, though both would likely heal within the hour. Jessica didn't feel inclined to apologize, but she did, stiffly. Amara acted as if nothing untoward had happened. As if she were caring for a child or a psych ward patient who couldn't be expected to behave any better. Then she proceeded to comb out Jess's hair, commenting on the way it naturally curled around her face.

It irritated Jess, but there was very little about the situation that didn't. God, she wanted free of these manacles. She'd hoped for a brief respite, because she assumed they would have to be removed to put on clothes. However, Amara produced a silver-and-brown-patterned two-piece sarong. The upper, scarflike piece wrapped around her torso, the excess rolled into silken ropes that crisscrossed her breasts and then tied around her throat, the tails trailing down her bare back. The skirt unhooked to allow Amara to place it around Jess's waist above the manacled wrists. A slit from knee to waistband let the fabric fall on either side of where her wrists were bound to her thighs. The garment draped and covered Jess's backside and front, but of course would ripple when she walked, so the shadowed hint of both would be visible. Accessible.

Yeah, she was supposed to think he was different. Vampires often had their servants wear such provocative outfits, because a primary, heady part of the vampire-servant connection was sex. Vampires had libidos like rabbits. Mason himself had noted that excessive exposure to him would be a risk. He'd stated it as the matter-of-fact truth he knew she understood. Regardless, it amounted to a threat in her mind.

"I also have several pairs of pantaloons slit like this. I use them for dancing. They'll be perfect while you wear the manacles." Amara affixed the chain between the two ankle cuffs and then released the clasp holding the two locked together. It gave Jess some degree of freedom, so welcome that she almost felt compelled to thank her. She didn't, instead adjusting her legs apart, barely resisting the urge to take them out as far as possible, like a dog straining on the end of her tether.

"You dance for his pleasure," she said sourly.

"Yes," the servant responded, meeting her gaze. "And for my own. I am a dancer, Jessica. That is what I was when Lord Mason and Enrique found me. Dancing allows me to connect more deeply to my own sensuality. When I surrender to it, it also becomes my lord's pleasure."

It gave Jessica an unbidden image, of Amara dancing for Lord Mason as he sat in the shadows. Opening his robe to stroke himself while watching her made her so wet and needy for him that her thighs were glistening when done. She came to her knees before him, begging for the privilege of him spilling his seed on her breasts.

Jess viciously shrugged off the image. What was the matter with her? *Amara* would do that. Not her.

Allah has blessed him. With no sisters or friends to giggle with about such things or explore her wonder about them, Farida had made her diary her confidant for her innocent reactions. *Thick, long and beautiful, his organ is a pillar that makes a woman's body grateful to clasp it.*

Amara rose after adjusting the skirt and ankle manacles and turned Jess toward a mirror. She affixed a choker of small jade stones around her throat, the hold of the collar making Jessica shiver, shadows in her mind shifting, uncertain.

"You are beautiful, Jessica."

But when Amara's hand trailed over Jess's back scars, Jess jerked away from her touch, avoiding her gaze in the mirror. "If I'd been smart, I'd have stolen Raithe's blood and scarred up my face, so he'd have killed me to avoid looking at me."

"Jess." Amara took hold of her shoulders, brought her back to the mirror. "I know our words mean nothing to you. Only time will prove the truth of it. But I swear to you that Lord Mason is not a vampire like that."

"You're saying he wouldn't throw me down and fuck me, if I showed even a second of willingness?" Jessica's gaze shot up, met hers in the mirror. "What about if I got in his face and pissed him off? They all have a limit on what they'll let us dish out. But none at all on what they'll take away from us."

Amara held her eyes. While there was no censure in her expression, her voice was even, firm. "Then test him, Jessica. Make him angry, the man who let you live even after you desecrated the tomb of his lover, who brought you here to help you heal."

Jess shrugged her off again and moved away from the mirror. Since she'd been used to shuffling for a while, walking with the manacles was much the same movement. But she wasn't that sick person anymore, so having to do so now because of her hobbles made her even angrier. She was going to lose her mind. "You know what? He told you to take care of me. That doesn't include talking. Dress up the demented little psych patient, sit her in a chair in the corner and stop feeding me bullshit about Lord Mason being a touchy-feely vampire."

"I did not say he was that. I was saying—"

"I don't give a shit," Jessica snarled. "Shut up, shut up, *shut up*. You can't be trusted. You're his. You'll say anything for him, do anything for him. I'm not falling for it. Dress me up for him. Keep me manacled, so when he comes to hurt me, I can't fight him. I'd say he can't do more to me than's already been done, but vampires always can. There's always something more they can do. *And . . . let . . . me . . . loose*."

The last words were a screech as she threw herself at the wall. Not because it made any sense, but because the energy was screaming through her muscles. Now she understood why a wild animal would fight a trap until he tore off a limb to get free. She had to be free. She couldn't tolerate this.

Enrique had apparently decided to watch over his wife more closely, for before Amara could act, he'd reentered the room. Moving swiftly, he caught Jess before she could rear back and slam herself against the plaster again. As he grabbed her around the waist and chest and pulled her back, his arms became many arms, his scent suffocating her, a stench of male lust closing in over her head like sewage water, drowning her. *"Let me go."*

As she shrieked, he sat her on the floor, going down with her. She writhed, biting, doing her best to get away, vaguely cognizant of Amara saying something and him releasing her, moving back as she flopped back and forth like a fish on the sand. Helpless. She was so fucking helpless . . .

Habiba, *stop it*.

When the thunderous command exploded in her head, it stilled her, as much as she didn't want it to do so. She stopped thrashing, but she couldn't stop the nervous rock of her body, back and forth, back and forth. *I'm not hurting them*.

You are trying to hurt yourself. That is unacceptable.

Why? Want the privilege of doing it yourself? Take these fucking things off. *I can't think. I can't . . . breathe, with them on. Please . . . take them off . . . I'll do anything . . . Just don't trap me, please please please . . .*

She pressed her forehead hard into the wood of the floor and the adjacent stippled edge of the Persian rug. Squeezing her eyes shut, she tried to shut it all off. In control for so long, and now she couldn't find the switch to get a grip on herself again, as if the manacles had unleashed a beast inside. If she had some control over herself, maybe she could find the control on her mind. She couldn't bear this; she couldn't handle the jagged ache in her chest that threatened to shut off her breath. Every escape route gone. God, what had she done to deserve Hell? It was a question she'd stopped asking herself long ago, realizing that there was something worse. No Hell, no Heaven, nothing but random chaos. Her life meaningless to anyone but herself, and she wanted to stop caring about that.

Silence. She realized Enrique and Amara were gone, but she wasn't alone. She could feel him watching her from the doorway. Managing to roll over, she made it to her knees, not wanting to face him from her back.

"You know, a vampire who doesn't get his full eight hours of sleep can be very cranky," he observed mildly.

Jessica kept her head down, her breath rasping in her throat. More tears had squeezed out of her eyes during her tirade, and she turned her face into her shoulder, trying to get rid of them. One had rolled down the side of her nose and itched.

When he went to one knee beside her, she noted he was wearing a pair of jeans and only that, versus the embroidered tunic he'd had belted over it earlier. The pants had been pulled on hastily, because the top button was still undone. Her vision filled with the expanse of broad chest, the planes of a flat, hard stomach, the stretch of denim over groin and thigh.

Those things shouldn't distract her, shouldn't mean anything to her. Rocking back, she tried to duck under his grip, but it came to rest on the side of her face, the back of her neck, controlling her head. He made a soothing noise and wiped away the tears with his thumb, then rubbed her nose where the itch was. When she teetered precariously, he steadied her.

"Stop this," she quavered. "Stop being nice to me."

His amber gaze rose from the track of his thumbs to lock with hers. "Is that what you want, *habiba*? Or would you rather see how I punish a disobedient servant, so you can stop worrying about it?"

Jessica swallowed and found herself unable to speak, to even think under his gaze. She was so very tired. Emotionally, physically, even down to whatever kind of exhaustion could inflict the soul. But, in contrast, her nerves were stretched tight as lightning-charged wire, and the panic of those bonds was choking her.

He stared at her a long time, and she had the oddest thought he was struggling with some decision inside himself. Then he touched the manacle on her right wrist, and it clicked, unlocking. He did the same to the left and freed her of the ankle hobbles as well. The restraints dropped from her body.

She was on her knees to him, and that was unacceptable, his own words. She tried to pull away, to rise. Instead he turned her deftly to swing her up in his arms.

"What are you—"

"Be silent." He carried her back into the bedroom, to a wing-backed chair. When he sat down, he flipped her so she was on her stomach on his lap, her upper body teetering over the edge, his denim-clad calves under her grasping fingers. While she struggled to move, he of course held her down with little effort as he pulled up the back of the skirt, exposing her buttocks to the air. "Jessica, I do not wish to be woken again today. You'll let Amara and Enrique care for you, with no more tantrums or interruptions."

Whap!

She'd had skin peeled from her back. She'd been flogged, burned, stabbed, electrocuted . . . Hell, name any torture that had been devised in creative human history and she'd probably experienced some form of it. One part of her had started to shut down as soon as she realized she'd been right, that he was going to hurt her. And this did hurt, but not the way Raithe had hurt her. This was . . . he was simply spanking her. With a strong, open palm that made her buttocks wobble and tingle. As she squirmed, he put his hand on the back of her neck, holding her there with a firm but gentle hand, and kept doing it. When she struggled, her movements rubbed her clit on his hard thigh, and damn if she wasn't getting . . . No. She tried to shut her mind down and couldn't, because what he was rousing in her was cutting through the fear.

She tried to push it back, preferring fear, but he kept up the spanking, alternating cheeks, sometimes striking both at once with a thrum of sensation. Then he put a hand between her legs, and exposed the shame that she'd gotten wet. He dragged that moisture up between her cleft and stroked her rim, making her writhe and cry out more.

Just a teasing touch, and then he spanked her some more, until she was gasping. She'd abandoned the flailing of her arms in favor of gripping his denim cuffs, squeezing down on her reaction, fighting her traitorous body as hard as she could. Unable to face herself, she pressed her face into his calf. Her sex was throbbing, her backside aching, and she needed release. She shied from that like a startled horse. Had she lost her mind?

Then he slid her down between his spread thighs, onto her knees on the floor, and opened the jeans. *Holy God.* Yes, all vampires were beautiful, but now she understood why Farida had felt as she had. From her position on his lap, she knew he was hard and erect, but seeing it stretch forth to graze his flat belly, his testicles temptingly outlined by the stretch of denim . . .

His large hand molded the back of her head, almost gently, and with his other hand, he pushed the organ down, bringing it in alignment with her mouth.

Let your mind go, habiba. *This is what you need. This is what Raithe should have prized in you, cherished and protected.*

She was too dazed to respond, to do more than accept. The broad head pushed against her slack lips, and then he was penetrating, guiding her down on him with a palm cupped at the back of her skull, letting her get the salty taste of him. Since she had no balance of her own, he held her steady, while the other hand gripped the base of his cock.

It was like a pacifier, God help her. Raithe, in those arousing moments that always, *always* were the precursor to something horrible, had taught her this about herself. When she knew there was going to be that horrible moment following, no way of escaping it, she'd learned to take what she could from the nonhorrible moments, even though it was still unwilling. And something about this position, on her knees, working a man's cock with her lips, gave her a trancelike escape, a frisson of personal desire that could belong only to her. At least until it was over and Raithe exploited it for his own purposes.

She liked the taste of Mason far better. Male musk, salt and the exotic scent suggested that he used a cologne on his testicles, much as he would on his clean-shaven face. And there was so much of him. Hard, driving into the back of her throat, and she was only halfway down his length. Automatically, she softened her throat muscles and took more, winning a growl of approval. Her sex was rubbing against her heels, and she was quivering with her building response. She moved faster, trying to gain a grip on sanity by doing something entirely insane. He was lengthening, thickening in her mouth, and her eyes were watering, even as she couldn't get enough.

But he pulled her off of him then, despite her mewl of protest, and brought her back over his knees, as if he was going to spank her again. Instead, he started rubbing two knowledgeable fingers up and down her wet opening, teasing her clit, and alternating that with more stinging spanks that had her crying out. When he sank three fingers into her, keeping the others working on the outside on her clit, the helplessness, instead of being born from terror, was passion. The energy that had been sparking on her nerves so uncomfortably, making her feel as if she couldn't survive another moment without doing violence wherever she could manage it, was channeling into something different, an even more explosive form of release.

Come for me, habiba.

She shattered, screaming. The powerful rush of climax came without the choking, bitter hatred of Raithe, without the utter certainty that it would be followed by pain and fear. But she was out of control, in the lap of Farida's vampire, sarong hiked up so she was accessible to him. Not only were vampires all the same, but she was as despicable with him as she'd been with Raithe.

As she came down, he was turning her again, to lift her into his arms. They were moving, out of the curtained room, away from the heat of the sun behind those panels. He was taking her down hallways and then stairs, winding down to a lower level, where it was dim, quiet and cool, the walls becoming stone.

She'd had kinetic waves of energy washing through her to the point of madness moments ago, but now she was struggling against heavy lassitude again. She tried to keep her eyes open, fearful of going to sleep in a vampire's arms. Where was he taking her? A dungeon torture room, no doubt. She knew it. Maybe it would be better if she could lose consciousness.

"Something a little nicer than that," he remarked dryly. *You have regained your grasp on your health,* habiba, *but to restore it completely you will need food, and lots of rest. Open your eyes, sweet one. Trust me.*

Slowly, she obeyed, and found they were in a bedroom. One equipped with a wide, king-sized bed in an antique, ornate wood frame, with full canopy and draperies.

"So you brought me to a nice setting to rape me."

The words couldn't deny what she'd just done, though. She couldn't have stopped him, so she could hardly say she'd allowed it, but she had participated. Had wanted to taste his cock, had wanted to . . . had wanted.

You say no, but everything I do to you, you want . . . You ask for it with your eyes, your mouth . . . You deserve it. Raithe's hated words.

"Jessica." Mason had his hand on her chin, a firm jerk, and she broke away from Raithe's voice, scrambling toward Mason's without shame.

"You do need food, but more than that, you're exhausted. You are going to sleep with me until dusk." He put her down, but reclaimed her chin, made her look up at him. "Until you fall asleep, I want you to think about this. A child will take candy from a stranger, or help him find his lost puppy, because that is the nature of a child. Children carry the gift of innocence, of joy. Of God, whatever name He is called. Someone who would abuse that gift deserves the worst fires of Hell. Whereas a child deserves only the embrace of the angels." His lips twisted in irony. "Unfortunately, you shall have to do with the poor substitute of mine tonight."

Uncertain how to respond to that, she watched him lift a slender silver bracelet from the side table and lock it snugly around her wrist. It had a length of chain attached to it that he looped around his forearm before he scooped her back up and carried her onto the bed.

As he lay down, she tried to scramble off, but with an artful yank, he tumbled her against him, curling her up in a spoon position inside the curve of his body. Keeping the chain wrapped around one hand, he folded his muscular arms over the front of her body. When she bit his arm, he chuckled against her neck. "Don't take too much of my blood, *habiba*. You'll make yourself sick."

"I'll wait until you're asleep and stake you."

"Thank you for letting me know." He tightened his arms around her, one coming across her bosom so he cupped her breast, tucking his fingers beneath it, and laid his other hand over her pubic mound, those fingers resting with maddening but potent stillness over her clit. "Think I've lived to be this old by being a heavy sleeper, hmm?" His breath stirred her hair on her nape. "You're tired, too. Sleep, *habiba*."

"I hate being called that."

"*Shrew* seems impolite for a guest. But I can go with that if you wish."

She was tired, and yet . . . the way he was holding her, his cock pressed against her ass, hands positioned where they were, made her very awake. So casually possessive. She was his, bound to his desire, his will, even though he said she wasn't.

I didn't say you weren't, Jessica. I said that I would help you choose the life you most want, when you're ready. That I wouldn't hurt you the way Raithe did. But this calms you. You may rebel against that, but I suggest you try to understand the why of it. It will tell you a lot more about yourself, and far less about Raithe and his type of monster.

"Raithe turned me into this," she said bitterly, trying to ignore how distracting it was to be held this way. "Like Pavlov's dog, he used pain with pleasure until it became part of me. That's the only reason pushing me onto my knees to suck your dick helped. It's a psychosis."

"I am in your mind, Jess. Raithe didn't impose that lesson on you. He took what was already there and twisted it, yes. But if you use your incredible bravery in another way, to look deep into your soul, you will see that this gift, which is uniquely yours, is what helped you survive. And I will use it, unapologetically, to give you a reason to live again."

Convenient for you. She thought it, even as she couldn't help recalling he'd denied his own release. *Stop reading my mind. Shut up and let me pretend you aren't there.*

Remarkably, she felt his mouth pull against her temple, a smile. It infuriated her. But being held in his arms like this . . . it didn't make her feel the way the manacles did, as if she couldn't sit still, was suffocating, though it should have. His breathing became even, suggesting he was sleeping, but she wasn't fooled. All vampires were light sleepers. If she tried to get up, she'd wake him. With the bracelet and chain, he'd made sure it wouldn't be a quick getaway.

But that wasn't the problem. He'd made her climax, and though her muscles had seized up in automatic reaction afterward, expecting the pain that would be extracted as a result, it hadn't come.

She couldn't trust, couldn't get pulled into this. She wanted to scream and weep, to tear her flesh away from her body, to stop being Jessica Tyson, this person whose soul had been torn into so many pieces inside herself that she felt like a bag of broken toys, unable to trust or believe in anything.

His lips pressed against her brow then, his body curving more securely around her, and it was a terrible, wonderful comfort. She was lost, fucking lost.

It's all right, Jessica. Sleep. You're safe. I promise.

I can't trust you.

You'll learn that you can. Time, habiba. *Give yourself time. You have all you need here.*

It did take time, but eventually Jessica Tyson's body began to relax in his arms, her exhaustion taking away her choices, much as he had, until she succumbed to sleep.

Mason knew she'd be surprised to know how awake he was. When he'd faced her in the bathroom, asked her if she wanted to know how he punished a servant, he'd seen the spark, flashing down to the tinder of her soul. Still, using his knowledge that way had been a terrible risk. Spanking and putting her on her knees to him had pushed her mind almost to the breaking point, and nearly broken his control as well. By Allah, it had been hard not to let himself climax in her throat.

A pretty face, an exceptional mind, the agile body and charisma—all of that had shone through her photo. But it was this, what Raithe discovered in addition to all those exceptional qualities, that had sealed her fate like the scent of fresh blood.

Most servants had at least a basic natural submission in their personalities, and were trained to open themselves up to even deeper levels of it. A true submissive's nature, however, was a complex treasure to a vampire. Couple that with a male vampire who was a fucking sadist, and Mason knew exactly why her mind had snapped, and why she couldn't be trusted not to try to take her life again. If he was in her shoes, he wasn't sure if he wouldn't do the same.

The true consequences of his impromptu test would come when she woke again. There was no emotional bond between them to let her believe that her reaction had been anything other than the sick, learned response she thought it was. While the agony of her struggle had taken his mind off his aching cock, he'd rather have borne ten times the sexual frustration than witness the beginning of this journey, knowing how long and agonizing a road she likely faced to believe in her own worth again.

10

When Jessica woke, she was back in her room. It was early morning, which said she'd slept through an entire day, since Mason had taken her to his bed during daylight. She was startled she'd slept so deeply that she hadn't been aware of being moved. Amara was reading nearby, but raised her head as she stirred. Her expression was wary, and when Jessica stretched, she remembered the manacles were gone. So, too, was the silver bracelet Mason had used to bind her to him while they slept.

Good morning. His voice resonated in her brain, a quiet reminder of his presence. *I'm trusting you not to do harm to yourself or my staff,* habiba. *If you betray that trust, you will wear the manacles again.*

She pursed her lips. *So harm to you is okay?*

A pause. *I will deal with that an entirely different way.* He filled her mind with the image of her naked rump beneath his hand, her slick cunt, the saliva that marked his jeans as she bit him in the throes of her climax.

Feeling her cheeks flushing, she scowled and pushed herself up on her arms, amazed anew at how sleep fell away from her, and her body vibrated with a desire to move. To stretch and leap. To play, as if she were eight again.

Amara still had not spoken, maybe to give her Master time to have his say. When Jess rose from the bed, though, finding herself in a relatively modest cotton nightgown, the servant spoke. "I hope you slept well, Jessica."

Jess managed a curt nod. "You don't have to be here while I dress and get ready for the day."

"I think I do." Amara set the book aside and rose. "Lord Mason feels that your periods of clarity are going to come and go. You might try to run away or hurt yourself."

Jess gave a bitter chuckle. "It's actually the hazy moments that are safer. The clear moments are the unbearable ones."

Amara's gaze darkened, but instead of commenting on that, she gestured toward the closet. "There is a selection of clothes for you, though Lord Mason noted he particularly liked the sarong."

Well, then, she was never wearing that again. She tried to push away the thought of how his body had felt, molded against hers in the thin fabric. In truth, his arms had been the most effective restraint of all, if the intention of the manacles was to keep her from a self-destructive panic attack. At least once she'd woken to find her cheek pillowed on his biceps, her hands hooked on his crossed forearms, holding on. In the nonjudgmental torpor of half sleep, it had been reassuring enough to send her back to dreamlessness.

He was a vampire. But he was Farida's Mason. How did she reconcile the two?

Jess moved to the closet. She reminded herself again it was time to pull it together. Several days ago, she'd been a dying woman with flagging energy. This morning . . . well, she didn't feel that way, and while it was damned irritating, she was back to paying attention, wanting to use whatever weapon came to hand to change her circumstances. Of course, now that she was fully marked, her mind told her escape attempts were futile, but she'd followed the instinct too long to abandon it. At least until she figured out a better strategy.

"So how did you come to Lord Mason?" she asked, pawing through the selections.

"I was part of a prince's household, valued for my dancing skills. Lord Mason was visiting the prince on business, and Enrique . . ." Jessica turned as Amara hesitated, then her lovely face creased in a smile. "We saw each other quite often during that visit. He was very resourceful. Then the prince presented me to Lord Mason as a gift, and I learned that Enrique had entreated my lord to bring me into his service. Enrique and I fell in love quite quickly."

Looking at the soft light in her eyes, Jessica didn't doubt it, though it was a peculiar relationship for her to contemplate. "But you . . . dance, for Lord Mason?"

Amara nodded. "I usually dance for him once each week, if you wish to watch. Lord Mason likes the performance as part of his meal."

"Thanks, but no. I don't have any interest in being near that." She shuddered involuntarily, remembering, and couldn't help flinching when Amara came close enough to touch her shoulder. "Not that I expect I have a choice," she added bitterly.

Today Mason's servant had her long black hair loose over her shoulders. Her skirt had melted colors like a sunset, over which she wore a belted tunic embroidered with tiny, glittering stones. Jessica wondered if she rose from bed this way, tempting and touchable. She'd no doubt that Enrique's French blood had gone to the boiling point at the sight of her. Most men's would. Hell, she herself had responded to the woman.

"Jessica, you do have a choice. You do not have to be there at all. But there's a screened balcony area and you could watch. Maybe it will reassure you. I think you should see the way a true vampire-servant relationship is supposed to be."

"I don't want to be reassured. I don't want to lower my guard. I just want out of here." Jessica shrugged off the touch and stepped farther into the closet, presenting her back to the woman.

"I understand that, but when the bond is true, there is nothing to fear. Even Enrique and I, having one another, have not achieved as deep a bond as most servants seek with their Master. That has been Lord Mason's choice, but we find great joy in what he offers us."

"I've seen that bond, Amara," Jessica retorted. "Raithe's servants captured my fiancé and delivered him into Raithe's hands. He killed Jack in front of me. If having a loyalty so unquestioning you'd use it to kill innocent people is a 'joy' to you, you're right. It's something I never want to know. And it doesn't matter if you tell me he's a fucking saint; he won't win my trust. I went far enough down that road, too many times, and I still bear the burn scars. Never again. So save your breath."

She could feel Amara studying her. "You're wrong, Jess," the woman said softly at last. "I do not wish to upset you, but you haven't seen that bond, for Raithe never offered it to you."

Jess curled her fingers in the clothes, a reaction to her surge of resentment, but decided not to respond. Most of the clothes were lightweight garb similar to what she'd worn the day before, but some were more modest. Jess chose a tunic top and matching long skirt, embroidered with tiny mirrors and beads. "Do I have any underwear?"

Amara directed her to a dresser with a selection of bras and panties. Jess searched through them until she found a turquoise satin set that at least provided grudging full coverage of her ass. When she took it all into the bathroom, she found an assortment of toiletries. While Amara did allow her to close the door for a few minutes for privacy, she had to leave it open while dressing. It could be worse. She could still be wearing the manacles. But Amara's hovering had a similar itchy feeling.

Once she was dressed, Amara took her through the sprawling estate to a large kitchen, introduced her to the cook staff and parked her at a butcher-block table. It was a relaxed, informal eating space, and the plateful of food they put before her reminded her vividly how long it had been since she'd actually felt hungry. Jessica stared at the fresh fruit, the sharp cheddar cheese, the single piece of chocolate sitting on a gold circle of foil on the corner. She also had a cup of ripe wine, and a tall glass of ice water. Everything had wonderful aromas and colors, but it wasn't too much food, not enough to stuff herself. Picking up each piece slowly, she inhaled it, closed her eyes to chew, entranced with food that tasted good again.

While the staff was not unfriendly, they didn't attempt to engage her in conversation. A few surreptitious glances came her way, but for this first meal, the scrutiny didn't bother her. As she ate, Amara and the cook chatted, the other three members of the staff moving about efficiently.

The import of that hit her, such that she dropped the chocolate, untasted. "Why are there so many of you?" she demanded.

Amara and the cook looked toward her. "What do you mean, Jess?" Amara asked.

"One vampire. No guests. Why are there three of you?" Jess was on her feet and backing away from the table, that need for flight kicking in as Amara rose from her stool. "He doesn't need a damn cook and three kitchen staff, unless he plans to have guests. Unless he's expecting other vampires to visit."

"Very few vampires visit me. You've had the good fortune to fall into the hands of the most unsociable vampire in the Western hemisphere. However, I am doing necessary renovations and have contractors to feed."

She found him standing behind her, leaning in the doorway, so her first view as she spun was a wall of chest. He was wearing a dark T-shirt, and as she lifted her gaze she saw his hair was loose for once, the strands enhancing the sculpted curve of jaw, temple and straight nose. She made herself focus on his vibrant eyes, and not the fact he was wearing the same jeans as earlier, and how distracting the fit could be to a woman's libido.

"I'm glad you approve of my fashion sense."

"Bite me," she snapped, then colored as his brow rose. "Stop it," she muttered. Pivoting on her heel, she marched back to the table and sat down. "Command your minions and then go away. I can't eat with you here."

"Always testing."

Jess stiffened as his body pressed against the back of hers in less than a blink. Leaning forward, he picked up the chocolate, bringing it toward her lips. With his chest against her back, his arm in front of her, she was effectively captured. "How long do you think you'll get away with issuing *me* commands, Jess?" he murmured. "You think you're pushing me to see if I'll become Raithe, but there's another reason you're pushing me, the one you won't face. When you're ready to do so, that's the last time you'll get to push me without immediate consequences." His lips grazed her temple and she shuddered. The cook and Amara were back to conversing by the stove, paying no obvious attention to them, but she was sure it was a deliberate move to give her a false sense of privacy. Not that she needed one with the fanged bully.

"The fanged bully wants you to try the chocolate." He brushed it over her lips, once, twice, the heat of his fingers making it melt and the aroma drift up her nostrils, heady, overwhelming. Like him. "Open up."

"Will you go away if—" Of course, she had to part her lips to speak, and he put the truffle on her tongue. Letting the pad of his finger slide against it ensured she tasted the chocolate that had melted on him. She had a sudden, desperate desire to hold on to it, to suckle on him the way she had his cock the day before.

He bent, pressed his lips to her throat below her ear. "You do not know what a temptation your confused mind is, *habiba*. But again, I am not Raithe. I will not take advantage of your mind for my sole benefit. Not until both of us would be pleased by me acting on your desires. Enjoy your day with Amara. I'm heading to bed, but will see you later. I will not be far."

In the next blink, he was gone, leaving an emptiness at her back, and the lingering heat of his breath at her ear, the taste of chocolate on her tongue. She savored it, telling herself it was the truffle she was appreciating.

How could she deal with having someone in her head and sorting through the truth or delusion of her own thoughts? With Raithe, she'd gotten to the point she didn't care. Both became a nightmare, what she could imagine he would do to her, against what he actually did.

For now, with a dearth of other options, she narrowed her focus onto the food, and pushed away anything else she couldn't face. Like her foolish craving to believe this was real, that she'd found a sanctuary. Nowhere was safe, but particularly not a place that held a vampire.

After Jessica ate, Amara took her on a tour of the grounds. She was relieved the woman didn't give her a choice, because while principle would require her to refuse if asked, she wanted to get out and *move*. It felt marvelous to eat, to walk straight with lithe strides, to know she wouldn't be exhausted by walking down the stairs of the back balcony that led to . . .

"Oh." Jessica stopped. Amara came to a halt with her, and a smile curved the woman's lush mouth.

"Yes, it has that effect. Wonderful, isn't it?"

Mason's home might as well be called a castle, though she supposed it would be considered a large estate. Years ago, as a child, she'd gone to Biltmore Estate in the mountains of North Carolina, and it reminded her of that, only this particular castle rested by the sea. Amara had explained they were in South America, on the edges of one of the few temperate rain forests, which explained the deep forest that came within a hundred feet of the front of the sprawling structure. But the back of the estate opened onto an oceanfront view comparable to the gates of Heaven. Mason had a layered series of wide verandahs that artfully led into winding marble staircases, down to a sloping lawn with myriad gardens dotted with fountains and statuary. Those gave way to sand and the ocean shore. In daylight it was breathtaking, but for some reason she imagined it through Mason's eyes, when everything was bathed in moonlight, giving the water, statues and gleaming leaves in the gardens a kissed-by-silver look.

When she recognized some of the exotic flowers, tears threatened. Their petals had been scattered in Farida's tomb. He grew them here.

Amara stayed silent, but Jess was aware the woman's hand brushed the small of her back, a reassurance. The tears weren't only because of the flowers, Jessica knew. It had been so long since her appreciation for something beautiful hadn't been destroyed by her justified wariness of it. Because while the vampires she'd known had accumulated beauty, they didn't understand its value. They used it as a tool, a weapon or a possession. This . . . Mason had built his estate in a solitary place that spoke of beauty far beyond the power or ownership of human or vampire, and the architecture of house and gardens appeared to pay homage to it. Yet there was the undeniable sense that it was a home. Amara and Enrique were comfortable here, as were the cook and staff. The kitchen, the bedrooms, all the living spaces, appeared to provide . . . a haven.

Taking a deep breath, she focused on less disturbing details. She saw he had spoken the truth about the renovations. On the western wing, a catwalk construction was happening on the second level. Above that, bundles of shingles were stacked, a roofing job in progress. She narrowed her eyes at the charcoal smudges along the siding, the piles of broken brick and discarded construction material below. "That looks like rubble from an explosion."

"Yes, it is," Amara commented matter-of-factly. "The Vampire Council gathering was held here last year. A small army of vampire hunters attacked and blew up this verandah, the ballroom and that western wing. Which, thankfully, is the final area requiring construction. The din has been horrible on some days. They'll clean up that debris as the last step."

Jessica blinked, turned to look at her. "Vampire hunters attacked a full gathering of vampires?"

"At dusk, no less." Amara didn't smile now. "They were of course defeated. Many of the hunters were killed and driven off, though they killed a handful of vampires and many servants. Please do not celebrate that in my presence, whatever your feelings," she added. "There were many lost that day who we considered friends."

Jess drew another breath. "Amara, I don't want to offend. I just want to leave."

"I know." Amara's dark eyes saw more than Jessica was comfortable with. "I wonder if you'll feel that way when he lets you leave. Because none of the others wanted to go."

"The others?"

Amara nodded. "Lord Mason has . . ." Her lips twisted, and now amusement flickered in her gaze. "He will punish me for teasing him in this way, but he has an unusual hobby. He has a harem. I will show you a place he has dedicated to them, in a manner of speaking, after we complete a circuit of the grounds."

"A harem? *Here?*"

"No, of course not. I say it that way because they are all very loyal to him." Amara started down the stairs, drawing Jessica with her. Despite herself, Jessica's curiosity was roused, though she managed to remain silent, glad when Amara continued without prompting.

"Lord Mason spends a great deal of money, anonymously of course, on educational programs for women in Africa and the Middle East. That, as well as fate and circumstance, has brought women in his path who need assistance to improve their circumstances. Some have stayed here for a time, to get back on their feet, much as you will do, before he helped them find their place in the world again."

At Jess's dubious look, Amara shrugged. "I know you think I'm telling you this to get you to trust him. If he was in my mind now, he'd likely forbid me to tell you any more. But I will still show it to you. While only time will convince you of Lord Mason's trustworthiness, perhaps it will help. For now, come with me."

When the servant led her down into the gardens without further conversation, thankfully, Jessica saw the landscapers hard at work, laying the new plantings. Amara explained this was more evidence they were in the final stage of the renovation, for of course the landscaping had been saved until after the main reconstruction, which required material laydown areas and troops of construction workers coming and going over the ground.

As Amara moved on to the statuary garden, Jessica noticed more than one landscaper shot a lingering glance at the two women, the pendulum swing of Amara's hips, but the foreman quickly barked them back to their responsibilities.

While she tried not to be caught ogling the statuary in the gardens, part of the reason Jess had loved Rome was for the sculpture. She lost the battle to maintain studied indifference when she reached a fountain topped by an impressive piece depicting three horses. One plunged forward, two others galloping alongside. The curve of head, the dainty nose that somehow meshed with the powerful body, told her the breed. "Arabians."

"Yes. Lord Mason has a great fondness for them. His two, Hasna and Coman, were brought back to the estate this past week. He boarded them inland until most of the hammering and sawing were done."

Jess turned. "He has horses? How is that possible? They're afraid of vampires." The lingering scent of taken blood, the nature of vampires as predators, made most noncarnivorous animals fear them. Of course, she recalled Farida's words. *As if they were one creation . . .*

"They are not afraid of Lord Mason." Amara watched her with those shrewd eyes. "Would you like to see the stable?"

Jess bit back her eagerness to say yes, and settled for a shrug, which she was sure didn't fool the servant a bit. Amara took her hand with a conspiratorial smile and led her swiftly across the lawn, cutting around the eastern side of the estate. The walk took them past a large gazebo with swings and a boardwalk out to the beach, as well as a man-made pond with another fountain in the center. There was a breathtaking variety of flower gardens, scattered with benches for contemplation. Myriad winding paths. Everywhere she turned, beauty to delight the eye, stir the senses.

The female eye, the female senses.

Brow furrowing, she stopped, freeing her hand, looking at it all again, thinking of the interior as well. "Did . . . Has Lord Mason always lived here alone, except for servants and staff?"

Amara met Jessica's gaze in understanding. "No. He built it for her. He wanted to give her a home worthy of a sheikh's daughter, and he did, even though she was already gone before the first brick was laid."

Jess had schooled herself to catch nuances in speech, slight shifts of body language, a necessary skill to survive. However, it had other uses. "You don't approve."

Amara's reaction intrigued her, because unless the woman was a superb actress, Jessica had caught her in a genuine uneasy moment.

"It is not my place to judge Lord Mason's actions. He is far older than I am, and sees things very differently. If—"

"But you think this is a waste, him spending all this money and time on a corpse."

"On a memory," Amara corrected, her mouth thinning. "I think three hundred years is a long time to grieve. To go without love."

Jess thought of the tomb. The gifts, the way he'd preserved her. Did he think one day she'd come back, and he would have it ready for her? No, that wasn't it. It was more like he was proving what he would have provided to her, that the promises he'd made had been honored, even if she was gone.

Or Jessica's damn mind was playing tricks on her again, trying to turn him back into the romantic hero she'd wanted him to be, not a bloodthirsty vampire.

Amara continued their trek to the stables. Around the building and paddock, Jess saw at least two groomsmen restocking the barn with hay. Her steps quickened at the sound of a snort, despite the fact she knew Amara would give her Master every scrap of information about Jess's reactions, her interests.

Why do I need that, habiba, *when I'm already in your mind?*

She almost started. Instead, she muttered a vile curse. *Don't you have other things to do?*

I am doing them. But seeing my home through your eyes is a pleasant diversion. Enjoy my horses.

Then he was gone again, but as he withdrew, it was as if he'd caressed her mind, an absent touch similar to him passing a hand over her hair or sliding his fingers down her arm before he moved away, only this was *inside* of her. It made gooseflesh ripple on her skin.

"What is he?" She brought Amara to a halt again with a hand on her arm. "I know he's a vampire, but what else? He's a magic user of some kind, isn't he? The preservation of the tomb—"

"That is for Lord Mason to tell you, not me. Look." Amara pointed. While normally she wouldn't have been dissuaded by the distraction, when Jess looked, she saw a snow-white head peer over a stall door. When the female Arabian saw them, she trilled, and abruptly a jet-black head was next to hers, the taller male looking out with her. Bright, intelligent eyes, soft noses, manes combed to silk. Jess's feet were in motion before she even thought about it.

Vampires liked keeping pets. Dogs, mainly. Predators with a pack mentality meshed well with vampires' dominant personalities. The Rottweilers had been castoffs from one of the vampires who bred the dogs. While he'd given that pair to Raithe because of some slight imperfection they had, he prized and babied the ones without imperfections. The line between brutality and pampering was very thin in the vampire world.

However, the Bedouins of the past had treated their horses as members of the family, and she saw that care here. When she put out her hand, the female touched first, bringing her muzzle to Jess's palm. "Oh, you're lovely, you are," she crooned, sliding her hand up the mare's forehead. "And someone gives you love regularly, look at you, you spoiled thing." The black pushed her arm insistently, so she gave a hand to each, stroking, rubbing, reaching up to the ears where she knew they liked it, the curves of their powerful necks, as their soft rubbery lips explored her shoulders and hair.

"Did you have a horse of your own?" Amara had taken a seat on one of the hay bales. The grooms kept a respectful distance, like the other staff members, for which Jessica was glad, but she wondered if they'd all been warned to give her space.

"Growing up," she relented. "Before I went off to school, my family ran a horse farm. We raised quarter horses, but the neighbors had Arabians, so I was familiar with both."

It was a taste of home, here so far from it, and not just geographically. She'd never see that home again. Even if she could safely visit again, she wasn't sure if it wouldn't look like some transparent, ghostlike reality. She was dead to that life now, or all who were part of it were dead to her. No. She was the ghost, not them. Jess put her forehead down on the nose of the white. A brief touch only, because Amara was watching her.

While Jess knew Mason didn't need Amara's eyes to see her, Jess took her hands away anyhow, reluctantly. "We can go on now."

~

Jessica learned that the estate was two hours from any town, so she could save herself the trouble of trying to escape on foot. While there were vehicles for the laborers to come and go, the roads through the forest were unmarked and twisting. Though it was her habit to note such things, she reminded herself again it was a moot point. A fully third-marked servant had no escape. Even if she had the fortune she'd had with Raithe, killing Mason would only kill them both.

Perhaps Mason had read her acknowledgment of that, for Amara surprised her at the end of the tour by indicating she had a few tasks to handle. "There are many more rooms I haven't shown you, but you're welcome to explore on your own or we can continue our tour later." Apparently reading her expression, Amara added, "Lord Mason wants you to consider this your home, until you are able to choose another. We'll be close, but you should be able to relax in your home, have some measure of freedom."

Jessica relished the idea of an hour or two on her own to get her thoughts in order, look at her surroundings without being so obviously under a microscope. That way, if Mason was studying her like a bug, at least she didn't have to acknowledge it.

"We'll cut through here to get to the kitchens, and give you another snack now. We typically take our meals at regular hours, out of courtesy to the kitchen staff, but for today, I think they won't mind making an exception."

Amara directed her through an arched portico that led to a breezeway. Jessica could see a segment of the ocean around this corner of the estate, feel the breeze through the pillars. As she walked, she trod on flat gray stones. Embedded in the interlocking design was an occasional golden tile. Words in Arabic script were on those tiles, made by different hands, if the shapes and sizes of the handwriting were any indication. The dates varied, from the past five years to more than two hundred and fifty years ago.

"These are names," Amara said. "Women's names."

Though Amara said nothing further, Jessica knew this was the harem she'd intended to "show" her. The walkway was paved with approximately forty marked tiles.

"None of them chose to stay with him, be his third-marked servant?"

"Some would have, if he'd only asked."

Jess looked toward Amara. The woman's eyes were reflective, a bit sad. "Most vampires prefer their servants willing, Jess, but the vampire must acquiesce as well. Lord Mason does not desire that singular bond with another woman. I was marked because I was already Enrique's, so to speak."

"So he never marked any of these?" Jess couldn't keep the disbelief from her voice. Amara shook her head.

"A few who were in more precarious circumstances when he helped them were second-marked, so he could locate them, hear their thoughts if they were in distress. But that is all. You are the first, since me, he has marked three times."

"He said he did it to save my life. So if I believe all this"—Jess glanced at the flagstones dubiously—"then I'm another damsel in distress. Wouldn't he have let you marry Enrique without being his servant?"

"Yes. But I begged to serve him eternally, share that responsibility with Enrique as part of our marriage. I do not think that is what swayed his decision, however. He wanted me to have a similar life span, rather than Enrique outliving me by so long."

Despite Amara's words, knowing the sexual drive of vampires, Jess was sure Mason had claimed Amara's body. He wouldn't be a vampire if he hadn't. "How did Enrique feel about you and Mason . . ."

"If you come to see me dance, that question will be answered. Enrique will be there."

"Do I have a choice?"

"As I said earlier, you do, but the question is, do you want your life back, Jess?"

Jess snorted, but the empty anxiety in her stomach contracted. She stopped on the breezeway and faced Amara. "My life is gone, Amara. My fiancé, my family, the career I intended to pursue. I can't go back to any of it."

"Your fiancé may be dead, but Lord Mason will work hard to give you back as much of the rest as possible."

"Sure he will." Jess turned in a circle, which made her feel slightly sick and more off balance. "Because he's miraculously different from every vampire I've ever met. I mean, he could have his own weekly TV superhero drama. There's a pilot and two seasons here on these tiles."

"Perhaps you should ask *her* whether or not he's different." Ignoring her caustic tone, Amara nodded. Between the next set of pillars a sandstone wall had been built, and there was a small alcove inside it at waist height. The recession held a shallow stone dish filled with water. The dish was ringed with stones, and a handful of lit candles floated in the water. Jessica approached it slowly, conscious that Amara stayed where she was.

The etching in the stone above the shallow pool was also in Arabic, but she'd studied enough to recognize Farida's name, though she couldn't decipher the script beneath. "What does it say?" she asked. Petals floated in the water. Somehow she knew no staff member was given the task of keeping this water clean, the petals fresh, the candles lit. Only one person did that.

" 'My heart, my soul, my life. Forever yours.' "

He couldn't have created all this just to fool her. She knew it, but it was far too soon to believe her rational mind. Raithe and death still hovered too close for her to have that courage. Amara had drawn close again, so Jess saw her in her peripheral vision.

"He put that here, so she could see them. This breezeway was not created for him to congratulate himself." Amara nodded to the pool. "It is for her. As he helps each one, he feels he is helping her, women like her, to have more choices than she did. It is one of the ways he honors her." She reached out and touched one of the floating candles, sent it drifting across the small bowl. "After all you've been through, I understand, truly, how you feel it is safer to believe all vampires are evil than to take a chance on a new truth. But being so adamantly sure of something is another way of making yourself vulnerable, isn't it? If that is always what you expect, it gives your enemy an opening."

Jess closed her eyes. "As much as keeping you guessing, shifting from perspective to perspective."

"So what's the choice? What do you do, Jess, when you can't afford to trust, but trusting may be your only way back to yourself, to something approximating the life you wanted?"

Jess couldn't answer the question, but then found it wasn't necessary. When she looked, Amara was gliding back down the breezeway.

She'd wanted time alone. But with more questions than answers now, Jess wasn't sure if she needed solitude. Particularly not before that sacred shrine.

11

"I don't want to question you, my lord, but are we sure she's all right alone?" Through the security cameras Mason had in the underground study level, Amara watched Jessica settle on a bench by the horse sculpture. At Mason's prompting, she'd reluctantly left the girl on her own for a while, though she was sure the vampire was monitoring her with his mind as well.

"We've got to give her some breathing room." Mason leaned back in the chair behind his desk and templed his fingers. Despite his words, Amara saw a worrisome brooding look around his eyes. It was past lunchtime, and though she knew Mason didn't have to sleep as much as younger vampires, it was still late for him to be awake.

He glanced at her. "She's very intelligent, Amara. Her instincts are honed for survival under extreme circumstances. So though she adapts quickly, that means the damage done to her adapts quickly as well. The manacles kept her from causing herself harm, but swiftly became a liability. Having you with her gives her a sense of stability, connection and information about her surroundings, but when she shifts into thinking of you as a jailer, it can become a destructive tactic. She needs to be able to stretch her mind to know she has the right to exercise it here. She needs time to think."

"That's what concerns me. She keeps returning to the conclusion that she'd be better off dead."

"Only because she doesn't dare to believe that she isn't with another version of Raithe. Or that Raithe hasn't irrevocably destroyed her spirit." He turned his gaze back to the monitor. "She doesn't realize how remarkable she is."

Jessica had reached out to touch the sculpture. She glanced over her shoulder, as if she thought somebody would tell her not to do so. Mason cleared his throat. "Her body is strong and healthy now, and it wants to live. That's the strongest ally we have against her mind's self-destructive tendencies. We keep it in the forefront. Let's give her activity, ways to burn her energy and focus on her natural passion to live. In order to beat Raithe, she has to do it herself, on her own terms. A woman strong enough to do as she has done, has it in her."

He swiveled in the chair to face his servant. "We have to believe in her, Amara, if she's going to believe in herself. Tomorrow, find her some barn clothes and tell her they need an extra groom for Hasna and Coman."

"Excuse me? Put her to work mucking out stalls?"

"She keeps waiting for the other shoe to drop, for me to torture her with sick games that turn her natural desires into nightmares." Abruptly he rose, headed across the room to a decanter of brandy. He waved Amara away when she moved to pour for him. "I'll get it. If I give her a job doing something else, it will keep her off balance, in a good way. The hard work will condition her body again, along with her mind. The stables need painting, sanitizing. Jorge will be delighted with the extra hands. I want her exhausted at the end of the day."

"And how will you occupy her evenings?"

Mason set down the decanter, gave her a sharp look. "Don't go too far, Amara."

"My apologies, my lord." Amara inclined her head. "I shall go let Jorge know and then tell Jessica." Turning on her foot, she moved toward the door.

"Allah save me from the pique of women," Mason muttered. "Amara."

"My lord?" She turned, arched a brow.

"It's about helping her."

"I've no doubt. Just . . ." Amara sighed, came back to him. When she reached out to touch his chest, she was gratified when he closed his hand over hers. He cupped her face, threading his fingers through her hair. Mason loved her hair, as did Enrique. There was nothing that gave her such contentment as the pleasure she could bring her Master and her husband. She wished Jessica could know the reward of that, of having the things one did out of love and a desire to please returned in full measure, with such caring and ardor. With love.

Mason shook his head. "You are lucky your love is so generous, Amara. And your beauty too staggering to resist."

She smiled up at him, but she couldn't help the worry she knew darkened her eyes. "Please be careful, my lord. I didn't see her savagery coming, when she knocked me into the tub. If I'd been able to resist her, she might have killed me. Raithe didn't see it coming, either."

"He had a moment of vulnerability."

"All of us do, eventually."

Mason moved his touch to her chin, gave it a light squeeze of rebuke. "Let me be concerned with that. You did well today. Now, about tomorrow night . . ." In his mind, he showed her what he wanted her to wear when she danced. Despite her intention to focus on the topic of Jessica, an anticipatory flush swept her skin. His gaze kindled, seeing it, his fingers dropping to a caress on her throat. "Did you invite Jessica to be there?"

"As you commanded. But I suspect she won't come this time."

"That's all right. Perhaps another time, if we leave the invitation open." He brushed her cheek with his knuckles, reclaimed his brandy. "Even if her life does not include vampires or servants in the future, I think seeing how it should be between them might help her heal."

Amara put her hands over his as he raised the glass to his lips. Mason stilled, looking down at her over the lip. "Like teaching an abused woman that not all men are evil, so she'll give a new one a chance?"

He lifted a brow. "Amara, you *do* know I can read your mind?"

"Yes, my lord. But sometimes I don't think you realize there are times we can read yours."

When his gaze shuttered, his mouth tightening, she removed her hands, took a step back. She'd told Jessica the truth, that she did not fear Lord Mason, but she also knew where the lines were drawn between vampires and humans. At a certain point, Mason would not be pressed, or defied. He was not a monster like Raithe, but he certainly could be as ruthless. Though it was the type of ruthlessness as provocative to a woman's senses as a seduction.

"I mean no offense, my lord. But we do love you well, and my intentions are—"

"I know what they are." He gestured, his desire clear. They were done. Suppressing a sigh, she turned for the door.

But as Amara left, she knew she wasn't mistaken. More was happening here than saving a "damsel," something far more personal. She'd always nursed the hope that Mason would open his heart again, but this damaged girl was not the choice she would have made for him. Despite her words, it wasn't physical danger that concerned her. For all that Mason had given her and Enrique, no one—except perhaps Farida—had accessed the deepest levels of his soul. Her loss had damaged that core, perhaps irreparably.

If Jessica found her way into it, there was no telling what further destruction she could wreak in the powerful vampire, the Master that Amara and Enrique both loved.

During her delightful third meal of the day, Jessica received the unexpected information that she'd been left jeans, boots and a T-shirt in her wardrobe, so that she could help out at the stables the next day. When she mulled it over, despite her suspicions, she found she liked the idea. Far too much. Though she knew Mason could read her mind easily enough, she still felt it necessary to think, *So you resurrected me because you were short on manual labor?* to see if he was listening in. But her mind was quiet tonight.

Amara explained during dinner he was otherwise occupied, which should have been soothing, because she knew vampires had an entirely different idea of dinner. If it wasn't for blood, it was for sex. She was having a hard enough time thinking about the invitation to watch his dinner with Amara and Enrique tomorrow night, never mind that she knew she wouldn't go.

Amara and Enrique ate with the rest of the staff when not needed by their vampire, so Jessica had found herself seated in an informal dining area populated by several tables and pervaded with the relaxed atmosphere of people who worked and lived together. She learned many had quarters here, traveling back to remote homes for their days off and vacations. After dinner there were drinks and games of cards. Others wandered off to watch television, read or enjoy arcade games in the staff entertainment room. Some worked out in an exercise room or used the adjacent indoor pool. It appeared all of the staff, with the exception of the aging cook, were trained in combat skills. Those workouts were overseen by Enrique, whom she noted had exceptional hand-to-hand skills. Once that was over, though, he retired to the couch with the local papers and to watch a televised soccer game.

Though it seemed the staff viewed Amara and Enrique as upper management, connected to the lord of the estate in ways they weren't, the two seemed accepted and liked. And they were comfortable as well. Amara read a book, her head on Enrique's knee, while he bantered politics between soccer plays with the grooms playing pool.

It was surreal. While Raithe had kept her on a very short leash—sometimes literally—she was fairly certain his small, handpicked staff had never had such a sense of . . . normalcy. Amara had explained earlier that Lord Mason's live-in staff was aware he was a vampire, and all were second-marked, to ensure their loyalty. Quite a few of them were from families that had served him in generations past.

In contrast, she felt like the heroine in a horror film, sitting on the outskirts of a campfire, the only one noticing that things were shifting in that darkness, prowling. The laughter, the announcer on the television, the *plock* of pool balls, as well as conversations that were so easy, so untroubled, began to grate.

There'd been some casual attempts to draw her into them, but she'd withdrawn to a corner to watch them all, leafing through a book to appear occupied and remain unmolested. Whether or not they believed it, they left her alone. But she still felt hemmed in, the more she stayed down here, as if she were being woven into a tapestry in which she didn't belong.

She rose abruptly, nodded her good-nights to Amara and Enrique, and was conscious of scrutiny as she left the room. What would they say about her after she left? Why would she care? She had to quell an urge to bolt into a run in the hallway, escape the shadows at her heels.

In the horror movies, it was always the one who left the campfire first who got attacked by the monster. She firmed her chin. The stairwell was lit, and she remembered her way well enough to take only one wrong turn before she reached the hallway with her room. When she slid into her room, the dim night lamp was on. Then she froze.

The French doors were open, letting in the sea breeze, as they'd been this morning to let in sunlight. Her rational mind told her that. Still, there was a big black hole of night yawning in the corner of her room like a vortex, and the darkness that had dogged her heels closed in. She pressed her back against the door and told her heart to calm its pounding. This was stupid. She could walk over there, close the doors, and the night would not reach in with grasping fingers. The shadows in the corners would not coalesce and grab her, blind her and hold her, come at her with pain and wicked whispers, sly laughter.

She slid down the door, wrapping her arms around her knees. Had it come to this? Needing someone in her room with her as if she were a child? She'd managed fine all those months when sick. Yes, because she'd had something worse to fear, and because she'd been careful to ensure she was in a well-lit room by the time night fell. She'd been here less than a few days and her guard was already slipping.

No, she was fine. She was going to get up, walk across the room and close those doors any minute now. Leaving them open wasn't an option. She couldn't possibly go to sleep with that dark eye staring, unblinking, at her. In the distance, there was a dotting of landscaping lights in the garden, a couple sconces on the verandah, but not nearly enough. She tried to listen to the ocean and be soothed by it, but instead all she heard were sibilant whispers.

Trying to get a grip, she looked over at the bed. It had been turned down, the sheet dusted with flower petals. Then she noticed the basket on the nightstand and, more important, the aroma that came from it. Keeping one eye fixed toward the opening to the night, she rose and sidled closer to the basket to fold back the cloth napkin.

Chocolate chip cookies. Warm from the oven, a full dozen of them. Of all the choices of comfort food, it ranked as king, particularly to an Ohio girl so far from home. It didn't matter that she'd had three small meals today, that her shrunken stomach was still full from dinner. Pulling the blanket off the bed, she backed to the far side of the night table. Wrapping herself up, she slid back to the floor, wedging in the corner, putting the table as a block between her and the open doors.

She slid the basket over to her with a finger hooked inside the edge. Cradling it in her lap inside the nest of the blanket, she withdrew a cookie and took her first bite. As she did, she fixed her eyes on the darkness outside the French doors and tried to see past it to the moonlight, the clouds shifting in the sky. Tried to calm herself with the smell of tropical flowers and quiet rush of the ocean, devoid of whispers.

Grudgingly, she had to admit Mason was right about one thing. He could heal her body, but her mind needed a lot of work. Okay, one step at a time. Tonight, being here in the corner was as brave as she was going to get. She ate another cookie, positioned her head on the wall and kept silent watch, bolstered by chocolate. Maybe she'd fall asleep in this position and wake when safe, fierce sunlight was bathing the room.

Jessica, you're not in your bed.

His voice, a soft murmur, didn't frighten her as she might have expected it to do. "Amara didn't tell me you imposed bedtimes. I'm *not* six." Even if she was camped on the floor with chocolate chip cookies and a fear of the boogeyman.

Get in your bed, habiba. *You will be more comfortable there. And I am here. Nothing will hurt you.*

"After I finish my cookies."

Now. Or I come tuck you in personally.

Muttering, she rose, holding the cover around her, but swayed, staring at the door. "I can't." *God, I'm pathetic.*

Here. I'll fix it. Don't be afraid. The doors slowly swung shut, and she heard a latch close. An automated shade rolled down, completely shutting off the outside view.

"How did you—" But of course it made sense for a vampire to have controls that could remotely seal off every door and window with the push of a button. In daylight, she might perversely find that frightening, because it kept her shut in. Now, it brought some comfort.

Into bed, habiba.

She slid under the covers, putting the cookie basket close to hand on the pillow beside her, re-covering it with the napkin. There were several pillows, and she drew one close to her body, holding on to it as she adjusted her head on the pillow above it. She lay facing the door, but brought the cover up so she could tuck her chin down and not see it. She *was* six, if she was pretending that hiding under the covers would keep her safe.

That might not keep you safe, but I will, Jessica. Anything that wishes you harm will have to come through me.

"Even your own kind? When will you tell them about me? Turn me over to them? I know that's why you're keeping me. You've probably already told them I'm here."

I will not be turning you over to the Council, Jessica. We will talk more of it later, but the only reason I am keeping you here is to keep you safe, until I can figure out how to let you live your life without being a fugitive from my kind. You may leave when I'm certain you will be safe.

She dug her fingers into the pillowcase, and for some reason the crisp, white fabric reminded her again of the bloodstained front of his shirt. She'd touched it, she remembered, felt the warmth of his body beneath it. It was a myth, that vampires were cold. Raithe had had an insidious heat that emanated from his pores. Like Satan. Heat and brimstone pouring from his skin, lips stretched back from fangs, a venomous hiss heralding fetid breath, even as he turned everything inside of her cold.

Jessica, stop that.

She snapped out of it, to find that she'd dug her nails into her arm, deep enough to draw blood.

"I can't believe you, Mason. I know you want me to. But I can't."

All I ask you to do right now is believe one thing. That you will sleep tonight without fear. I will not let anything happen to you for the next eight hours. Can you do that? I am with you.

She felt it again then, that warm touch on her mind that spread through her body and settled over her like a cloak. "How do you do that?"

Magic.

"Right." She tried for a snort, got a yawn. Burrowing deeper into the blankets, she stretched out her fingertips to touch the basket. She should thank Amara for the cookies tomorrow. It was a nice touch, even for a vampire's servant whose motives she mistrusted. "What are you doing, anyway?" she mumbled. "Other than being a Peeping Tom."

If that was my intention, it appears you're sleeping in your clothes. And your shoes. Very disappointing. I'm sorting through contractor invoices.

Her lips curved in a sleepy smile, but she worked her toes under her sandal straps, let them slide off and fall out from under the covers to the floor, then curled her feet back under the comforter. Her mind drifted. "You're sitting at a desk somewhere in this opulent palace, doing paperwork?"

Unfortunately, my magic does not extend to having checks write themselves. Or handling contractors trying to take advantage of my abundant wealth.

"How did you get so rich?"

Strip dancing in Vegas.

She achieved the snort this time, then she sobered, her eyes drooping further. "Those gifts, the ones in Farida's tomb. They were beautiful."

A silence this time, but it was almost as if she could hear him breathing. With her eyes closed, she imagined him beside Farida. Beside her. His breath stirring her brow, his hand stroking. He'd worn a heavy signet ring then, something amber, she remembered. The cool metal of it had touched her sometimes when he'd caressed her.

Sleep, my love. I'm here. His arms wrapped around her body, her head tucked under his. She'd never been happier than when he did this, held her so close, their legs tangled so one of his was between her thighs, one of hers wrapped around his hip as they slumbered, as if even then they tried to be as closely connected as possible. Sometimes her last prayer of the day was to the old gods and goddesses, the ones she still believed moved in the shifting sandstorms or hid in the cool waters of the oasis, living under Allah's indulgence.

Great Beings, thank you for this perfect moment, which shall make all other moments bearable. Let me always do your Will, in gratitude for this great happiness you give me. To be his. To have his love.

She drifted to sleep, imagining herself with long dark hair that spilled over his arms as he held her. The sound of the desert wind rose outside, fluttering against the tent sides.

On the other side of his estate, Mason had his eyes closed as well, elbows braced on the desk as he drifted in that dream with her, felt the touch of long, black tresses mixed with the image of short, brown curls. Trusting dark eyes against wary gray ones, a lush, curved body giving way to a lean, small-breasted torso. It had been difficult not to go to her, especially when she'd started to hurt herself, her mind floundering. But she'd managed it—by immersing herself in her fantasy. It had been so powerful, she'd taken him right with her.

Amara was right. Jessica Tyson wasn't like the others. He just wasn't sure what that made her to him yet.

12

To those who'd never known a bond with horses, Jessica knew the idea of spending her days mucking out their stalls, sanitizing the wood with gallons of bleach, laying down fresh straw and then grooming the beasts, trimming their hooves, combing coats, manes and tails, would seem more proof of her teetering sanity. But the next two weeks were the best she'd had in a very long time. At times, if she closed her eyes, she could almost transport herself to her parents' barn, imagine that Jorge was her father, moving around in the loft. She'd hear her mother calling out to him from the front office, asking about someone interested in a foal.

But of course, when she opened her eyes, that wasn't where she was. The fears and worries, shadows and darkness would creep in and squeeze her heart in a painful vise. Jorge and his grooms were very careful around her, never coming up on her unawares, and always speaking in easy tones around her. On one hand, she appreciated it. But in another way, it reminded her that she was walking on quicksand, never knowing when those choking fears would take over her mind.

It had happened often over these two weeks. Brief panic attacks for no reason, that mind-altering catatonia that kept her locked in one place, oblivious to the passage of time. She'd snap out of it, the pitchfork held in a death grip by trembling hands, her back pressed to the wall. But she'd avoided doing herself or others harm. Obsessively focusing on just this task, this job, had helped her manage them, push past their hold.

If Jorge or his groom saw them happen, they didn't mention it. They left her alone, but stayed close enough to encourage conversation, if she sought it. A couple times she did. Just innocuous things, like their mutual interest in the horses. But both times she brought herself up short, and retreated again.

Only a couple weeks ago, she'd considered death a mercy. But she hadn't been physically strong then. She could damn Mason all she wanted for it, but he was right. While the desire to kill herself, take herself out of harm's way, simmered at the back of her mind as an instinctive escape plan, it was no longer her prime directive. There was a vast difference in outlook when one was cheerfully heaving slabs of dirty straw into a wheelbarrow to add to a compost heap, versus feeling sick, fatigued and on death's doorstep.

She had a routine, something she could count on. Each day passed without her being harmed, without anyone trying to frighten her, play with her mind. Unlike her first couple days, Mason was only a distant presence, oddly reassuring in his occasional comments in her mind, but otherwise leaving her to her own devices. Amara and Enrique hadn't pressured her when she chose not to accept the weekly invitation to watch Amara dance. Instead, they drew her into the evening activities with the other staff, so that she dared a game of pool or cards or a few minutes with the television, listening to the others comment, before making the trek up the stairs to her well-lit, secured bedroom.

She knew it was a lull before another storm, whether that storm came from the decisions she needed to make or those Mason would force her to face. But since this appeared to be a neutral time, without pressure to think or choose, she grabbed it with both hands, let herself live in stasis. It worked as an effective anesthetic, and her bedtimes were filled with her fantasies where she was Farida, Mason at her side as the romantic lover she'd long hoped he was.

~

Day Fourteen. The sun was starting to go down. She forked the last of the straw into the stall, making sure it was evenly spread. Then she headed out of the barn to find Jorge and let him know the stable was ready for the horses.

The two Arabians were in the paddock, cavorting and playing with each other. She climbed up on the rails to watch, sending a cautious nod to Gregorio, the groom who was keeping an eye on them.

Was there anything more marvelous than watching two strong, beautiful creatures do this? Enjoy the life God had given them, each moment just about *that* moment, and nothing else?

"This is a particularly refreshing look for you."

It took her a second to realize the voice wasn't in her mind, and when she did, she started. His hands brushed her waist, steadying her, before they were gone and he was climbing up next to her.

She didn't want to, but she couldn't help staring. Mason was wearing fawn riding breeches that molded his muscular ass and powerful thighs like skin, the pants tucked into polished black boots. With the white shirt he wore open at the throat, and his hair tied back, he looked like the kind of bad boy rake from Victorian romances that made women swoon.

"You're not going to swoon, are you? I can catch you, if you give me enough warning."

"If you don't stay out of my fucking head . . ."

"Language," he rebuked mildly. "And I can't help that your tongue rolled out of your mouth when you looked at me."

She'd acted on instinct versus thought for a while, so perhaps that was why she took him by surprise. Herself as well. She lifted one manure- and mud-encrusted boot, planted it on his thigh and shoved, knocking him off the end of the fence.

He landed on his feet, of course, as quick and lithe as a cat, but the narrowed glance he sent her had her scrambling off the fence. Her bootheel caught and she let out a yelp. However, instead of landing headfirst in the dirt, she was in his arms, holding on to his biceps, his face intensely close. Her foot was still tangled in the fence railing.

"I told you I could catch you if you warned me."

"You're being juvenile," she retorted, trying to ignore her shiver. She called it fear, instead of something far more confusing.

"Really? Did I just smear horse manure on *your* clothes and knock you off a fence?"

"Let me up." She squirmed, and he didn't budge.

"If you were of a mind to be civil, I'd take you for a ride on the beach."

She stilled, and despite herself, desire leaped in her breast, so strong it registered in the pleasure filling his own gaze. That in turn added another kind of desire to the feeling. God, he smelled good. Like the desert, exotic and mysterious. *Ignore it. All vampires emanate the fuck-me vibe. It's physical.*

He cocked his head, obviously reading her thoughts. He didn't say anything about it, though, just gave her that faint, sexy smile again. Holding her up in one arm, he freed her boot and lowered her feet to the ground, keeping one arm around her waist. Belatedly, she noticed she was still gripping his arms. She jerked free and stepped back, her cheeks warm. He was right. She *did* feel like an adolescent.

"So do you need a saddle?" he asked.

She shook her head. She'd first been put on a horse when she was three years old. It was one of the pictures on her mother's desk, behind which was a wall of blue ribbons and trophies. She'd taught her daughter as much as she was willing to learn, and unlike most girls, Jess had never grown out of her horse stage. Squatting, she began to unlace the boots. While being shoeless around a horse wasn't always a good idea, she couldn't resist the idea of riding bareback and barefoot, along a sandy stretch of beach sparkling under the stars.

Mason was speaking to the grooms, and a bridle was brought out, slipped on the head of the white mare. Jorge led them both out of the paddock. They were already prancing, crabstepping, knowing where they were going. Ears pricked forward as Mason approached, spoke to them in Arabic.

Jess straightened. She couldn't imagine a more breathtaking picture than the two Arabians, heads held high, manes tossing, feet stomping, and the man holding them, weight shifted to one hip in the snug breeches, broad shoulders flexing as he stroked their muscular necks and then glanced back at her. He said a word to the black and led the white forward. The black stayed where he was, watching with interest.

"Hasna's name means 'beautiful.'" He smiled down at her. "Very appropriate for you."

Jess ignored that and his offered hand, took a handful of mane and rein and swung up with a lithe twist of hips that felt so damn good she almost laughed aloud. Hasna pranced about, but a horse sensed a rider who knew her business, so she quickly settled as Jess spoke to her and adjusted the reins.

She noted Mason's look. Having taught riding before, she knew that expression. He was gauging her experience level to ensure she would be reasonably safe on the mount he gave her. It surprised her enough that, when he touched her leg and crooked his finger to have her lean down, she did so. Sweeping off her bill cap, he combed his hands through her sweat-stained hair to loosen it from her skull and then took his hands away before she could get more discomfited by the casual contact.

"So you can feel the wind, *habiba*." He gave her a quick smile before he turned the hat over to Jorge. Then the vampire turned and spoke another Arabic command. Coman came forward eagerly, and Jess noted he had no tack at all, not even a bridle. Mason swung up, just as lithe.

Farida had been right. Jess saw it, from the instant he completed the mount. So easy, so relaxed, the horse barely registered he had a rider. The powerful thighs flexed on the black's sides and he was moving forward, Mason taking the lead toward the beach. In this position, she could see him lay his hands on his thighs, guiding the horse solely with his knees. Watch that excellent ass shift with the horse's movement, making it impossible not to imagine it bare, flexing in a coital rhythm.

If Mason heard her embarrassing thought, he at least had the courtesy not to show it. To all appearances, he was taking in the night sounds, his attention on the shore up ahead. What in the hell was she doing? She'd been fine these past couple weeks, until he appeared. But how many times had she fantasized about him, guiltily stepping into Farida's body as she imagined what he might do to it, what soft, seductive things he would whisper to her late at night?

That was a different Mason, Farida's Mason, a storybook charac-ter she'd enhanced in her mind. It didn't mean she wanted this one, but it was logical that she would respond to his presence, particu-larly with those vampire pheromones swirling around him, like flies swarming a corpse.

That damned diary. It was confusing things. Raithe had never confused her like this. She wanted to say she was sorry she'd ever found it, but she knew that would not only be a lie, but an insult to Farida's memory she couldn't permit. She'd had the strength to sur-vive Raithe because of her.

She would resist Mason, like she'd resisted Raithe. Though Raithe had known how to get around that, just like Mason did, exploiting the weakness of her own body.

You say you hate it, you filthy cunt, but your slit is wet . . . Fuck her ass, Trenton. She'll cry from the pain, but she'll still come all over your balls and lick them clean afterward, like an eager little bitch in heat . . .

Hasna whinnied. Jess jerked out of the memory, flinched from Mason's touch on her shoulder. He'd brought Coman alongside and had his other hand on the mare's rein.

"Easy, *habiba*. Stay right here with us."

There was a strained note to his voice, though, and she wondered if he was regretting his decision to let her ride one of his prized horses. Then she raised her attention to his gaze and realized it was something else. Fire, the rage of Hell in the depths of his eyes, but not toward her. Coman shifted restlessly beneath him, but he stilled him with the movement of his knees. "Come here, *habiba*. This one time, I'm going to outrun those memories of yours. For both our sakes."

Before she could protest, he'd plucked her off Hasna and sat her before him on the black. He slipped off the white mare's bridle and tossed it over a salt-encrusted bush. Hasna followed them as he put the black into an easy trot toward the water's edge. His arm slipped around Jess's waist, making her far more cognizant of his heat at her back, the solid chest, the feel of his groin and her buttocks snugged in against it. A soft command, and the horse was cantering, the wind building in their faces.

Male vampires didn't have facial hair, and she'd missed that during her captivity, the rasp of a man's five o'clock shadow. However, she didn't mind the smooth, firm line of Mason's jaw, pressed against her temple. She put one hand on his forearm across her stomach, and had no place other than his thigh to put the other.

"Would you like to go as fast as he wants to go? Feel his wildness call to your own, *habiba*?"

"I would love it," she said, before she could think to be more reserved.

"Good. I would, too." His arm tightened around her waist in approval, and she couldn't help but compare the muscles that flexed against the back of her shoulder to the musculature of the horse's crest. "Now, as he runs, move with me, no stiffness. I won't let you fall."

Of all the scenarios she'd imagined for herself, combining one of her favorite pastimes with the company of a vampire had been far off the radar. But now, she made a concerted effort to relax her body into his, giving herself tacit permission to enjoy the forbidden, without interposing the memory of Farida to keep him at a safe distance. "Go," she encouraged.

He smiled against her temple. Another word, that musical language she didn't know, and she gasped as the horse's feet lifted off the ground in a joyous response. Coman leaped forward, Hasna on his flank.

The silver line of moonlight on the water wavered into jagged lightning as the body between her legs moved with all the reckless power and speed the stallion had been blessed with. She'd seen horses run wild in pasture, but the fence curbed their speed. When given limitless stretches of ground, horses became the favored animal of the gods, fire on their fetlocks, thundering them to the heavens to do battle for Zeus.

Coman went faster and faster, as if on the next breath he was going to leave the ground in truth. As exhilarating as that was, feeling the male body behind her added to it. Mason moved with Coman, united with that horse's exuberant spirit. He let out a wild yell, like a Berber raider coming over the dunes. It made her laugh and tremble at once, her fingers digging into his thigh and forearm, her head thrown back on his shoulder, fear for once gone from her mind when his arm cinched around her. Remarkably, they went even faster. His breath was at her ear, body pressed in hard against hers. She was so alive. Damn it, she was *alive*. Nothing could touch her like this. Nothing except what she wanted to touch her.

Perhaps it was only a few minutes, but when he brought the horse back to a half gallop, then to a canter, she was breathing hard, as if she'd been the one running. A long time ago, she'd galloped her palomino, Deena, through forest meadows. As they cooled down by the river, Deena would walk and Jess would lie back on her rump, letting the reins go slack, because Deena knew the way home. Jess had stared up through the screen of trees at the blue sky, listened to cicadas and frogs, and dreamed about the marvelous, heroic woman she would be, never realizing she should have treasured the girlhood, because her ability to dream for herself was a loss she would never get back.

You don't know that, habiba. *Your life is far from over. And you are* that marvelous, heroic woman. Keeping his arm around her, he lay back and brought her with him, her shoulder blades against his upper abdomen, head pillowed on his chest. The distracting press of his impressive groin adjusted in the small of her back. But he had no demands of her, allowing her to use him as a prop as she stared up at the stars and moon. Then at Hasna, for the mare's head filled her vision, ears pricked forward as she nosed Jess, curious about her position. It made her chuckle, stroke the long nose until the horse snorted and nosed Coman instead. He gave her a playful nip, but stayed to a walk, mindful of his master's will. Mason's thighs were warm beneath Jess's palms and she had to make a conscious effort not to stroke the long muscles as she might Coman's flanks.

"She stayed right with him," she said, desperately hoping he would continue to ignore her thoughts, or at least not comment on them.

"She can run nearly as fast. His legs are just longer. They've been together since they were babies. They're very devoted to one another, gentle as lambs, for all that their high spirits make them a bit of a handful."

"They're magnificent."

"Thank you. Coman's name means 'noble.' Their bloodlines go back centuries. Far purer than mine. I think they know they outrank me, but they're tolerant."

It made her want to smile, but she restrained herself this time. When she turned her head to look out at the sea, it pressed her cheek to him, so that she felt the bump of his nipple, distractingly close to her lips. She noted again that he smelled good, like cinnamon and a male musk, as well as a trace of the tropical flowers she'd passed in his gardens. He smelled like his home, as well as the desert.

He'd let his arm slide to a resting spot on her hip, and she was aware of the pressure of his long fingers there, how easy it would be to slide upward beneath her T-shirt. Or down, beneath the loose waistband of her jeans to tease her between her legs. Then, using a modicum of that impressive strength to lift her, he could turn her over and let her rest on her stomach, his heartbeat in her ear, her legs tangled with his behind the horse's shoulders, her fingers curled into his shirt at the ribs. She could sleep this way, moving in a fantastic dream of moonlight and horses running under the night sky.

"Sit up, *habiba*, and I'll turn you over."

"No," she whispered, staring at the sea. "Don't. My thoughts don't mean anything."

Of course he didn't listen to her. He lifted them both to a sitting position, and as she sat tensely, he guided one leg over so she was sitting sidesaddle, legs draped over one thigh, and then the next step, turning her to face him, straddling his lap. She'd gone numb, her mind not working. She was afraid, but wanting, too, caught between her dream of him and Farida—

"Jessica." He curved his palm over her cheek, but she wouldn't look up. She stared at the open collar of his shirt, at the column of his throat, the smooth skin revealed there. He paused, his breath stirring her brow, then he reached between them and, before her eyes, he slipped two buttons, so she saw more of that muscular flesh. Lifting her hand, he placed it inside the fabric, against his heart, warm male flesh.

"Being with Farida, it was a dream. A beautiful one. I don't blame you for escaping there when the awful memories you've had to carry become too much. But this is you and me right now. Can you face that?"

Sometime during the ride, his hair had become unclipped and the wind rippled it forward over one of his shoulders, teasing her cheek. Reaching up, she caught it, twined her fingers in the copper strands, but she shook her head. "I don't know what's real or a lie anymore, Mason. I don't think I even want to know. Can you please . . . just let me pretend for a little while?"

Before he could answer, she slid her hands under his arms, pressing her palms into his back, laying her cheek with wonder on the warm flesh. *This is Lord Mason, Farida's Mason. That's all that's important.*

Her tension eased as he sighed, folded his arms around her and lay back again, taking her with him. "This is not helping you, Jessica." His deep voice thrummed against her upper body, through her chest and stomach.

"For right now, it is." She turned her head so she could look at the shore again. Coman was unconcerned by their movements, nosing Hasna, having a horse conversation of some type. He kept to a walk in a floating silver world of water and moonlight, and the rush of water passed over his hooves as he moved along in the shallow surf. Occasionally, as higher waves came in, it lapped up to Mason's boots. She curled her wet toes against them. His body was warm and strong beneath her, his arms a bulwark against any fear.

Her mind stirred uneasily, wanting to remind her he was what she feared most of all. She hushed it, because she knew. She knew what he was, what he was likely to become. But he was giving her this moment, whether or not he would use it as a weapon against her later.

Maybe she'd accepted that something vital in her spirit had broken, when she realized she'd escaped Raithe only to walk back into a vampire's hands. Whatever the powers that be were, they didn't mean her to be free of vampires, perhaps ever. She would never have a lasting peace, a life of her own choosing, a life without fear. So all she could have were moments, and those moments only at the behest of whatever Master she was forced to serve. So fine. Whatever his game, he was giving her this one.

Given his effect on her senses, she shouldn't have been surprised to find that her body was starting to want more out of this moment than tranquil moonlight. It was impossible to ignore the feast of male beneath her, her legs straddled over his groin. Despite his undemanding touch on her back, his cock was hard against her belly. She had the absurd idea to make a slow rub against it, tease him, see how far his restraint went.

"I wouldn't advise it, love." His hand cupped her head, stroked the cap of hair, caressed the shell of her ear, a soothing rhythm that made her as sleepy as the evidence of his desire stirred her. In that dreamlike reaction, she slid her fingers up to his throat, traced the line of his jugular, that place that was so arousing to vampires. Deliberately baring a throat to a male vampire was as provocative as stripping. Maybe more so.

"You are killing me." He tipped her head and took command of her lips, his arm constricting around her back so every part of her from breast to thigh felt the hard planes, curves and demands of his body. She whimpered in the back of her throat.

It was the damnedest thing Mason had ever seen. Even after being so traumatized and abused, her sexual nature refused to be denied. It had to offer itself, wanting so desperately to trust, though her damaged mind was far from ready to handle a man's lust, and definitely not a vampire's. He didn't want to frighten her, but he had only so much control.

He'd stayed away two weeks, thinking that would help him gain perspective, as well as give her breathing space. Instead, he'd been instantly, painfully aroused by the spark in her eye when she knocked him off the fence. Despite the flash of fear, she'd maintained bristling challenge and awaited retaliation, to see if he would hurt her. Her laughter as they'd run had been an unexpected treasure, and now this, melting in his arms . . . While he knew her mind drifted in the pages of that damn journal, putting her into the safe place she imagined that to be, it was far from safe, because of the raging need she created in him.

He didn't coax open her lips. He simply demanded entry and she opened. He swept inside and devoured her, taking possession without hesitation. What a lovely, delicate mouth she had. Perfect for kissing, plundering. It was impossible not to imagine her lips closing over the head of his cock, since she'd already done it once. Only now he imagined her head tilted back over the end of his bed so he could drive in deep, come hard, watching her throat work as she swallowed. Her body would be spread and tied on his mattress, cunt lips glistening as she made moaning whimpers like this, wanting him to take her after she served him well.

Dear Allah. His arm slid down her back, his hand cupping her backside, moving her against his cock.

The need became too much. She jerked back, the soothing swirl of thoughts invaded by darkness, violent demands. He was able to stop her before she scrambled blindly away and toppled off the horse, or spooked Coman into shaking her loose. Fortunately, the horse trusted him, and a soothing word kept him steady as he caught Jess. He didn't force her to stay, but ensured she had a controlled slide off the horse's side to a stumbling landing on the sand. Backing away, she had her hand pressed flat against her belly as if she were calming the wild animal there.

Good luck with that, love, he thought. His own beast was barely held on a leash. However, Mason schooled his face to calm as he swung his leg over Coman's neck and dismounted. He released the horses with a word, let them canter ahead, cavort along the shore. They were well trained enough to come at his whistle and these miles of beach were his.

Perhaps something vital wasn't broken, habiba. *Only changed. Learning and growing. You must not give up on yourself so easily . . .*

Jessica spun around and started walking down the shoreline, trying to shut him out. She couldn't get this close to him, couldn't relax her guard. She was too fucked up in her head. Hell, she could barely keep reality and fantasy separate. She wanted a man's touch, a man's body, and his happened to be every woman's fantasy. He was a savage, bloodthirsty beast who would turn into a monster.

Farida had felt differently. Or she'd been the same as Raithe's servants. Deluded, stupid women, like those crazy cult members who popped up on the news all the time. The ones who drank poisoned Kool-Aid after bearing the psycho leader twenty kids apiece. Or followed him into someone's house to murder an entire family.

But Amara didn't seem that way. Jessica rolled her eyes at herself. Oh, yeah, Amara was Suzy Homemaker. Her husband shared her body with a *vampire*. Hell, Mason had probably fucked Enrique, too. Vampires were notoriously bisexual. Notoriously sexual, period. He'd probably screwed his precious horses.

"Now you're being nasty."

She snapped out of her mental rant to see him walking alongside her, his hands clasped behind his back, keeping easily apace with his longer legs. "I have never had carnal relations with either of my horses. I expect they would knock me through a barn wall if I became so desperate." He considered her with a sidelong glance. "I do admit there was a winter storm in Russia where I had to share a hut with a sheep for five days. While she did get exceedingly attractive, on several different levels, I managed to restrain myself."

"Is this charm?" She stopped, faced him, her fists clenched. The skin of her face felt tight, and there was an ache high in her throat.

"I'm trying to tell you there are no absolutes, *habiba*."

"Oh, horseshit. That's what people say so they can live in a gray world and rationalize what they do."

He sobered. "I didn't say there is no right and wrong. I said there are no absolutes. Right and wrong is in each man's heart. And that can differ between culture, circumstances. For every religious tenet, I can give you an example where breaking that tenet is the right thing to do. That's why you missed that I was a vampire, in Farida's writings. Your experience up until that moment was that all vampires are incapable of love, compassion, feeling."

"Each person deciding what's right and wrong doesn't always work," she argued. "What about sociopaths?"

At his look, she folded her arms over her chest. "I'm not saying you're one. I'm just saying."

"Faith can be a moral compass. I'm not talking about religion," he interjected, cutting off the derisive sneer on her face. "Though I prefer the name of Allah, I've never settled on a religion. I've seen enough commonality among all of them to suggest a man's spirituality rests inside himself. Perhaps that is what life is about, the journey to embrace and explore our own unique and yet common faith."

"To what purpose?"

His gaze had wandered ahead to the horses but now came back to her. Giving her a faint smile, he responded, "So that maybe we can go back to Eden, and finally be at peace. Jessica, you have experienced love. Can you honestly see what it inspires us to do, and think it's not worth it, just because we don't know if death is the beginning of some divine journey, or dust and oblivion? Love is probably the closest we'll ever get to understanding what divinity is. The same way hatred is the way we understand evil."

They walked in silence for a few moments, before he added, "And my ultimate point is that a healthy young woman feeling desire should be nothing for you to fear."

"It is if what I want is twisted, perverted. God, I know what you are."

"You may know what I am, but you don't know who I am." His jaw hardened, the amber eyes flickering.

"Still, vampires all have that need to . . ." She swallowed, because it disturbed her to say the word while looking at his handsome face, the stern set of the firm lips.

"Dominate? Yes. For that reason, vampires look for humans who have a compatible personality. A natural desire to submit. To serve. Hence, servants. You've been denied a true understanding of what that relationship is meant to be, Jessica."

"So Amara said. So you say. But you're trying to take up where Raithe left off, manipulate me into believing this is how I am, what I have to accept."

"If that was true, you would not be so angry." While his eyes still showed temper, there was compassion there, too, which made the jagged ache in her chest worse. "I have no intention of forcing you to accept anything, unless it concerns your safety. I only recommend, strongly, that you not shut yourself down to the possibility that your submissive nature existed long before Raithe met you."

"Why does it matter?" She swung away from him, facing the ocean, the surf far less turbulent than her thoughts. "It doesn't matter anymore."

"Yes, it does, and you know why. You cannot take control of your own destiny until you realize your own value. Until you know, in your soul, that who you are, not what Raithe tried to make you, has led you to this moment."

She swallowed, continued to watch the frothy overlay of water. "I can't believe anything you tell me. I can't trust anything."

She wasn't sure what she was seeking, but his words still took her by surprise. "No, you can't. But I know that Raithe tried to destroy a diamond. Sometimes the more you put a diamond through, the more it glitters, defying you to dim its inner fire. The wise Master would dedicate himself to polishing it until it shines, not shattering it."

She turned and met his gaze. Ten feet between them, but he felt much closer. She wanted him much closer . . . and far away, at the same time.

A muscle flexed in his jaw. "You have the choice, Jessica, to deny or accept any part of who you are. We all do that, to be the person we think we must be. The one we can face in the mirror, so to speak." His lips tugged ironically. "I merely want you to understand you have the freedom here, and the safety, to explore that choice."

∽

He started walking again. Jessica rolled his words over in her mind, watching him move ahead to the horses. God, he was a strange one. As he bent to pick up a piece of coral, he examined it in the moonlight, then skipped it across the water, a maneuver men usually perfected as boys.

She wasn't used to being curious about a vampire's past. For her, monsters sprang up from the underside of the mind and had always existed, fully formed evil. But the past couple weeks, and perhaps the unanswered strands of Farida's diary, had made her wonder. She already knew from idle staff gossip that he was a born vampire, not a made one. The Council had met in his home, which suggested he was a vampire of some standing.

In vampire hierarchy, a born vampire was accorded greater status than a made one. Raithe had been a made vampire, turned by a female vamp at thirty. Most born vampires, on the other hand, came from a human and vampire parent combination. She wondered how much older Mason was. She knew he was at least three hundred, but in truth, other than his efforts to preserve Farida's grave, she only knew about two years of his life. Even that had been indirect, through Farida's journals and the other documents.

While Mason didn't like her need to draw from their shared memories, only inside the pages of Farida's book did Jess feel stirrings in her *heart*, something that made her physical desire her own, her own choice, as he'd intimated. Watching him now, walking slowly along the shore, she remembered Farida writing of a night she'd walked along the edge of an oasis lagoon, and Lord Mason held her hand. The two of them joined like children in the night, until he turned to her, and all thoughts of childhood fled under the demand of his embrace.

This was him. The man she'd loved so much. A vampire. Jess rubbed her temple. Maybe each day she'd understand it a little better, but there was no way she was going to be able to take it in all at once. He'd said to give it time, and she admitted that was not bad wisdom. Already, the past weeks had given her a steadiness that, while dangerously tenuous, was more than she'd expected.

The more you put it through, the more it glitters . . .

Until she'd felt his desire stir so hard and urgent against her belly, and her own response had frightened her off the horse, she'd had a stolen moment of peace. She'd learned a lot about breaking commandments. Steal, lie, kill. But perhaps that kind of stealing wasn't so bad. Maybe Mason was telling her not to make herself the victim of her own crimes.

Oh, the hell with it. She quickened her pace, and then broke into a light-footed jog to catch up with him. As she reached him, he gave her another sidelong glance out of the vibrant eyes, his sensuous lips quirking at her expression. His hair rippled across his broad shoulders. What was it like for Farida, having that amber gaze settle on her with love and adoration? Just being looked at like this tied up her tongue.

After a moment, he reached out a hand. Like the journal. But as she began to reach out, he made a quiet noise and she paused, looking up at him.

"You take my hand as yourself, Jessica. Right now. Not three centuries ago."

Her fingers trembled. She shook her head, slowly pulled them back to her. Turning away without meeting his eyes, she broke into a run again, one that took her ahead of the horses.

Mason let her go, though he kept her in sight. While logically he knew he'd had only a couple weeks with her, and Raithe had had five years to undermine her confidence, he'd never been a patient man.

She'd internalized so much of Farida's journal, at times it was as if she was following it like a map right into his soul, in the quest to find or run from her own. But he'd been telling her the truth. The strength he saw in her was entirely her own.

Unfortunately, he desired her, and not merely to help her rediscover her passion. When he touched her, he wanted to keep her. The last time he'd wanted that had been . . . too much of a damn coincidence. He needed to haul back on his own reins. She didn't want to be another vampire's possession. At least that was what he told himself, even as he remembered the way she'd looked up at him, her gaze floating across his throat, as if wanting to taste him. She bore his mark on her inner thigh. She *was* his.

But not his to keep.

13

Jessica followed Amara up the winding staircase. "I really don't want to do this," Jess said.

"So you've told me. Twelve times since we left your room. But you were the one who told me yesterday you'd changed your mind and *did* want to come this time." Amara stopped, faced Jess. Since she was on the step above her, looking down, it made Jess feel somehow small and childlike when the servant laid her palms on her shoulders. "You made the decision, Jess," she said gently. "No one is forcing you. I believe you do want to do this. You're just frightened. No one is going to hurt you, or make you participate in any way."

As Jessica stared at Amara's midriff, covered with a silk robe, she was filled with misery. She couldn't face the terror of going up or the disgrace of going back down. The woman's brow creased in concern and she brushed knuckles against Jess's jaw. "How about this? Stay at least fifteen minutes, once we start. If you still don't feel comfortable about it, you can slip back down the stairs and go do as you wish. Can you do that?"

Jessica drew a deep breath, closed her eyes. When she'd washed off the day's stable work in the opulent bathroom, she'd found a new jar of body cream on the counter. It had smoothed onto her skin like liquid silk and left a jasmine scent lingering on her skin, as if made with the flowers in Mason's own garden. She wasn't sure if inhaling the aroma helped, or made things worse.

It was like living in an enchanted castle in a fairy tale. Over the past several weeks, each time she returned to her room, she found certain things changed, reflecting her likes and dislikes, as if the staff could read her mind. Since she was all too aware who in the household could read her mind, she knew who was ordering those alterations. She wasn't sure why he was doing it, but somehow the horseback ride together had changed things.

While he was back to staying at a distance, somehow he'd taken a couple steps closer. As the days passed, she admitted, to herself at least, if everything going on around her was a ruse, it was the most elaborately planned ruse she'd ever witnessed, with a large cast of consummate actors. But her life had been uncertain for so long, only unpredictability had become predictable. To give herself permission to expect something to remain a consistent truth was like stepping out onto a decaying bridge and believing it wouldn't crumble under her feet. In her life, the crumbling had been inevitable. It was just a matter of when it would happen.

But time had also given her more courage. She hadn't survived this long by sticking her head in the sand. Maybe that was why, when she overheard Amara and Enrique discussing her next "dance" for Mason, she'd had a moment of blind courage—or utter foolishness—and told Amara she at last wanted to come and watch. It would be evidence that she could handle herself, manage her own fears.

"Jessica?" Amara prodded her.

"Fifteen minutes. I can do that," Jess admitted grudgingly. Amara smiled, recaptured her hand and tugged her upward again.

Jess wore a modest island dress she'd found in the closet. This one stopped above her knees, the top a halter style that showed a discreet amount of cleavage. With the pretty lavender and gray color, it was something she would have bought for herself. However, the delicate silver ribbon choker on the same hanger had given her pause. With amethysts and quartz crystals dangling from it on threads, it teased her throat at every movement.

Amara had said it was a wonderful compliment to the dress when she saw it, and Jess couldn't disagree. But from the day she'd been enslaved, Raithe had made her wear a heavy steel collar with links for various tethers. She'd had it cut off as soon as she'd run far enough, but it had taken a long time to wake in the mornings and not feel naked without it.

Putting on the ribbon choker she knew the master of the house had selected for her, she had that same feeling at first, as if she might not be fully clothed without it. For that reason she almost ripped it off, but looking at it in the mirror, her nervous fingers stroking the delicate strands, awakening the skin beneath with the caress, she didn't. Instead, she was distracted by a fantasy of Mason behind her, clipping the fragile choker in place. Putting his large hands over it, reinforcing the hold, its meaning.

It could be pulled free with one tug, and yet, when accepted willingly, it could symbolize something so much more binding.

God, now she was thinking like him. Or maybe that *was* him. Sometimes she didn't know, but she knew she had no experience in willing subjugation. That was why she was here, right? To see it.

She tuned back in as Amara pushed back a tapestry on the right side of the corridor. Jess found herself in a cozy nook containing only a wide, low couch scattered with comfortable pillows. A tray holding her dinner had been left on a side table with a carafe of wine. Music, a mysterious woodwind composition, wafted up from somewhere beyond the plush velvet blue wall hangings on the other side of the nook.

Amara pulled them back, showing that there was no wall, only a wrought-iron rail through which Jessica could see the ballroom below. Jess drew in a breath, for it was one room she hadn't yet visited. Like so much of this place, it was a fantasy. More of the tall beveled-glass windows, their gold dividing lights gleaming from the candles grouped beneath them. The walls in between were hung with panels of blue silk shot with gold, and the chandelier reminded her somewhat of her choker, individual diamond pendants of light that hung free like stars against the ceiling, which was a basilica. The dome had a starburst pattern of glass to show the night sky, and the glass was interspersed with panels of marbleized blue and gold. The floor was acres of polished wood.

"Seems like a lot of room for dinner."

"My lord Mason likes the dancing done in this room. Otherwise he takes his dinner in his private quarters or the dining room for guests."

Jessica swallowed, feeling herself pale, despite her valiant attempt not to react. Amara bit her lip, but Jess drew back, evading her touch. "I'm fine," she said testily. "Go do your thing."

"Jessica, Lord Mason has very few guests. And when he does—"

"Didn't we cover this before?" Jess snapped. "There's nothing you can say I'll really believe, so it's kind of wasted breath, isn't it?"

She hadn't meant to snap, but despite the calmness with which she'd made her decision to watch this, the actuality of it was stretching her nerves out tight, fraying them. Amara's reminder of how vampires socialized only exacerbated it.

Amara pressed her lips together. "Lord Raithe did terrible things to you, Jessica, so I can understand your fear. But you choose to be rude. No one here has been anything but civil to you. It is not too much to ask the same in return."

"Yeah, actually it is. Because I didn't ask to be here, did I?"

Habiba, *behave, or I will address your behavior personally. Not hurting my staff includes not hurting their feelings.*

Oh, Jesus Christ. She glared at Amara. "Fine, I'm sorry. I'm sorry I'm not being all civilized for your 'dinner' where he'll suck your blood and fuck you in front of your husband."

The slap was surprising, but she'd had her fill of standing still while being hit. Jess caught the woman's wrist before she made contact. Amara swept her legs, startling her with the speed of the movement. Jess landed hard, but fortunately on the bank of pillows behind her. She twisted and kicked, but in a maneuver she didn't expect from the gentle Amara, she found herself rolled on her stomach, the woman's knee pressed with convincing aggression against her spine, her arm held behind her back.

"I have told Lord Mason this is a women's fight, and his interference is not needed," Amara said between her teeth. "You have been badly treated, Jessica. I, like my Master, would do a great deal to undo what was done to you. You are testing us; I understand that. But the relationship I have with Lord Mason, and with my husband, is sacred to me. If you cannot see that after what you see tonight, then we will know a different approach is necessary to help you. But I will have your apology, or I will happily tie you down and shave your head."

Jessica couldn't shake Amara's hold unless she wanted to make this struggle far more violent and bloody. However, at that threat, she stilled. "You'll shave my head?"

"Yes. There is no greater threat to a woman than to her vanity. And you have lovely hair. It would make a beautiful weave to add to mine, when I wear it up. I'm sure Mason would enjoy rubbing your bald head for luck, if nothing else."

"You bitch."

"Exactly," Amara said pleasantly. "Would you like to apologize now?"

"So, being tortured for five years is no excuse for rudeness."

"There is no excuse for rudeness."

Jessica couldn't help it, she started to laugh. While harsh and grating to her own ears, it wasn't the panicked hysteria she knew often accompanied her laughter. She actually felt some loosening of the tension in her belly. Amara's touch eased and the woman drew back. Jess turned over, looking at her from her reclining position while the woman cocked her head. The stern look still lingered in her eyes, but there was a light smile on her face as well.

"Let me guess. You were a kindergarten teacher once."

"Schooling the prince's children was part of my responsibilities." Amara's dark eyes twinkled. "I did not know that wrestling technique when I cared for them, though. I wish I had."

The older servant had gone to her knees to manage the offensive maneuver. The robe had fallen off her shoulder, leaving it bare except for a glittering strap of whatever costume she was wearing, and showing a hint of bosom. Remembering the night Amara sang to her, and following impulse, Jessica reached out, touched the bare shoulder. Beneath Amara's robe there was an outfit meant to please Mason as she danced for him, raise his bloodlust, harden his cock. And maybe to arouse her husband as well, the man to whom she'd pledged her troth, a man who also belonged to Mason. Jess didn't understand why the thought drew her nerves taut, in a not entirely unpleasant way.

No, that wasn't true. Under a layer she wasn't yet willing to lift and examine, she was afraid she completely understood it. Which might be the real reason she wanted to bolt.

. . . you have the freedom here, and the safety, to explore that choice . . .

Amara's expression had become quiet, watchful, as Jess's fingers turned over. Her knuckles followed that line of exposed skin down to the ripe curve of lifted breast, the swell bared by the robe. Amara's breath drew in, her wet lips parting. Her body, prepared for an evening of pleasure for her Master and husband, was likely already damp.

Jessica, while watching the two of you would be every man's fantasy, what you are touching is mine. And you do not have my permission to enjoy her. That pleasure is mine tonight.

Her touch stilled. Jess raised her gaze to meet Amara's. For that instant, it was as if their desire was linked, and it coiled tight in her belly, galvanized by his words, his control.

Perhaps later, if you ask, I will allow you to taste her, tease her to climax with your hands and mouth, as you are imagining.

She drew back, a tremor running through her hands, and shook her head. Though in denial of what, or who, she wasn't sure. "I'm sorry," she whispered.

Amara's eyes softened. Leaning forward, she brushed a kiss over Jess's open mouth, gave her a teasing taste of tongue. Pressing her forehead to Jess's, her long-lashed dark eyes glittered with desire and challenge. "I think one day we should defy him. I doubt he would put great effort into stopping us. More likely he would decide to punish us . . . afterward."

With a wink, she rose, nodded toward the open blue curtains. "If you're more comfortable, you can close those. They'll form a small crack through which everything can be observed, without feeling as if you're on display."

Then she was gone, slipping out from behind the tapestry, leaving an impression of silken hair and liquid eyes, myriad things to stroke the senses of touch, scent, sight and taste. Had Jess wanted to defy him as well? Take his servant and overwhelm her, because she was feeling overwhelmed? Amara would let her keep the control, and help her find satisfaction in a safe place. That sounded reasonable, not insane at all. Except Jess knew she was using it as a substitute for what her body truly craved, who it truly craved. And that *was* insane.

Fortunately, she had time to collect herself. She ate the dinner, studied the empty ballroom and obsessed over what she was going to see below. Whenever her breath started to shorten, a warning of anxiety, she reminded herself that very little of her experience with Lord Mason had matched the unpredictable cruel menace of Raithe.

That didn't stop her throat from closing up, her mouth drying and stomach lurching, when the staff finally began to set up the dining area. She drew the curtains as Amara suggested, watching through the crack as the ballroom lights were dimmed, leaving illumination to the window candles and sconces placed upon short pillars set up in a circle in the center of the large room. A divan was carried in, cushions were scattered about and several statues placed at different points of the circle. Erotic, elegant sculptures, life-sized artwork. As the stage was set, she was reminded how much vampires enjoyed presentation. Her heart accelerated. Fifteen minutes, once it started. She'd said she'd stay fifteen minutes. She could do this for fifteen minutes. She'd done far worse, for far longer. And she was way up here, and they'd said she didn't have to participate. She didn't even have to wait fifteen minutes. She could go now.

No. She *would* do this. Because it wasn't about complying with her agreement with Amara. It was about her facing her fears, not letting them run her life.

Incense was lit and a staff member used a fan to disseminate the aroma in the room. Jessica inhaled vanilla and sandalwood. Several screens were brought in, draped with transparent fabric, and arranged on three quarters of the circle, so it was as if Jessica were gazing into a sheikh's tent.

Was he purposely creating a scene from her imaginings, and if so, was it to help ease some of her fears or draw her deeper into a dangerous fantasy? He'd seemed opposed to her immersion in Farida's memoirs, but had he changed his mind, decided it could work to his advantage?

Leaving that disturbing thought, made more disturbing because she wasn't repelled by either idea, she studied the people who came and went. Human servants were intriguing, of course, for their willingness to bind themselves to monsters, but neutral staff held a mystery of their own. Most, like Mason's, carried one or two marks for security purposes, but typically they were not called to serve a vampire's more intimate demands for nourishment. They simply worked for a supernatural being as they would a human employer, collecting their paychecks. She knew some of Mason's staff had families, children.

The ideas vanished, swallowed in a black hole of uncertainty in her mind as Amara entered the ballroom. She opened a panel in the far wall, revealing the sound system, and made an adjustment to the track, slowing it down, making the exotic selection even more seductive. When she came to the center of the room, she sent an absent smile up toward Jess's corner, despite the curtain being pulled. Sliding off the wrap at last, Amara tucked it discreetly under the pillows, then began her stretches, rolling her head and shoulders.

The tingle in Jess's fingertips returned as she remembered touching Amara's perfumed, silken skin. The brief bra top she wore was the coin style, lifting and displaying her breasts prominently. A matching coin belt, low on her hips, overlaid the slitted transparent skirt that showed the cleft between her buttocks and the hint of her sex. The anklets she wore were also laden with delicate coin chips and an interesting accessory, a slender chain that ran between the two, a subtle manacle that allowed her only a certain range of stride, almost like what was put on Jessica for her own protection.

Jessica shifted her glance at a movement at the French doors, and Enrique slid in, joining his wife. Her eyes widened as she realized he was also in a form of dance costume. The harem pants and arm braces made of metal showed to good advantage the rippling, muscular physique, the tanned, smooth skin. While Amara didn't look toward him, Jessica sensed her awareness as she stretched, practicing spins, shimmies, loosening up. When he came up behind her and slid his palms over her hips, she undulated against him in a graceful move, creating a musical sound of silver coins as she looped an arm around his neck and they turned together.

Jessica noted then that their third marks were the same, the tattoo-scar outline of a wolf. Enrique's was on his upper abdomen, to the left over the rib cage, and Amara's was on her back, so that as their bodies came together the marks were pressed to each other. A mated pair. A quiver ran through Jess as she thought of the tiger mark on the inside of her own thigh, and the one high on Mason's shoulder.

When Enrique at last let Amara go, it was with obvious reluctance. He sat then, taking an unobtrusive place on the cushions next to one of the screens.

Jess was glad for her curtains. As she gazed out the narrow opening, the music and incense drifting over her, the tightness in her belly waffled between desire and fear, taking her on a merry-go-round of anxiety. He'd set this up perfectly. The right amount of privacy and titillation to tempt her to her own destruction. But she couldn't look away, couldn't think of leaving now.

Particularly when Mason arrived.

A desert tiger he still was. From her time in the desert, Jess knew men of wealth often wore the belted tunic over a robe. He'd chosen the belted tunic, the wide sash emphasizing the lean power of his upper body, but wore no robe beneath it. Even his feet were bare, as he stretched out on a hip and one elbow on the divan, opposite from Enrique. His attention centered on his female servant.

He reclined so easily, like a cat in truth, all lazy power and grace. Propping up one knee, he lifted his plate off the adjacent table and set it before him, a small selection of meat and fruit. Vampires didn't eat food, but they enjoyed the taste and smell. She knew all of this, because she'd been to the ritual of a vampire dinner hundreds of times. It reminded her, even though she was holding her breath, taking in his every feature, that she was supposed to be fearful of what she was about to see, despite the aesthetic props. But that uneasy stirring couldn't break her motionless anticipation.

At his nod, Amara began dancing to the music's haunting strains. Jess watched his eyes follow her. Had he commanded her to wear this particular outfit? Was that why his eyes had scanned over her functionally at first, ensuring she'd followed his direction, and then taken his time on the return trip, lingering on the bounty of pleasures the view offered? Jess's thighs tensed in an unexpected way at the thought. Lifting the first piece of meat, he inhaled it before he took a sparse taste, though his gaze never left his servant.

As riveting as he was, she made herself go back to Amara. She didn't know much about belly dancing, but Amara had offered to teach her some of the moves. Though she'd refused—for now—she couldn't help but imagine what it would be like to dance like this for Lord Mason, as Amara was doing.

If you do not understand that I consider my relationship with Lord Mason and my husband sacred . . .

Amara's attention was wholly on her vampire Master as she executed the effortless spins and shimmies that drew the gaze to the movement of hips, the arch of the body, the undulations that made the breasts quiver and the coins sing. She did it all without jerking the short chain between her ankles, keeping it barely slack, working with joyous grace and beauty within the limits of her bondage.

She approached Mason in a series of lithe, erotic movements. When he crooked a finger at her, she spun to her knees and fell back so her skull was caught in the cup of one large hand. Leaning down, he gave her the food he had in his mouth, transferring it with a long, sweeping kiss that stole Jessica's breath away again. Then he released her and she was up again.

She maneuvered around him, moving with fluid grace to one of the alabaster statues. It was a male nude and Amara presented her back to it, working her hips in a rotation that had her brushing the top of the inanimate male's thighs. Turning, she trailed her fingers, the points of her nails, across the anatomically correct genitalia. Another dip, sway and turn brought her to a female statue. Her lips passed over the tip of the breast.

A leap and unexpected fluid flip brought her back to the divan. Her stomach arched up to him, hands and feet on the floor, head dropped back so her hair brushed the floor. She held there, quivering, as Mason poured wine on her bare belly and licked it off, teasing her navel piercing, catching it in his teeth as she moaned. She held the position, however, as Mason balanced two small empty cups there, nodded to Enrique.

Now the other servant rose, came to Mason and dropped to one knee between his wife's straining thighs. Pouring what appeared to be coffee in the small cups, he offered one to Lord Mason. The two men drank for a bated length of time while Amara served as their table, then Mason brushed the front fold of her skirt away. Revealing her sex, bare except for the silver ring of a clit piercing, he tipped the cup. A few drops of hot liquid landed on the small bud of flesh, making her shudder, a soft cry coming from her lips. At a nod from Mason, Enrique dipped his head, began to tease her with his mouth as her sounds of pleasure and shaking increased.

Jessica was quivering herself, low in her belly, her hands curled into the pillows as she watched them.

"Stop," Mason said at last, and though his voice was a seductive growl, Jessica heard him clearly. When Enrique paused, Mason gripped his shoulder, eased him upward until, though still leaned over his wife, Enrique's mouth was about eight inches above her glistening lips.

"Dance for him this way," Mason commanded. "Enrique will be still. You must bring yourself to his mouth on every rotation, to earn the barest touch of his lips, his tongue. And you must follow the proscribed form of the dance." His eyes glinted. "I will know if you deviate."

Amara began to perform the hip circles. It took her several tries, for Mason obviously had a diabolical knowledge of her range in this position. But at last she reached Enrique, and she cried out softly as she made brief contact with his mouth. Her body arched up, a work of erotic art, every circular motion straining with the effort to bring her labia and clit back to Enrique's lips for one exquisite, short taste, then down again.

As she performed for him, Mason's expression was unreadable, but Jess saw him trail a hand down Enrique's bare back. As Amara's arousal increased, she nevertheless followed the tempo of the music that had been chosen. Even from here, Jess could feel how much the woman wanted to move faster, faster and faster, until her hips would be a shimmying blur, so flexible in her need that it could not help but be likened to frenetic fucking.

However, despite being forced to the slower tempo, it was obvious when Amara was getting so close to a pinnacle that one more simple contact would detonate her. Mason's palm drifted down to

Amara's belly, teased her there again and brought her to a halt, trembling. "Both of you, dance for me," their Master commanded.

When the vampire settled back on the divan, Enrique slid his arm under Amara so they came up together in a supple movement. Amara began the shimmy and Enrique turned with her, moving in behind her body to adopt a similar movement, synchronizing the masculine and feminine forms, the spins coordinated as if they were inside each other's minds. Perhaps, with their link to Mason, and their love for each other, they were. Amara twisted between the two men, rubbing up against her husband, then spinning to her knees to Mason for a caress and another mouthful of food. Back to the feet of her husband to press her lips in fervent adoration against his thigh, before coming back to her feet so she danced once more for Mason.

When Jessica could feel perspiration beading on her upper lip, her thighs so slick she had trouble holding them against each other, Mason rose from the divan, moving into the dance.

Amara spun, as if attempting escape, and Mason caught her waist, trapping her in Enrique's embrace. Her husband took her mouth as Mason unfastened the coin halter and let it fall to the floor like a shower of treasure, his hands replacing it. Jess was awestruck by Amara's control, for her hips continued to move in a figure eight, rubbing with irresistible seduction between the two men's arousals.

She'd been shared by Raithe before. But this was different; she couldn't deny it, no matter how she wanted to do so. Enrique bent, licked Amara's nipples between the vampire's fingers, then took Mason's fingers into his mouth as well. Mason caressed the man's nape with a free hand and then dropped it along his back. Enrique's loose pants were slit on the side all the way to the hip, open to the creature to whom they were both bound. Mason's hand slid into that side opening and tightened on one muscular cheek. As he did, Amara put her hands behind her back, tugged open the tie holding Mason's tunic closed. Then she raised her arms, slid them around Mason's neck to lift herself.

Because Jess was so soaked, if she'd been in Amara's stead, Mason could have done as he did to her now, simply dipped his fingers, already wet with Enrique's mouth, into the hot pool of her need.

Then, as Amara clasped her legs around Enrique's waist, Mason used the accessible position to lubricate her rear passage with those fingers. Amara closed her eyes, made more of those pleasured sounds in her throat, her breasts thrusting upward in reaction, winning the absorption of the two males.

It was as simple as that. In one smooth movement, Mason drove into her backside as Enrique thrust into her sex. Amara screamed at the dual sensation. When Enrique let out a guttural sound himself, dropping his forehead onto his wife's shoulder, Mason leaned over him and sank his fangs into Enrique's neck.

Jess dug into the pillow she held, white-knuckled. Her breath was shallow, her skin on fire with shuddering heat. She wanted to condemn herself, call herself no different from those vampires who had so avidly watched her be shared by Raithe and others, but she couldn't. When Mason had joined their dance, it had been seamless, an acceptance so immediate, it was obvious there was no conscious need for choice from either servant.

He drank deeply, then moved to Amara, and did the same. A thin line of blood trickled down Enrique's throat. Amara had one arm bent back, her fingers clutching Mason's shoulder, while her other held on to Enrique's. When Mason bit her, those fingers convulsed and her eyes closed, her building crescendo of moans revealing how close to climax she was.

Mason was fastidious and relentless, moving from one to the other, catching that trickle on Enrique's shoulder and licking back up to the bite area, wasting not a drop as he suckled and bit again, increasing the pleasure and pain. He and Enrique kept up a rhythm inside Amara that made her wordless pleas echo through the ballroom, a never-ending cycle of just-at-the-knife's-edge release.

"Now," Mason commanded, and Enrique went over that edge, hips jerking spasmodically beneath Mason's guiding hand. The rapture of his wife elevated to one long, blissful scream of climax as she joined him. She bowed up in their grasp like a graceful bird, mesmerizing in her flight.

Jessica wanted Mason to come, to release. She wanted to see it. A moment later she did, hearing his animal groan while Amara clung to her husband with one arm and Mason with another. The woman rode her aftershocks on their wave, both of them making primal noises of encouragement matched by the pounding heart ricocheting in Jessica's chest.

The quivering in her stomach had become a shaking throughout her body. Need was drawn dangerously tight, hovering between desire and anxiety. She couldn't move, was afraid the shuddering would become something else she couldn't contain, couldn't control.

You don't need control, habiba. That's my job. Lie back on the pillows, and give yourself the release you so desperately need. Put your fingers into that soaking wetness I can smell, imagine it's my cock and let yourself go. I want you to spread your legs wide, as I would do, massage your clit with your thumb.

"No, no . . ." He didn't look toward her, didn't distract the others at all, but she wanted to close her eyes anyway. She couldn't, though. She had to see Mason withdraw, so gently, from Amara, help Enrique ease her to the cushions. It wasn't lost on Jess that she herself was as weak, as if she'd been mentally taken and left as limp, even without the release her body craved. She was glad she was on the pillows, because she wasn't sure she could rise.

Enrique stretched out on his wife's body, giving her long, drugging, postcoital kisses. He penetrated her again, his cock still erect. In this position, Jess could see his buttocks, the pantaloons pulled down to his thighs, moving in a slow, up-and-down rhythm, building again, or maybe just giving her the pleasure of aftermath stroking.

As absorbing as their tableau was, her attention left them. Mason had moved to the edge of the circle, where a basin of water, cloth and soap had been left on a short pillar. It had been placed on a thick, circular rug to protect the floor from water. Since his robe was still open, she watched him soap his hands and clean his semierect cock.

It wasn't as if he was flaunting himself. He wasn't even turned all the way toward her, but that made it even more tantalizing, seeing him half in profile. Had Enrique or Amara ever done this for him? Sitting on their knees before him, cleaning the folds, the ridge under the head, teasing him with the wet cloth and stroke of their hands, their mouths, to bring him to arousal again? Vampires had a much faster recovery time than human males. Though third-marks apparently did, too, if Amara's gasps and the increase in Enrique's thrusts were any indication.

I'm waiting, my love. Bring yourself pleasure. Give that gift to yourself.

Was he teasing her deliberately, pointing out the detested obvious she couldn't deny, that she craved the release of a climax, but only at his direction? Her body trembled again as his amber gaze lifted at last, pinning her through that tiny slit in the curtain. His hand still rested on his cock, his body so virile and powerful, revealed by the robe. His hair was loose, brushing his shoulders.

Give that gift to me.

Because she couldn't look at him any longer, she crept back to the cushions, but then she was easing herself down on them as if his hands were taking her there, her fingers finding herself under the dress.

Legs spread, habiba.

She adjusted, but tears pricked her eyes, her heart torn between betrayal of herself and what her body seemed determined to accept.

Shhh, my love. No thinking. Give in to your pleasure. My demand for it.

The moment she touched herself, any struggle, no matter how token, was over. Her clit screamed for friction, her mind filled with the images she'd just seen, the connection between the three below. The way Amara had moved, dancing for them both. Dropping to her knees before Mason and bending back in that vulnerable move, offering her whole self to him.

From her position, Jess could still see through the crack. Mason had set aside the cloth and reclined back on his divan. He left the robe open, immodestly male as he propped on one hip, one forearm resting on a crooked knee. His cock was hard and thick again, probably leaving a damp, heated track across that section of his abdomen, the remains of his last release. He waited for her to serve his pleasure with her cries.

She moved her fingers over herself, dipping into the wetness, stroking it over her clit, imagining without any conscious thought his mouth on her there, or his broad head, about to push in and stretch her. Raithe hadn't liked to fuck her there. He preferred her ass, her mouth. And his horrible friends . . .

Here, habiba. *It is my mouth on your clit, teasing you. Licking your honey, cherishing you as I prepare you for my cock. And when I thrust in, deep and strong, like Enrique with Amara, I would lie upon you, holding you down, surrounding you. With my fingers tangled in your hair, my thumbs on your lips, I would drown in your eyes . . .*

"Oh, God . . ." She dropped her head back as he switched to Arabic in her mind, the flow of sensual words drowning her as well. She didn't need to know what he was saying, because the music of it was taking her where he wanted to go. Where she wanted to go as well. The climax seized and shoved her over, over the fears of her body and mind, over all the terrors and pain, but she couldn't get high enough for them not to tear jagged holes in her vulnerable soul. She was like a parachutist jumping from a burning plane, the wreckage falling all around her flimsy chute. Safety, the hope of rescue, was an illusion.

I can't, I can't . . . Help . . .

Pleasure this overwhelming had to be a threat, taking her away from herself, as Raithe always took her away from herself. She'd climax no matter how revolted, frightened or in pain she was. Afterward, her tears were his prize. Eyes were the window of the soul, and whenever she'd had to look in a mirror, she saw it dying. He'd prolonged her life with his marks while shredding her soul.

She couldn't stop it. She was frightened, falling, burning. Her mind, always trying to save her, scrambled for Farida, but she couldn't quite get there, couldn't reach the fingertips of the long-dead woman.

The climax yanked her out of range like an opening parachute in truth, bringing a pain beyond bearing, a pleasure that was so lonely, desolate tears poured down her face. She rippled and bucked in the clamp of the ruthless orgasm, a release for a body that hungered for any fulfillment, no matter what consequences the poison she consumed would bring.

It would be the lash this time. A barbed cat-o'-nine that pulled ribbons of flesh from her belly and breasts, her thighs. He stood over her, watching her scream. His cock rose, becoming a rod of steel at the sight of her combined pain and orgasm. He'd fuck her even as she bled.

Jessica. "Jessica." The thunderous command jerked her away from

Raithe, tumbled her through her darkness and dumped her back onto the balcony, crying and hunched into herself, tearing at her face, trying to get out of her skin, because it was burning, he was burning her . . .

Strong hands circled her wrists, and she was pulled up into a male body, one that didn't smell like Raithe or his sweaty, fear-filled dungeon. But he would take her there, to that dark place, and leave her there for days with no light. Silence brought its own horrors, but the dungeon was rarely silent. He bred rats and spiders down there, so she heard the rodents' scratching movements, the scrapes on her bare toes as they tried to climb up her body. He'd suspend her a few inches off the ground so they had to leap. She was screaming to be freed, feeling the spiders in her hair, on her shoulders . . .

It's me, habiba. *Mason. Farida's Mason. Shhh, come back to me. Come back here. You're with us, and we won't let anyone else harm you.*

There were other hands on her. She struggled at first, but then realized they were gentle, soothing, stroking her back, surrounding her. Amara. Enrique. Mason. She wasn't in the dungeon. The three of them were holding her together, protecting her on all sides, like a fortress of flesh and bone, instead of a prison. Not apathetic, not standing back leering, laughing or bored with her agony. Being noticed was no longer a bad thing.

"Easy, dearest." Amara's voice. Enrique was murmuring to her in soothing, musical French. And Mason's strength was around her, his body closest of all. Holding her against him, almost as though they'd been on Coman, outrunning the past, him calling out that wild yell, defying fear and darkness.

She drew in shuddering breaths, trying to pull it together, glad when rationality started seeping back into her cracked consciousness. Jesus, God, that had been a terrible one. Her last panic attack that severe had been in a marketplace in Egypt, when she thought she'd been spotted by one of Raithe's friends. She'd stumbled away, not sure where she was going, and woken up hidden in a vat of trash, with maggots crawling over her skin . . .

"Stop. Look here, in my eyes." Mason lifted her chin, made her look into the brilliant amber gaze. "Jessica, this is going to stop, right now."

Why was it his touch helped? When everything about him should repel her? Why did he make her feel safe?

"Because I will die to keep you that way," he said. "I will tolerate no more of this. You are safe here, and well, and you are going to learn to trust us."

Despite herself, Jessica blinked, and something else filtered through. A wry, weary humor. "Why didn't I think of that before, my lord?" she said hoarsely. "Command the fear and nightmares away and *pffffft*"—she managed to spray a light saliva on him—"it's all gone."

Amara's hand caressed her nape. "It's a male thing, dearest. They can't stand to see us in pain, so they must order us to stop, as if we are doing it deliberately to disturb them."

She caught Enrique's serious, quiet smile in the corner of her eye, but Jess didn't see any smile in Mason's eyes. Instead, he glanced at the other two, his mouth firm. "Let's get her to bed. And I don't want her left alone. Amara, stay in the room with her."

Jessica tucked her chin on his chest as he lifted her. Closing her eyes, she shut it all out. Not only because she couldn't bear to face any more tonight, but because she couldn't understand why what she most wanted was for *him* to stay in the room with her. And, knowing he could hear her thoughts, she wondered why he remained silent and unresponsive, even as he carried her as if he'd carry her to the ends of the Earth to keep her safe.

14

God, that had been embarrassing. As she ran a currycomb over Coman's flanks, Jess forced herself to consider it a blessing that she hadn't seen or heard from Mason for the past several days. When she'd told Amara the next morning that she was fine, she was better, and she really didn't need her to stay in the room when she slept, she expected Amara to smile and babysit her anyway. Instead, when the woman simply bid her sweet dreams the following evening, Jess knew that Mason had allowed it, since Amara would not counter her Master's order.

It was interesting to Jess because, since he could see into her mind, he knew as well as she did that she really *wasn't* fine. But she did have a desperate need to feel like something was under her control. After relying on herself for so long, that fleeting moment of wanting him to stay with her had sent her into a tailspin. Have a bloody *vampire* take care of her?

She'd thrown herself back into the routine she'd carved for herself, anything to help her settle the shitstorm that night had roused in her. Working with the horses, taking her lunch in the gardens, reading in her brightly lit room at night, and trying not to listen for footsteps outside the door or unexpected voices in her head, actually did her good. So she told herself.

Maybe she'd been right, and wrong, all along. Maybe Mason and his servants *were* different, but she needed to leave everything about vampires behind in order to bury that past. And burying it was the only solution. There was no therapy that would make her comfortable with life in a vampire household again. Therapy worked for people who could anesthetize their brains into the belief that life was supposed to be this fucked up. Or those whose biggest problem was an unsatisfying marriage, inexplicable middle-class depression or suicidal kids. Manageable problems.

Her best short-term approach was to compartmentalize it, pretend it happened to someone else, and stay away from anything that might bring it to the forefront of consciousness. And then maybe, somewhere down the road, she might be able to forget it even happened, or at least not let it rule her life anymore.

She'd had only one goal with Raithe—survive each night, pray for dawn. And she did it day by day. She had to do the same thing here. Create short, manageable tasks, bite-sized pieces of life. Prove she could handle herself, handle her own life. Then, if Mason could convince the Council not to summarily execute her, he would let her go. If he lived up to his promises . . .

She worked her way back to Coman's haunches, brushing vigorously. Oh, and she needed to stay away from explosive climaxes that resulted in psychotic meltdowns.

Easy enough. After all, she'd been defiled enough to last most women ten lifetimes. But that sex had been all about violence, torment, humiliation. What had happened in the ballroom . . . it had been a fantasy come to life.

Jess stopped with a snarl at herself that had Coman's head swinging around, the white of his eye showing as he rolled it in her direction. She pressed her hands to her forehead, willing the thoughts to go away. She couldn't afford fantasies. Her fragile mind was having enough difficulty managing reality.

No. It was getting late. She needed to finish grooming Coman, help with the feeding, then she'd go inside, eat dinner, read a book . . .

~

Enrique turned from the window, from which he could see Jessica Tyson sitting by the horse fountain in the upper-tier garden, her favorite place. Though night had come, the area fell inside a wash of light from the windows of the staff leisure area. The girl obviously had an aversion to darkness, though they'd all noticed it wasn't the night itself she feared. She was more apprehensive of dark rooms, or the darkness that lay outside a room, which turned windows and doors into openings into her private Hell.

A vampire household had odd hours. While he and Amara often slept in the afternoons in preparation for the evening, most of the staff, like the maintenance and stable help, had gone to bed by now. However, he noted they'd left the back lights on, for her specifically. She spoke little, but was often close to one or more of them during the day, as if she yearned for human contact but could not bear for it to be too direct. A vampire's staff tended to be sensitive to undercurrents, so they'd stayed accessible if she needed anything, but were never overt in their attentions. Jorge in particular was growing very fond of the girl.

Enrique was sure she was oblivious to how many of the staff were taking a personal interest in her progress. He was also certain she didn't have a clue how deep the interest of the lord of the household ran, enough to eclipse the interest and concerns of all the other staff members combined, to a multiple of ten. If she knew, it would probably scare her to death.

Suppressing his worry with effort, Enrique looked toward Mason. The disturbing darkness simmering in his gaze had been there in greater or lesser degrees since Jessica had become hysterical on the balcony. Tonight, as on past nights, Mason had been conferencing with several trusted contacts close to the Council. From his expression as he cut the connection, his efforts on Jessica's behalf were still on the fence. But they now knew he had her, for he'd taken the leap and told Lord Uthe, second-in-command of the Council, that she was in his care.

"They will allow me to keep her here, until I come and speak to them about her situation." Mason put the cell phone down on the desk. "We've made an appointment to do so. They wanted me to bring her, but I indicated she was in no condition for that."

"It will take time, my lord," Enrique said quietly. And he meant not only the Council efforts. "This kind of trauma can take months to heal, even years. It's a miracle she's functioning as well as she is, after only a handful of weeks."

In fact, Enrique suspected they'd not yet seen her worst breaks. She was still too busy protecting herself, and her defensiveness was likely her mind's best glue right now. When she truly realized her ordeal was over, he was certain it would dissolve, and her memories would turn on her in a far more drastic manner. Her ambition to live independently might be far down the road. Or possibly never.

"She doesn't have that kind of time." Mason spun the cell phone in circles. From his moody stare at a Rodin bronze on his desk, Enrique knew his Master might have heard his discomfiting thoughts. The amber gaze lifted, locked with the Frenchman's. "It's a chicken and egg dilemma, Enrique. In order to fully heal, she needs to be away from anything remotely connected to vampires. But I can't let her go, not only until I get this cleared up with the Council, but until I know she's safe from herself. She spends too damn much time crafting her own manageable reality. She can't face down her demons and regain herself again." With a frustrated sound, he rose from the chair, paced to the window and stared down as well, though Enrique noticed he stood to the far right of the window, where she wouldn't see him if she looked up.

"Are you certain, my lord? She may be able to heal fully in this environment, if she learned to trust it. Is it possible her pain is clouding your judgment?"

Mason's attention cut sharply to him and Enrique shrugged. "Forgive me, my lord, but her torment appears to be drawing you back into some dark memories. When you've helped women in the past, it's been clear you haven't been doing it out of some misguided notion that you are saving Farida. It is to honor her memory. But there is a tie with this girl, something that has the potential to become an obsession. There is too much in common."

When Mason only stared back down into the garden, Enrique pushed on. "Is it possible that what happened the other night is a good thing? Maybe she needs more of it. She needs to know she can lose control and be safe. It's like an infection that needs to be split open and drained, over and over, until it starts to heal."

Mason shook his head. "It hurts her too much."

"Her, or you?" When the vampire cut him a warning look, Enrique locked gazes with him. It was not a privilege Mason always granted, but when they spoke, male to male, Enrique knew the line could waver. "We worry whether or not you can handle the agony of watching her go through that, and what it may do to you."

Mason's gaze narrowed. "You should leave the meddlesome advice to Amara. I'm less likely to take a strip of her hide for it."

When Enrique's jaw hardened, a flash of temper in his gaze, it reminded Mason that, though his servant had the male tendency not to analyze or question the actions of another male in the way a woman might do—the way his well-meaning wife did—it was therefore far more significant when Enrique did choose to speak. He was doing what he'd done since Mason had met him—told him the truth of his mind, and the Frenchman had damnably good intuition.

With a sigh, Mason reached out, gripped the man's shoulder, though in truth he felt more like ripping something limb from limb right now. "I know you are both concerned, and I appreciate the love you show me. But do not worry yourself further. I know what I'm doing. Go to your wife. She misses you."

He had no need to placate either servant. They served him, after all, but he couldn't have their worry pressing in on him while he was fighting his own demons. As Enrique slipped out of the room, Mason was already back in his head, remembering Jess's thoughts that night on the balcony. She'd wanted him to stay with her, share her bed. Until then, he'd been Farida's Mason, the fantasy in which she could lose herself, hide from what she was, reconcile it with what Raithe had done to her. But in that moment, she'd been herself, seeing him for what he was, what she wanted. While it was progress, he also suspected it was what had sent her into a catastrophic spiral.

The next time she was that aroused, he would be with her, every step of the journey. She needed someone physically with her who could straddle the line between her nightmares and fantasies and bring her back into a pleasurable reality. Unfortunately, he was so linked to her fantasy, he couldn't fault Amara and Enrique for their suggestion that he needed to step back.

But damn it, that wasn't what his gut told him. It was more than what Enrique implied, a cold hand reaching through three hundred years to remind him of the worst memory of his life, a memory that had directed so much of his life ever since.

By Allah, he was tired of thinking about it. He'd done nothing but brood the past few days. Glancing back down, he saw Jessica had left the fountain. Even as he searched for her through his mind, he knew she'd gone to the workout room. She went there daily to rebuild her muscles and practice sparring techniques.

Mason knew Raithe had sculpted her hatred like an artist, letting her train, letting her believe she could devise ways to fight him. He'd never believed he would have a vulnerable moment when her relentless training would kick in and serve her at last.

Both Enrique and Amara were combat-trained. Amara had been more reluctant at first, as it went against her perception of herself, but Mason and Enrique saw to it. For though Mason knew his servants had little chance against vampires, his world had other, human opportunities for peril. No matter where her journey would take her, he approved of Jess having skills to defend herself and the brain to use them.

Another woman would have given up in despair. Would have stopped practicing the defensive and offensive techniques, or trying to resist Raithe's mind. Eleven stripes on her back documented how long it had taken her to give up on simple escape. But she hadn't really given up, had she? Or Raithe would not be dead.

He'd never seen such a fighter. Or a female more desperately responsive to a Master's touch. It was too intoxicating for him to stay away.

~

The staff's workout room would rival an urban center's most up-to-date gym. Weight machines and hand weights, as well as mats to keep from slipping or damaging the polished wooden floor. Various weapons were displayed on a rack—nunchakus, quarterstaffs, swords. A row of mirrors hung on the back wall to study her form. When Jess looked in them, she saw a cautious-eyed woman staring back, wearing a black cotton tank and stretch leggings to allow the full range of movement. Her feet were bare.

She liked the rows of tall windows that didn't open to the night, but one touch of the curtain control allowed a panorama of the nighttime shore. Usually she'd see the lingering colors of the setting sun, but she'd stayed out by the fountain too long. It was full night, and the room was unpopulated. She told herself she preferred it that way. None of the staff was intrusive, but she often felt their scrutiny, and didn't want to be curious about what they were thinking, or feel tempted to talk to them.

She'd use music for company instead. Going to the sound system, she scrolled through the vast number of playlists and digital music selections. This system was as high tech as the one in the ballroom. Whatever he'd done to get his money—Berber raider, strip dancer in Vegas—Mason must have been successful at it. *Very* successful.

While the music selections were likely staff choices, it amused her to think of Mason with an account at a music download site. Did he visit chat groups? What would his call name be? ISuckBlood46? Fangboy24?

Actually, I considered Vladimir666, but it seemed cliché.

She hated the fact that her heart leaped at the sound of his voice. *Don't you have better things to do than invade my head?*

There was no reply to that, but she didn't expect any. He had stayed out of her head, for the most part, since that night on the balcony, but occasionally she'd hear a short comment like that, smoothly inserted into her thought process so it didn't startle her. *Here, then gone.* She should be grateful he spoke to her so little, shouldn't desire contact with him at all.

As she seated herself on a bench and listlessly began to do triceps pulls, she knew what the problem was. Okay, she had myriad problems, given the peanut brittle state of her brain, but her overriding issue was lack of focus. Making the journey to Farida's tomb, expecting to die there, had been like running a marathon, pushing the body past its endurance to reach that twenty-sixth mile and cross the finish line. Everything disappeared except that finish line, the heart exploding in the chest, head pounding, legs trembling. But now that finish line had disappeared, and not only was she uncertain in which direction the race lay, she wasn't sure she had the energy left to continue running it.

There were too many dangerous moments when she wished she could stay like this, in this stasis of not going forward or moving back. No race of any kind left to run.

Another form of cage, habiba. *One of your own making. You have so much more to give to yourself than that.*

She should view his interjections as a reminder that she was watched, guarded. A prisoner. But then, she'd expected the third mark to be utilized as the second had, to exploit her strengths, deepen her weaknesses, expose her vulnerabilities. Instead, Mason appeared to be using it as a way of knowing when she needed reassurance. When the dark shadows were starting to claw at her, his bits of dry humor drove them back again. When the shadows fell upon her like an ambush, the comforting embrace of his firm command helped her take a deep breath and get a grip.

There were worse things than a cage of her own making, weren't there? Sometimes she just wanted to get away, as far and fast as possible, for there was no way a vampire could be this trustworthy. She was trapped between catatonia and a beast's mindless need to run from any perceived danger. Her desires and needs vacillated between the two, her fucked-up head turning on her.

With no answer for that, and feeling darkness rising with the frustration, she rose from the bench to begin her sparring routine. At least she was starting to anticipate the psychotic episodes. Maybe, like a journey through a minefield, if she could keep rerouting herself around the explosive patches, she'd be okay.

Punches, kicks, twists, lunges, turns. Retreats, aggressive advances. In addition to the fitness equipment and weapons, there were several attack dummies and a sizable punching bag. Much better equipment than she'd had at Raithe's. She'd been like Rocky Balboa there, willing to use slabs of hanging meat if needed to keep herself sharp.

Here, everything was provided, except there was no way to lock the doors of her mind against what she fought, keep it from creeping in a red haze to the forefront of her mind. As she turned, twisted and rolled in the prescribed movements, the crescent gathering of dummies became faces. Raithe. His friends. Laughing.

There was one who'd had horrid breath, like stale blood and rotting flesh. He'd insisted on kissing her, and broke her nose when she couldn't take it anymore and bit him. While she writhed on the floor in agony, he pinned her down, tasted the blood coming from her nostrils and kissed her more. With the threat of more pain, he forced her to kiss him back and act as if she were enjoying it. When he at last tore away her clothes and fucked her, her stomach was heaving, her senses more repelled by the aroma than the violation.

Afterward, they'd flogged her for her initial resistance, but she knew they loved how much she fought. They got off on proving to her that there was no strength that prevailed against them, that couldn't be turned to provoke their sick desires. Or her own. But still she fought, because it wasn't about proving something to them. It was about proving to herself she hadn't given up.

At that point, under those conditions, she'd been isolated, one person with a million voices in her head, all the different fragments of herself they unearthed but she discovered, learning how to deal with the unthinkable. But now she didn't know how to end her own isolation, how to escape those voices.

Snarling, she hurled herself at the dummy, hammering it with her fists, driving it back on its sturdy base, the rubber grips for floor protection squeaking in protest. As the memories continued to crowd in, she hammered harder. Her breath labored and she started to scream, rage. She let the episode take her, knowing she was safe to lose control here, surrounded by weapons and no opponents, things willing to take her wrath.

But that reality disappeared quickly, the moment she gave herself over to it. She wouldn't be happy until she took it down, took him apart. Grappling with it, she tore at his flesh until sawdust spilled forth, bone marrow and blood in her mind's eye. She yanked at the cord binding it to the frame, ripped it loose and took it to the ground. It felt good to kick and pummel it some more, straddle and hold it between her thighs. Make him feel what it was like to be helpless. How long would he have to be tortured before he'd create a nuclear bomb in his soul, one that could turn the world to ash if he were given the chance to use it?

At the brush of contact behind her, she whirled, one arm striking out, her leg coming up and around to take out a knee, even though she didn't have a grip, let alone a position, on the opponent. Mason flashed her a feral smile, just out of range. He took a combative stance. "Go, *habiba*," he said.

A *real* opponent. Blood and bone. Her mind registered he was vampire, and therefore undefeatable in hand-to-hand, but the other part of her was as eager to fight him because he *was* vampire. She spun forward, punching, and he was ready, blocking the moves, countering with defensive techniques that left him open to further attacks. She was willing to accommodate, coming at him fast and furious.

He caught the roundhouse kick, spun her off her feet. She landed like a cat, sprang back at him, almost managed to connect with his temple before he turned, letting her slide past him, his hands briefly clasping her waist, thigh brushing her buttock before he faced her again. A growl and she closed in again.

So it went, up and back the length of the room, as she practiced every move she had. He countered all of them, but moved back from none, letting her use her full strength and skill. Raithe began to fade, along with the cruel faces of his companions, and her focus sharpened on Mason, the shift of his eyes, his body language. Trying to anticipate his graceful warrior movements, she tried new combinations, learning as she went, emulating some of his maneuvers.

He started placing directions in her mind, hints to deal with his greater height and strength. If she overextended herself, he'd catch her, his capable hands steadying the leg, palm sliding with intimate familiarity along the back of her thigh or hip before he released her. He often turned her punch with an inside block and a twist that would capture the wrist. He'd twist her into his body, holding her back against him for a brush of lips along her temple before he let her go, fingers trailing her arm, and they engaged again.

Because it was the first time she'd plumbed the depths of her new third-marked abilities, she found her speed had tripled, her strength as well. As she pushed those to the limit, she found she felt almost invincible, dangerously so. But she didn't care. It was exhilarating. All easy, flowing movements, no pauses, like a continuous dance where the music never stopped. Yet, by the time she was gasping for air, she wasn't sure if it was the physical exertion or other reasons that had her breathless. He was the one who at last called a halt to it.

"Enough, *habiba*. Get some water and walk it off." He nodded toward a pitcher on a small bistro table that had apparently been brought in during their sparring.

She drew a deep breath, letting her mind go blank as she turned away. Spinning, she brought her foot around in the roundhouse again, only this time she connected with that perfect jawbone, snapping his head back and causing him to stumble before she finished in a ready pose, hands up, one leg back. A follow-up was futile, for he could take her down in an instant. The point was she'd gotten one in under his guard.

Mason straightened, swiping a thumb along his bottom lip to see the blood where his fang had speared his tongue. One fucking hell of a kick. She'd caught him with the blank-mind trick, something that wouldn't have worked if he'd been anticipating, because her intent would have flashed through her mind before the move. However, he'd been too damn worked up watching her fight, how she kept the anger and passion channeled. He couldn't help but be stirred and distracted by the athletic precision of the slim body, how she pushed until her muscles trembled.

He bared his teeth in a smile. "Nice one. But a cheap shot, if this was an honorable match."

"Honor doesn't mean shit," she said bluntly. "Winning does."

"Well, in that case . . ."

Jessica knew it was coming, reflexively tried to dodge, but of course that wouldn't work. He took her down to the mat on her back, sweeping her legs, but catching her on one arm, so she landed with all the violence of a babe being laid in her cradle. Which of course put him above her. The copper hair he had clasped in a tail at his nape fell forward, brushing her face.

She saw the challenge in his vibrant eyes. She'd wanted that, damn her damaged soul. She, who'd hungered for her freedom such that she'd tear the flesh from her bones to get it, needed to feel the tautness of Mason's leash on her body. It made no sense.

Weary with it, she closed her eyes. "I know. You're going to tell me not to think."

"Your thoughts can be a liability to you sometimes, Jessica. You've been through a great deal. The soul knows how to heal itself, but often only through instinct. The mind derails it."

"You know, your whole Yoda thing is really annoying." *Particularly when it's obvious you don't take your own advice.*

Before he could respond to that, or she could feel moved by the shadows that passed through his gaze, she rolled away and bounced to her feet. Her body was on the tip edge of exhaustion, but she needed more. Her muscles were vibrating from the match. Or maybe it was the proximity of his body, those amber eyes that had her thrumming.

At his arch look, her gaze narrowed. *Big deal. Basically it's the taste buds responding to the smell of chocolate. Any chocolate. It doesn't mean anything.*

He cocked his head, but she was already backpedaling. Retreat was the better part of wisdom, to her way of thinking. "I'm going for a run on the beach. Unless my jailer has an objection?"

"I think he'll run with you," he said, thwarting her escape attempt.

Muttering a curse, because stifling it was pointless with him in her head like a parasite, she took the nearest exit to the verandah. Not bothering to wait for him, she followed the winding steps at a quick trot, and loped across the lawn until it became sand. She reached the darkened beach with the reflection of moonlight on the pale sand guiding her.

As she moved to the wet, packed ground, she started to run, falling into a familiar, steady rhythm, recalling her daily workouts from her Rome flat. A morning jog through the narrow, uneven streets, nodding to people she knew, hurdling or sidestepping the cats. One of the most amazing things to her about Europe had been its vast age. Particularly Rome, part of ancient civilization, a place that had seen so many things grow and change. It was a society built on history, not philosophy. As a novice archaeologist, the contrast with the States, miraculously built on principles, fascinated her.

The vampire running behind and to the right of her had been alive for hundreds of years as well, seeing things grow and change. And yet he'd fallen in love with a young girl who'd known only the desert, her father's tents. Maybe he'd found what all students of history did—the situations changed, but people didn't. She wondered again how old he actually was.

Eight hundred, habiba. *Give or take a few decades.* As he pulled even with her, a frown crossed his face. *I think I am coming up on nine hundred, but I'm not certain.*

Holy crap. Raithe had been three hundred. She shot Mason a sidelong glance. Though he could move faster than any animal on the planet, and probably most cars, he was matching her pace with a comfortable stride, a little longer than hers so that she was competitively trying to keep pace with him, pushing herself harder. The manipulation should annoy her, but it didn't.

Vampires gained in strength and power as they aged. The oldest known vampire was Lady Lyssa, the last queen of the Far East clan. Raithe had discussed her with his companions, though Jess had never met her, for of course she was far above Raithe's station. He wasn't influential enough to be invited to the gatherings where Region Masters, overlords and Council members would be. Since she resented that, Raithe claimed not to care about the trappings of civilized hierarchy. To him, they were a farce. Regardless of his motives, since she was regularly subjected to his savagery, Jess couldn't agree more.

But Raithe hadn't completely destroyed her reasoning skills, at least not when she could exhaust herself with physical exercise and distance herself from her fears. Whether or not bolstered by Farida's writings, her rational mind had told her from the beginning there was something different about Mason. The Council and their rules did exist, which suggested vampires might have an order of sorts. Restrictions on their behavior.

She'd felt power from Mason that would eclipse Raithe's *and* that of all his friends. What did a vampire do with that kind of power? *Whatever he wants,* the frightened part of her mind told her.

When he lengthened his stride again, she cursed him. "You're playing with me."

"Helping you stretch out. Show me how fast you can run. Test the marks. Turn yourself loose like one of my horses. I want to see you fly."

She considered him out of the corner of her eye. While he wasn't wearing typical exercise clothing, she didn't think he'd be kicked out of any gym, considering the way the blue jeans hugged his ass in the right way, and the black T-shirt stretched over his broad shoulders, revealing hard curves of biceps that she had a sudden desire to bite with her nails. At his sidelong look, she frowned and lengthened her stride.

He dropped back a couple paces, so she lost him in her peripheral vision. As her stride lengthened, she felt that third-mark ability kicking in, increasing her speed far beyond what she expected. She was running. Really, *really* running, soaring, bare feet barely hitting the wet sand, the sky and ocean stretching out before her.

There was no Raithe waiting. No sickness or death. Just her, just Jess, running under a wide-open sky, her muscles burning and stretching, and yet begging for more. She dug down to see if she could give them more and miraculously, her body responded, lengthening out, arms pumping, lungs laboring. She *could* fly.

In high school, and then in her first years of college, she'd been a cheerleader, a cheer coach. She'd loved the lift, the toss through the air, remembering the clasp of team member hands as she came to rest with perfect balance on their shoulders. Then the forward leap and flip, into the cradling arms of two male cheerleaders.

She ran faster, thinking about the honest enthusiasm of the crowds at the football games, how it would carry them all away. The roar of approval that came with the dramatic flips, twists and pyramids. An illusion, but an illusion that had been real.

Jessica . . .

She was already in motion when she heard his warning. She took the triple front handsprings, with a twisting layout finish, at a third-marked servant's speed and strength. As she came over, too fast, out of control, she had the fleeting thought it had been a long time since she'd attempted the maneuver with her familiar levels of strength and speed, let alone the enhanced versions.

Oh, crap.

She came down wrong, her right leg twisting and buckling beneath her. The sharp stab of pain, certain to be a fracture, jolted through the calf and resonated up to the thigh, wresting a cry from her throat.

She rolled across the sand, but before she'd gone more than one roll, he had her, holding her while she caught onto his shirt, gritting her teeth. "Ah, goddamn it all, that hurts. Damn it . . ."

"Foolish girl. But you were running like a gazelle up until that moment, *habiba*. It was a sight to see." Cradling her in one arm, adjusting so she was propped against the inside of his thigh in his kneeling position, Mason lifted his wrist, bringing it to his mouth.

"What are you doing?" she gasped through eyes tearing with the pain, though she knew.

"If you take my blood, you will heal quickly. Within a matter of minutes, in fact."

"A third-marked servant can heal without the Master's blood. So . . . don't . . . need it." She tried unsuccessfully to pull herself from his grasp as she spoke through clenched teeth. The agony rocketing up her leg was incredible. Wasn't adrenaline supposed to numb the pain in the first few moments?

Cupping her face with a broad palm, he forced her to look at him. His silhouette against the night sky was intimidating, implacable. "You will heal faster with my blood. You're being childish."

"Fine."

"No, not fine. I will not bear your pain, Jessica. I can't. You'll take my blood or I'll force it down your throat, but you *will* take it."

His voice sharpened, the words becoming an undeniable command. Startled, she focused through the discomfort and saw tension in his jaw, a hardness to his eyes that she suspected masked something that could unravel her. They were close enough to the tide line that saltwater spray had gathered along the strong column of his throat, the pocket where his collarbones met.

"Fine," she repeated, ungraciously. Seizing his hand, the one cradling her face, she sank her teeth into his wrist.

"Holy . . ." He hissed between bared fangs. "I could have sliced open a vein, rather than you using your dull bicuspids. Like butter knives in the mouth of a pit bull."

Whine, whine, whine. Poor baby vampire doesn't like pain. If you'd used the vampire faster-than-a-speeding-bullet shit, you could have caught me in midair.

Mason narrowed his gaze at the crown of her head, thought about strangling her, though he knew she was right. He'd been too entranced by watching her and quite simply had missed his cue. He was glad she couldn't read that out of his mind. "I'm going to start calling you Kate," he decided. "Shrew."

Bastard.

Letting out a sigh, he stroked a hand over her head as she drank. She stiffened at the touch, but didn't draw away. Her irascibility was probably good, because if she let down all of her defenses, he might not hold the rein on his own control. Despite her brutal approach, having her mouth settle on his flesh so he felt the suction of her soft lips, her tongue brushing him like a feather as she drank, couldn't help but fire his blood. It made him want to take her under him on the soft, wet sand. Not necessarily to fuck her. No, something more devastating. Have her lie beneath his body, that incomparable intimacy of feeling the press and give of every soft curve, while he offered every hard and needy plane and angle of his. He'd kiss her mouth until she was gasping and writhing. He knew he could. He knew she would.

"Enough, *habiba*," he murmured, running a light finger under her chin. "That's plenty." When she lifted her face, the bemusement in her eyes was too much. He brushed his mouth over hers, but pulled back before she could do it first. At her look, he swiped the tip of his tongue over his lip. "You had blood on your mouth," he said.

"And you can't carry a handkerchief like most men born in the Middle Ages?" But her gaze lingered on his lips, her own pressing together. Then she extended a trembling hand toward his face.

Mason stilled, aching for the confusion in her expression as she caught a strand of his hair in between her knuckles, slowly twined her fingers in it. Exerted downward pressure.

Mason took his time leaning forward, letting her keep up her pull, holding back on her until it was more impatient, insistent, but he was torturing himself with the sight of her mouth drawing closer as well. Then he hovered above her lips, lifting his gaze to meet hers.

"I don't know . . . ," she said, a sheen of desperate tears in her eyes, her fight with herself.

"Yes, you do," he said quietly, and closed that distance, taking command of her mouth, giving her the illusion of taking her choice away. He knew that was what she needed right now, when she was afraid to comprehend her own needs.

His own weren't much easier to understand, though. He wanted to take her to this mindless place, wanted to sweep his tongue into her mouth, feel her response, the tightening of her fingers on his arm, the grip on his hair. Farida had loved his hair. He'd hacked it all off once or twice, when he thought he'd go mad with the dreamlike illusion of feeling her fingers slip through it while he slept. For nearly a century, he could hardly bear for a woman to stroke it because of the memory.

But Jessica's touch only made him crave more. If it wouldn't have required breaking the kiss, he would have turned his face into the slim palm, the fragile fingers. He'd only been speaking truth. He couldn't bear her pain. The fracture of her leg bone, feeling the flash of startled pain, had nearly driven him mad. It had been all he could do to take the time to reason with her, gain her sullen capitulation, rather than forcing the blood down her throat in a way that would have healed the leg quickly, but scared her half to death with his near violence. During these few minutes it was necessary for her to stay on the ground, letting the fracture heal, he wanted every second.

Teasing her lips open even farther, he penetrated deeper, so her hand curved up around his neck, found his back and dug in. She pulled away the band holding his hair so it fell over one side of his face, and hers. When she arched up into him, the smell of her was maddening, blood pulsing in the artery so close to his nose. He settled for scoring it with his fangs, countering her surprised reaction to that by the more shocking act of cupping the heat between her legs.

She cried out, her throbbing response immediate, pulsing against his palm, insistent. *Oh,* habiba . . . He closed his eyes, pushing back the insistent image of stripping her naked and letting the damp sand cling to her body, the salty foam of surf merge with the scent of her cunt's musk as he plunged into it.

No, no . . . I can't . . .

You can. It is what you want.

Regardless, her rising panic was as inexorable as the tide behind him, and he cursed his own needs. She was no virgin, but she was as jumpy and fragile as one. Even now, she was beginning to fight him, trying to shove his hand away, wriggling.

Trapped. Please, don't . . .

He removed his hand, but continued to hold her, compelling her to calm beneath his touch, but that black tide in her head was eradicating her rational responses. Nothing would help but freeing her completely.

With a silent oath, he forced himself to do so, sitting back on his heels. Jessica scrambled away several feet, crabbing back and showing her leg was mending. She was panting, poised to run like a rabbit. But he didn't move.

Jessica stared at him, kneeling in the sand, his now empty hand curled tensely on his thigh as he studied her, fire simmering in his eyes. The aroused tension of his powerful body was unmistakable. He was going to move forward, take away her choices, and she couldn't move fast enough—

"As I told you from the beginning, I am not Raithe." Now he rose and stared down at her, not offering her a hand, not moving toward her at all. She didn't like the chill that moved over her skin. "More than that, I will not allow you to make me into him, in order to shield yourself. If I ever take you, it will not be rape. You may count on that."

The arrogance in his voice was what brought her to her feet. While her calf twinged, he was right. The pain was almost gone. She clenched her fists nevertheless. "No one will ever take me anywhere I don't want to go."

"I believe that is what I just said."

She had the urge to slap him, and might have, if it had been merely barbed banter. But the humorless regard, the set of his stern mouth, suggested she'd offended him. It didn't make her afraid, exactly, but it did make her hesitate to push the effort. So she did the only thing she could. She bolted. Or rather, started jogging again, without him.

Mason let her go, noting with approval the leg could bear her weight, though she was treating it gingerly. She'd felt the hammering of his heart, had noted his obvious arousal, but hadn't acknowledged her own. The scent of it was in his nostrils, strong as blood and as potent. It made him want to go after her still, take her down beneath him.

She thought he was angry with her reaction, and he was, but not with her. He needed to push past this useless fury at a vampire far beyond his reach. Raithe's justice had been meted out at the hands of the very woman he'd wronged, but every time the fear rose in her, it closed on her with strangling hands, dulling that sharp mind and desperately defensive barbed wit. It paralyzed her, left her a desperate, mindless animal, and made him want to hurt something. Cause eternal agony to those who had hurt what belonged to him, what mattered most to him.

Closing his eyes at the thought, he shook his head. Perhaps he was as bad as Jess, merging past and present. By Allah, she messed with his mind, but whether it was for good or ill, he didn't think it mattered. Because he wanted *her*, Jessica Tyson. And he hadn't wanted a woman, for more than the release of cock or the needs of blood, in a very long time.

15

AFTER her shower and change, Jessica couldn't sleep. Despite the late hour, she prowled the house, hoping to distract herself by exploring some of the areas she hadn't yet. She discovered a solarium, an odd choice for the sun-averse master of the estate. However, remembering her conversation with Amara, she knew it wasn't an odd choice for the female servant he'd wanted to live here with him. Farida would have loved the ocean view during sunset.

She also discovered a music room, complete with a variety of musical instruments she wondered if Mason played. Then there was his art gallery, a long corridor lined with precious pieces that occupied an hour of her time. He liked horses; that was for certain. Desert scenes. Very few of the works depicted images of human beings, or vampires, save one. Jessica spent some time in front of an impressive oil painting showing a vampire female with vibrant jade eyes and long dark hair. She knew she was a vampire, because there was no human in the world that preternaturally beautiful. And Mason had a portrait of her.

She didn't want to deal with the roil of feelings that thought produced, or address the hopeful, petty idea the impossibly beautiful female might be dead. So instead she moved on and found a small den. The massive wooden chair and weapons on the wall suggested it was a male retreat for some long-dead Scottish laird. There was even a fireplace to make the chamber cozy on a cold night. Over the man-tel was another gorgeous horse sculpture, this one in some kind of smooth jet stone she couldn't help but touch.

She imagined Mason in the chair, long muscular legs splayed while he read, his strands of copper hair glittering in the firelight. She'd be on the rug, leaning against his leg, gazing into the fire as his fingers stroked her hair. Her mind would drift, becoming sleepy un-til he found her throat, teased her face up for a kiss. He'd bring her into his lap to straddle him, take him deep inside of her in a dream-like state, the firelight licking over their bare skin . . .

Was she deranged? More than a month ago, she was certain vam-pires were evil incarnate. How could one handsome vampire—which was redundant, of course—with a veneer of civility change her mind? Had she learned nothing?

Even the way he'd said it: "If I ever *take* you . . ." Vampires saw themselves as dominant and superior over humans. It would never occur to them to woo or court a woman. They simply overwhelmed with force or seduction, took what they needed. Why thinking of Mason doing that could make her tremble with a sharp-edged arousal, while Raithe committing the same violation brought fear and revulsion, she didn't care to face. That line of thinking led to peril.

Leaving that room, she found an archway to a set of downward-spiraling steps. Plaster walls gave way to stone as she descended, propagating the idea of a castle. Given the recent attack by vampire hunters, it made sense for Mason to maintain a sturdy fortress. Still, she admired the hunters' bravado, launching a vampire attack dur-ing a full gathering.

She paused, thinking. Was that a career for her? The underworld of vampire hunters, sparse as they were, would welcome someone with her knowledge, as long as they didn't know she was connected to another vampire. And as long as that vampire didn't use his con-nection to her to betray the hunters' plans. What would Mason think, if she went that route? His reaction wasn't a foregone conclu-sion, because vampires didn't tend to be incredibly loyal to one an-other. Remembering in vivid detail the leering faces of every one of the sycophants that had enjoyed her torment, she knew she wouldn't mind devoting a few years to hunting down specific targets. Perhaps it would bring her closure.

But how about vampires other than them? Unbidden, Amara's words came to her. *There were many lost that day who we considered friends.* What if she joined a band of rogue hunters, and they decided to hunt Mason?

Oh, Jesus. What did it matter? As if she was in any position to be plotting out career plans. Tuning back in to her surroundings, she realized she was belowground now. Mason's bedroom would be down here, but as vague as her memory was of the night he took her there, she remembered it had been at the other end of the vast estate, so this level was apparently a large complex. As with the protection of the automated windows and doors, it made sense for a vampire, having plenty of underground space. He probably even had escape tunnels going off the property. It wouldn't do any harm to know where they were or where they went.

Of course, she didn't really care for underground spaces. Farida's tomb had been the exception of course, because of her reasons for being there, and because in her deluded mind, she hadn't believed anything there could hurt her. Raithe liked taking her underground, to that terrible dungeon room where he'd toy with her endlessly, without the inconvenience of dawn.

Light switches still illuminated her way, but the fixtures were sconces embedded in the stone walls, holding electric lights similar to torches. Even so, shadows were gathering in her mind with her descent, as if she were traveling into the darkness of her psyche. As a hard tremor went through her, she realized she needed to stop, go back.

Go through one more door. Prove you can do that much. Like Amara coaxing her into fifteen minutes more on the balcony, or Mason telling her to stretch out and run rather than letting her memories have her. Firming her chin, she faced the door ahead of her. It was heavy oak, like an English castle in truth, but the ornate doorknob turned easily enough. Switching on the light from the panel conveniently located to the left of it, she pulled the door open.

As she stepped over the threshold, her mind froze. Time had slipped away from her before, when pain or fear made something incomprehensible, so when the gears of her mind lurched into motion again, she had no idea how long she'd stood there.

Her idle explorations had not been idle at all. She suspected, in the subconscious way she marked her surroundings and escape routes, she'd been seeking proof to support or refute her confusing opinion of the vampire who'd supposedly rescued her. Perhaps her rising apprehension as she descended the winding staircase had been because she knew she was going to find it.

The short set of steps led down into a large dungeon chamber. An impressive and expensive St. Andrew's cross, the adjustable straps dangling. The wood was so well-oiled it gleamed. Hazily she wondered which staff member was responsible for its upkeep. Spanking benches. A wall of floggers, paddles, cuffs, gags. A rack for various spreaders, posture and yoke bars. She knew all of them, had experienced most of them. The adjustable metal pole anchored to the floor could be fitted with a pair of dildos at the top and impale the slave, the loops for ankle and calf cuffs securing hours of vulnerable, standing torment. It had been one of Raithe's favorites. For a male, it could be fitted with a clamp around his balls, holding him fast at anus and testicles.

Blindfolds. Chastity belts fitted with painful phalluses to stretch the ass and cunt, make the slave move in that humble, shuffling walk she detested. Snug mittens, which, when pulled over the hands, could be locked at the wrist, so the fingers were immobilized.

All the best quality items for the master of the house and his visiting vampire guests. Everything for a vampire who wanted to indulge in torturing his servants. His slaves.

True to a dungeon, it was windowless. But the walls were hung with velvet tapestries, so it was warm, not drafty. A curved walnut bar in the corner held waiting wineglasses, ice bucket and cushioned stools so vampires could belly up to the bar while they observed. The glass sparkled. This room was used. There were no cobwebs. No dust.

Her breath caught in her throat, a sob she refused to let come out. *I am not like Raithe.* That was what he had said. But he was worse than Raithe, because, despite everything she'd been through, he'd been diabolically clever. He'd actually made her hope.

He'd said she could leave, eventually. She was an eternal fool. He'd third-marked her. There was no leaving that. Before her was proof they were all alike. Whether they seduced or forced a human to it, this was who they were, and what he would eventually want from her. Pummeling her about her nature, and yet denying his own. God, she wanted to hate him, but she couldn't summon the energy for it. What was that absurd saying? Fool me once, shame on you; fool me twice, shame on me . . .

The hoarse laugh that tore out of her throat might have been another sob. She didn't know, didn't care. Mindless calm settled on her limbs. She wasn't even shaking, she realized, though she felt very, very cold. This time she wasn't out of control, driven mad by fear or uncertainty. She was past all that. It had all gotten too tragic, too ironic. The world was some mad stage for insane gods, and she was ready to exit the theater. Maybe she would be lucky and escape their attention, an old, broken toy they didn't care to play with anymore.

But they had one last joke to play on her. As she moved down the steps and her fingers touched the gleaming wood of the cross, the truth exploded in her chest, so violently it drove her to her knees. It wasn't what she had or hadn't believed that boiled from her heart, invading her brain like fire ants. Even suspecting the truth, she'd wanted him. Hell, knowing the truth now, she *still* wanted him.

There was no leaving the stage. She'd become a minion in Hell. Though Raithe was dead, he'd successfully turned her into one of his mindless drones who couldn't stop craving a vampire's mastery. Try as hard as she could to pretend otherwise, she was forever lost. Mason could bind her in these things, whip her flesh until it bled, and she would still want him in some sick, twisted way, would want to beg him for pain, for pleasure, to overpower and master her in all ways.

No. She'd been an archaeology student, Jack's fiancée, the daughter of Harry and Eleanor Tyson of Marion, Ohio. She'd been an honor student. Her ninth-grade history essay won a state contest. She . . . she was talking about someone she didn't know, someone who was killed more than five years ago. Her face twisting in an ugly snarl, she forced herself to her feet, lunged for the oak door. It closed and bolted with an iron bar like in the movies.

Even if it was true, that a servant was bound to his or her vampire into eternity, she'd have some time before Mason died, right? Maybe if she got to the afterlife first, she'd escape him. Though she fervently hoped there was no Heaven or Hell. Dust and oblivion suited her fine. Anything was better than this.

Lunging across the room, she ripped one of the knives from the pegs. The weapon was thin bladed, likely used to make blood lines, the sharp point useful for jabs into mortal flesh. Vampires did enjoy their knife play.

Aware she was sobbing outright now, her way-too-healthy body trembling, rebelling, she increased her grip on the knife. She didn't want to die in a place like this, but like so many other things, she had no choice. Didn't she?

No. There's no other way. Thinking otherwise is part of the lie, too. Please, let me be free. Finally.

Gripping the knife in both hands, she positioned the tip between the two ribs she knew guarded the heart, and prepared to shove it in with all her strength.

~

After she left him, Mason walked the beach for a time by himself. Hoping to give her some space to unwind, he'd stayed out of her mind awhile, though part of it was that he didn't want to increase the disturbance of his own thoughts with whatever was going through hers. When he at last made it back to the verandah, Amara told him Jessica had taken a shower and was exploring the house.

Mason nodded. "Ask Enrique to cut some of the new roses and put them in her room. The yellow and white ones."

Amara raised her brow. "I thought you said you didn't want the new bushes used for flower cuttings until they were more mature, my lord."

Mason gave her a narrow look. "Do I look like I suffer from senility, Amara?"

"No, my lord," she said demurely. "I'll ask Enrique to take care of it."

"And while you're at it," he added, "pen a correspondence to Gideon and remind him that next time his vampire hunters attack my estate, they could have the decency not to blow up expensive landscaping. My rosebushes were innocent of offense, unless he deems them guilty by association."

"Yes, my lord." Amara tucked her tongue in her cheek. "Anything else?"

"No. Yes." He stopped in the doorway and looked back. "In my private reading room, there's an onyx sculpture over the fireplace."

"From the Rae collection?"

"Move that to her room, since she likes horses." He continued toward his upstairs study, throwing the last instruction over his shoulder. "And Amara?"

"Yes, my lord?"

"Stop being smug. It's very annoying."

Stepping into the study, Mason eyed the stack of invoices waiting there. He toyed with the idea of threatening to rip the roofing contractor's throat out if he didn't repair his shoddy work on the pool house, versus having to find a replacement for his crew, but then discarded the idea of dealing with it at all. He didn't want to do this right now. He wanted to find Jessica, spend more time with her, even though that was probably the last thing either of them needed.

As he reached out to her, looking for her whereabouts, fear and distress flooded his mind. Terror. Her madness closing in, along with a terrifying resolve.

Cursing his inattention, Mason bolted out of the study, already knowing he would be too late.

~

She missed the first strike. She'd made it so determined and vicious, the blade punctured skin but hit the rib bone and skittered off, the blade going in at an angle. The pain was intense, but she jerked it out, blood spattering over her hands, and prepared to stab herself again.

Jessica, for the love of Allah. Don't do this. Don't let him win.

"He's already won." She snarled in frustration as the weapon slipped out of her grasp because of the blood on her hands, her despicable shaking. She'd crumpled on the ground beneath the weapons rack, so it fell in her lap, jabbing her thigh, creating another bright bloom of blood. She fumbled for it.

Talk to me, Jessica. Please talk to me.

"I'm broken, Mason. I want you . . . I want you to do the same things to me that made me kill him." Though her desolate voice echoed in the empty chamber, mocking her, she spoke aloud because she couldn't bear being in her own head. "You're— I don't know what you are, what you want, but I can't go through it again. I'm too frightened, too weak . . ."

You are not weak. You are one of the strongest women I have ever met. You are strong enough to get through this.

"I don't want to be strong anymore." She screamed it, harsh fury splintering her words, tearing her throat raw. "I was a s-student. I was supposed to b-be m-married . . . travel around in a sailboat . . ." She cried now, her chest aching around the wound. "I wasn't supposed to be anything special or different, or b-brave . . ."

Gripping the knife again, she fumbled to position it correctly this time. Her heart beat frantically, a bird pounding to get out of a cage before she took away all choices. As she'd beaten on the bars of her cage with Raithe, hoping for a choice. This choice.

Jessica. Hold on to my voice. Please.

She shook her head, but it was difficult to hold the blade steady. Dully, she realized the blood from the first puncture had soaked the front of her shirt. Had she gotten a lung after all? Her breathing was labored. She couldn't talk anymore.

What will help, Jessica? What can I do or give you that will help? One thing. Think of one thing. Don't give up on me.

She closed her eyes and leaned forward. The tip went in, an inch's worth of pain. *What are you afraid of, Mason?*

Right now, I am very afraid of losing you, habiba.

No, not that. Are you afraid of anything?

A pause. *Yes. I am afraid of . . . I do not care for small spaces.*

Perhaps it was the hesitation that caught her attention, the fact that his male pride, even in this terrible moment, made him revise the way he said it. "You're claustrophobic?" Her eyes opened, and though wavering with tears, she blinked them away. The blood from her shirt was forming a small pool in the vee between her bent legs. Looking at that was easier than looking at what else was in the room. Her hands stayed locked on the dagger, but she didn't go further, yet.

With the tip in, all she had to do was push. No one could stop her now. "Well, that's . . . pretty typical. For humans."

She giggled at her own joke. Now she felt the darkness of his worry, his urgent pull at her to put down the knife. She cradled it closer, but the motion dislodged it. It raked a stripe down her abdomen, parting her shirt. Dizzy, she rested her wrist on her knee. Dropping her head on top of the steel pommel, she let it press into the concave bone over her eye. It was likely a lie. Vampires feared nothing. But she was curious, in a drifting sort of way. What story would he tell her? He'd told Farida stories at night.

When I was young, I played with the children of my parents' staff members. They had read the human stories about vampires, how they slept in coffins. When a born vampire is young, we sleep heavily during daylight hours. You cannot rouse us. So as a lark, and a curiosity, they put me in a wooden crate and buried it in a hole in the back garden. They were not intending to be cruel. They were children.

She eased down to her side, curling into a fetal ball. Cool stone lay against her cheek, while she stared at the polished upper points of the St. Andrew's cross in front of her. *Don't believe it, Mason. It's always about cruelty. Power. Even when they act like it's just play. Just harmless fun.*

No, habiba. Not always. My parents found me. I'd figured out how to escape, but it took a while. I kept passing out from the panic attacks. They found me as I was emerging from the ground with bloody and torn fingers. Fortunately at night.

Are they still alive, your parents?

No. They were killed a year later, by vampire hunters. Jessica, open the door.

"Can't," she said drowsily. "Can't get up. Heartbeat . . . putting me to sleep."

Then don't be alarmed.

Before she could process that in her sluggish brain, the floor shuddered. Thunder reverberated through the chamber and the door splintered inward. The iron bar hurtled free, stripping the screws on the braces. It clattered down the stone steps amid a froth of wood pieces. In the next moment, the wreckage of the door was screened by Mason's wide shoulders, his concerned, handsome face as he bent over her.

"Give me the knife, Jess."

As befuddled as she was from blood loss, she realized he could take it from her. But he waited, his mouth a thin, hard line, his eyes fierce as his gaze swept the blood soaking her shirt. "Jessica, right now."

When she lifted a trembling hand, his fingers closed over it. As he lifted her in his arms, her heavy head lolled against his shoulder. "You're angry," she whispered.

"Of course not. I should thank you. I was thinking two hours of paperwork were going to be torment. You quite selflessly proved something else could be far worse."

"Could help," she managed. "Good at paperwork."

"Consider it added to your current stable duties." Sitting down on the top step, he cradled her in his lap. He still smelled like the sea, where they had walked earlier. When he shifted her in his arms, she watched him nick the artery in his throat with the dagger, then toss it away in a jerk of movement.

"You've lost too much, *habiba*. You need to drink from a richer source. Now." He'd placed pressure on the wound in her chest, but with the other hand he cradled the back of her head, holding her steady and bringing her up to his neck.

The smell of it was too intoxicating, and she was too far gone to resist or despise herself. She latched on to his flesh and drank him in, aware of how his breath left him, his heart rate increasing, the thigh muscles hardening beneath her as his grip around her back and waist also constricted. His strength flowed into her for the second time today.

Every time she took more of him, it increased the binding between them. She knew that, but she didn't know how not to crave that. It brought tears and desire surging forth at once. *I'm broken, Mason.*

No, habiba. *Nothing can break you. You need time, and rest. You need to stop worrying so much, learn to trust me.*

But you have this room. Like him.

His lips brushed the top of her head. "Jessica, every tool can be used for good or evil. When you look at the things in here, what I see in your mind *is* evil." He paused as a growl entered his tone, an underlying fury she sensed him trying to contain before he continued. It made her glad her face was hidden where she couldn't see his. Not because she feared his anger, but her reaction to it. She was all too aware it made her feel protected, not afraid as it should.

"But imagine this," he continued. "Imagine I have bound you on that cross. I kiss your wrists, below the cuffs, teasing your pulse with my tongue. Then I do the same all over your naked body, pleasuring you as long as I wish, until you are begging for release, but not release from that cross. For a climax, at my touch, at my command."

Her body quivered, nerves warring with reaction to the sensual picture. She was done drinking, though her lips still pressed against his throat. He rested his cheek on her head, continued in that husky murmur.

"After your climax, I would adjust the cross so you are lying down, and use warm fragrant water to bathe your skin, still vibrating with your release. My touch promises you more of the same, over and over again, until you are as exhausted as you are now, though from something far more lovely. Your own mesmerizing responses."

"But why would you want to do that?" she whispered. "Why wouldn't you want to hurt me? He liked making me come while he hurt me. And sometimes, with you . . ." A shudder of denial jerked her against him.

Mason stroked her hair, his fingers delving deep to fondle her neck in a slow, soothing rhythm. He knew he had to keep it like this, casual, relaxed, balancing her again. Even though they were both soaked in her blood, and her memories were making his own boil. The hated knife still lay too close to them, but too far for him to give it a vicious kick.

"Raithe and his kind were monsters, *habiba*," he managed. "But you do take some pleasure in pain. It is part of who you are. I could put you on the cross, do as I said, but also introduce some pain into it. Perhaps a light flogging that striped your pale skin with faint red lines, or a nipple clamp that pinched you enough to make you gasp. The very act of binding you, taking away your control with the straps, is a form of torture, but one you would embrace, if done the right way, by the right person."

By him. Only him. He pushed away the possessive surge. "But it is your pleasure *for* the pain and restraint that would drive me, not my need to see how much power I could take from you, how much pain I could inflict upon you. It is a key difference. Willing submission is a gift of the gods, *habiba.* Forced servitude comes straight from Hell. It is not you who is broken, Jessica. It was Raithe. If I could help you believe one thing, it would be that. What you have is a gift to a Master."

She shook her head, wearily closed her eyes, her mind. "I don't know what's right or wrong."

Mason drew a deep breath, hitched her more securely into his lap, worried by how pale she was, how limp in his arms. "Remember the night with the cookies, how I asked you for only one thing?"

Slowly, her cheek moved against him. A nod.

"I shall ask it again now. Learn to trust me. I promise you, if you can do that one thing, you will be able to use that trust to trust yourself again." He raised her shirt then, relieved to see the wound was closed. "Good. Let's get you into some different clothing."

She was too weak to walk without aid, so Mason carried her through the house, back to her bedroom, where Amara was waiting. As the servant cleaned and dressed her, Jessica was too drained to do anything but lie there like a doll. Mason was at the periphery of her awareness, but she was beyond wanting to think, to look at him. She should have finished the job. She was so tired. Too tired. How many episodes like this had she had in these past weeks? How many more would she have, and would she ever get a grip on her life again? She knew these things took time, a great deal of time. But she'd lived ten lifetimes in the past five years.

"Sorry about that," she mumbled. "Sorry about door."

He bent over her then, Amara stepping back. As Jessica lifted her lashes, she was conscious that her upper body was bare, Amara having removed her bra and shirt. Mason's gaze slid over her breasts, the pink nipples, before returning to her face. His expression was unreadable, but not frightening. Putting a hand on her forehead, he held her gaze in his. She wanted to cling to it like a cradle in a tree, forever rocked by the reassuring whisper of his breath, the warm blanket of amber sky. "Don't worry, love. Sleep now."

"I hate this. I hate being weak."

His jaw tightened. "You are not weak, Jessica Tyson. Just impatient. Though I am happy my mark made you physically well, it might have been better if your body had improved by degrees, instead of all at once, to give your mind time to catch up. Time is no longer your enemy. What did I tell you?"

She swallowed. "You said to learn to trust you, and use that to trust myself again."

"Good." He bent, and his lips brushed her forehead. "Do that, and all will be well."

But it didn't work that way. There were no knights in shining armor to come and surround her with safety and care, hold her in their arms, real and metaphorical, until she could stand on her feet again. They didn't exist. Even if they did, they came too late. The evil had circled, waiting to puncture her with its claws, poison her mind with insidious whispers, and it had succeeded, again. It would never let go. She'd never feel safe again. No one could make that go away.

Even as she had those thoughts, though, her hand closed on his wrist, clung with desolate hope.

Mason shifted to the right to allow Amara to finish, but covered her hand, stroking her knuckles as her despair gave way to uneasy unconsciousness. Amara glanced up when she realized Jessica had passed out, but her words died in her throat at the expression on her Master's face. "My lord?"

"She's right," Mason said flatly. "We are always too late. And I am goddamned sick of it."

He knelt. Because he wanted to be sure she heard him on all levels, he spoke aloud, though he was aware of Amara's intent gaze upon him. "You have a candle in your darkness, *habiba*, one that will never be extinguished. You saved *yourself*. Even if a hundred knights in shining armor had come, you are your own savior. Because it is not the body that resists and defeats the evil and despair wielded by someone like Raithe." *Or Farida's family.* "It's not even weapons of steel and wood, or fire. It is the spirit, and each spirit wages that war. What we have is each other, to make that war worth fighting."

He drew her from Amara, held her close. He willed his own heat into her, and thought their heartbeats might have synchronized. "Your war is over, though you have fought so long you cannot see it yet," he murmured. "What I can give you now is rest. Let me protect you for a while. Do me this honor, and I will not fail you. I swear it, even if I have to destroy my own spirit to make it so."

∽

But his words did not ease her dreams. While Mason forced himself to leave the room and go change, assigning Amara to remain at her side, he stayed closely linked to Jess's mind. He was determined not to withdraw until his heart stopped racing from their near miss, which likely meant he'd be in her brain for the next century.

Therefore, he didn't need the servant's communication when Jessica started tossing and turning, crying out in her sleep. The nightmare that had started in the dungeon area was returning to haunt her, with more crowded visions of blood and pain, cruel laughter and helpless agony.

How could she escape being drowned completely in such madness? She was capsized in an ocean of it, and each time she struggled back into the flimsy boat she'd created, another wave could submerge her again.

And how could he bear it? Her every cry, every wave of fear and pain, resonated inside him as if it were his own. Was she right? In the end, would it have been better to give her the mercy killing she wanted in Farida's tomb? When Farida had died . . .

He drew back his lip to snarl at himself. *She isn't Farida. She can beat this, if you have faith in her.* Perhaps that was why Farida had suffered as she did. Perhaps he hadn't been strong enough to endure what he must. *Perhaps that is why Allah has sent her to you.*

Ah, by Allah indeed, he was losing his mind, as surely as Jessica was.

Amara, ease her. She responds to sensuality, and a woman's touch will not frighten her as mine does.

He sensed a hesitation from his servant, a flicker in her mind he ignored because there was no room in his churning brain to hear it, but then Amara rose from the chair where she'd been reading. Going to the bed, she settled on one hip next to Jessica's restless body.

She stroked the young woman's hair, traced the delicate shell of an ear, picking up her Master's desires and following them, a conduit for his need to touch the troubled girl. Down the throat again, a fingertip sliding on the artery, then out to the collarbone. She'd put her in a light cotton gown, so it was easy for Jessica's flesh to feel the caress.

Mason stayed in both minds, his willing servant and unwilling one, weighing the dual responses. He'd made it no farther than his upper-level study, but now he was back outside her room, sitting in the hallway, no more than fifty feet from her bed. Dawn was still far off, and he wasn't going to go below anyway, not when she was like this.

Jess's dreams paused, disrupted by Amara's skillful fingers. The woman moved down the sternum, to the abdomen and back up, letting the hint of intimacy draw the attention of Jess's body in an easy, dreamlike way, taking energy away from the nightmares. Returning to the neck, she caressed Jess's throat and the girl's chin slowly lifted, arched in an unconscious invitation that made Mason's fingers curl in a fist on his thigh. The throat was one of the most erogenous zones she had, always craving a collar, whether it be of flesh or gems, steel or velvet.

The buttons of the cotton gown slipped free under Amara's hands until the two sides fell back and Jess's body was bare, her legs moving restlessly for a different reason. Amara cupped her breasts, thumbs moving slowly, not quite touching the nipples, the teasing touch making them harden and Jessica's thighs loosen further.

Amara's mind said she could smell the girl's arousal. She was wondering where her touch and Jess's dreams had taken her. Mason knew, and it took willpower to stay where he was. If Amara's stirring caresses had taken Jess deeper into the twisted carnality of her nightmare, he would have commanded her to stop, but the images in Jess's mind were now of him. His mouth drifting down her skin, his hair tangled by her fingers as he moved between her legs, tasted the sweet honey gathered on her labia. His tongue nudging her clit, so she arched and spread further for his pleasure, her body begging to be swept away, given pleasure that would drown her, that would not bring fear and pain in its wake.

Amara's mouth was on her now, following that track, following where his mind had unconsciously bade her go, and he closed his hand into a fist as she molded her hands on Jess's hips, and Jess's fingers found Amara's luxurious mane. Amara loosened her barrette, let the dark tresses of her hair fall against Jess's flesh. The sleeping woman sighed with pleasure, feeling the fall of Mason's hair against her skin. Amara made another nip, a tender kiss above her mound, brushing the sensitive bone with her chin. But when Jessica moaned, Amara stopped, for a name had slipped from between the young woman's lips. Mason.

My lord, come to her. She does fear male touch, but she does not fear yours. You are what she wants.

When Amara straightened, keeping a hand on Jess, she turned her head to find her lord already in the room. She would have smiled, but there was a powerful yearning hovering in the air. Bowing, she slid off the bed, giving way to him. She did not wait for the order to leave, but gathered her book and slipped out the door, closing it behind her.

Mason put a knee on the bed, staring down at Jessica. She was not the most beautiful woman in the world, though she was lovely. It was the strength in her face, the resilience in the chin, the fire in her eyes when open. Allah, her tears alone had the power to strip him raw, for they were hard tears, tears of fury and anger with her own weakness, not the easy tears of a woman who trusted herself enough to let them fall.

It was not her pain that held him mesmerized, though, but her capacity for pleasure despite it. He had told her to learn to trust him, and here they were, him knowing consciously what that meant, and her unconsciously. It wasn't what most people understood trust to be, what it meant in the dark regions of her soul. That was the part of her he had to reach to help her trust him, utterly and completely. Consciously, as well as in her dreams.

He hadn't demanded such faith from a woman in a long time.

For three hundred years, he'd been afraid to do so. But at the heart of it all, vampires were closer to beasts than men, and he didn't question instinct. Territory. The need for blood or possession.

Bending, he placed his lips on her abdomen, and it contracted beneath his mouth. *You are so lovely,* habiba. *Give yourself over to me. Let me give you pleasure, take away your nightmares.*

She stirred, coming out of her dreams into the reality of him, and he sensed her mind drifting between the two. Her fingers found his temple, drifted across his hair.

It's dark. "I'm afraid. I need the light."

"No, *habiba*. You only need to know the dark can hold more than pain and terror." His lips returned to her belly, soft, persuasive. The heat of his tongue traced a lazy circle, so that she couldn't help herself. Jessica did as she wanted, tangling her fingers in the thick copper silk of his mane.

When her hand touched his head, it was a benediction, inspiring thoughts both sacred and profane. Mason took his time, nuzzling her, working his way lower, toward that slick, heated well that spoke of her craving need, which called out to his own.

But she needed him other places as well, and he responded, sliding farther onto the bed so that he could close his hand over one sweet breast. Amara's gentle touches had not been enough. She needed demand, that barely leashed, near-violent lust that the right female roused in a male, to sweep her away. And though she didn't trust a male for that, Amara had been right. In this dreamlike state, exhausted, for this one precious moment, she was letting herself trust him.

He read her surprise that he'd anticipated her desire to have her breast touched, and he smiled against her flesh. *You fear having a vampire in your mind,* habiba, *but you have not been taught the benefits. Anything you desire I can see, feel. It need only cross your mind and I will give it to you.*

He pleasured himself with the weight of the small curve, the sensitive tip that hardened further at his touch, eagerly pressing into his palm as she twisted and arched again. When her thigh rose, a pale column in the semidarkness, it fired his blood further as she tried to hook a heel around his side, pulling him to her. He closed a hand on it, so he could mouth his way along the inside as she shuddered beneath his touch, unable to pull free as he used his strength to hold her. A subtle reminder that she was all his, the dominance too much a part of him to put aside. He had no desire to quell it. With her, he found himself raging to use it in ways he hadn't in some time, ways that would prove the differences between what she'd experienced before, at the hands of a male who never should have been allowed near her. No male should. Only him.

Her aroma was too much. He turned his face into her waiting pussy and indulged in a long, leisurely lick, gathering her sweet cream on his tongue and relishing her cry of response, the aggressive tug on his hair from her slim fingers. Sliding her leg over his shoulder, he raised her hips to his face, causing her to reach up and grasp the railings of the headboard, an unconscious surrender and anchor both.

Penetrating her with his tongue, he flicked, suckled and ate at that succulent fruit that offered juices to his laving tongue until he was growling. He wanted to score her thighs with the tips of his fangs, make tiny marks of his ownership over the tiger-shaped third mark. It was an urge he barely managed to suppress, conscious on the rising tide of his own desires that she was teetering on a fragile line.

In her mind, he heard whispers of incomprehensible things—needs, fears—and yet one thing for certain. *More, more, more.* She'd been forced to climax so many times, but never had she been given true pleasure, true fulfillment. Her body was so eager, so hot for it, that as he drove her higher and higher, as he'd hoped, it shed the shadows, began to burn fierce and bright, moving eagerly toward what the young female muscles and heated blood wanted.

He turned her then, in an effortless move, bringing her up on hands and knees, and covered her, pressing his still-clothed cock against that damp juncture as he reached beneath her and claimed her breasts again, knowing the blood flow rush would make the nipples even more sensitive. He scraped her nape, but didn't bite. This had to be all about her, though he wouldn't deny his own desire was building to a point beyond which he wouldn't be able to recall himself. He was lost in her desperate need, so strong it overwhelmed his senses. So many things flooding her mind, jumbled emotions, desires, a five-year tsunami too torrential to be handled in one night.

She would need release, night after night after night, until it would ease to a downpour. He would gladly help her weather the storm.

Clothes . . . naked. Want you.

When he lifted off her to unbutton his shirt, she surprised him by turning around on her knees, lithe and quick. Grasping both sides of the open collar, she tore it. Her mouth fastened on his chest, tasting him, licking, and when she found a nipple she bit, pressing her body urgently against his, her stomach against his steel erection. Her hands were there now, trying to find the workings of his trousers.

Those whispers were becoming comprehensible, damn it all. She didn't want to be in this reality. She wanted to be in some strange, out-of-control dream where she could pretend in the morning it hadn't really been her wanting him this much, wanting to feel like this. She wasn't ready. Truth be told, maybe he wasn't either. The intensity swirling in this room wasn't all from her.

He caught her hands, stilling her. *Jessica.*

She looked up at him with wild eyes as she pulled against his hold. *Don't stop. Don't stop.*

"I have to," he said quietly.

"No." She bared her teeth, tried to yank herself from him, tried to fight him. The things in her head became far less complimentary. In fact, outrageously inventive, such that he would have been impressed, except he was swamped by the raging heat of her frustration and his own.

Scooping an arm around her, he brought her forehead firmly back to his bare chest, cradling the side of her face to hold her still. She struck at his midsection, but he had the advantage in strength and balance on the mattress. While she subjected her body to a fierce struggle that left her panting, he waited her out. At length she drew her arms in against her, like a bird's wings crossing over her breasts, hugging herself. He tightened his grip then, creating a cocoon for her against his body. She was still vibrating with her need and it burned in his lower belly, like searing fire held to a vampire's flesh.

Judging her calm enough, he eased her back to the sheets. She stared up at him, so much swirling in the gray eyes. But as if she couldn't bear to look at him directly, she turned her head into his fall of hair as he stretched out on her, fully clothed. He guided her face back to him.

You keep looking at me, habiba. *Or I will stop.*

Jessica caught her breath as his hand moved between them, found her wet folds, and began to manipulate her there with consummate skill. She was furious with him, for all she'd wanted was him inside her, and yet at that touch, she couldn't deny him. She was glad he hadn't returned there with his mouth, for that, while incredible, had not met the emotional need of having him up here with her, his body on hers, his gaze close. His broad shoulder leaned over her, his leg trapping one of hers as his booted foot kept the other spread to give him the access he desired. Her lips parted, and her breath clogged in her throat. Fumbling, she found his arm, dug her nails into the hard biceps. She couldn't bear to look into that face that knew so much about her, but she couldn't bear for him to stop. So even though she wanted to bury her expression in that acre of muscular chest, so close and emanating heat against her, she stared in his eyes as he'd commanded. An excruciating, sweet torment, seeing how he saw her.

As he built her higher and higher, the breaths and gasps, cries and pleas, wrenched from her throat. It was too much. When her face contorted with her desire and she turned it away, into his neck, he stopped. His hand covered her mound and labia, in a way that had her twitching uncontrollably.

The true purpose of a chastity belt, love. That broad strap, fitted for the shape of your pussy, softened so it will not chafe, cups you. Yes, it locks you in until your Master wishes to access your sweet pleasures, but because of its restraint you think of his hand there at all times, possessing you, claiming you as only his. Now look at me. I want to see your face as you come. Watch you as you scream for me.

So close to that precipice, her body compelled her to obey, face that intent expression and the stern set of his lips. The concentrated demand there alone, as well as the impressive hardness pressed against her thigh, was almost enough to contract her muscles, send her over. What was she—

"No thinking, *habiba.* There is only us. Only this moment."

He began to work her ruthlessly, the fire in his eyes growing as she bucked, a wave working up from inside her, increasing the pressure in her lower abdomen, her chest, her eyes glazing from the effort of holding his.

"Don't stop . . ." She gasped.

"Don't look away," he returned, merciless. "I want to see your eyes while your cunt spasms against my hand."

"Aahhh . . ." When her cry escalated into a scream, the climax cut over anything else she might have thought or said. His fangs gleamed in the darkness, giving her a thrilling shiver. Keeping the perfect rhythm against her clit, he never faltered. The teasing pressure of his fingers inside her lips, tickling and increasing the sensation, intensified her screams. Because he kept her legs forced open, she had to experience the full contact. Writhing, twisting and gasping, she held his amber gaze, clinging to that connection she needed to feel, so it wasn't merely an empty physical release. He was here with her. He was here.

Always, habiba. *I will not let you fall, unless I am there to catch you.*

16

ROMANTIC nonsense, of course. The things that men and women said when they were in the throes of passion together. So Jessica told herself as she opened her eyes to a setting sun. Mason had left her, with great reluctance, sometime before midday, when the heat of the sun could be felt through the curtains. While she loved the light, she'd felt a little isolated after he left, a little more alone in the bed than she wanted to be. She'd sensed he wanted to take her back to his chamber again, and she wasn't sure she didn't want the same.

Madness, of course. But she'd faced that terrible dungeon room, the memories it held for her, and he'd talked her away from despair. Whether or not it was wise, she needed to believe in something. It was the irony of her life that it had to be another bloody vampire. Scrubbing a hand over her face, she propped herself up, realizing belatedly she was still naked, for at a certain point, he'd stripped the open gown off her shoulders.

The sheet's touch on her sticky thighs reminded her of what they'd done. Or more specifically, what Mason had done to her. She wanted more. She wanted something more than those fingers, devil-blessed though they were.

But here in the daylight, she knew he'd been right. She hadn't been ready, running toward him from nightmares. If he'd followed through, she might have woken up feeling far more wary and mistrustful of him than she already was. Of course that explained it only for her. What about for him? He was male, for Heaven's sake. How many would have resisted a woman throwing her legs open and saying "take me now" like that? She'd been too much of an exhausted puddle when it was over to even offer to reciprocate with her hand, or mouth. And she couldn't believe she'd had that thought, or trembled from the imagining of being down on her knees again, like that first night . . .

Okay, Jess, this isn't a high school date. He's a vampire, a nine-hundred-year-old vampire. He can get his rocks off with his two third-mark servants anytime. He doesn't need to . . .

Oh, bollocks. He'd been hard as iron against her leg last night, and based on the size of that iron bar, he'd wanted her as much. So why had he held back?

A sense of honor. Of course. It was the only explanation that made sense. She scowled. Bloody honorable, saving-the-damsel-in-distress, irritating bloodsucker. She didn't want to be the damsel in distress. Okay, so maybe she did need his care during her way-too-frequent meltdown episodes, but still . . .

"*Aarggh.*" Throwing back the covers, she put her legs over the side. The truth was, she didn't know what she wanted, who she was or if she was a fucking insane psychotic or simply a damaged soul right now. Maybe she was both. But she did know he'd wanted her. Part of her had wanted to prove she could get him to give in to that desire. But had it been because she wanted him, or wanted that sense of control?

"You must not be in my head right now," she said aloud, glaring around the room as if he were there, hovering like a ghost. "You'd have made some smart-ass comment by now."

She waited, and only silence was forthcoming. He might still be sleeping, of course. She'd kept him up past his vampire bedtime. But the attempt at humor didn't dispel the twinge of isolation she felt at the silence. Therefore, she wasn't entirely unhappy to see Amara come in, bearing a tray loaded with food. God, she was pathetic. Afraid of the dark, afraid of being alone, afraid of trusting . . .

"How are you this afternoon?" Amara sat down next to her, comfortably reaching out to smooth Jessica's rumpled hair and glancing down at her breast to see the now-faded mark of the knife. "You gave Lord Mason quite a scare last night. All of us, in fact."

Before Jess could formulate a reply to that uncomfortable observation, Amara had picked up the satin robe on the end of the bed and shook it out, holding it for Jessica. Jessica put it on but belted it herself, adjusting her position to sit cross-legged on the bed. "There's enough here for two of me," she ventured.

"I thought we could share an early dinner together." Amara folded her flexible legs into a mirror of Jess's seat and picked up a croissant. "These were just baked. They'll melt in your mouth."

"More babysitting?"

"No, actually. I brought you something, other than food." She produced a clothbound book from the pocket of the tunic she wore and laid it on the covers. "That came from Lord Mason's library. Farida had two journals. He lost the one you found, many years ago. This one he still had."

Jess stopped, the croissant halfway to her mouth, her gaze snapping to the book. The wrapping was silk, a painting of a desert scene on the front, the imprint of an orchid in the foreground.

Wiping her hands on the napkin, she picked it up with careful, loving hands. "Nothing I found indicated she had two of them. In fact, I never even found out how she learned to read and write English, which was one of the main reasons I sometimes doubted the memoir was even hers. But her words . . . the way she wrote, it was as if she were speaking. How she'd repeat herself, or ramble on about him . . ." A light smile touched Jessica's mouth, but the thought brought sadness as well.

"It is what a woman in love does, not a professional writer," Amara finished quietly, meeting her eyes. "Lord Mason does not speak of her often, but Enrique told me once that Farida's mother had some connection to a British family, by blood. She taught her daughter to read and write English before she died. Sheikh Asim allowed it, because his wife had proven useful in preparing correspondence with outside trading contacts. He was a man of some standing already, but that ability increased his influence with other tribes."

Jessica wondered if that was why Farida was often allowed to listen in on his meetings with male visitors. She stroked her hand over the book again. Another piece of the puzzle solved, but it created even more questions. Had her mother been full British, maybe an explorer's daughter who fell in love with Sheikh Asim, converted and became one of his wives? Or perhaps Farida's mother had only been part British, the next generation of such an unexpected union. How wonderful it would be to explore this new branch of Farida's family tree, ask Mason the questions burning inside of her—if she wasn't determined to get as far away from vampires as possible before this was all done.

"When Lord Mason noted how she liked writing in her journal," Amara continued, watching her face, "he picked up this second one for her, from a caravan. He thought she would run out of pages eventually in her first journal. Instead, she was so pleased by his gift, she switched between them randomly. It might be somewhat confusing to follow the timelines, but he thought you might like to read it."

"I would," Jessica murmured, passing her hand over the silken cover, imagining Farida's hands cradling the book. "Amara, what does he want from me?"

The sloe-eyed woman met her gaze. "I can't speak to that, Jessica. But I do know he is more concerned about what you want for yourself."

Jessica's irritation spiked. "That's typical."

Amara merely forked up a bite of mango and put it on her tongue. "Mmm. You should try this."

Jess put the book aside. "I don't accept that."

Amara paused, lifted a brow. "I'm not following."

"I don't want to be some fucking damsel in distress. That's not who I am, damn it. I'm not a victim. Okay, yeah, so terrible things were done to me. But that's . . . I don't want a bloody, fucking V stamped on my forehead, as if that sums up everything I am. And he should have . . . I wanted . . ." She scrambled out of the bed, nearly upsetting the tray. "I'd rather live in the stables as a groom, with Jorge, than be treated like an abused pet he has to handle like glass."

"I see." Amara chewed thoughtfully. "Perhaps you would feel better if you got out."

"I'll go to the stables later, but—"

"No. Not what I meant." Amara put down her fork and cocked

her head, as if deciding whether or not to continue. "There's a private club in the city Lord Mason visits. We go about once a month. It's a short charter flight from the estate. Perhaps you would join us."

Jess studied her face, came back to stand by the bed. "What kind of club?" Though of course she already knew, because the blood was draining out of her face, dizziness gripping her so that Amara was off the bed and capturing her arms, easing her back to the mattress.

"Jessica, it's all right."

"It's a fetish club."

Amara bit her lip. "Yes, for Masters and their slaves. There are a few other vampires who visit, but it is primarily human, so of course we do not reveal what Lord Mason is there."

She'd wanted him to take her over last night, and yet she couldn't even mask her reaction to a suggestion, a harmless suggestion. "I can't . . . ," Jess said faintly.

"No one is asking you to do so." The crisp voice came from the door, sharp as a knife blade. Jessica lifted her gaze, finding Mason there. He had a small bundle under one arm and wore his usual house garb of riding breeches and loose white shirt, causing her pulse to accelerate. However, she also noticed the temper snapping in his golden eyes. So did Amara. She dropped to one knee, bowed her head. "My apologies, my lord."

"Leave the tray and go."

Jess rallied, pushed her trepidation away. Hadn't she said she didn't want to be treated like glass? "Don't get all mad at her. She was just trying to help."

Mason cut his gaze to her, his attention dipping to the loose wrap of the robe, then rising back to her face. "I realize that. Her motives were inappropriate."

Amara had already risen, giving Jess a reassuring look and a quick press of her knee before moving to the doorway. When she reached it, Jess drew in a breath, for Mason's hand flashed out, grasped the woman's throat. Amara stilled, unresisting, her gaze meeting his briefly, before it swept down, her lashes fanning her cheeks. "Do not forget your place, Amara," he said, low. "I will be by shortly to get my dinner, and I am not likely to be kind about it."

She nodded, a flush rising in her cheeks, and then she slid past him, her body brushing his. Jessica noticed that flush wasn't fear, any more than the feeling that uncurled in her own stomach at the rebuke. Then she remembered him poised over her, a few hours earlier, and crossed her arms across her chest, feeling an inexplicable irritation. "What was that? Vampire code for 'I'll fuck your brains out if you forget that's your main purpose in my household?'"

"Astute," he observed. Jess started at the hard edge in his tone. But when he looked down at the bundle in his hands, flexing his fingers on it, she narrowed her gaze.

"You're mad because Amara's motives had nothing to do with me. It was about you."

A brief flash of surprise was replaced by that infuriatingly unreadable look. "It's something I shall resolve with Amara. It doesn't concern you. This, however, does." Coming to the bed and sliding the tray out of his way, he put down the bundle and settled his hip next to her, his gaze again sweeping her in that tantalizing way that made it hard for her to concentrate on the tension between him and Amara, and its potential source. But it was even harder, now that he was so close to her, to forget the implicit threat to his third-marked servant. Farida had not feared his punishments, nor did Amara. Deep inside that well she feared, Jessica knew why they didn't fear it, why they might even embrace it. It turned over in Jess's stomach, giving her a sour taste in her mouth.

She couldn't tell if he heard her absurd and confusing thoughts, but his mind was elsewhere. "Jessica, I know you are an intelligent woman. You know, despite your wish for it to be otherwise, that your hold on reality is very tenuous right now. Psychotic episodes will continue to occur, with the right triggers."

He had his fist braced on the bed, on the outside of her hip. She wanted to be defensive, but his scent and heat were too close, and he didn't give her time to rally from that sensual input. "What has been done to your mind would exceed the ability of anyone, even an exceptional woman such as yourself, to heal itself alone. Once I can clear your name with the Vampire Council, there are resources out there, people tied into our world, who can help you with professional counseling. Until then, I have an idea of how to protect you from yourself."

The praise had loosened some of the tension in her belly, but now it returned, spreading out in her chest. He put a hand over hers. "Don't get nervous. You've wondered how I accomplished the spell-casting over the tomb, preserving Farida's body, and the more perishable gifts, all these years. Yes?"

Cautiously, she nodded. She hadn't felt comfortable asking him about the details before, not knowing how he felt talking about Farida, but now the archaeologist in her stirred.

"I'm afraid it's not a very scientific explanation. At a certain period of my life, before Farida, I fell in with a mage, an exceptional magic-user. Another being thought by humans to be mythical," he added with a humorless smile. "He helped me do what you saw in the tomb. Because I am vampire, and had a blood connection to her, I had powerful energies he could channel for that purpose. Then, probably for his amusement, he taught me some small things I could do with that energy without causing harm. Illusions, binding work."

He folded back the velvet cloth. Jess lowered her gaze and swallowed, that tight coil constricting in her lower belly.

"Jess, don't be afraid." Mason lifted two silver cuff bracelets. "What I've done is spell these with that small magic, and my blood, so you are unable to hurt yourself intentionally. It will protect you if I'm not close enough to do so. They don't lock to one another. They simply lock around your wrists and your throat." He glanced down at the last one, a delicate silver collar that had a jigsaw clasp. "You will have as much mobility as before."

"I don't want to wear them. Will you make me?"

He nodded, his mouth settling into an implacable line, reminding her of his sternness with Amara and rousing confusing butterflies in her lower belly. "Yes, *habiba*. I will not allow you to hurt yourself again."

"You have no respect for a woman's independence." She meant to say it caustically, but her hands balled into tense fists. A loss of control, again, reflecting her inability to care for herself.

"It is my job to protect you," he said quietly, "and I will do it, your independence be damned."

"I didn't ask you to protect me, did I?" she fired back. "I didn't even ask to be taken out of that tomb. I wanted to die there."

"You don't want to die now." His gaze sparked, making her realize he wasn't as calm as he was trying to appear. *Good.*

"That's not the point." When she stood up, Mason rose as well. Since he was a hell of a lot taller and broader, Jess realized she was boxed in the corner. The silver bracelet dangling from his fingers was a lovely, delicate thing. Probably a secondhand trinket that belonged to Amara.

"Then what *is* the point?" he asked.

"You can read my fucking mind. Why don't you tell me?" As he continued to regard her with that dispassionate stare, she knew she was pushing it. But why shouldn't she? He said she could trust him not to hurt her. "Amara's good enough to fuck, but I'm not?"

"Amara is a servant, Jessica," he said tightly.

"I'm a servant."

"Because circumstances dictated it to save your life. You did not choose to serve me and I would not make that demand upon you."

"You didn't demand a damn thing. I practically *begged* for it last night. You were the one that backed off."

He turned toward the bed, picked up the other cuff. "I won't discuss this further. You're not emotionally ready to know what it is you want. Give me your wrist."

She knew he spoke only the truth, but after he'd practically turned Amara into melted hot wax in front of her eyes, it grated to hear it. Amara's lips had parted, her gaze gleaming in anticipation as much as she bowed to the rebuke. It made Jess so angry she wanted to spit at him like a cat.

"Your trust in me is a very fragile thing right now, Jess." He was continuing on in that reasonable, insufferable tone. "I won't endanger it over a moment of lust. You have too far to go."

"How noble of you, my lord. My God, I didn't think it was possible, but I've discovered a vampire saint."

A snarl was the only warning she received. In a heartbeat, he'd seized her under the arms and lifted her up against the wall, pressing his body in between her thighs so she had the full impression of his aroused cock. Equally intimidating was his furious countenance, inches from hers. He took her mouth in a savage kiss, plundering. It transformed everything from the juncture between her thighs to her

mind to quivering need. Another, deeper part, trembled at his barely
leashed violence, the power in that preternatural body. She felt his
hunger. It was time for him to feed. She reveled in it, her need suddenly as savage as his.

*Feed from me. At least give me that. Don't take from Amara and
Enrique today.*

She had no time to be startled by her thought, because she was
stunned at his response. Gripping her short curls, he pulled her head
aside to sink his fangs into the pumping artery at her throat. He was
angry and did it roughly, so that Jess cried out, but she gloried in it,
in not being treated like glass. Though one part of her was running
wildly, a rabbit mad with terror, the rest of her constricted her arms
and legs around him, holding him as if he were an oak in a storm. He
crushed her against the wall, rubbing himself against her with unmistakable intent, putting that hardness against her bare clit, because her robe had fallen open, leaving her blissfully naked against
his clothed body. God help her, she was still damp from last night, as
well as the juices gathering now. When she strained against him, he
let go of her arm, letting her grip his shoulder. Her thumb brushed
his throat, her mind marveling at how it moved, swallowing her
blood, letting her nourish him, as he'd nourished her last night to
heal her wounds. His lips were magic at her throat. *Powerful vampire
energies . . .*

"I want to go to this club," she whispered, closing her eyes.

No.

"I'm frightened, but I need to do it. I need to defeat Raithe on his
own ground. Please, my lord."

No. Be still.

She remained silent then, submitting to his needs, keeping her
arms and legs twined around him as he finished his meal. The insistent throbbing between her legs caused tiny whimpers in the back of
her throat, but the hard pressure of his body taunted her without allowing her any movement against it. And she understood then that
his punishments could be severe, leave a woman begging and wanting until she promised to obey him in the future. Perhaps she didn't
envy Amara as much as she thought.

At last, he lifted his head, after bestowing a lingering kiss on her throat to seal the wound. Firming her lips, trying to shift away from the raging desire he'd reignited, she gestured to the manacles, the collar. "You've made sure I won't hurt myself. Give me the chance."

Mason suppressed an oath, though at her persistence or his lack of control, he didn't know. Did she realize she'd called him "my lord" twice now? Her struggle between her naturally submissive nature and her memories, as well as his own, were going to make him push her down a path before she'd made up her mind honestly about what she wanted. He couldn't seem to keep his hands off her. Hellfire, he'd just *fed* off her on nothing more than impulse and anger.

And for that matter, what had compelled him to offer Farida's other journal to her? Yes, he understood how important Farida's story was to her, but that should have been tempered with his understanding of how often she used the pages of her journal as an escape.

Not yet responding to her, he eased her feet back to the floor, but held her there as he reached back, picked up the cuffs. "Lift your wrists, Jessica."

She put them out to either side of her against the wall, making him want to groan. He really needed to sate his lust with Amara and Enrique, several times. The blood she'd given him had been too sweet and potent. He was aching to consummate the giving act with a strong, possessive fucking.

Instead, he put a leash on his wayward cock, pushing against her trembling body, and clasped the first cuff around her delicate wrist. He'd had Amara measure her throat and wrists in her sleep, and one of the maintenance staff was a silversmith, so they all three fit well. Since he was all too aware a snug fit stimulated a submissive who craved evidence of a Master's ownership, he had only himself to blame when he saw the shudder run through her body. On second thought, it might be best not to have Enrique there for his session with Amara tonight. Mason had a feeling he was going to rut on his wife like a beast.

Then the collar. Oddly, a tremor ran through his own hands as he lifted that one. She bowed her head, so that he could see her nape, find the lock. He swallowed, securing it around her slim throat, his hands settling beneath it. He spoke the words, keeping his eyes on hers as she lifted her head again. She started at the brief flicker of heat energy, the warmth now pressing into her skin. A reminder of the spell that was there. A reminder of him.

"Lord Mason?" Her gray gaze was on his, imploring. "Please let me go."

I'm not sure if that's an option for either of us anymore. Then he realized she was still speaking about the club. "I'll think about it," he said curtly. "Now get yourself cleaned up and go see to the horses. Jorge can use the help with the evening feeding. Gregorio had to go into town."

Turning on his heel, he left. Though his high-handed dismissal had annoyed her enough that he suspected he was going to be treated to a succession of deprecating thoughts for the next hour, thoughts that would include words like *arrogant bastard* and *fucking vampire*, he couldn't summon a smile. He knew his departure for what it was. A scrambling, cowardly retreat from what this troubled woman roused in him. The same thing that made him decide not to partake of Amara after all. Instead, he sent her the message that he did not have need of her and descended to the underground tunnels for the remainder of the night, locked away from all of them.

17

*M*Y lord has known such loneliness. It took time to get him to speak of it. To my surprise, I discovered he was born a vampire, to a vampire mother and a human father. His father was his mother's servant. Unfortunately, his mother was killed by vampire hunters when he was very young, ten years old. Of course, with his father being her servant, he died at the same time. My lord Mason had to grow up on his own, without mentor or sire. Though he speaks little of this, from what he has told me, I think this was extremely difficult. While vampire young are so rare they are prized by their parents, vampire males are very intolerant of adolescent males not their own, those unprotected by a father or other guardian. At best, such an adolescent would be treated as a slave or pawn to older vampires, or at worst, killed outright by them.

However, over five hundred years later, he has earned his place among their ranks. I suspect he is a vampire of no little standing, but whatever road he traveled there left him very contemptuous of his own kind. He shows little interest in bringing me into that world. Though I wonder about it, right now all I want is to be with him, every waking breath.

Sometimes I see him looking at me when I am brushing my hair, sewing or even cooking, and there is such a yearning in his eyes. He is not always an easy man to fathom, but I think I answer a need for him *that no child ever outgrows, even when he is a man of over five hundred years. Belonging. As his wife, as well as his servant, I can give that to him. My father may think I have turned my back on all things, but I know what a good wife is.*

I will accept him in all ways, his dark and his light. My lord is far more learned and well traveled than I am, but I alone can give him a home.

Jessica closed the journal, put it to the side. She'd read most of it the night Amara brought it to her, but like Farida's other journal, the words kept calling her back to them. Now the reading had an enhanced significance.

She'd brought it here, to Mason's upper-level study. Of all the indoor spaces, she'd found she liked this one best. It had shelves of books to read, comfortable deep chairs, a couch for napping. She told herself it merely reminded her of working at the college, the professors' offices. It wasn't because this was obviously his preferred room. Or that his scent lingered here, and the reading chair most broken in was the one she'd curled up in to read the journal and doze, more than once.

The room also offered her something else. She'd resisted it the first few times she'd been here, but today the research assistant in her could take it no more. His large desk was covered with papers. Scattered, but partially stacked as well, as if the documents had once been well-ordered and then a flock of pigeons had flown in and knocked them into disarray. More stacks were grouped like mushrooms around the legs of the desk and beneath it. In some cases, she suspected they'd been flung there in annoyance. She couldn't help but start to shuffle through them.

He could check into her mind at any point, see what she was doing and tell her to stop. Since after an hour of working, she hadn't heard any thunder of protest, she happily immersed herself in work she hadn't done with such pleasure in years.

In one of the cabinets, she was amused to find brand-new boxes of untouched folders and empty hanging files. She labeled and organized, spreading out all the paperwork to group and categorize, developing a filing system for what was on the desk. Correspondence, invoices and jotted notes with questions for follow-up. Not only did the paperwork relate to the house renovations, but she discovered he had myriad other business concerns. Several wineries, including one in Italy and one in California. He was a silent partner in a nightclub, and she wondered if it was the club Amara had briefly mentioned. He even owned a portion of a horse sanctuary in the American West.

She discovered he had a broker who handled investments for him. Jess suspected that broker was as slavishly devoted to Mason as any third-marked servant, based on the enormous quantities of wealth the vampire possessed. She'd apparently stumbled into the clutches of the Howard Hughes of the vampire world.

Finding his transfer book, she spread out the checks he needed to sign, based on the invoice due dates. After some initial hesitation, she even placed some phone calls, following up on those jotted questions. Of course, she introduced herself as his assistant, not revealing her identity. By the time she finished the fifth phone call, she was giddy. It was ridiculous, how doing such normal, productive things sent her into a euphoria.

Amara had peered in once. When Jessica raised her gaze, wondering if the woman would chase her out for doing what she'd not been asked to do, Amara instead gave her a nod and retreated without further discussion. Jess was glad for it, because she wasn't sure what she'd say, which had nothing to do with the paperwork.

The bald fact was she hated that Mason had gone to Amara to slake his lust, if not his blood needs. There was no way any male, let alone one with the enhanced carnal needs of a vampire, would have just gone off to bed without taking care of his arousal. Amara must have done her job well, because Mason had barely sent her a thought since.

She had no right or reason to feel the way she did about that. It was more of her poor mind's war with its own sanity. But the fit of the silver bracelets and collar were a constant reminder of him, their heat on her skin. And that reminded her of what he'd said about the chastity belt, stirring a far more intimate region of her body.

"'You don't know what you want,'" she mimicked under her breath. "Well, that's for me to say, isn't it? Not you. I don't need a father."

She scrubbed her hands over her face, propping her elbows on the desk, then a smile twisted her lips as she thought of another passage in Farida's second journal.

There are times he is so . . . old. Like he knows best about all things and I am nothing more than a child. Perhaps that is so, but I have found that when I bathe, and take more care than usual with the cloth, cleaning those tender regions of my body he enjoys so much, he comes to me, and I feel the hunger in him. Not only for my flesh, either. I hold his heart inside of me, and we are both ageless then.

If she could cloak herself in Farida's thoughts, a woman completely, deeply immersed in her love of one man . . . *Lord Mason has a wonderful laugh. I must seek ways to coax it from him, for he tends to be too somber at times.*

"Jessica?"

She started up from the chair, hitting her knee with a painful clunk, her eyes springing open. Something flickered through the metal at her throat and wrists, a warning that was almost . . . arousing.

"Easy." Jess struggled to focus past that and saw Enrique at the study door. He held up his hand in reassurance, though he didn't come into the room. "I knocked on the door panel, but I thought you might have gone to sleep sitting up." His glance swept the much cleaner desk. "Mason's paperwork has been known to have a narcoleptic effect on the most hardy."

"No, I was just thinking." Jess put a hand over the circlet at her throat, her fingertips testing it. Just cool metal. She hadn't thought to ask exactly how the restraints would prevent her from hurting herself. She was starting to get an apprehensive—or anticipatory—idea of it.

"Amara requested you come to the back balcony. There is someone here to see you."

Jessica frowned, dropped her hand. "To see *me*?"

"Someone Lord Mason had brought here to see you."

"Oh."

Enrique nodded. "I'll leave you, then." And he was gone, just like that. But the uneasiness spawned by how he'd come up on her like that, unawares, made her go to the French doors and push them wide-open, enabling two exit points from the room.

It was ridiculous. Enrique meant her no harm; she knew it. Still, as she drew in the sea air, the memory gripped her anyway. Raithe suspending her by a chain, and allowing . . . commanding the human household staff to gang-rape her. One man after another, from a young, frightened-looking boy who could barely maintain an erection, to a grizzled maintenance man with hard, cruel hands.

She'd been able to handle the evening gatherings in Mason's house because there were as many female house staff there as male, and no vampire directing things. But this one moment, with her and Enrique alone in the room together, brought the fear back, unexpectedly.

She dug into the wood of the frame, a splinter piercing her forefinger. Warmth licked across her wrists, her throat, that sensual admonishment again, only stronger this time, breaking her out of the memory. The inhibiting magic, intended to keep her from going down that self-destructive slide of thoughts, was amazingly like Mason's touch, his presence. Though she didn't want to acknowledge it, it did ease the paralytic grip of the remembrance, the fear and revulsion. It also made her want to hurt herself again.

Sick. She was sick.

"Jessica?"

The French doors led out to the wide back verandah and the stairs down to the gardens. Amara had come seeking her, with a slender, elegant man. Jessica noted black silk hair tied back in a long ponytail and jewel-toned green and golden eyes. His white linen shirt and well-cut slacks made him look as if he'd escaped from a fashion magazine, his face sculpted like a young Valentino. "This is Robert," Amara said, pronouncing it in the French fashion.

Jessica slid a glance from the man to Amara, then back. "It's nice to meet you, Robert."

"A pleasure." Stepping forward, he took her tense hand. Jessica noticed he had a series of intricate tattoos across his fingers that made it appear as if he were wearing rings. There was a similar Celtic design around his neck, inked in black, with a dark cross in the hollow of his throat. When he brushed a kiss across her fingers, it was startling, but not threatening, not with Amara here. Still, Jessica retrieved her hand, pushing down the lingering uneasy feeling. He arched a brow. "May I see the area in question?"

At Jessica's blank look, Amara cleared her throat. "I don't believe Lord Mason had an opportunity to inform her. You *are* early, Robert."

He shrugged, typically Gallic. "My plane made better time than expected, and fortunately we weren't attacked by wild animals on our way to your desolate outpost." He said the last drolly, sweeping his glance over the back balcony and the breathtaking beach panorama.

"Robert is a very gifted tattoo artist. Lord Mason thought you might want him to design a tattoo for your back." Amara's expression said clearly she'd expected Mason to tell Jess about this, which said she wasn't aware of the argument they'd had. The volatile blood taking, followed by his abrupt dismissal, his "run along and play and don't bother me" routine. Jess suppressed the desire to grind her teeth.

"Robert, let's go have a glass of wine." Amara spoke over her silence. "We'll let Jessica finish up her paperwork. We've caught her in the middle of things and she needs time to change direction."

"*Certainement.*" Nodding, he squeezed her hand. Tension thrummed through her arm, more strongly this time, so that Jessica had to quell the desire to yank it back. "But I will say, it will be a pleasure to work on so lovely a lady."

Her back was many things, but lovely was not one of them. The only good thing about the scars was she couldn't see them without twisting around like a contortionist. But she was well aware of them, the way they pulled against her healthy flesh, as constant a reminder as Mason's bracelets and collar now. And how were they different, really?

No. They *were* different. Each time Raithe took a strip of her flesh, he'd followed it with an experience to hammer home the lesson that she couldn't escape him. The rape by the household staff had been stripe number four.

"Jessica?" Amara drew her out of her thoughts with a light touch that made Jess jump. Robert had left them, headed back to the verandah area. The woman settled her hand on her forearm, a reassuring grip above the silver manacle. "Lord Mason has decided to allow you to accompany us to the club next month. You have several weeks to think about it. If you change your mind, you're welcome to stay at home. You go only as his guest, to enjoy the dancing and entertainment. You will not be expected to participate in the club's activities."

Amara's gaze flickered downward. Jess realized she'd reversed their grips and was clutching her arm hard, that same white-knuckled response she'd had last time the club was mentioned. At one time, she'd liked to dance, so dancing sounded good. But at this club, she couldn't avoid seeing others perform the acts that terrified her to the bone. Even if done consensually, they would suck her into her memories like a drain.

Letting go of Amara, she forced herself to get a grip on her emotions. She'd asked Mason for this, as a way to face her fears. She had to learn to take care of herself. She couldn't be afraid of every man's casual touch. "All right," she said. It was several weeks off, after all.

"Robert is also your decision. You are not required to do anything. My lord thought it might be something that would please you, however."

It was on the tip of her tongue to say no. *I don't want him touching me. I especially don't want that part of me touched.* Still, Jessica gave a nod. "Let me think about it for a few minutes."

"All right." Amara squeezed her arm. As the woman turned, she hesitated, looking over one bare, tanned shoulder, her black and dark green patterned sarong enhancing her willowy body. She looked like an enticing, exotic tropical plant. She belonged in this dark and mysterious world, was at home here in a way Jessica never could be.

"Mason did not come to me last night." Her gaze flickered over Jess's throat. Though Jess knew the collar rested over where he'd pierced her artery, and the puncture scars had healed already, it felt as though Amara could see them. "I thought you'd want to know that."

"Why?" Jess crossed her arms over her body.

Amara cocked her head, her lovely fan of ebony hair rippling in the breeze. "He is different with you, Jessica. You have been through a great deal, so I don't tell you this to make you change anything about who you are or what you want. But have a care with him. He does not open himself to others easily. You might not see it as a gift, but do not abuse it, if you can help it."

"He's going to get really pissed off at you if you keep handling him."

"Yes." Amara inclined her head. "But I love him too well to say nothing."

She moved away then, leaving Jessica staring after her. Even Raithe's devotees had been smart enough to fear his anger, his wrath. But there was a difference between an abused dog that tried to love her master, thinking if she remained devoted, he would eventually stop beating her, and the prized pet who'd never known a reason to be afraid of him. Perhaps Amara wouldn't appreciate the analogy, but for the first time Jessica realized Amara did not fear Mason, because he'd given her no reason to.

In fact, in the short time she'd been with Mason, he'd given Jess no reason, either. It was the overlap of her memories with Raithe, the nearness of them to her present-day existence, that instilled fear in her. This, despite the fact that Mason's age, strength and power made Raithe look like a bumbling fledgling in comparison.

"Not might *is* right. Might *for* right." She murmured the quote from *Camelot*, the play her parents had taken her to see for her sixteenth birthday. She'd been enthralled with King Arthur, knowing she'd have never left him for Lancelot.

~

Enrique was waiting for Amara around the corner. When she reached him, he cupped her neck, drew her against his body for a lingering kiss. Amara smiled against his lips, enjoying his hard chest, the lean hips under her caressing hands. "So how did she react?" he asked.

"He hadn't told her, so they must have quarreled. Do you think she realizes she's being wooed?"

"As much as he realizes he's wooing her," Enrique observed. "He's slept deeply today. I haven't heard from him."

"No." Amara's gaze shadowed. "He is troubled by her."

"It's for them to resolve," Enrique reminded her, bending to nuzzle her throat. His hand slipped down to cup a buttock. Amara swayed into him as he nipped her, sharply enough to cause a gasp. "Try to stay out of it, or you'll feel Lord Mason's lash."

"And won't you enjoy watching that?" Her lips curved, but she sucked in another breath as he increased the pressure of his grip.

"Go to Robert and don't tease me. Otherwise I might wield the whip myself."

"Promises, promises, my husband."

~

Jess saw the embrace between the two servants, though she couldn't hear their exchange. A few moments later, Amara slid away to rejoin Robert, though Enrique caressed her arm and then her wrist, holding her briefly, a casual possessiveness before she maneuvered free with a smile. Having lived in the company of vampires, Jessica's notion of traditional monogamous relationships had forever been scrambled. Still, the bond between husband and wife, existing under the umbrella of the vampire's sensual demands on them both, was an enigma she wasn't sure would ever make sense to her.

However, she needed to think about Robert, and what Mason was offering to her. She wished he'd taken the time to tell her about it, so she'd have more time to consider it. A tattoo . . . she wasn't sure what she thought of that. But when she thought of Robert bending over her, touching the stripes, reminding her of their presence, laying his hands on her . . .

Would it make you feel better if I was there, habiba?

A flood of reassurance came with his voice, so strong she knew the magic of her collar and cuffs had been a mere shadow of it. But she squelched her reaction. "I'm not talking to you. You were an ass last night. And yes, I would feel better. But no, I don't want you there."

Even inside her mind, a woman is still incomprehensible.

"Oh, bullshit. You understand perfectly. Whatever it is you're doing to me, I don't want it. I don't want to feel better having you around. I don't want to be dependent on you. I don't want to be here, and I don't want him touching me."

A sudden quiet told her she'd made that last remark at a near shout, enough to still the quiet chatter from the nearby verandah where Robert and Amara were, perhaps even to reach the roofers who were working on the west wing. Biting her lip, she turned and exited the back stairs, striding across the gardens and breaking into an easy run, headed toward the ocean. Maybe he was like a cell phone. If she got far enough, he'd lose reception.

You're right, Jessica. I do understand. You don't want them touched, because you don't want to be reminded of them, but they are there, every day, a reminder whenever you move. You think I don't feel your discomfort? This is a way you can make them yours, if it pleases you to do so. Robert is an artist, as gifted as any of the old masters. He simply uses the human body as his canvas. At least talk to him, and then you can make the decision. If it helps, he prefers men exclusively.

"You don't seem to have much problem with that side of the fence yourself. Sure us girls aren't in the way?"

Irritatingly, she heard a chuckle in her mind, not the annoyance she'd been intending to rouse. *Habiba, male vampires do not share the insecurities of human males about touching another man. However, whatever pleasures I've experienced with a male body, my bonding preference has always been female. I think you are very aware of that, and if not, I'll be happy to prove it to you.*

It wasn't fair that he could make his voice that low, seductive whisper inside the chamber of her mind. But then his tone changed.

Do something that makes the scars belong to you, rather than the mark of the one who inflicted them. You say you want to depend on no one. Prove it. Make this decision for yourself.

With that curt admonishment, he went silent. She didn't know if he was still reading her thoughts, but he'd left her as alone as she could expect from him. Dropping to her knees in the sand, she turned her face up to the afternoon sun, felt the damp sand against her bare legs. She was in the most beautiful setting she could wish. She loved the ocean, the horses, the rain forest . . . all of it. Yet vampires, with their unnatural beauty and their penchant for such settings, had taken away her unquestioning, easy enjoyment of those things.

At one dinner party, the table settings had been exceptionally exquisite, the napkins formed into swans, the centerpiece an ice sculpture of a unicorn. One of the female vampires had worn a blue dress with a silver mesh overlay, the most gorgeous thing Jess had ever seen, even on movie stars. That same vampire had held Jess's arm over a brace of candles until her skin blackened and charred, fell away. She remembered the sparkle of the woman's sapphire necklace, the intricate connecting beads of jet and silver. She'd probably bought it from Tiffany's, for a price that ensured they sent her a fruit basket every Christmas, never knowing fruit was not her preferred truffle.

Putting her forehead down on the sand, Jess let the tide rush against her body, her face, so she could drown her tears there. It couldn't swallow her sobs, though, leaving her soaked and rocking on the sand. Maybe because she truly didn't want anyone near her this time, no one came. She cried and sobbed until she retched up her latest meal, until she was too exhausted to crowd her mind with anything else. When she reached that point, she stretched out, her toes still at the tide edge, and stared up into the sky. Stripping off her shirt so the damp sand pressed against her back, she spread her arms out to either side of her, lying there in her shorts and sports bra only.

Crying was getting easier and harder, both. The tears often took her by surprise. Like when she was in the barn, finding herself suddenly flowing like a leaky faucet. Or when she'd wake up in the mornings, her face stiff with the dried tracks. She needed to run now, let the miles and physical strain take more of the unbearable weight off her mind. Perhaps she'd been better off when she'd lobotomized herself, gone completely blank and numb. Then she didn't care, didn't feel.

But when that moment in the alley came, she'd cared enough to grip that weapon and strike with all the fury and rage of a stolen life. If she was brave enough to do that, she had to have the courage to believe Mason was giving her another chance. She couldn't squander her time in fear that it was all a cruel joke.

Had she become like the bird that feared going out the cage door, finally opened? Was her attachment to Mason because the limitations of an imprisoned life were safe, known? No. Okay, maybe. But there was another way to look at it. He'd told her she was a smart woman, that she understood the fragile state of her own mind. Maybe she needed the reassurance of his guardianship, to build her up to true freedom again. Give her the bravery to move beyond Farida's tomb, reinvent herself.

She hadn't balked at using anything necessary as a tool of survival before. Why should she resist what he offered because he was a vampire, or because she couldn't resolve how she felt about him? She couldn't become a coward now. Sitting up, she pushed back her wet hair. He was right. She did want to make these marks hers.

However, the design that came to her mind was disquieting, reflecting the struggle in her own mind. Rising and rubbing her face with both hands, she drew a deep breath. She would run and think. Brainstorm. She'd come up with something different, something that was hers.

Even as she had the thought, though, a new wave of despair washed through her, like the tide's inexorable return. It might be too late to consider herself free. Maybe that had ended long ago. Maybe she needed to accept she only had the courage to accept a benevolent dictatorship now. True freedom was forever beyond her grasp.

~

Mason's study window was becoming a favorite brooding ground, Enrique noted as he entered. "My lord?"

Mason didn't turn. "You've had news?"

"Yes." Though Enrique knew he could read it from his mind, he spoke the words anyway. "The Council liaison said that they welcome your arrival, but not to anticipate success. It would be unprecedented not to execute a human servant for the death of her Master."

"Like dogs. It matters not how cruelly they were treated, it won't be tolerated." Mason's tone was low, cold. Enrique wisely stayed at the door.

"She has accepted your gift, my lord," he ventured at last. "Robert will be back to perform the work in a few days."

"Of course she has. She thinks she has no choice. She thinks Raithe has permanently broken her, and any gratitude or feelings she has toward me is part of . . . an affliction." Mason's fingers clenched into fists behind his back. "We need to resolve this with the Council soon and get her away from here. She cannot see her own strength in the shadow of mine."

"With all due respect, my lord, I believe you are wrong."

Mason looked toward the handsome Frenchman, standing in the

shadows. He hadn't turned on any lights since he didn't need any, but a candle sconce flickered as Enrique lit one now. "Neither one of you is giving yourself enough time," his servant said.

"What do *I* need time for?"

"You've not responded to a woman like this since I've known you." Enrique doused the lighter, put it aside, and glanced toward the desk where Jessica had been working most of the day. "She calls to something in you. And you to her. I think she is your true human servant."

Mason stared at him a long moment. "You are speaking plain tonight, Enrique."

"You know my thoughts, my lord. There is no need to hide them. And perhaps I am saying what you wish to say yourself."

The vampire snorted, a harsh sound. "I will never seek a servant like that again, Enrique."

"Do you think Farida would wish you to be alone forever, my lord? Don't you think it's odd this woman, who draws you so much, was found in Farida's tomb?"

"You're not going to get ridiculously metaphysical on me, are you?" Mason lifted a brow, though his chest was constricting. "A gift from the grave, Farida's way of telling me to move on, after three hundred years?"

"Amara and I only wish you to have . . ."

"What the two of you have?" Mason took a step toward him, his face hardening. "I do have it, Enrique. You both belong to me. The emanations of your love and devotion touch me every day. It is enough."

Enrique met his gaze without flinching. "Once a man has been given what Amara has given me, what Farida gave you, anything less is never enough."

"You're right. Anything less isn't enough," Mason snapped.

"Unless what you could have had with Farida, cut short by Fate's cruelty, lies waiting for you in a bedroom in this very estate."

"Did Amara send you to bedevil me this way?" Mason stalked to the desk. "You're both getting on my nerves."

"No, my lord. But if I have served you well, I ask that you let me have my say."

The piercing eyes were those of the determined young resistance fighter Enrique had been when Mason met him, helping to smuggle Jewish refugees out through occupied France. Since then, he'd fought at Mason's side, protected his back. However it wasn't until the moment Amara had crossed their path that Mason had appreciated the depth of the man's loyalty.

Enrique's father had been French, and that was the country of his birth, but he also carried a Spanish name, thanks to his mother being a Spaniard. Like Frenchmen and Spaniards both, Enrique loved women. As much and as often as possible. But when he saw Amara, everything he'd ever loved about women had come together, channeled toward the lithe form of the astoundingly beautiful woman who'd danced for them as part of their host's entertainment. Mason had felt the click of something different in his servant's mind, a tumbler that fell into place. It might happen once in a man's life, if he was lucky.

It would have shattered Enrique to leave her behind, this woman who was obviously his mate in all ways, but Mason had read in the man's heart that he would, if that was what his service to Mason required.

Still, for form's sake, Mason sat down, templed his fingers and scowled. "You have served me well, Enrique. But your speech had better be short, or you may use up the favor quickly. Sixty years is barely a breath to a vampire."

Enrique moved to light another sconce. "All those years ago, when you brought me into your service, I'd never known or craved a man's touch. I thought I'd mistaken my desire for women, but you quickly proved my lust for them had not dimmed. If anything, you took it to a higher level, by showing me the pleasures of serving a Master."

Mason sharpened his attention on him, but Enrique stayed half turned, as if it were easier to say the words to the flickering flame. "I came to you after Farida, so it took me a long time to understand, but bonding myself to Amara helped. When Farida was taken from you, something shattered. Ever since then, you've re-created yourself, a piece at a time, but you exist as if you think your soul is glass that can break and destroy you from the inside. Except you can't die that way, so I think what you fear is facing that pain again."

Putting the lighter down on the corner of Mason's desk, he raised his dark gaze to his Master's. "You and Jessica are drawn together for many reasons, but that may be the most important. If it was only on her side, I would say you might be right, that she cannot hope to gain her own feet as long as you are there to lift her onto them. I know how difficult it was for you while she cried today, to not even speak in her mind or send one of us to reassure her."

"How do you know that?"

"Because I *have* been your servant for sixty years," Enrique said. "Because I know almost everything about you, including the fact that if I push you too hard, you will strike me back down into my place. But I also know that, after Amara, I love no one better."

He paused when Mason rose now, the two men gazing at each other over the desk. "In fact, I cannot even quantify it that way," Enrique continued softly. "You let me have Amara, knowing I needed that kind of love, a true family of my own. I share her with you. My wife. At your behest, yes, but because she is willing and understands my love for you. The love of a human servant for his Master, which is something that cannot be described. And in return, you never take my wife alone, always using me to help sate your hungers. It is to protect your glass soul, yes, but it is a respect for me I have never failed to appreciate."

Mason came around the desk. When he let his knuckles drift down the man's sternum, Enrique's fingers closed on Mason's biceps with strength, a reminder of past sensual wrestling matches. As he'd told Jessica, women had always been Mason's preference, but on occasion the power of a man, the aggressive way they fought before willing surrender, had appealed to Mason, perhaps because of how different it was from a woman's slick heat, her enchanting fragility and yet fathomless maze of desires. Mason had taken Enrique down on his hands and knees in more than one sweaty bout. His servant would offer his body to him, here and now, in whatever manner the vampire demanded.

Given the emotions he'd stirred, it was tempting. But just as he knew where his male servant's heart truly rested, so, too, did Mason know what called to his tonight.

As if reading his mind, Enrique nodded. "If you need her as

much as she needs you, there may be nothing better for you both than to face your demons together. Because that is what two people who love one another do. You make one another stronger, better, more whole. And I see the potential of that, when I see the two of you together."

Could he believe it could happen twice? If so, why did it have to be a human again, that most fragile of species? And Jessica, who carried a special type of fragility with her?

"Where is she now?" Mason said at last.

The Frenchman's sensual mouth curved. "You know that even better than I, my lord."

"Enrique, I can make your life Hell on Earth."

"Yes, my lord," he responded demurely, his fingers sliding from Mason's arms. "I am simply saying I expect you can find her more quickly with your mind. And, on rare occasions, you are not a patient man."

Mason narrowed his gaze at him. "I am not saying you are correct, but I thank you for your counsel. Ultimately, this decision is Jessica's."

"My lord, you left the decision to me as well. It did not make me any less yours, in the end. Perhaps that is the secret of it. There's no temptation greater than the *choice* of binding yourself to another forever."

Mason decided not to respond to that, instead returning to their original topic, moving back around the desk. "Contact the Council liaison. Tell her I understand, and look forward to discussing this further when we meet in Berlin. Also, reemphasize their discretion is vital, that it is imperative they don't discuss this matter with anyone else until then."

Enrique snorted. "You think they'll listen?"

Mason allowed himself a grim smile. "Likely not, but lesser miracles have happened. Regardless, it might be wise for me to go as soon as possible. And Enrique?"

"Yes, my lord?" Enrique paused at the door.

"With respect to Robert . . . remind him she's to be sedated during his work. I don't want her to feel any pain or anxiety."

"She might refuse."

"Which is why I made it a command, not a request."

With a nod, the servant turned and departed, leaving Mason staring across the desk and out the windows again, toward the border of the property, the depths of the tangled rain forest. It was an accurate reflection of his mind. He was going to have to make amends, because she was still out of sorts about the other night. What she'd seen as an argument, he'd considered simple good manners, especially when he'd decided to leave rather than strangle her. Or worse, take her down beneath him and punish her in a far more sensual way. But women tended to be oblivious to the great sacrifices a male made on their behalf.

It almost made him smile. As he rose, the warmth spreading through his chest told him he'd made his decision, if not to agree with Enrique, to at least give himself the pleasure of spending more time with his troublesome new servant.

Jessica stepped away from the wall, trying to hold the posture. It felt odd, all her weight settled back like that, but Amara had said it was essential to learning the foundation steps of belly dancing. She tried a hip bump, left, then right, then a hip twist. Her arms were supposed to float for the time being, but for fun, she tried the snake arm move, because Amara had also said the dancing was best when intuitive. Taking it too seriously could make it stilted.

Jessica moved forward across the empty ballroom. She could have practiced in the staff recreation area, but she'd been too self-conscious. One step, twist, one step, bump. Then she tried a figure eight and botched it entirely, and went back to the twists and bumps again.

Of course, she could have wanted to practice here because of the beauty of the walls, the mural paintings, the reminder of the setting that Amara had created here for her dance for Mason.

As Jess turned, she let her restless thoughts take her into a richly appointed sultan's tent, deep in the desert. The wind kicked up the sands outside with a soft murmur of sound. She rolled her head back, willing the thoughts to take her away from the darkness that had driven her into some kind of activity as the shadows gathered outside. It was a reflection of what was happening inside her, her psyche on its never-ending, out-of-control roller-coaster ride.

In a few days, Robert would come and do the tattoo design. She had come up with a couple ideas, different from the disquieting image that had first popped into her mind, and Amara had communicated them to him. But her mind's insistence that she'd been right with her first idea gave her another reason to escape into her faraway imaginings.

She turned and twisted, thinking of Amara dancing, and how Mason had watched her. Drinking wine off her belly, feeding her grapes . . . She pushed away the present, and transformed it into the past. Transformed herself into the past.

The same imagining as she always had. She was Farida, her sable hair loose on her bare arms as she danced for her love, her lord, who lounged on the cushions. His face was in shadows. Because he did not speak or smile, just watched her with that intent expression, it made her determined to please him, increase his desire to the point his reserve would break, and he would come to claim her. It was a sense of power and surrender at once, a dual sensation that took over her movements so she didn't have to think about them at all as her arms swept gracefully about her, her hips moving in the intricate movements that couldn't help but draw his gaze there. The heat of his attention gathered desire between her thighs, but she became more languid. Slowing it down like the act of lovemaking itself, drawing out every movement, every offering. She inhaled his scent and her own, as well as the exotic aroma of the candlelight and incense. She'd soon savor the flavor of the wine on his tongue when he brought his mouth to hers, the provocative scrape of a sharp fang.

She came closer, then fell back, using the full perimeter of the tent, as if she was seeking escape, then came back in, teasing him. She undulated her hips, turning in a flowing movement so the veil she held would stroke his jaw. Using it to hide her face, she swept it over the tops of her breasts, temptingly displayed in the brief top.

In the coup de grace, the one she knew would bring him off the cushions, she worked it into her dance so it became wrapped around one wrist, then the other, each sinuous hip and body movement or turn of the arm taking it in another wrap, until she'd brought her wrists together in a full binding, the finale of an elaborate dance between restraint and freedom. She finished on her knees, her arms extended, the loose end of the scarf trailing, enough length for him to pick it up, draw her to her feet.

Jess stopped, breathing loud, and found herself on her knees, her wrists held together and offered up to the male who stood only a yard away from her. Like her imaginings, his face was wreathed in the shadows of the dim room, but she saw enough to be lost. The flaming amber eyes, the unsmiling mouth, the jaw flexing as if with some internal struggle. His body was tense, the leashed power vibrating. His arousal was impressively evident, particularly in the snug riding breeches he seemed to prefer as casual wear, thank the gods.

He was every bit the man he'd been when he'd met Farida, as if time had not touched him. Jess couldn't imagine him on a crowded city street, in a shopping mall, or even driving a car.

"Amara is teaching you to dance." He broke the silence at last. Reaching down, he came up beneath her outstretched hands so her fingers turned and hooked over his palm like a falcon's perch. She stared up at him, struggling between her memories and her present existence, not certain in which reality she preferred to handle this moment. "You show promise."

"I'm still having problem with the figure-eight move."

"You're forcing it. It's a flowing, easy move." She blinked when he executed it flawlessly, as Enrique had done, with the leashed energy of a warrior rather than the seductive power of an houri. "Here." Lifting and turning her away from him, he placed his hands on her hips. "It's also easier if you use someone's hands, like this, to guide the maneuver. Try it now . . . Yes, like that."

With his body behind her, her mind shut down entirely, and her body followed on instinct, rendering the movement in a flowing twist that had her blinking again. His hands drew away, slow, leaving her skin tingling. "Good."

She swallowed, but before she could respond, he'd turned her again, drawn her attention up to the flicker in his gaze. "Your reality is right here, Jessica. Do not fear grasping it."

"I'm afraid of everything, Mason."

"But it hasn't stopped you from reaching this point. That's courage, *habiba*. A fearless man cannot prove he is brave. Or woman," he amended, a trace of a smile crossing his face.

"You know a lot," she whispered. "But can you tell me what I truly want?"

Those amber eyes flamed, and her lips parted, needing more breath than she could possibly provide herself in the oxygen-evaporating heat between them. "I'm more concerned with what you need."

"No." Perhaps it was the spell woven by her dance, imagined in a faraway desert tent, but her gaze lowered with deliberate brazenness, sweeping his body. "You're not. You're just trying to tell yourself that."

His mouth firmed and he took a step back. "And you are trying to make a fantasy come to life."

"Aren't you doing the same?" she asked, stung. "You're here, aren't you?"

A muttered oath. She didn't see him move, but then he was gone. Even as she sank back down to her knees, a little overwhelmed by her boldness, the satisfaction seemed a hollow victory without his presence. She'd pushed him, and yet all she'd wanted was for him to stay. The constant push and pull of her emotions was going to tear her into pieces. She wished she could become two people, though she was painfully aware that she may have already done that.

He could be right. She'd created a dependence on Farida, needing to step into a dead woman's head and be her, in order to deal with her own unbearable memories. That could be the sole reason for her attachment to him, and her pride just didn't like to hear it.

What if it was a double-edged sword, though? What if that was what drew Mason back to her so often? And why should that bother her? Wasn't it easier for both of them in a manufactured fantasy, rather than the stark reality where Farida was long dead and Jessica was a victim of trauma, poised on the brink of insanity?

When she got to her feet, the ballroom echoed her movements, underscoring how alone she was. If she even partially believed Mason's words, the assumption was she would eventually leave here. But where did she go, what did she become, when she'd been what she'd been? How would she ever find anyone who could touch that part of her, so deep inside, that had once known how to love and surrender to another, if they couldn't understand who and what she'd become to survive?

Feeling the hated tears threatening, and sick of preoccupation with herself, she left the dance behind. Maybe she'd just sleep for a while. A very long while. At least there, she had half a chance of getting immersed in a dream where being someone different wouldn't be interrupted or questioned. She wouldn't have to face a solitary existence, seeking purpose in a world where things didn't happen for grand, cosmic reasons. Where Darwin's law, of brutality and chaos, was all there was.

18

UNFORTUNATELY, it wasn't Farida's dreams she fell into, but her own nightmares. Her worst one—the dungeon. The darkness, the rats' claws pricking her legs as they climbed her bare body, trying to reach the fresh blood hung in a bucket around her neck.

It was the blood of a teenage boy Raithe had killed, as part of his annual quota. While vampires could live on blood without killing humans, all vampires had to mortally drain a human at least once annually to maintain their mental acuity and physical strength. Vampire law, however, allowed vampires to kill up to a dozen humans a year, in addition to the annual kill.

Raithe had found the boy and his girlfriend making out in the park. He liked interrupting lovers, like some clichéd horror movie monster. The teen had screamed for Jessica's help as she stood mutely behind Raithe, watching him take his victim down, drain him into shock and then cold, blue-tinged death. Then he'd told her to pick the boy up, put him in the trunk so they could go home. His girlfriend had run off.

The rats made chittering noises. Roaches, also attracted by the food, crawled across her hair, over her eyes. They all gathered around the bucket, the rats adding to the weight when they balanced on the lip of the steel pail, their claws scratching her chest. She tried not to make a sound, but of course it didn't matter. Raithe could hear the screaming in her mind.

It was the darkness that always broke her, though. What started as a whimper became a moaning cry and then a scream, as the rats tested her with the scrapes of their fangs, seeing if her flesh was edible as well.

No, no. Get off. Go away. Please . . . leave me alone. Please, Raithe. Let me go.

She hated it when she begged him, because that was of course what he most wanted to hear. So she cursed him, too, which resulted in him leaving her there, hour after hour in the dark, fighting off the rats with as much movement as she could make with the jerks of her restrained body.

Bastards, get off get off get off stop stop stop stop . . . There was screaming now, high, endless, agonized. And an unbearable weight, the smell of dry earth and rock . . .

"Jessica. Jess."

Female hands, a female voice, oddly reminiscent of her mother in its soothing, firm reassurance. "Wake up, lovely. It's a dream. Come back to us. Wake up."

She came out of the bed, rolling away from Amara instinctively and hitting the floor on the balls of her feet, her hands raised in defense. As she gazed wildly around the room, she knew it wasn't just her in the darkness. The smell of earth and rock, the screaming, continued, though she knew she was awake.

"Jessica." Amara again, but Jessica shook her head fiercely, shoved past her.

"Mason. It's Mason."

Before Amara could stop her, she was out the door and running down the hall. She didn't have to remember the way to his room. She could feel his mind, could follow it.

It was about nine o'clock in the morning. It had been after one in the morning when she'd seen him in the ballroom. He must have gone to bed about dawn, which was unusual for him. At his age, he usually went more toward midday. Had he been seeking escape as she had, and found darkness instead?

Oh, God, the blackness. It was absolute, pressing, crushing down so that even the rats couldn't reach her. They were crawling around and over rock and her flesh at once, in that illogical way dreams had.

"Jessica." Amara was on her heels as Jess hit the lower level and raced for his door, another oak door like the one on the dungeon. Jess tried the door latch. When it gave way, she would have made it all the way through, except the servant caught her at last. Seizing her by both arms, Amara swung her around and slammed her against the wall of the corridor. "Jessica, *listen to me*."

"Let me go. It's him. He's having a nightmare."

"Yes, he is." Amara shook Jessica hard enough to snap her head back against the stone, and the sharp pain of it helped Jessica focus past the fear and darkness. *But, gods, that endless screaming...* The servant seized her face in both hands, made her look at her. "He has had them before. He will not recognize you, do you understand? It is why his door is solid eight-inch-thick oak, and why he sleeps so far removed from us. He will kill you if you get in his way."

Trapped. He can't breathe. And by Allah, please stop her screaming...

With a fierce snarl, Jessica shoved Amara hard enough to dislodge her. "He needs me." She yanked on the door latch and stumbled into the room, because Amara threw herself forward to try once more to pull her back.

She vaguely remembered Mason's room from that first night, shelves of books, a fireplace with a small flame leaping to cast light over the room. Weapons and expensive artwork on the walls; heavy, dark sculptures decorating the side tables. A high bed with thick, carved canopy posts. The lair of a civilized predator.

They were fleeting impressions only, for as she came in he bolted from the bed. Wholly naked, a savage rage on his face, he flung himself at the wall, tearing down a tapestry so it twisted around him, a confusing net.

Though the fabric was thick brocade, he tore free of it in the space of an indrawn breath. He was snarling, his fangs fully exposed. The powerful body had always been impressive, but in a state ready for violence, all muscles bunched and tensed, he was a Titan reborn.

Amber eyes had gone to solid, hellfire red. It gave her pause, but only for a moment, because she could feel what was happening inside of him. Mason's control of the block between their minds had dropped and she felt his terror . . . not for himself. *I have to get to her. Have to help her. She's hurting. Screaming . . .*

Jessica clapped her hands over her ears, even knowing it was coming from his mind, pouring into hers. On her way here, it had been muted, but in the same room with him, the unearthly screeching of a woman in agony could shatter a soul. Forsaken, tormented . . .

"Mason, I'm here." Jessica staggered forward. As Amara grabbed at her, she dodged, darted forward. She could feel Enrique on his way, for it appeared all four of their minds were linked, jumbled with the vampire who'd marked them, bound them to his thoughts.

"I'm here." She cried it out more forcefully, trying to get through those screams. As he erupted from the shredded fabric, she ducked under an arm, sheer luck, since it was moving faster than she could follow. Throwing herself at him midbody, she tucked her head against his chest and wrapped her arms around his back.

In hindsight, she knew it had been an incredibly stupid move. If he'd caught her in the face, he would have broken her neck like a twig. While as a third-marked servant, it wouldn't have killed her, she was sure it would have been extremely unpleasant. But she couldn't be sensible. Somehow her nightmare screams in Raithe's dungeon had meshed with Farida's and made them far worse, so he was being ripped apart from the inside by them both. All Jessica knew was she had to help him, and she wasn't letting go.

He thrashed, his heart thundering under her cheek, the strands of his loose mane brushing the top of her head. If he'd wanted her off, all he had to do was toss her away, but that was the one thing he didn't do. As she clung like a burr he let her, backing into the wall violently enough that she muffled a cry against his chest as her fingers hit the flat stone.

Bare muscled flesh flexed under the coil of her body. Several weeks of working in a barn and a third mark were worth something, though, because she was strong enough to hold her lock on him. *Mason, I'm here. Right here. Stop. Stop.*

When he swayed against the wall, she bit her lip as he rocked over her knuckles. She was pretty certain the bones of her fingers were now like a crushed snack bag of crackers. But slowly, he settled, his chest expanding and deflating beneath her cheek, a fierce bellows.

Farida?

It lanced through her, the raw longing in his mind-voice, the hope and desperation, so unlike the coolly self-possessed vampire she'd known thus far. Even the various levels of his temper were easier to handle than this. She wanted to tell him yes, feeling in some odd way it was true, but it wasn't. She couldn't be Farida to him.

Jessica. "It's Jessica," she murmured against his skin, closing her eyes in relief when his arm circled her back, his palm cupping over her shoulder, then sliding up to the side of her face, grazing her jawline, orienting himself.

Mason blinked, gazing around him. He found Amara and Enrique at the doorway. Enrique was holding a sizable steel baton. At Mason's look, he gave a wry shrug. Mason, understanding his servant would have plunged in to protect Jessica or Amara as needed, nodded his thanks and meant it. His servant tipped the baton in return. Then he withdrew, taking Amara with him.

They were familiar with his nightmares, and knew he couldn't block his mind during them. But he hadn't thought about Jessica experiencing them. He also hadn't expected having such a horrible convergence of her nightmares with his own. It was as if his mind had reached out to her in his sleep, and he'd pulled hers in. Even thinking about it now he couldn't bear it, the way the two women's screams came together, hammering at him, at his failure to protect either one of them. It shuddered through his body, his stomach heaving in a way that made him wish he could vomit.

"Hey. *Hey.*" Jessica's sharp tone jerked his attention back down to her. With a worried expression, she placed one hand on his jaw, her fingers stroking through the long strands of hair at his temple. She attempted an annoyed look. "Haven't you heard of pajamas? Sweatpants, flannel boxers, anything?"

Staring down at her, he realized she was leaning against him, and his own body, heedless of his nightmare, was beginning to react to that. He should send her away, but he didn't want to yet.

"That's okay." She managed a nervous smile. "I'll trust that you can control your mindless lust if I stay. I won't vouch for controlling mine, though."

He closed his eyes. Allah, he hadn't shut down the communication between their minds, and his thoughts were still leaking over into her head. "I'm sorry, Jessica."

"For what?" Her voice was soft, and he opened his eyes again to see concerned gray eyes, a kissable mouth.

"I would think that's obvious."

"No, not really." Her brow furrowed. "It's okay for you to soothe my nightmares, but not for me to return the favor? You're a vampire, Mason. Not Superman. And even Superman had his weaknesses."

"Obviously, since Doomsday killed him."

Her eyes widened, and a sparkle went through them. "*You've* read 'The Death of Superman'?"

"Of course not. I perhaps heard something about it."

Her mouth spread into a smile that brought light into his soul, driving back the hunched, vicious shadows lurking there. "You liar. You *have* read it."

"I have a friend who enjoys comic books," he allowed. "I might have spent some time reading one while visiting him."

Her hand was still on his jaw, her fingers moving in his hair, stroking in a reassuring and yet tempting way, making him want to press his face into the slim, feminine palm, brush his lips over it. And then go further, for all she wore was a thin cotton sleep shirt, falling off one smooth shoulder. She smelled like jasmine. But then he noticed her other hand, the one gingerly curled on his chest.

He enclosed the hand gently in his. "I hurt your knuckles."

"I'm sure they will heal in no time." She shook her head. "Don't get that look. You're about to get all aggravated because I rushed in here with no thought for my well-being, and you could have broken me like a doll, or gone after me with fangs—"

"All of which is true."

"But you didn't," she pointed out.

"Jessica, I have these nightmares. Amara and Enrique have learned to wait them out."

"This was different. You co-opted mine. I wasn't going to let you feel that, in addition to what I could tell you were already feeling." She shrugged irritably. "Mason, do you honestly think there's anything you can do to hurt me that would be worse than what I've already experienced?"

Jessica had hoped to ease his concern with that bald statement, but something stilled in those amber depths so that it stilled her as well, her fingers resting on his bare shoulder now. The male was a wall of hard, aroused muscle, and all she wanted was to stay right here against him.

He'd obviously received that thought loud and clear, if the convulsive jerk of the organ pressed against her belly was any indication. "Yes, I could. I could betray your trust. You fear that above anything else right now. If that turned out to be true, I could destroy you." When she would have protested, he shook his head. "I'm in your mind, Jessica. I know it's the truth."

"You're wrong. I don't trust you at all. No further than I could throw you. So there." She didn't care if he knew it was a lie. When she tilted her head and fired a defiant look at him, she was pleased by the hint of a smile on his firm mouth. "But I'm no longer confused about one thing. I know all the synapses aren't firing right in my brain, but you're not Raithe. I promise I know that, Mason. I wish you'd believe me. I *need* you to believe it."

Taking a breath, Jessica took her hand to his mouth, traced his lips. Mason froze, that magnificent, muscular body going still as she outlined the sensual shape. He was right. She'd never thought about this benefit of a third mark, of having a vampire in her mind. So, in elaborate detail, she could imagine how that mouth felt on hers, on her body. How she wanted to touch him.

She shifted. With him leaning against the wall, he had one leg braced out long and straight, the other bent. Now she put her hip into that bent one, which brushed her abdomen against the part of him again that was most interested in her proximity. She knew it was easy to feel her nipples through the cotton shirt. Her thin panties didn't shield her at all from the heat building in his groin, and she wondered if he felt the responsive heat in her own. Since his breath drew in on a near growl, she assumed he did.

For once, she was more than willing to use her knowledge of vampires for her own pleasure. Knowing what got their engines running on all cylinders, she teased his bottom lip, tracing wet heat with her fingertip, and grazed a fang with her knuckle, letting the tip score her skin, enough to produce blood.

"Ouch," she whispered, turning the digit so it was in his mouth, dallying with the curl of his tongue. He tasted her, the amber eyes brilliantly intense on her face as he soothed the cut. Mason's fingers flexed on her back, above the band of her panties, bunching the cloth of the shirt in his fist.

"Will you hurt me, Mason?" She asked it in a voice she was surprised to hear quaver. Maybe this was one of her crazy moments; she didn't know. All she knew was, as much as she didn't want to go back to her room to the lingering vibrations of her nightmares, she didn't want to leave him here with his. She didn't want to think about those screams, what they meant. Sometime soon, she would want to know, but not right now.

"Only if you beg me to," he responded in a dangerous voice, thrilling her with the matching flash in his gaze, the strength of that arm cinching in so she was pressed hard against him. She closed her eyes, a shudder running through her body. His other hand moved down and gripped her buttock, winning a soft mewl of desire from her lips. Lifting her body, he rubbed her against his cock in a way that slid her clit against it, the sensation heightened by the friction of the clothes between them. When he groaned, she gasped herself, the bolt of sensation startling her. She desperately wanted him, needed him, inside of her now. Her panties were already soaked, and she knew he could feel it, sense it, smell it.

Her body couldn't care less about the folly, the complexity and the irony of her attraction to a vampire. Every time she was in proximity to him this started to happen. Starved for his touch, the rest didn't matter, past, present or future. She didn't want a self-pleasuring, or Amara's mouth, or even Mason's provocative thoughts. She wanted his strong hands, his heavy cock, the weight of his body demanding everything from her. Total surrender of thought or choice, whether madness or not.

He had her by the wrist now, her fingers free of his mouth, but he was . . . oh, God. He was kissing her wrist, one fang sliding down her frantically beating pulse, the long, slick side of the enamel, not the sharpened point, teasing her. Turning his gaze back to her, he reached out to the wall beside him, where a pair of crossed daggers was mounted. He pulled one free of the scabbard without even glancing at it. Before she could get apprehensive about his intentions, he took the blade to his throat and pricked the artery there. His other hand cupped her face.

"It will help your fingers heal more quickly." His molten gaze held hers. "No argument, *habiba*. I burn to feel your mouth on me."

Rising on her tiptoes, since he'd lowered her back to her feet to pull the blade, she found she couldn't quite get there. Giving him a disparaging look, she raised a brow. "A boost would be helpful."

Never mind her voice was a bit breathless. A spark of humor went through his gaze, but it was lost in the fires of lust that weakened her knees, making her need the assistance even more. The hold of his arm increased, his knee pressing between her legs, compelling them to open. As he slid her up the hard column of his thigh, she cried out. *Oh, God.* That flexing muscle between her legs, the spasms that rocketed through her clit. She curled her arm behind his neck, undamaged fingers digging into his shoulder, and brought her mouth to the cut.

At the first touch of her lips, he tightened everywhere, muscles rippling along chest and arm, cock convulsing where it was trapped beneath her hip bone. To a third-mark, the smell of blood was appetizing . . . but only the blood of the Master. She licked at the dagger mark, feeling him harden further against her as his mouth brushed her ear.

Take me to bed, Mason. I want you inside me.

Giving orders, habiba? He nipped her sharply and electricity strummed through her.

Please, Mason. I need you.

You need many things, love. But I'm not sure if that's one of them.

She bit and he growled, swinging her over to the bed and taking her down on her back, pinning her with his body as he cupped her head, holding her to his neck until he deemed she'd had enough. It felt glorious, the length of him stretched out on her. Lifting her legs, she tangled them over his hips, those bare buttocks, so taut. Straining up so her damp center rubbed against his cock, a swatch of thin cloth separating them, she willed him to tear her panties away, to simply take her.

"You can feel how wet I am for you," she gasped. "Do it."

But she could already see it happening, that thing that had happened every time they reached this point, and she wanted to howl, wanted to have his strength so she could force him forward. The doubt collecting in his eyes, the decision swinging another way, despite what it was obvious both of their bodies wanted. He caught her face in both hands, held her still.

"Goddamn you," she snarled. "You want to. I can feel it. Get over yourself. It's not that big a deal. Just fu—"

Stop it.

"I'm not her," she shouted in his face, not caring that temper flared in his eyes. "I'm not your precious, never-say-a-foul-word, submissive Farida. I'm not perfect and beautiful, trapped in your memory like some freaking zoo animal. You're the one who keeps drawing away."

Mason pushed her legs off his hips and stood, countering her swing at him and moving back, leaving her in the middle of his bed, panting and wanting nothing more than to skewer him with one of those blades.

"Whereas you keep slamming down on the gas without looking to see if you're hurtling over a cliff," he retorted in a near shout. "If you want me to take your body, it means I will *take* you, Jess. I have been patient and tolerant, because of your situation—"

"Oh, to hell with that. I'm sick of—"

"You will be *quiet.*"

His thunderous snarl reverberated through the room. More than that, he injected the command into her head, into the very marrow of her bones, stunning her into silence. She'd known Raithe was far less powerful than Mason, but she hadn't seen such an active demonstration of it until this moment. Vibration thrummed through her like the aftermath of an electric shock, leaving her staring up at him, frozen.

Mason turned away from her, snarling a stream of curses in Arabic she was sure it was best she not understand. She had a fleeting moment to regret the loss of view as he shrugged a robe over his broad shoulders and the tiger mark, before he belted the garment with a sharp jerk. He turned back to her. "Sit up."

Swallowing, she did so, but he kept his distance. "Jessica, I am glad you know I am not Raithe. But I am a vampire. If I want you, a human woman, I will have you on my terms. Of all people, you know exactly what that means."

She wanted to block it out, deny it. Suddenly she wanted to go back to her room, but he wasn't going to let her off so easily. He took a step toward her, commanding her attention.

"You keep pushing the boundaries. That's acceptable, given your situation. I want you to know, no matter how much you test me, you can trust me not to harm you as he did. But let me lay this out quite clearly for you."

Coming back to the bed swiftly enough she didn't have time to gasp, he cupped her skull, gripping her hair hard enough to yank her head back. It put his mouth at her throat, her eyes staring at the ceiling. She thrashed against him, but she couldn't throw him off, could only clutch the sleeves of his robe to prevent the sense of falling, though he held her rigidly enough. "Put your hands on the bed, on either side of you, palms down. Do it. Now."

With that voice resonating through her, she did it before she even thought to resist. His breath was hot on her wildly pumping neck artery, the hand in her hair tight, making it clear he was entirely in control of the moment. "If I decide to take you," he said in a husky tone, "fuck you, as you were so crudely going to put it, I will demand your unconditional surrender. I will restrain you. I will want you to get down on your knees and take my cock in your mouth. You will ask my permission to come, always. There will be times I use pain to elevate your pleasure. Spankings, floggings. Not what you experienced with Raithe"—there was a slight easing of his touch, and she thought one fingertip might have stroked across her sensitive occipital bone, making her shiver—"not torture. It was as I described it in the dungeon. This would be to put a pretty flush on your delicate skin, sensitize every nerve ending, so when I followed up with my mouth, you would writhe and beg to serve me in any way necessary to get that permission to climax. Again, not some humiliation like Raithe. My demand would be that you experience the highest, most unbearable pleasure possible, reach the top of the highest roller coaster, before I let you go over."

He adjusted his stance so now his face was over hers, eyes burning, refusing to let her look away. "But in your mind, can you honestly separate the two yet? Can you truly say you are willing to surrender to another Master? A vampire, at that? You aren't, and you and I both know it. I'm not here to satisfy your itch. You're either mine, or my guest. You will not be both. I want you too much to compromise."

After that startling revelation, he released her. With surprisingly gentle hands, he lifted her to her feet, taking her off his bed, setting her at a safe distance from it. Jessica was numb with shock and more as he traced the line of her temple, caught a curl in his fingertips and spoke in a calmer voice. "I thank you for coming to my aid. It's been a long time since someone soothed me out of a nightmare. Particularly someone selfless enough to help me, while still trembling with her own."

Leaning in, he brushed a kiss on her forehead, as if the raging carnality of the past few moments had never existed. As if she were a child being sent off to bed, he said, "Good night, *habiba*. Enrique is outside the door with a robe and slippers to escort you back to your room. The halls in the lower level are too cold for your nightshirt only."

Dropping his hand, he turned away, moving to the small fire. Jessica stood, swaying. One part of her was ready to bolt, but another part of her wanted to stay. She didn't have to be cold. He could stoke up the fire and she could curl up in his lap while he read, idly stroking her hair, just as she'd imagined. He'd said it wasn't about brutality. It was about pleasure. Could it also be about tenderness, love? In all of Farida's pages, not once did she take the upper hand with Mason. She always belonged to him, submissive to him, and yet she'd felt cherished, protected . . . loved.

But he'd made his terms clear, and he was right. Jess wasn't ready to accept them. It might be many, many years before she could accept them, his all-or-nothing threat, or offer. Empty and now cold in more ways than one, Jessica moved to the door. When she stopped and looked back, Mason was staring into the fire. It was obvious he'd left her in his mind, because he showed no reaction to her thoughts. For one insane moment, she wanted to cross the room, go to her knees, ask him to help her understand. Why did she feel so drawn to him, have such a fierce desire to be his, if she wasn't ready to surrender? But he turned farther away from her, a subtle denial that twisted in her chest like a knife.

Maybe it was the drama of the moment, the aftermath of their powerful nightmares. In the morning light, she'd be appalled at her own weakness, or consider this another episode of instability. From the beginning, she'd thought Raithe had made her what she was. From the beginning, Mason said her former captor had only fucked up what was already inside her. Who was right was a question only she could answer, and she didn't know yet. She'd been willing to trade self-awareness for desire, and the illusion of warmth and safety. She wasn't sure if that was appalling, or the best deal of her miserable life.

Forcing herself to turn the latch of the door, she stepped out, into a cold that was an emotion, not a temperature, a desolation even Enrique's kind, concerned smile couldn't temper.

$\sim$

Mason let out a breath, unclenching the hand he had braced on the mantel. Her thoughts were truly going to kill him. Since his own were supposed to be blocked from her, being with him by the fire was a mirrored desire. He'd love to hold her while she slept, wearing one of his shirts so she'd be cloaked in his scent. Then he'd lay her on the soft mattress and take her body, her nails raking the sensitive flesh over his tiger tattoo as she arched for him.

If he barely pushed the issue, she'd be his. And then hate him forever for making her choice for her.

"You can't have her," he muttered. "She's not for you." As the two pairs of screams revisited him, he shuddered and crouched in front of the fire like an animal in pain, crossing his arms on his knees and dropping his face into them. If anyone tried to hurt her, he'd rip them limb from limb.

He didn't know if Jessica Tyson was crazy or not, but she was definitely driving him to insanity.

19

MAYBE she should handle her own sexual frustration. Lock her bedroom door, slide her hand between her legs and bring herself to climax. She wouldn't imagine Mason. Her fantasy man would be . . . She swung a dagger gaze around the barn, and pinned Winston, Jorge's top groom. He was a handsome young man with curly dark hair, who right now was wearing only a pair of jeans. His smile was sexy and absorbing as he worked with Hasna.

She forced herself to hold the image of her fingers tugging on his dark curls, not coil away toward a more familiar, firm mouth. With an oath, she stabbed the pitchfork so hard into the hay it reached wood, the impact singing up her arm and drawing Winston's attention.

His smile became a nervous nod as she snarled at the simultaneous sensual reverberation from the wrist manacle. Clucking, he took the mare out of visual range. Cowards. All men were cowards.

Helping the landscapers dig out trenches for a new maze garden, washing the gazebo siding with the maintenance men and even helping the household staff and Amara clean all the chandelier glass in the ballroom was not the surefire remedy for irritation and an overdose of sexual frustration she'd hoped. Not even the passage of three days had eased it.

She hadn't heard or seen Mason, which was typical, but disconcertingly, this morning she'd felt nothing, as if he weren't present on the property at all. Which made her wonder if that was why she couldn't follow through on her fantasy. A sly, shameful part of her wanted him to command her to think only of him, and then reinforce that by branding every inch of her skin with his clever mouth, his hands, his cock.

Oh, Christ. She pulled off her bill cap and swiped it over her face as Enrique arrived with a lunch tray for her and the men. She wolfed it down, oblivious to table manners. The male aversion to an agitated woman was universal. Even Enrique offered nothing except cautious and brief pleasantries. He did remind her of her appointment with Robert for the afternoon—right before he collected the tray and departed beneath her stony regard.

God, she'd forgotten. She toyed with backing out of it, but in the end, she attacked more stable work. She'd exhaust herself to the point she wouldn't care to make any decisions at all, though she was all too aware that underscored Mason's point. She wasn't ready to make choices. Ironically, the key difference between Raithe and Mason was now her biggest thorn. A Master controlled everything, except the submissive's decision to belong to him, the most important decision of all. That was up to her. Damn male vampire.

Okay, fine. So he's right. For too long, her life had been about survival and reaction, instinct. Now, when analytical reflection was needed, her skills weren't merely rusty—she'd forgotten how to use them.

So start exercising them again, damn it. Think about it. Putting down the pitchfork, she planted her backside on a hay bale. When Hasna dropped her nose over the other stall door for attention, Jessica petted it absently.

First truth. Anyone who'd endured what she had over the past five years had to have a shrink's compendium of phobias, complexes and syndromes. Could she really trust her feelings? Her rational mind said the most intelligent course was the unlikely hope for Council clemency, Mason's offer of setting her up somewhere on her own and then a great therapist. By the time she turned seventy or eighty, she might be ready to handle a healthy relationship with a guy again. Not a problem. She was a third-mark, after all, so she should still have a firm body and great skin.

Second truth. If she went with the assumption that Mason was right, that Raithe had exploited something that was already in her nature, then it was obvious why she responded so strongly to Mason. He was a Dominant, and she'd formed an extremely fragile bridge of trust with him, which continued to stand only because he hadn't done anything yet to disrupt it. He had a vampire's magnetic personality and physical beauty, and on some odd level, that was now what she knew best. The familiar.

Both truths made logical sense. But maybe because she *had* lived on instinct so long, and trusted it, something about her conclusions felt wrong. When she'd responded to his nightmare, she'd known she *had* to help him, even if she had to mow over Enrique and Amara. She couldn't bear his pain.

It would be easy to make a romantic leap and think she carried some of Farida's spirit inside her, returning to a mortal form to bring Mason love again. But she wasn't much on past-life nonsense, and it seemed too coincidental for Jess's tastes, too schmaltzy. And while she felt a strong bond with Farida, she was Jessica, herself. So something else was fueling their bond. Something about how Mason had lost Farida called to Jessica, told her he understood her losses, in a way very few would.

Or maybe she was just hormonal as hell and he was a hot-body vampire who wore *eau de pheromones* in a way she couldn't resist. Her lips curved. She'd replayed his bare-assed stalk across his bedroom to get his robe a few hundred times. If her mind was a movie player, the digital media would have worn out by now. But every time she saw that tiger on his shoulder, she wanted to stroke it, feel the muscles shifting beneath the design.

Despite the fact she'd been forced to have sex countless times over the past five years, she craved it with Mason as if she'd been celibate all that time. And maybe, in a way, she had been. She sighed. So what if Mason was right? While she'd abhorred the vampire inflicting it on her, being restrained and commanded to serve him may have capitalized on something that belonged to her, not Raithe, making her feel as if she was betraying herself. Raithe had destroyed her self-esteem, her self-confidence. He'd caused her to hate herself in a way that had made the wasting disease eating at her skin feel almost deserved.

She swallowed, the ache of tears threatening in her throat. She didn't want to hate herself. And Mason understood all that. He *was* trying to help her reclaim herself, putting her needs before his own, even as it made him a target of her anger and frustration. Maybe he was as frustrated as she was. While she was petty enough to take some satisfaction in the thought, some warmth came with it, too.

Letting the fatigue of her frenetic work marathon close in, she curled up on her side on the hay bale and thought about him. Coman whuffed into her hair from the opposite stall, and she reached up, touched his velvet nose. So gentle and fierce at once. He could kill her with his strength and power, but he didn't. Much like his Master.

Because she was pretty sure he was beyond the reach of her mind, she dared to send her thoughts to him. *I miss you, Mason. I don't understand what I feel for you, but I know you've gone off somewhere, because there's an emptiness inside me. How could I know that, if all I have are misplaced, broken emotions? What if the key to finding out what I want is linked to what you want, and you won't reach out and grasp it?*

Maybe she did need therapy. Or maybe she was just the product of a therapy-happy society. Her mind might have all the answers, if she was brave enough to look.

Her eyes drooping closed, she let herself sleep, watched over by the two horses and Jorge. The old groom came in quietly, retrieved the pitchfork and finished up the few chores, keeping a watchful eye over the troubled, hardworking young woman he was beginning to hope would be around awhile longer—and not only because she was cutting his daily workload in half.

～

In her dreams, she was Farida again, or at least moving in Farida's mind, watching Mason. He stood at the cave entrance, looking at the desert sunset from the safety of the shadows. The wind blew the open robe back, showing his bare chest and the trousers he wore beneath. Putting aside the pot she'd been cleaning, she came to his side.

"You deserve more," he said. "Soon we'll go to my family home, and this will be a distant memory."

"I hope not. It has been the happiest time of my life." Tilting her head back, she met his amber eyes, his beloved, brooding face. She wanted to make him smile. "I was raised in wealth, my lord. It brings comfort and sparkling things. But sometimes it brings a fog as well, and raises walls between hearts. I suspect a queen may wander through many, many empty rooms, wearing her jewels, and yet feel so lonely she wishes to die. I cherish this moment, for it is the one I surely have. Everything else is unknown."

"I will never let you be lonely." He drew her close, taking her inside the robe so she pressed against his bare side, her hand slipping up the back of the robe to settle on the tiger scar. "I will also weigh you down with jewels and give you many rooms. But I will be with you in all of them."

She smiled then, lifting on her toes to brush his mouth with her own. "Take me out into the night with you, my lord. Let me see it through your eyes. That is all I care about. I will not be truly happy until every breath you take is mine, every thought is shared. Until we have become one creation, so that we cannot be parted without destroying us both, as if we are one body severed into two."

~

Jessica opened her eyes. Amara was sitting cross-legged on another hay bale. As she woke, the woman's eyes crinkled. "You looked so peaceful there, I didn't want to disturb you, but Robert will be here in about an hour. I thought you might want to take a shower."

"Amara, what if my feelings are true? What if I've been falling in love with Lord Mason all along, ever since I found that first journal? Do I trust it? Do I risk it? Will he even believe it or . . . would he reject me?"

At Amara's startled look, she struggled to a sitting position, trying to shake off the fog. "Sorry. Just ignore me. I'm still waking up."

Instead, Amara shifted from her hay bale to sit beside Jess, passing a fond hand over her rumpled curls and retrieving the bill cap that had fallen to the floor during her nap. "I don't know how to answer, Jessica. If by 'falling in love,' you mean it in the traditional human sense, no vampire would admit to holding a human in equal status to himself. Human servant is the closest relationship we can achieve with one, at least in the eyes of the vampire world. That's why those of us with submissive tendencies tend to do best with them, perhaps understanding the role of Master-servant better."

Jessica shifted uncomfortably at being included in the "those of us" category, but Amara was continuing. "As I have said, he's different with you. Mason has been alone for so long, without a true human servant. I am sure he is afraid of hurting you, Jess. Don't be angry at him for trying to protect you."

"Maybe he's trying to protect himself as well."

"Perhaps." Amara gave her an even look. "Is he wrong to do so? Can you truly say you are ready to commit your life to another vampire? They don't do things by halves, Jessica. They might compel a short draught from someone for a dinner, but the humans in their homes have clearly defined roles."

"That's pretty much what he said." Jessica blew out a frustrated breath. "I get it, but I swear, it's like being a mule and having this really pretty carrot dangled in front of your nose and then jerked away, every time you've made up your mind what you want to do with it."

Amara chuckled. At Jessica's narrow glance, she shook her head. "I'm sorry. That was an interesting . . . visual."

Jessica felt her mouth relax into a tentative smile. "I wasn't intending a sexual reference."

"Which made it all the more amusing." Amara gave her upper arm a gentle rub. "If you decide you truly want him, then I think Lord Mason will be hard-pressed to deny you. You will leap for that carrot, and no matter how high he holds it, you'll climb up his body to get it." Laughter flitted through her beautiful dark gaze. "Though he is formidably stubborn himself, particularly when he thinks he's doing the honorable thing."

Jessica mulled it over. "Where is he? He's not here. I know that."

When Amara's face shuttered, Jessica's stomach flooded with alarm. "Amara, where did he go?"

"He left for Berlin last night. He's meeting with the Council about you." Amara caught her arm when Jessica would have jumped up. "You're safe, Jessica. You have nothing to fear. He will never turn you over to them."

"But what if they come here? What if—"

"He will not permit that. If the worst happens, he will notify us. We already have the arrangements to take you to another safe location. But Lord Mason is doing his utmost to get you exonerated for your actions so that won't be necessary."

"So why didn't he tell me he was going?" Jessica tried to calm her jumping stomach. "Never mind. I know the answer to that. Damsel in distress again. Damn him."

"He didn't tell me to deny you the truth if you asked his whereabouts, but he didn't want you to worry. Consider this, Jess." Amara squeezed her shoulders. "If the Council pardons you, the choices you make from that point forward will be based on your own wishes, whatever those choices are."

Jessica swallowed. "But will I ever know what those wishes are, Amara? Will I ever be able to trust myself?"

Amara's gaze filled with sympathy as she lifted Jessica's face with a light finger along her cheek. "From what I have seen of you, Jessica Tyson, I say yes. A resounding yes." The sincerity of her smile flooded Jessica with warmth. "The mind is complex, but it is easily derailed. The heart is very consistent. If you can learn to separate the two, I think you'll have your answer. At least which path you most want to follow."

"And if it dead-ends?"

"It is still the choice of the heart." Amara shrugged and rose, drawing Jessica up. She guided her in several dance steps around the barn, winning a reluctant smile from Jess, while the horses watched quizzically. "We don't live life by being fainthearted. A long time ago, I left behind the life I had merely because a handsome Frenchman swore that he saw his entire life in my gaze."

At Jessica's incredulous look, she laughed. "It was definitely a decision of the heart. Believe me, I'd been exposed to beautiful men before, so it wasn't that. In Enrique's gaze, I saw truth, destiny, things I couldn't define with my mind. In fact, my mind was overflowing like a volcano with all the reasons it was totally absurd for me to agree to go anywhere with this virtual stranger." She spun outward, came back in and guided Jess under her arm. "But my heart told me to go, and I never regretted it, though for quite some time I was fearful of my choice. The mind is a clever impostor. It can imitate the heart, lead you astray. But if you strain to listen to the heart over the machinations of the mind, it will never fail you."

Jessica slowed to a sway, thinking. Amara linked their fingers and they moved together like reeds, back and forth, back and forth. Then Jess looked up. "Amara, when Robert first came, I had an idea for my design, but it was different. If I wanted to do that instead, could Robert do it today anyway? And will he be angry?"

Amara pressed her palms flat against Jess's, holding a mirror pose with her. "He's an artist. They're all temperamental. But perhaps"—her studied look disappeared, replaced with a sly smile—"given Robert's preferences, Enrique will convince him for us. Are you sure?"

"Yes. No. Yes." Jessica took a deep breath. "*Yes*. Though I may regret this."

"Or you may not."

Right, Jess thought. Which was even more terrifying.

≈

As predicted, Robert expressed his irritation in dramatic French fashion. However, through his tirade, which Jess watched with trepidation, Enrique employed charming remarks and smiles, even some blatant flirting and innuendoes that had her eyes widening.

Regardless, it achieved the desired result. The tattoo artist disappeared, muttering, to cloister himself in one of Mason's many rooms and work out the new design, indicating he would be back in several hours. Accordingly, Amara thought it prudent to have Jess in place a half hour before that, to avoid delaying the man further.

So now Jess found herself lying on her stomach on a massage table set up by the indoor pool, looking out the glass windows toward the forest and a small sliver of ocean. Robert's case of inking tools was on a side table, waiting for his use. A small fridge was brought in, which she assumed held drinks to replenish them as needed.

Despite Robert's preferences, rationality had nothing to do with her memories, so she was glad for Amara's presence. She was completely nude beneath the light covering, since the scars followed her spine from nape to tailbone. As the woman adjusted the sheet over her shoulder to keep out the draft, Jess couldn't help the quiver of nerves.

"I'm here," Amara said, for perhaps the third time.

"I know," Jess said. Turning her head, she pressed her cheek to the table. Amara sat back in a wicker chair, her bare feet drawn up beneath her, toes unconsciously pointed, like a graceful ballet dancer. "I'm glad."

It was perhaps the first time she'd expressed to Amara something approaching a frail trust, and she was gratified by the woman's warm look. How long had it been since she'd had a female friend?

Amara pulled the chair closer and enclosed Jess's willing hand in her slim-fingered one. "Lord Mason called me a little while ago."

"Oh?" It sent a beam of light through her fears. "What did he say?"

"He asked how we all were, particularly you. He said you must stop overdoing it in the barn, or he will fire Jorge, because he won't waste three grooms when only two are needed. You will be responsible for turning an old man out onto the street."

"Ass," Jess muttered.

"He was concerned for you," Amara added, chuckling. "I told him you were fine. He also wanted me to tell you . . . your family is safe."

Jessica's eyes popped open and she jerked up from the massage table, heedless of her nudity. As she scrambled to a sitting position, she grabbed Amara's hand again. "What?"

One-handed, Amara helped her guide the sheet back around her upper body, retaining her modesty, then stroked Jess's hair back with an understanding, gentle touch. "He knew you were worried about them. So he checked and found they're all alive and well, and quite oblivious to the existence of vampires. They still believe they lost one of their daughters to a car wreck in Rome five years ago."

"So the Council didn't go after them to find me. I was so afraid . . ."

"No." Amara shook her head. "The Council is very careful about their interactions with the human world, Jess. When they hunted you, they did check out your family. They have been monitored throughout your disappearance, but you were smart enough to give the Council no reason to involve them. It was quite obvious they believed you were dead."

Her relief at hearing her family was alive was shadowed by the meaning behind that statement. A family in grief . . . Her mother.

"They had your sister and brother." Amara, ever intuitive, held her grip on Jessica's hand. "While I imagine that cannot replace a lost child, I'm certain it has helped."

"Oh, God . . ." Jessica crumpled back down to the table, her cheek against the cool surface again. She drew her hands tight against her breast, her erratically pounding chest, as Amara ran a soothing hand over her back. "I stopped hoping or wondering, because there was nothing I could do to save them. At certain times, I was sure he'd done it, merely because he could, but he wouldn't have been able to keep that to himself. He would have enjoyed telling me too much. Then, after I killed him, I worried—if they were still alive—that they would be tortured to find me, or killed by Raithe's fledglings in retribution. I couldn't do anything to protect them. All I could do was to stay away and hope like hell they were left alone. All those years, I knew, if they were harmed, it would be my fault. Like Jack. I almost didn't want to know. How cowardly is that?"

"Jessica." Amara touched her face. Jessica realized more of the endless tears were leaking out of her eyes. "You may very well get to see your family again."

"I can't hope for that. God, Amara—I couldn't even think about whether they were alive or dead. I can't . . . I mean, it would be beyond my dreams." To be in her mother's arms, feel her father's awkward touch on her hair, hug her younger sister and brother. They'd both be in college now. "I wanted so much to call them, so many times. Just to hear my mom's voice on the answering machine . . . I—I . . . j-just couldn't bear it . . ."

"Shhh . . ." Amara was blotting her eyes with a tissue, but Jess couldn't hold in the painful ache in her chest.

"I've got to sit up again." When she did, Amara was there, enclosing her in her arms, letting her cry it out. It had been so hard to bury those fears, accept the helplessness, blocking out what someone like Raithe could do to her family. More than once, he'd threatened to torture her until she offered him her mother's life to get him to stop. They'd never reached that point, but it had been another fear he'd cultivated in her, in a garden of terrors.

As she tried to get her emotions under control, another thought brought a renewed flood. Mason had asked about her family. He'd done it without her knowledge, preventing an agony of suspense and terror. Even the way Amara had approached it now, soothing and quietly inserting it in the conversation, had kept her emotional response limited to regret and relief.

Despite the confusion of her thoughts about Lord Mason and vampires, she was ready to hope, more than ever before, that she was lucky to have him on her side. If nothing else, she no longer harbored any doubts about the design change.

"I think we are at last ready. Unless she's changed her mind *again*." As if on cue, Robert's long-suffering tone reached her. He came into the pool area, shuffling his drawings. His expression transformed as he took in her tears, how she was held in Amara's embrace. "What has happened? Amara, you didn't tell her I refused, did you? Look, *ma cherie*, I have done your beautiful design. Look here."

Jessica was taken aback, though not in a bad way, as Robert rushed to her side, tossed the design to the table and took out a handkerchief to pat at her eyes. "There will be none of this. Whatever you want, *cherie*, it's yours. You want the Sistine Chapel on your back, it will be so. I am Michelangelo reborn."

That made her laugh, and as she saw the crinkle around his sapphire eyes, she knew that had been his plan. "I'm all right," she said.

And she was. She was all right. Raithe had tortured her, broken her mind, again and again, but he hadn't broken her spirit. He hadn't broken her. Maybe Amara was right. Maybe the heart safeguarded truth like hidden treasure when the mind was broken, and all the mind had to do was find it again.

Deep in her soul, Jessica Tyson knew what she wanted. As unlikely as it seemed, as fraught with peril and stupidly impulsive as every brain cell told her it was. But she'd gone down far more frightening roads than this one, with no hope at all. For the first time in a very long time, she allowed herself a spark of hope, allowed herself to believe the choice she was making was truly hers.

Amara had picked up the top paper and was staring at the design she'd chosen. The servant looked up, met Jessica's eyes. Amara didn't smile, but something powerful and reassuring emanated from her as she cupped Jessica's face, leaned in and kissed her mouth.

"Yes," she said. "This is perfect."

~

When she readjusted herself for Robert, she realized the purpose of the portable refrigerator. Given the reason for the tattoo design, she should have remembered—vividly—that scars on a third-marked human servant disappeared unless the wounds were mixed with the vampire Master's blood. Though she'd been only second-marked with Raithe and therefore could still scar on her own if the wound was grievous enough, he hadn't taken any chances. When he stripped the skin from her back, he'd marked her with his blood, and it had burned like acid.

A panic attack surged to life at the thought, while Robert prepared his needles and took the small vials of blood out of the fridge. Mason's blood. The panic was replaced by another feeling, not exactly unpleasant, as she imagined Mason drawing it from his body for her, for this. Reaching out, she touched the lip of the now open vial, enough to get a drop, brought the finger back to her mouth and tasted Mason.

"Jessica?" She shifted her gaze to Robert and noted he'd lifted a different vial and syringe. "Lord Mason wants you sedated during the procedure, so you will feel no pain."

She shook her head. "No, I want to be awake."

"With his blood, it's going to be quite painful." Amara's hand touched her head.

"I know. But that's okay. I want to feel it. I'm not afraid." She turned her face so she could look up at the other woman. "I know he told you to make me, but he did it so I wouldn't feel afraid or hurt too much. I promise, if either of those things happens, I'll ask you for the sedative. Please. Let me have this choice."

Amara's gaze rose, obviously meeting Robert's over her body. "Let's respect her decision on this, Robert. I'll take the consequences if Lord Mason is displeased."

Shallow breaths, shallow breaths. As Jess heard the whir of the needles being tested, she gripped the metal table frame beneath the cushioning. A burr in the steel cut into her finger.

The cuffs on her wrists and around her throat warmed, sending their intertwined strands of pleasure and reassurance, a mild electrical jolt of rebuke. Her lips curved. Even better than sedation. It reminded her of his hand in her hair, his mouth so close to her throat. *I will demand your surrender* . . .

There were two ways to surrender. One was by coercion, as Raithe had done. Taking her by brutal force, threatening those she loved, subjecting her to unspeakable pain and humiliation. The other way was by willing desire, knowing being enthralled to a particular Master held something that could not be found somewhere else. A fulfillment, and oddly, a tranquil peace. She saw it in Enrique and Amara, and though she'd never experienced it directly, the understanding of it was there, in a culmination of things. The activation of her restraints, the design she'd chosen, the choice Amara let her have.

She tried it again, pressed her finger against the sharp edge, a patient administering her own morphine, a tiny, secret dose of pain followed by pleasure. As the shiver went through her body again, she imagined his touch, comforting and demanding at once.

Amara rubbed Jess's shoulder. "I'm going to fold back the sheet for Robert. Are you ready?"

Jessica nodded. She heard Robert draw in a breath. While she'd sketched what was there, this was the first time he'd seen the reality of it. *Please don't ask me, don't ask me* . . .

"The world is a terrible place, *cherie*," he murmured at last. His gentle fingers lighted on the center scar. The emotion pouring from his voice wasn't sympathy, but rather cold outrage. "If whoever did this is not dead, I hope to God that Lord Mason leaves no strip of skin on his cowardly body."

If Raithe still lived, she believed Mason would have done exactly that. She'd seen it in his face, more than once, when he'd tapped her memories. As gratified as she was by that, she wanted more than his vengeful honor toward a damsel in distress.

As Robert bent to his task, began to wipe her down with a

cleansing solution, she turned her head back toward Amara with an expectant look.

"Yes, love?" Amara leaned forward. "Have you changed your mind?"

Jessica shook her head. Letting go of the table on the nonburred side, she threaded her fingers into the beautiful fall of Amara's tresses, enjoying the pleasure of touching it, almost as much as she enjoyed Amara's pleased expression when she offered the spontaneous affection.

"The night we go to the club, I'll need help, getting ready."

She might not be sure what she wanted long term yet, but she was quite sure what she wanted short term. And she wasn't going to wait for it anymore. For five long years she'd waited for her life to change, until she'd given up that it would ever happen. She wasn't going to waste any more of it agonizing.

When Amara nodded with a knowing look, Jess closed her eyes and let Robert take her a step closer to owning her life again. Or having the ability to give it to whomever she chose.

20

Mason rubbed his eyes. "I hate politics," he stated emphatically. "All politicians should die lingering, torturous deaths. Ants should gnaw living flesh from their bones."

Lord Brian, barricaded by racks of test tubes and microscopes, glanced up from his notes. A faint smile crossed his usually serious features. "Then you have placed yourself in a masochistic position, my lord. Taking over in Lady Lyssa's capacity, and now challenging Council law regarding human servants who take the lives of their Masters. However, I still don't understand why you'd want to know about our Cleves research." He nodded to a sheaf of papers. "If the girl's Master is dead and she wasn't third-marked, research on reversing the third mark wouldn't be relevant."

"I third-marked her to save her life."

"Oh." Lord Brian considered that. "And you do not wish to keep her for your own. Understandable. Keeping a servant who'd staked her previous Master could be discomfiting, to say the least. You'd feel compelled to stay in her mind constantly, afraid she might get in a pique and stake you for a glass of wine demanded at the wrong moment."

At a delicate cough from the other end of the room, Brian sent a narrow look toward Debra, his research assistant and third-marked servant. "I'm sure that was lab dust."

"Of course, my lord." She sent him a beatific smile and bent to her work again.

"That's not why I'm interested," Mason snapped. He slid onto one of the stools across from the vampire scientist. "She deserves a choice. She didn't choose this life."

He waved a hand at Brian's raised brow. His annoyance wasn't with the scientist. As Enrique had predicted, word had leaked out, and the halls were crawling with the fifteen made vampires Raithe had sired. While, in recent years, the Council had severely curtailed the practice of making vampires, it was a few decades too late, in Mason's opinion. Made vampires were notoriously more volatile, with far less impulse control.

Mason understood that the incidence of born vampires was dwindling, so population concerns were not entirely unjustified. Still, he didn't see that any vampire needed more than a dozen "off-spring," particularly when it seemed they didn't have enough brain cells between them to constitute one intelligent being.

Mason gestured to the papers. "What does the name mean?"

Debra lifted her head. "Cleves, after Anne of Cleves, the wife Henry VIII divorced after six months because she was too ugly." A smile touched her lovely pink mouth. "He thought she looked like a horse."

"Debra came up with the name for the serum. Clever, if a bit impudent." Brian's eyes glinted, but his gaze lingered on the slim nape of his assistant as she measured a viscous substance from a beaker. It reminded Mason that Brian was still fairly young. Debra was likely the first servant the born vampire had chosen without his parents' input.

However, while Brian was not yet a century old yet, his dedication to scientific inquiry for their kind, begun when he was little more than a teenager, had led to an entire division of the Council's headquarters being committed to his research. He was now spearheading at least eight different projects, handled by a variety of like-minded vampires, their servants and even some humans carefully recruited from the scientific community, an unprecedented step.

"Can you tell me how it works in a way I'll understand?" Mason's dry tone brought the younger vampire's attention back to him. Brian slanted him a grin.

"Probably not. Suffice it to say, we use different composites to remove the three different marks, essentially washing the blood clean of the vampire's presence. No bond left between him and the human. So far it has shown guarded success in the cell modeling, but it will only be effective on third-marks during their first ten years." Brian frowned suddenly at something in his notes, lifted a test tube to the light and made another note. Mason waited through several minutes of scribbling. Debra glanced up a few minutes later and cleared her throat, a faint amusement in her expression.

Brian's gaze came up, and Mason realized the male had gotten lost in his research again and forgotten he was even there.

"How soon can it be used, Lord Brian?" He couldn't help the edge in his voice, but since it focused the other vampire's attention, he didn't regret it.

"Oh, very soon. It took some time to get the Council's agreement for the test, but your interest has come at an opportune time. My two volunteers and their Masters are en route to Berlin."

"Good. I suppose you don't have any idea when the Council will sanction its usefulness, if it works?"

Brian lifted a shoulder, a shadow crossing his handsome face. "Unfortunately, you are the first to see the usefulness. Most of the Council believes an impetuously marked servant should be killed, to protect our world. However"—he brightened—"I have a theory, based on the mind-link between vampires. I believe it's possible that the vampire Master or Mistress could impose a memory block by tapping into that region of the brain before the serum is administered. Debra and I have been working up possibilities, and if the Masters coming are willing, we're going to try it. I don't see how the Vampire Council could oppose its use then, if we're successful."

"Hmm." Mason propped his crossed arms on the counter. "So the servant would remember nothing."

"Nothing."

"And if that's unsuccessful, do you think putting the servant down is the best course?"

Brian lifted his head, met Mason's gaze. While not the most physically impressive vampire, he wasn't fainthearted, and Mason appreciated that in him. His hesitation appeared to be due to careful consideration. "I'm not sure," he admitted. "The scientist in me is often far more interested in the challenge of doing the impossible than the implications of overcoming that challenge. I leave that to the politicians, such as yourself." That smile twisted his lips again.

"Careful, boy," Mason growled. "Or I'll snap you like one of those test tubes."

"I don't fear you, Lord Mason." Brian gave him an arch look, reminding Mason as well how often the two of them had communicated during the volatile period when Jacob, Lady Lyssa's former servant, was transitioning to his new powers. "I know I'm useful to you."

"Yes, but my temper has been known to exceed my good sense." Mason settled back on the stool. "What's the background of the two volunteers?"

"We were very fortunate. Their marking was an impetuous decision made by a pair of forty-year-old vampires who hunt together. Now their Masters no longer want them. They were contemplating the termination solution, but they were open to another option, if presented, and came to the Council for guidance. The humans are willing, for of course this may be their only chance to get out of this alive."

"Half of our kind need babysitters," Mason muttered. "Or an ethics committee."

"To promote the façade that we're civilized, the same way humans pretend to be?"

Mason studied Brian's dispassionate expression. "A cynical scientist."

Creating a new slide, Brian shrugged. "Cynics and optimists both consider themselves realists, my lord. Perception is everything. At your age, I expect there are very few methods of brutality you haven't seen inflicted by the strong upon the weak."

Remembering Jessica, the marks on her back, the scars on her mind, Mason's fingers tightened on the counter. She'd gotten the tattoo yesterday. He remembered how she'd said she didn't want him there. Or rather, she did, but she didn't. He should have been there.

"I've studied the mythos of religions," Brian continued. "The

Genesis tree of the knowledge of good and evil was of particular interest to me. At some point, the first humanoid life form took a step
out of the natural order, toward the wells of knowledge beyond
survival and instinct. They couldn't resist exploring them, because
that is how our brains are wired. Whatever that first humanoid
embraced—call it evil symbolized as a serpent or whatever you
wish—it infected us. The shadow companion of our so-called advanced intelligence is the temptation of sadism, a compulsion the
nonhumanoid world does not seem to experience . . . except as an
aberration. Or as the victims of it."

Brian paused as Debra brought him her results. Mason watched
their heads bend together over the data. As she murmured something to him about vectors and isotopes, her hand naturally rested
on his thigh. Leaning over him, she pulled a sheet of paper closer to
point something out. He nodded, pursed his lips and ran a casual
palm down her back, lingering on her hip. "Try this run again." He
indicated something on the sheet. "Use the control group this
time."

She nodded, glanced briefly toward Mason and retreated. All
servants knew the potential to be shared with another vampire was a
courtesy their Master or Mistress might offer, even in an unusual
setting such as this. Mason suspected not many vampires were
tempted, though, due to the lack of comfortable places to sit, let alone
recline. And this lab was a reminder of the weaknesses they faced, as
well as the strengths. It was not a place to indulge sensual pleasures,
at least not for him.

Watching the two of them together, however, he suspected this
was their second home. There likely wasn't a surface where Brian had
not exercised a vampire's carnal needs on his pretty assistant and
servant. Why did the thought irritate him, like a deep, recurring itch
he wanted to scratch but couldn't reach? Or worse, as if he knew that
scratching it wouldn't ease the cause of the abrasion?

Turning his attention back to Mason, Brian added, "I'm not as
cynical as I appear, Lord Mason. Vampires acknowledge their need
for power and control more honestly than humans do. They embrace it, give it outlets. Humans still try to pretend their core nature

256   JOEY W. HILL

is that of some peaceful guru sitting on top of a mountain, calling out 'ohms' to the sky. While it is something to strive for, at least vampires recognize it is a highly disciplined state, contrary to our true natures, not a route back to them."

Mason gave him a grim smile. "Know thyself."

Brian nodded. "Exactly. Anyhow, to more practical matters. If effective, the serum would be viable for use in less than a month, but it will depend on Council. Unless I can figure out a memory block, they are not likely to endorse it."

Mason studied the vials again. "Brian, have you ever employed magical systems in your work?"

The vampire scientist paused. Even Debra straightened and turned. Brian's brow furrowed. "It is not beyond the realm of possibility. I have on occasion sought counsel from wizards, witches and shamans who practice in a discreet way in human society. I did not clearly state my nature, of course. It would be difficult, therefore, to seek their input on this."

"Hmm. There's one who is aware of our existence. His ancestor grandfather taught me some rudimentary things several centuries ago, and we made a pact. He is a powerful wizard." Mason raised his gaze to Brian. He was not in the habit of revealing his past, or for that matter, his present, to anyone, but this was important. He steeled himself against the invasive curiosity reflected in the other man's face. "I helped deliver an old enemy into his hands, and he agreed to be of assistance to me if I had need." Turning Brian's notebook around, he jotted down Derek Stormwind's name, the way to reach him and the word Brian would need to gain his help. "Call him, tell him what you seek. He knows a great deal about manipulation of time."

"He can turn time back?"

"No." Mason felt an old, dull pain. "But he can give you the ability to forget, if you have the desire to do so."

Brian's sharp eyes were on his face, but fortunately, the arrival of the Council liaison saved Mason from any further questions. Or Brian from having an appendage removed for asking. The young woman paused in the lab doorway and bowed to Mason. One of Lord Uthe's attendants, he recalled. "Lord Mason, the Council is ready to discuss your request."

"Good luck," Brian offered as Mason rose. Mason glanced at the papers again.

"If it works, and you gain Council agreement, I will want a dose for Jessica."

"Of course. But human physiology can be inconsistent, so I'll need some specifics on her beforehand. Have your servant e-mail mine and Debra will tell them what I need. Or you could bring her here for examination."

"Enrique or Amara will contact you." Mason headed for the door. He sure as hell wasn't bringing Jess here. The made vamps of Raithe's, here to champion him posthumously, were one thing. But there were others here, older vampires adamant that rogue servants should be summarily executed. Their attitude toward him had been that of tense courtesy, but there was no doubt this was a hostile environment.

"My lord." The woman looked hesitant, sharpening Mason's gaze upon her. "My lord Uthe also wanted to inform you ahead of time that the Council has agreed Lord Raithe's defenders could be present for your audience."

She stepped back into the hallway before she could stop herself, a reaction to his expression, he was certain. Allah strike them all down, he was not exceptional at diplomacy on a good day. Uthe wasn't known for pulling underhanded tricks like this, so he suspected this was Belizar's doing, using his right-hand vice-chancellor as the fall guy for his own trickery, inciting Mason's temper.

Mason looked back at the scientist, who had likewise stilled, though he was watching him with less tension than the human women. "Sometimes, Brian, I think we underutilize those sadistic tendencies. Wiping up the floor with the blood of dissenters is far less painful than trying to reason with them. For me, at least."

Grim humor flickered through Brian's gaze. "Another reason I'm not anticipating running into you on top of a mountain chanting, my lord."

Mason grunted and turned his attention back to the young woman. She'd gone pale as a sheet. "I was speaking in jest," he said impatiently. "By Allah, the lack of humor in this place is as stifling as all the hot air spouting through it."

As he brushed past her, he thought of Jessica. Except when she was too tightly clasped in the clutches of her fears, she never hesitated to make a wry remark or take an impudent jab at him with that sharp tongue of hers. Whether it was a coping mechanism or not, it was one of her braver ones.

When he'd touched base with Amara tonight, she'd reported that Jess was pleased with Robert's work. Some of his irritation was replaced with something more pleasurable when he remembered what else Amara said. "She demanded—her words, my lord—that as you fly home and come into range of our minds again, you abstain from looking into hers. She wants you to get the full effect of the design she chose, in person."

"Women," he responded. "You are all alike in your vanity."

"As males are in their arrogance." Amara had a smile in her voice. "She misses you, my lord. She wants you to come home soon."

"She is all right? Her nightmares—"

"You mistake me, my lord," Amara cut in gently. "It is not what I observed, though it is obvious enough. She asked me to tell you that."

It had been ridiculous how much those words meant to him, the spear of reaction that went through his chest. He was nearly nine hundred years old. But though he made himself go over all the dampening things he'd told himself about Jessica ever since their first twinge of connection, it didn't change the strength of his desire to see her, his growing impatience with being here.

Stay levelheaded. You are guaranteeing her future. What Brian was working on could conceivably sever every tie she had to the vampire world, and truly allow her to live her life as she wished. He would of course make sure she was watched over, protected, but if Brian's idea worked, or Derek was able to help him, she wouldn't remember Mason at all.

Or Raithe, he reminded himself. He could take away her nightmares.

I miss you, too, Jessica. Recalling the sensual hip movements she'd practiced in the ballroom, he wondered if she'd practiced any more. Or taken Hasna for a canter on the beach. Followed the landscapers around and asked them questions about the flowers, or gotten on her knees to help them plant or trim. Easy things, the things that added up to a contented, happy life.

He had to do this for her. Damn it, he wished Lyssa was here. She was the one trained as queen and diplomat, after all. As he had the thought, he cursed his shortsightedness. Of course. *Who better to help?* He wished he'd thought of it earlier, but then he hadn't known he was being summoned before an audience more likely to raise his homicidal instincts than his diplomatic ones, meager though the latter were.

Stopping, he gestured the escort to go on. "Tell the Council I will be there in a few moments. I need to make a call."

Stepping into a side room, which appeared to be a small, unoccupied study, he removed his rarely used cell phone and took a bracing breath. Hit one of the five permanent numbers he'd had Enrique program into it, since he had little patience with such things.

The world is outgrowing you, old vampire. Perhaps you need someone young to keep you on your toes. He curled his lip at his subconscious as the phone rang an ocean away. It was picked up almost immediately, the male voice on the other end filled with amusement.

"Okay, when's the end of the world happening, and do we have time to fix dinner before it happens?"

"Jacob." Mason allowed himself a smile, already feeling a loosening in his chest. "I need to talk to your Mistress, and unfortunately my time is very limited."

"Hold on a second. She owes you. She lost the flip for diaper duty, so you just saved her from the consequences."

"*Lyssa* is changing diapers?"

"A cardinal from the local diocese is rushing over even as we speak, to record the miraculous event—ow."

Mason grinned, imagining what blow Jacob had absorbed. While he didn't count many male vampires as friends, Jacob was the exception. Though Jacob had acquired most of Lyssa's remarkable strength and speed on the bloody, terrible day she converted him to a vampire, Mason still had difficulty thinking of him as a nonhuman, probably because Jacob retained much of the casual mannerisms of his mortal roots.

Jacob's turning by his Mistress had been an act censured by vampire law. While she'd been pardoned for it, given that she'd also saved the Council's asses in the same evening, she wasn't welcome to sit as the Council advisor anymore. The main reason for that was because she'd more fully embraced the Fey half of her lineage since then, and the vampire world was largely purist.

Through Mason's efforts and those of her allies, the Council was softening in their opinion toward her again. Allies such as Lord Brian, who had worked with Jacob after the extraordinary event and whose father was a Region Master with great pull with the Council, and Lord Uthe, who was on the Council and a faithful advocate of Lyssa. While their support was vital, she'd also since given birth, and born vampires were too rare to be snubbed. He hadn't yet seen the child, but he understood she'd had a boy.

"What is it, Mason?"

It was the same imperious tone, wrapped up in a sultry voice that went straight to a man's cock. He winced as she huffed out a soft chuckle.

"One of these days, Mason, you will visit often enough to remember our minds are linked. And that my range is far greater than most."

"My apologies, my lady."

"Accepted. Explain what you need."

It made it easier, giving it to her in his mind, concisely summarized. Jessica Tyson. Rescued, given three marks, and now he was trying to get Council to pardon her. How should he approach?

"Was her Master's death accidental?"

"Opportunistic. He kidnapped her and forced her to serve him, Lyssa. And not service in the way we honor it. She was tortured for five years. I've seen things in her mind that . . ." Pausing, he gave her brief flashes of Jess's memories.

"Great Goddess." The hollow shock in Lyssa's voice reminded him, too late.

"My deepest apologies, Lyssa. I didn't think. You and Rex—"

"Rex did nothing that I did not allow him to do to me." She cut across him sharply, shutting the avenue down, though Mason cursed himself for his own insensitivity. It seemed his desire to help Jessica had shut out everything else of consequence.

"Rex broke my heart," Lyssa continued, in a more dispassionate tone. "But I gave it to him. This girl gave nothing. It was all taken. Now, make sure the Council is aware of this. Lead with it, and get Uthe on your side first. If he can bring Belizar along, the others will mostly follow. Three are very conservative on the issue of servants killing their Masters. All the more reason you need to convince them of the uniqueness of the situation, and, most importantly, that she will not become a rallying point for other human servants to murder their Masters. Emphasize how exceptional a situation this is.

"She managed it with Raithe only because she was *extremely* lucky. There is no exaggeration in that. In any other reality, she would be dead. And Mason"—her tone sharpened again—"do not lose your temper. That will not serve you in this instance. The more emotional you seem, the worse it will go. Do you have feelings for this girl?"

"I don't see how—"

"You certainly do. Goddess, I should have known. Another rescued maiden, and once you've risked all to save her, you'll go back to ground like a mole again."

"It's not like that," Mason snapped and then cut himself off, realizing he'd just underscored her point.

At the pause on the other end of the line, he was uncomfortably aware she might be plumbing things in his mind he himself didn't want to face. "Hmm," she said at last. "We'll see. I'll believe it when I don't see you brushing cave dirt off your backside. Regardless, you must push any feelings you have for her aside. They have no place in that chamber. Your approach should address Raithe's lack of judgment only. The reason she should be pardoned must logically benefit the vampire community. The benefit to her is secondary. Do you understand?"

"I do. You're still a pain in the ass."

"At least my head is not stuck up mine."

He bit down on a retort. But at the sound of a squall, followed by Jacob's deep murmur of reassurance, warmth swirled in his chest, replacing the annoyance. "Are you going to bring that child to meet me sometime soon?"

"Anytime you wish."

"You're always welcome, Lyssa." He paused, thinking ahead. "Actually, how about very soon? If things don't go well here—and with my gift for diplomacy, we know that's likely—I'll need to work out a way to protect her. Your resources might help."

"So if the Council rules against you, you won't turn her over."

He knew she could read it from his mind, and in these echoing halls, he had the presence of mind not to say it aloud.

As long as I have life to defend her, she will never be harmed again. The unexpected surge of determined rage, the bloodlust that accompanied it, blocked out everything else for an unsteady moment. Lyssa was silent on the other end as he got a handle on it. "I wish you were here."

"Mason, you can do this." Rather than soothing or encouraging, her tone was reassuringly impatient. "You are far more adept at politics than you wish to admit, and you know it. This girl's life is at stake, and you are more than capable of saving it. Don't doubt yourself."

"Yes, my lady." A smile tugged at his mouth when she continued briskly.

"Fine, then. We will come, if you don't mind us bringing Lady Daniela. She and her servant Devlin are visiting."

"All right. I'll send a plane for you. I'll have Enrique transfer you the itinerary."

"Good. Your staff should set up a nursery for us." A hesitation, and then, "Am I seeing this correctly in your mind? You found her in Farida's tomb?"

"Yes."

He heard Lyssa murmur something to Jacob, and then she came back to the phone. "We'll be there in a few days. Watch your step, and *don't lose your temper.*"

She clicked off. Like most monarchs, Lyssa saw no reason to continue beating a point once she'd made it. And of course she had diapers to change. Shaking his head at the irony of it, Mason headed toward Council chambers. As he strode the corridors, he relaxed his shoulders and worked on a mantra to keep him calm. *Ripping out throats won't help Jessica. Bashing in heads does not change minds.*

Damn it, he wished Lyssa was at his side. Of course, last time she was here, she'd threatened to kill them all, including him, a prime example of "Do as I say, not as I do." Holding that reassuring and amusing thought, he stepped into the chamber.

21

Two hours later, he decided there was no virtue in restraint. Unless by restraint, one meant applying shackles, followed by a great deal of bludgeoning.

The most outspoken of the vampires Raithe had sired was Trenton. The youthful vampire was vaguely familiar to Mason, though he'd not yet placed him. He was backed by a handful of cohorts with expressions of smirking contempt behind an aura of righteous indignation. As Trenton rebutted Mason's comments, or responded to Council inquiries, their burning eyes fixed upon Mason, tips of fangs showing in an aggressive way that revealed their immaturity. Probably not one of them, including Trenton, was more than sixty years old, but given the gravity of the matter, their plea wouldn't be summarily brushed aside.

Keeping his gaze off Raithe's proponents as much as possible, Mason explained in an even tone the details of her kidnapping, the death of her fiancé, the faking of her death for the local papers, Raithe's threat on her family. None of those was technically against vampire law, but all were considered serious lapses of judgment, due to the hazards of exposure they presented for their kind to human society.

Uthe, as well as the two less conservative Council members, reacted as Lyssa had, with distasteful shock. Belizar's expression remained unreadable, as expected. He was leader of the Council for a reason, and would give nothing away. Lady Helena was not so circumspect.

"It is an unfortunate occurrence, Lord Mason. But no matter the circumstances, the law is very clear about a human servant who takes a vampire's life."

"Yet it is such an unlikely scenario, it's a wonder we have a law about it at all, rather than dealing with it case by case," he pointed out. "In our documented history, we have had *four* instances of it. In every instance, the servant in question was forced into servitude, and suffered extremes of brutality from the vampire. Out of those four, three were third-marks who died with their Master or Mistress, so there was no one left to punish. Jessica Tyson is the only servant to *ever* survive killing her Master."

"As such, she could become an inspiration for those second-marked or even suicidal third-marked servants who harbor similar desires." That from Lord Mortimer.

Mason lifted a shoulder, making sure his attention passed over each face on the Council with equal gravity and appeal. "I like to believe, as I hope you do, that our relationship with our servants is symbiotic. Most servants who will hear of your decision have no desire to leave their Master or Mistress's service, because it was their choice. They have not been subjected to what Raithe did to Jessica Tyson."

He then relayed a select few of those atrocities. In preparation for this meeting, he'd had to sift through those visions, pick the ones he knew would have most influence on this group. It had enraged him, the idea that one type of fear and agony would be weighted more highly than another. That anger resurged now as he showed them the skinning as punishment. The repeated rapes and humiliations. The dark dungeon with the rats and spiders. The group in his peripheral vision stirred with irritation, but he kept his gaze locked on Belizar, reminding himself of Lyssa's words. *No emotion.*

Lady Helena blinked. He noted it when she swallowed, a sign of discomfort. Uthe shook his head, anger crossing his gaze. While Council usually met without their servants present, Mason knew they all enjoyed close relationships with them, as he did with Enrique and Amara. He couched his explanation of the torments in those terms, suggesting the Council imagine their own servants being so treated. When there was a muttering from Trenton and his companions, Belizar cut a sharp glance at them.

"Our right to exert our will over a human servant who has bound his or her life to ours is unquestionable," Mason continued. "They are ours to do with as we wish, but we are guided by the symbiosis I mentioned, that deep connection. As such, we are all familiar with the human mind. A mortal cannot be pushed to the point of unbearable pain and despair, and not be expected to attempt escape. That is what Jessica Tyson did. She didn't act out of retaliation, but the desire to get away from Raithe. Because, as we all know, the only way for a servant to escape her Master is to kill him.

"Most vampires *want* a strong connection with their servants. When it doesn't occur, frustration can escalate to brutality, particularly if the human is taken unwillingly, or without a reasonable comprehension of the role. While I am pleased to hear that Lord Brian is working on a way to reverse the marks chemically for these infrequent instances, it is no substitute for a vampire using good judgment."

His tone hardened. This time he cut a deliberate glance toward Trenton. "Raithe exercised deplorable judgment, and continued to compound the problem. Even had Brian's solution existed, Raithe would not have availed himself of it, because he allowed himself to be guided by the baser, more savage instincts we all possess."

It flashed through his mind again, those terrible days after Farida's death. He'd kept them safely locked away for years now, but since Jessica had come into his life, many of them had started to break free. Blood. Screams. Death.

Focus. He could almost hear the snap of Lyssa's voice, and given her uncharted range of powers, he couldn't be sure it wasn't her.

Rising from his chair, Mason moved to the center of the room, meeting Belizar's eyes for a long moment and then briefly traveling over the Council members again. He ignored Trenton and his group now, the way he'd disregard children playing around the feet of their parents. "When we claim a position of superiority over another species, we must always remember the baser instinct we, as vampires, possess. Many atrocities can be rationalized and justified. We enjoy the power we exert over our servants, and, in truth, it's a mutual pleasure. But for some vampires it becomes a destructive desire, to see how far that power extends. They take the relationship into darker realms that do not bode well for our anonymity. There must always be limits on our behavior. It is the only way we live together in a crowded world."

"So you want to turn the girl loose?" Helena's brows rose. "Her crime against her Master aside, it's dangerous for a marked servant to be loosed from our world, unsupervised."

Mason cocked his head. "This girl wants simply to be left alone, reconstruct whatever life for herself she can. Do we not owe her that?"

"We owe her nothing," Trenton snapped. "That human bitch killed Lord Raithe."

Mason wondered if Lyssa would be proud of him, the fact he stood motionless, ignoring the young whelp as if he hadn't spoken. Instead, it was Belizar who surged up from his chair, his lip curling back in a snarl.

"You will *not* speak out of turn here." His voice reverberated through the chamber, so thunderously it vibrated through the floor. "Do so again, and I will have you buried in the earth for a week."

For the first time, Mason was glad for the attack on his home that had destroyed his west wing and his landscaping. The vampire hunters had been used as a tool by a faction of mostly made vampires seeking to overthrow the Council at that gathering. Since then, the Council had demonstrated an extremely short fuse for disrespect of any kind, particularly from made vampires.

Trenton subsided with a sullen look. When the Russian vampire turned his attention back to Mason, his eyes still glinted with a hint of red. As Brian had said, the façade of civility was useful only when everyone wished to play nice. Mason wasn't sorry for it right now.

"Lord Mason, do you have anything else?"

"One more thing." Mason met Belizar's gaze, held it, knowing he was the one vampire who had to believe his next words for him to have a chance of winning Jessica's case. "I give my personal guarantee to Council that pardoning Jessica Tyson will not adversely affect our society." He paused. "If the Council will not pardon her to seek the life she wishes, forbidding any repercussions against her from our society, then I ask they allow me to keep her as my third-marked servant, living under my guardianship."

Once everything died down, he could set her up somewhere, doing whatever it was she liked. He'd buy a mansion wherever that was, and that could be her home. She'd never need to see him, but to all appearances, she'd be living as his servant. Time would pass, things would change, and she'd be all right. Eventually he would go back to his desert, his hole, as Lyssa said. After all, Amara and Enrique stayed in South America for months at a time without him, while he drew blood from the occasional oblivious Bedouin traveler who crossed his path.

It all sounded very reasonable. Except the idea of leaving Jessica alone like that didn't sit well with him at all. It was a passing feeling, he told himself. As she did better on her own, he would be bothered less by the idea.

"If Brian perfects his serum"—Lord Uthe pinned Mason with his shrewd gaze, bringing his attention back—"and finds a way to erase her memory of her time in our world, will you accept that, and allow us to handle her placement?"

"I will accept the administering of the serum, with her knowledge, but I will help with her placement. She is under my protection. That cannot change."

Damn Lord Uthe for being as smart and well informed as he was. But as he held the other male's gaze, Mason reminded himself that Lyssa had said this Council member would be his greatest ally, if he dealt with him fairly. The silence stretched out as he sensed each Council member mulling over his words.

"Lord Mason, if we disagree with you, and wish the girl brought here for justice, how will you react?" This from Belizar, asking the one thing that would expose where Mason's true loyalties lay. The Council looked toward him expectantly. *Your feelings for the girl have no place here* . . . Lyssa's words resounded in his head.

"I'd of course bring her here," he lied, "according to the Council's wishes, though I would continue to argue for a merciful judgment. We are not a compassionate species, but I believe we are a fair one.

Do not rule against her, my lords and ladies. Let her live in peace. That is all she wants."

Even above his own desires, he wanted that the most, for her. While he would, in fact, take her to the ends of the Earth to protect her from this group or any other, not only did he not want her to be a fugitive again, he wasn't sure she had the mental strength left to be one.

"Thank you." Lord Uthe nodded after a quiet moment. "I admit, I'm surprised you would capitulate to such a directive, given your adversarial stands against this Council in the past."

"I doubt you will ever find me very accommodating," Mason observed dryly, and noted he won some small smiles from the Council. Even Belizar's lips twitched. "But there is one thing that our esteemed Lady Lyssa helped me understand, though I perhaps was not as quick to understand it as the more astute minds on this Council. Every man or vampire should make an effort to obey the law, even when they disagree with it. Resistance should be reserved for things that strike at the very core of who we are. This is about a human. While I believe a grave injustice was done to her, and that she deserves to be pardoned, she is still just a human."

He paused, watching them exchange glances. The knot of Raithe supporters positioned on the left side of the room was shifting like a hive of bees about to erupt, but he knew they would stay in that tight knot as long as Belizar held sway here.

Mason thought of Jessica, crumpled on the sand, the tide bathing her legs as she wept. The fears that chased her waking moments as well as her dreams. Her wry smile, her slim hands moving capably over Hasna's mane as she braided it. Her unexpected burst of laughter as they raced over the sand on Coman's back, the clutch of her hand on his leg, the gasp of exhilarated breath.

He swept his attention over the Council once more. "But for the benefit of our species, I beg your consideration of one last point. We've devoted much time to the fate of one servant. I think it would be wise to give equal, if not more, time to improving our laws, making it illegal to force a human into the role of full servant. While I feel the punishment for breaking that law should be as proportionately harsh as the trouble it can cause, at the very least, the human should not have to pay for the vampire's folly, any more than she already has."

At the uncomfortable silence, the sharp looks from Helena and Mortimer, Mason wondered if he'd pushed it too far. But Belizar merely inclined his head. "We thank you for your time, Lord Mason. The Council will now clear the chamber to deliberate this matter."

Mason bowed. "I look forward to the Council's decision."

~

Since the Berlin site for Council operations was an ancient castle, he strolled along the parapets, desperate for the fog and cool night air after the stifling environment of the Council chambers. Bracing his palms on the stone, he gazed out over the lighted town nearby. He thought about using the cell phone again, only this time to call and speak to Jessica directly. He'd had to resist the urge to do so numerous times since he'd left, and now he wondered why he had. Why *shouldn't* he call her?

Because it was weak, and unfair to her. He knew that. Sighing, he looked down the steep wall to the clumps of shrubs below. The more he reached out to her, the more likely it was he wouldn't let her go, that he would be no better than Raithe in that regard. What would she say, if he had her on the phone? Would she tell him what she'd been doing or be terse and quiet, since the last time she'd seen him he'd thrown her out of his room, aching and unsatisfied? Of course, she'd told Amara she missed him.

He should get her a gift while he was here. He didn't know if she liked jewelry, but he knew she appreciated beauty. No, something that appealed to her interests. Perhaps a book on the archaeology of this region. That would be good.

"Why do you defend her?"

There were humans and vampires moving within and without the castle, so he'd paid only peripheral attention to them. Obviously, he needed to sharpen his senses, if he'd let this son of a sway-backed camel creep up on him. Turning to face Trenton, he saw four of his companions were with him, hostility emanating from them. A desire for violence.

All Mason's intentions to remain even-tempered shattered as Trenton's green eyes narrowed, for in that moment Mason remembered why he seemed familiar. He'd seen him in Jessica's nightmares.

Raithe had given her to Trenton when she was bloody with lash marks, so dehydrated and in pain she kept fainting. While the vampire fucked her, he'd slapped her awake, again and again, until he was done, until the blood from her nose had dripped on her breasts, painted her with crimson lines where he rutted upon her.

The images crowded in quickly now, making it clear that Trenton had been one of Raithe's most devoted sycophants. He'd wagered on the dogs as Jessica fought them for food. Helped string her arms up in chains for the stable rape, stayed to watch.

After hours of aping civility in that damned hot chamber, everything was washed in red. Mason's fangs lengthened in his mouth, preparing for this kill. He would tear flesh, immerse himself in the cleansing numbness of savagery on Jessica's behalf. Did Trenton see something in his face? His cronies certainly did, because they were backing up.

You kill him here and now, and Jessica will never be safe. Never exonerated. She will be a fugitive forever.

There was no doubt this time that the voice that exploded in his head was Lyssa's. He knew of no other vampire who could speak in another vampire's mind with the sharpness of cut glass, slashing through brain matter like butter. He almost yelped.

You're nine hundred, not a fledgling like these whelps. Control your reaction. Goddess, you need a sitter.

It was the command mixed with the exasperation that recalled him, that made him retract the fangs. Whatever happened here, Mason knew Trenton would disappear in the next month or so, never to be seen again. He'd make sure of it. While a dead vampire had to be investigated, little was done if one disappeared, for vampires were notorious for going to ground for long periods of time. Trenton was far too low on the food chain to merit a search party.

Mason didn't miss the irony of that. Once, he'd been low on that food chain himself. He, of all vampires, knew how easy it was to become the victim among vampires. But he had no problem using that to his advantage now. That, too, was the nature of a vampire. Yesterday's weakness was today's strength. He'd learned patience the hard way, taking time to strike at the opportune moment.

He forced his lips to curve, showing the now retracted fangs, knowing the moonlight was catching the red glint in his eyes, though his voice came out remarkably mild. "I defend her because it's the right thing to do. Humans cannot be underestimated."

"They are weak, puny—"

"Insignificant against our all-powerful selves. Blah, blah, blah." Mason shrugged. "Yet our human servants help us manage our bloodlust and blend into a world overrun by mortals. Abusing that relationship to the extent Raithe did is unwise. Use your mind to do your thinking, Trenton, not your hot blood. And remember you were once human yourself."

It was a deliberate insult to point to a made vampire's humbler origins. Trenton whitened with fury. Looking at this pathetic gathering of Raithe's offspring, Mason knew they hadn't had the guidance and mentoring they should have. Raithe had likely turned them, taken their new, wildly fluctuating bloodlust and created sadistic monsters. While Mason might have felt pity, they'd had a choice. Unlike a human being taken as a servant, vampire law said a human had to give his or her consent to be turned, and only *after* the Council approved the action.

The boy was stupider than most made vampires. He snarled and lunged forward. Mason couldn't be happier as he leaped to meet him.

The others closed in, but he'd already caught Trenton by the throat and slammed him against a stone turret, so hard the rock crumbled beneath the impact. The others came to a stumbling halt and spun around, realizing he'd passed them by and now had their ringleader pinned against stone twenty feet behind them.

"Stay back," he hissed. "In the time it takes you to think about crossing the ground between us, I will have killed every last one of you."

"My lord Raithe deserved better," Trenton rasped over Mason's hold, his eyes burning.

"Your lord Raithe deserved far worse, and the lot of you with him. You've lost your meal ticket. An older vampire has already taken over his properties and thrown you out." Mason bared his fangs as Trenton scowled darkly. "That's the true reason most of you are here, hoping to get scraps from another table. Figuring I'll buy you off to support my position. You severely overestimate your own value, and underestimate the Council's wisdom. Go ingratiate yourself with another rich fool."

But those words were directed to the angry vampires behind him. Now Mason brought his face close enough to Trenton's that he could see death in his eyes, the gleam on Mason's fangs. As the young vampire hissed, frightened and trying to wriggle free, Mason held him effortlessly, dropping his tone so only the boy could hear him. "For you, Trenton, that's a wasted effort. Enjoy the short life you have left."

He dropped him then. Trenton thudded to the stone, but rolled and scrambled past him, back into the ranks of his friends. As Mason turned, he wished they'd rush him so he'd have a reason to kill. But they didn't. There were a few mutters and grumbles, some foul glances, but then he was alone again beside the parapet. And still wishing he had the courage to call Jessica on the phone, like some idiot teenager.

"Ah, damn it." He retrieved the phone, furrowed his brow, then figured out how to call back the last number.

"How did it go?"

He bit off a sigh. "I hate cell phones."

Lyssa's voice was amused. "You didn't mean to call me?"

"No. I meant to call last number received, not dialed."

"Well, since you're here . . . ?" She paused.

"Thank you," he said, grudgingly. "Some of Raithe's young whelps followed me out to the castle walk. I didn't throw them off. Ah, bollocks. I should have thought of that. It wouldn't have killed them, but it would have been satisfyingly painful."

"And as I said, you need a babysitter more than Kane does."

"You allow a babysitter for your child?" He was alarmed at the thought. A vampire infant, one young enough to be passed off as someone else's, was a tempting target to infertile vampires who wanted the status a vampire child brought to them.

"Of course not. Remind me to hurt you when I see you, for thinking I'm that irresponsible. Either Jacob or I am with him at all times, but Danny and Dev have offered to give us a night out. It would be nice to go hunting, and enjoy other primal pursuits." The warmth to her tone told him she was looking toward Jacob. The yearning in his gut twisted further.

"All right. See you in a few days, where I can thank you even more properly. I need to call . . . Amara." He clicked off before Lyssa could call him a liar. Holding the phone up to the dim moonlight, he figured out how to redial his own number.

"My lord?" When he swore and turned, he found he'd made the Council attendant pale for the second time this evening. "The . . . the Council is ready to give their decision."

"Fine. I'll be down in a few minutes. Aren't you Uthe's servant?"

"I am one of his assistants, but I belong to the castle, my lord. Part of the second-marked staff that serves the Council. My name is Gretchen."

"Are you here of your free will?" When she nodded, he scowled at her. "Then learn how to mask your reaction to vampire temper. Most of us are quite irritable. Your jumpiness makes you look like prey, and vampires feel much less cranky if we've fed."

Since she went three shades whiter, his well-meaning advice obviously wasn't perceived that way. Then he heard a voice in his hand.

"Hello?"

He brought the receiver up to his ear, realizing he must have hit the dial number after all. "Jessica?"

"My lord, it sounds like you're frightening someone half to death."

"Why are you answering the phone?"

"Amara said it would be you. That you were calling back to talk to me."

He shook his head, waved Gretchen away, holding up a couple fingers to indicate he would be down in a few minutes. He waited until she departed to speak. "I wanted to check on you. I know I left rather abruptly."

"You did. Amara said you're meeting the Council."

The underlying tension in her voice was easy to read. "I am. But whatever the outcome, Jessica, you will be safe. I promise you that."

She paused a long moment. "None of us is safe, my lord."

There was a sadness to her tone now. Daylight would be waning there, and twilight was often when she felt most vulnerable, too close to her past, as if that veil between day and night held the power to call her back to Raithe's world.

"You *are* safe," he repeated. "I won't accept anything less."

"As Farida was safe?" When his mind froze, she continued, her tone thoughtful. "I'm not trying to be cruel. It's like you just said to that girl, heavy-handed though it was. You were trying to teach her what the reality of life is. We can rely on each other, we can rely on ourselves, but a certain portion of Fate is out of our hands. You reminded me of it, when you rescued me. The best thing we can do is cherish every moment of joy and safety we have and not be afraid to live our lives, no matter how long or short that is."

Easing a hip on the wall, he looked out over the lights of the distant city. He missed the sea, the rain forest. The smell of Jessica's hair and skin. He wanted to make her smile. "Heavy-handed, hmm? Maybe I should show you how heavy-handed I can be."

"You have done so in the past, my lord." He was pleased her tone changed, became prim. "You spank like a girl."

He laughed then; he couldn't help it. Allah, he missed her. "You say that only because I'm not close enough to prove you wrong."

Her voice lowered, but he heard the tremor in her words, words that drove away all humor and left him feeling far too lonely in the foggy night air. "Farida was lucky to have you for the short time she did. A lifetime wouldn't have been enough. When I leave, I will think well of you, my lord. That's something I never thought I'd say about a vampire."

"Jessica." He stood, but she'd already hung up. He wished he had Lyssa's range, enhanced by her Fey abilities, because he'd have sent thoughts to Jessica that would warm all parts of her, not merely the lovely curve of her bottom. Drive that melancholy away, convince her . . . of what? How could he send her the feelings that her words had stirred, when he didn't know what they were himself? *When I leave . . .*

"Get on with it," he muttered, pocketing the phone. "Nine hundred years old and gone stupid over a child. Go help her. Let her live her life."

22

STUDYING herself in the mirror provided in Mason's private plane, Jessica pushed down anxiety. She and Amara had worked together with the cook, who was an expert seamstress, to alter the dress, which had fit Amara's taller, more voluptuous frame, and she had to admit the results were impressive. But she wasn't used to seeing herself like this. Hell, even after two months, she was still surprised to see a healthy young woman looking back at her.

It had been a long time since she'd made herself beautiful for someone she wanted to see her that way, rather than dressing at the command of a vampire who wanted her paraded like a show dog. Of course, beyond the decision to dress up, she didn't even have a strategy. Her nebulous intentions would likely disperse like frightened birds when confronted with the reality of him. Then he'd withdraw from her again. She didn't know if that relieved her or made her want to scream.

Straightening, she laid a hand flat over her abdomen, stilling the butterflies that seemed to have razor blades for wings. Meeting her own flashing eyes, she noted the lift of her chin, the stubborn tightening of it. "You will *not* see a damsel in distress tonight, my lord."

They'd used the off-road vehicles to get to Mason's private airstrip, taking his plane to the nearby city where the club was located. Mason had called Amara two days before and let her know he was wrapping up the details in Berlin. Though he was running later than expected, he'd gallantly refused to have them reschedule the club visit. He'd told Amara he'd charter a plane to the city's airport and meet them there tonight.

He hadn't relayed the Council's decision to Amara, or asked to speak to Jessica again, not since their one and only intriguing conversation. Which meant Mason would deliver the decision in person, and he wanted Jessica to hear it first.

She wasn't overly eager to hear the decision. From the beginning, the Council had been little more than a distant concept to her. What mattered was he'd promised she'd be safe, and she wanted to believe him. Whatever the decision was, she'd manage it. But she wanted tonight just for this.

"Do you know what you're doing?" she asked her reflection, knowing her color was a little too high, her pupils too large. If nothing else, her nervousness about the tattoo she'd chosen, the way she'd dressed tonight, and thinking about how Mason would react, had helped take her mind off the kind of club they were visiting.

Enrique and Amara had both assured her the limo would be available to bring her back to the plane if things got to be too much. With its security contingent, fully stocked bar and snacks, and cable television, she'd be comfortable. There was even a rack of movies. Rifling through them, she'd wondered if they were solely for Mason's human passengers, or if he really liked *Sleepless in Seattle*. It brought a smile to her face, imagining him switching to cable, tempted by shopping network purchases or considering the plethora of male enhancement drugs.

A vampire on Viagra. Good God. A lethal weapon, for certain.

"I'd ask if you're ready, but if you get any lovelier, we'd all trip over our tongues." Amara peered in, her own breathtaking face wreathed in a smile. Surprising to Jessica, she'd abandoned her flowing and tailored garments for provocative club wear tonight. Black liquid latex pants with silver cat buckle ties down the sides showed flesh from waist to ankle. They were paired with a white silk top, cut into long strips from the high throat to the belted waistband so the curve of breast and lines of the ribs were revealed as she turned. The high throat was collared with a filigree silver slave collar, matching the design of the belt. The liquid latex was so tight and thin that when Enrique had put his hand on her hip earlier, Jessica had noted it was like closing his hand on his wife's buttock, the flesh as soft and malleable beneath his hand as it was when naked, only now polished with that slick surface layer.

"Lord Mason has called to say he's at the club, so we can head over there. He'll meet us out front. He said we've picked a popular night. There's quite a crowd."

She didn't have anything for her nervous hands, because Amara was carrying the small bag with the few toiletries they might want. Mason of course was paying for everything. So it was Amara's hands that closed over her cold, tense fists.

"I don't want to have a panic attack tonight. *I don't.*" Jessica turned pleading eyes to Amara, as if she could prevent how her own body might turn against her. Crowds of people, all of them into subjugation, suffering . . . dominance.

"Jess, shhh. You won't. Remember what Lord Mason told you, about submission?"

When Jessica shook her head, Amara rubbed a soothing thumb over her knuckles. "There is a tremendous difference between the beauty of willing submission and the horror of forced servitude. This club only permits the former, so it's like visiting a surreal, magnificent garden of aroused bodies, perfumed with their desire to please one another."

"I feel like a weed, then."

Amara smiled softly, but she shifted her touch to Jess's bare shoulders. "You *know* the difference, Jess. You may not in your head, but your heart knows. That's why you're here. I know you're ready for this. You may stumble tonight. You may even have to come back to the plane, but the very fact you chose to come this far says you believe in your ability to heal. Everything tonight is your choice. *Everything.* Don't let Raithe take that away from you."

She remembered her thought when looking in the mirror only minutes ago. She wasn't a damsel in distress. Raithe was dead. *She'd* killed him.

Everything would be her choice. Even if her choice was to surrender to Mason.

Amara was looking at her closely. "Better, love? Less nervous?"

"Yes," Jessica said, and realized she meant it. "Yes, I am."

Amara's eyes shone in approval. "I've met many admirable women, Jess. You're one of them."

Before Jess could get over her surprise at that fierce statement, Amara gave her a mischievous smile. "Enrique, Mason and every person in that club will be delighted with us. And more importantly, we are going to be delighted with them." Dropping her hold to Jess's hand, she interlaced their fingers like favorite teen girlfriends. "Come *on*. I want to dance. This club has the best DJ you've ever heard. And the blackberry mojitos . . ."

~

When the limo stopped at the left side of the crowded parking area, Enrique bade both women to wait. Jess watched as he stared into space, then he nodded. "Lord Mason will come open your door, Jessica. Amara and I will meet you both inside."

Amara touched her knee, then Enrique handed her out of the car. Jess watched them go, Enrique settling a possessive hand on his wife's hip, the sway of her agile hips attracting more than one interested glance.

As they left the car, the noise of the people entering the club poured in. She saw several Masters crossing the lot with elegant slaves on collar and leash. One was wrapped in a lush velvet cloak, but another was barely clad at all, in a web of straps and silver chain links. Both were stunning women with impassive faces, women who could have graced model runways. Being gorgeous was apparently a requisite for membership in such an exclusive club.

Focus on Mason. Just Mason. She could do this. *You will be there as Lord Mason's guest. You are not required to participate . . .*

A shadow fell over the window. She didn't have to look. She knew it was him, from the way her pulse leaped and her palms dampened. As the door opened, her gaze was down, so she saw his dark slacks, the polished boots beneath. He was apparently playing the urbane billionaire tonight, but in her pounding heart he was still the desert djinn. She wasn't sure if she wanted to be swirled away by him in those scorching sands, or if she should try to run.

"Jessica?" His hand extended into the vehicle. Broad palm, long fingers. Such a big man. Raithe hadn't been that big, for all that, she realized. Perhaps about five ten, and she'd found his shoulders somewhat narrow. Because he'd dominated her world for so long, he'd become larger than life. Mason was the real thing. Placing her hand in his, she let out that held breath when his fingers closed over hers. Firmly possessive and gently protective at once.

After Mason's third mark healed her body, she'd rediscovered the pleasure of eating. Every mouthful of food had compelled a sigh of pleasure, a moan of response. His fingers closing on hers made her feel that way about his touch, and he'd been gone only a short time.

She didn't dare look up at his face and see what he was reading from her mind. Instead, then and there she made herself a deal, knowing it was a dangerous one. Tonight she wasn't going to analyze her feelings for him, whether they were from some sick dependency or something far more terrifying. Tonight, as Amara said, she was going to enjoy everything the night had to offer, including him. *Whether he liked it or not.*

And she hoped he *did* get that thought.

Mason didn't receive her challenge. His mind had stopped functioning. He had been exposed to countless breathtaking females, vampire and human. Amara herself was one of the most physically beautiful human women he'd ever known, and Lady Lyssa would have eclipsed ten Helens of Troy. However, he couldn't remember the last time a woman had spent time on her appearance solely to please him, and him only. Amara did it for him, but also for Enrique. It was also in her nature to enjoy her own beauty.

The black dress was short and clung to every curve, emphasizing her lithe, toned body, the elegant strength of it. It was sleeveless, the shoulder straps keeping a distractingly tenuous hold on the neckline's plunge between her unbound breasts, the nipples a subtle invitation against the dark fabric.

His sight, quicker than a mortal's, won him a flash of the lace tops of her black stockings. She'd slid out of the vehicle carefully, trying to maintain ladylike modesty in the short dress, but sometimes enhanced senses brought divine rewards. The garters were embellished with a tiny, pale pink rose on each connecting strap. The spike heels with ankle straps she wore made his fangs sharpen in his mouth, thinking about nipping her above the strap, sipping from her, then working his way up each perfect leg.

He inhaled her. Powder, soap, shampoo, a fragrant body spray she'd applied in places that suggested she expected a man's mouth nuzzling there. The only jewelry she wore were the silver bracelets and collar he'd put on her.

"Welcome home, Lord Mason." She raised her gaze to his face and held it there. Gray, long-lashed eyes. They'd been highlighted with silver eye shadow. He was in danger of falling into those enigmatic pools, no matter how troubled the waters, and letting himself be sucked into her very soul. Her short curls were styled around her face in a way that made it impossible not to want to touch the delicate wisps and tendrils. There was a hint of gloss on those pink, kissable lips. Lips that a man would kill to have wrap around his cock.

By Allah, he'd gone right from appreciating her beauty to wanting to rut upon her like a savage, territorial beast. As he held her hand, studying her, he used the long pause to struggle for control. He wanted to drag her into his arms and kiss her senseless. He wanted his scent, his mouth, branded upon her. He'd been worried about the effect this place would have on her. He should have realized what it would do to him.

"I brought you a gift from Berlin." He cleared his throat. *You idiot, you're supposed to tell her she looks stunning.*

But he felt the tendril of wary pleasure that uncurled in her mind. Keeping her hand, he drew the necklace from his pocket. A Swarovski crystal, formed into a disk and etched so it appeared to capture the crescent moon in its sparkling depths. The faint pink glimmer to the faceted glass would look devastating on her, particularly if she was wearing only it and her stockings.

"I think you lied." A hint of a smile touched her somber features. "You looked to see what I would be wearing tonight."

"Just a fortunate guess. Allah didn't want me to do anything to mar your beauty, so He guided my hand."

She tilted her head, and though that nervous flush remained in her cheeks, the tiny smile played around her mouth as well. "I didn't realize you were a religious man, Lord Mason."

"A woman can compel a man to a worshipful state," he rejoined. "Particularly when she looks like you. Turn for me, *habiba*."

Her pulse thudded against her throat, both from the command and the name. She *had* missed him. It was there in her mind, wanting to be said, but she didn't. Instead she turned on her heel, so his gaze fell on her sweet nape. Then his attention shifted lower.

He'd forgotten the primary reason she wanted to surprise him tonight. The tattoo. The back of the dress was a dramatic contrast to the front. For one thing, there was hardly any back to it. It plunged to no more than an inch, if that, above the cleft between her buttocks. Every time he guided her through a doorway tonight, he could settle his hand in that shallow curve, caress bare flesh. A surprising part of him wanted to cover her, conceal her from male eyes. However, before he could get disturbed by his jealousy, he was riveted by the design she'd chosen.

Robert had transformed the straight, long scars into stalks of bamboo. They'd been embellished with delicate leaves that did not detract from the tiger's amber eyes glowing out from the depths of that mysterious forest, the shape of his face and hint of powerful shoulder. One paw reached out as if through the bars of a cage, and where it disappeared, it was obvious that paw would be on the top of her buttock.

"Would you like to see the rest, my lord?" Her voice was a whisper he would have missed if her spoken thought wasn't also in his mind.

"Yes."

Standing within the open door of the limo, her body was shielded by the car and his body. She slid the straps off her shoulders and eased the snug fit of the dress down past her hips and the rise of her buttocks, until she showed the tiger's paw fully. The claws dug in to the crest of the left buttock, and several red drops of blood marked the slope. She'd enhanced them tonight with tiny slivers of ruby that sparkled, attached by one of those mysterious adhesives women used. She wasn't wearing any panties, nothing to mar the design.

Her head was down, angled to the right, so he saw her waiting

profile, the fragile curve of neck beneath his collar. When he realized she was holding the position until he indicated he'd looked his
fill, until he told her she could dress again, something in his chest
constricted with hunger. Not that he needed to breathe, but if he did,
he knew he would have been unable to do so right now.

Mason tested her resolve, bringing the crystal over her head as
she stood in that tempting pose. She held it as he latched the chain,
followed it with his fingers and nestled the pendant in the crevice
between her breasts, registering how her own breath elevated as his
fingers brushed the top of the left curve.

He didn't tell her to put the dress back on. He did it himself, curling his hands over hers. Both of them stretched the dress back up her
torso. Then, because he could, and because he wanted to do so more
than he wanted life itself, he smoothed his hands down over her
breasts, to her waist, and finished at her hips, tugging the skirt back
into place.

"Do you like it, Lord Mason?" Her voice was barely a whisper.

"You know I do. You overwhelm me, Jessica."

She turned then, those gray eyes full of intriguing shadows. The
crystal sparkled. "Are you . . . do you have to tell me tonight?"

He didn't have to ask her what she meant. Mason pressed his lips
together. "Not if you don't wish me to. I should have taken off the
collar," he added gruffly, reaching up to touch it. "The bracelets will
be sufficient, and it won't detract from the necklace."

Her hand fluttered up, alighting on his. "Leave it?" she asked. Her
words were somewhere between a request and a plea. *I feel better . . .
knowing I'm clearly marked as yours here. Safer.*

She was going to test his resolve until something broke inside of
him; he was sure of it. He already felt like a wild animal in a dangerously flimsy cage. But he nodded.

She let out a small sigh, her chest rising beneath his palm. "Are
you ready to go in, my lord?"

For a second, he entertained a fleeting thought to drop her at the
door with Amara and Enrique and wait for them back at the plane.
She'd certainly be safer. But at the question, the direct lock with his
gaze, he discarded that idea like smoke. For one thing, there was no
way in hell she was going in there without him. Yes, part of it was

possessiveness; he couldn't deny that. But he remembered what she'd said about the tattoo. *Would you feel better if I was there, habiba? Yes, I would, but, no, I don't want you there.*

When he was in Berlin, he'd known he should have been there, despite her answer. Tonight he wasn't going to make her answer the question. He was going to be at her side. At her beautiful back, that design taunting him with a message that he wanted to answer, fiercely.

"Yes. But first, you need to wear this."

When he removed the item from his other pocket, Jessica recognized a mask. Instantly, she recalled the full head masks Raithe often made her wear, closing all the holes so she could barely breathe. Or sometimes just the eyes and ears, so she'd be forced to stumble about as they taunted her in a masochistic version of Marco Polo. They'd make her think she was about to fall down stairs, or prod and poke her with things she couldn't identify, things that hurt. Though knowing what the items were wouldn't have changed anything, she knew that any knowledge helped. Managing fear when you lost all vestiges of control, even of your mind and body, was impossible. It was the ultimate victory for a master torturer.

"Jessica." Mason cradled her face, bringing her eyes up to him. Now he was very close, his body vibrating against hers where she'd retreated into the corner created by the open car door. "Jess, stay here with me. Like the bracelets and collar, this is for you. Be easy. Trust me."

Slipping a long arm around her waist, he brought her forward again. Jessica welcomed the distraction of his arm against her bare back, the heat that filled the small space between their bodies. "It's for your protection. To hide your identity."

Closing her eyes, she pushed back the roar of memories. "I want to enjoy tonight, Mason. I don't want to be afraid."

"You won't be. You're here with me." *You should feel safe under your Master's protection. That's the way it's meant to be. If you will trust me, I will give you that gift tonight.*

At her bare nod, he brought the mask up. It wasn't a stiff leather head mask that could suffocate and chafe. The black velvet eye mask had a froth of dangling onyx, pink and silver gems sewn along the lower edge, so that the various lengths of strands tickled her cheeks and the corners of her mouth. Sequins were sewn in a tapestry around the eyes to enhance them like exotic makeup. The mask was soft, the long string ties fanning out on either side of her head but coming together in a point in the back, where he laced them together, the mask slowly tightening, molding to her features like her own skin, giving her a shortness of breath that wasn't entirely unpleasant, reminding her of when he'd locked the collar on her neck. The long tie ends that drifted like ribbons over her shoulders were also sewn with glittering sequins. The curls on her forehead now fell over black velvet, glittering with traces of silver and pink gems and sequins.

Mason traced the edge of the mask, then teased her lips open with his thumb, making her mouth that much more sensitive. His voice was sensual velvet, like the fabric. "As much as I love your beautiful face, you cannot imagine how provocative this makes your mysterious gray eyes and that tempting mouth. But this mask may also help you deal with your fears, ease your inhibitions. You can be whatever you wish to be tonight, safely."

Her gaze flickered up to him, startled. Mason squeezed her hand. "I will not make any demands of you related to the preferences of this club, *habiba*. That has not changed. But this night is for you, your pleasure and enjoyment. I am encouraging you to take full advantage of it. Now go join Amara and Enrique. They're waiting at the door. I'll be there in a moment."

The curve of her pink lips beneath that mask had the potency of an experienced seductress. But the way she'd turned and let him put on the necklace and then the mask, trembling but trusting at once, wasn't calculated at all. He had to remember how fragile she truly was. Yet when he looked into her mind, he realized she *wanted* him to forget, putting a further strain on his floundering control.

Those gray eyes were watching his face. "You're shutting the gate again, aren't you?" she asked. "You tell me to seek pleasure for myself tonight, but you put yourself out of bounds." *Does that mean another male should touch my body, tease my flesh with his tongue—*

He'd closed his hands on her shoulders before he thought. She gasped at the bruising power of it, but her lips parted, her eyes seeking his, alight with something that wasn't all fear. With a mental oath, he released her and took a step back. "Don't push on that gate, Jessica," he warned. "There's no such thing as a housebroken vampire."

Studying him for another long moment, she surprised him with a cool nod. "We will wait for you at the entrance, then, Lord Mason." But then she closed that step, and her fingertips slid up the thin fabric of his shirt, two fingers briefly caressing a strand of his hair. He closed his hand on her wrist, a warning, but she merely held his gaze, her body leaned into his.

Maybe I want you off the chain. In case you haven't noticed, my lord, this outfit suggests I have left the gate wide-open.

With a fiery toss of her head, she slid past him. The gauntlet she'd thrown down, as provocative as it was, was nearly eclipsed by the impact of her departure. In the spike heels, the short, formfitting dress and with that tantalizing tattoo, she was erotic art in motion, the mask adding the perfect touch of mystery. It was impossible not to be tempted by her. One man walked into a parked car. Another hit a Mercedes as he parked his Escalade, setting off a security alarm. She was going to cause a riot before she reached the door.

But as he struggled past his own reaction, Mason detected something else. She was holding the connection to him, her consciousness reaching out to him. A human servant was often not aware they were doing it, but the vampire could feel it. Like reaching through the darkness of dreams, trying to find his hand, the reassurance that he was still there.

The damnable woman goaded him past all sense. Damn it, damn it, *damn it.* Lyssa was right. He needed to pull his head out of his ass. She was both, irresistible temptress and damaged girl. She was surrounded by noise, people. Men. Lots of them, and many here with their submissive slaves, chained in a variety of ways, from elegantly sensual to hard-core bondage. The thread between them was helping reassure her. As she drew closer to that door, her trepidation was increasing. When she saw even more graphic displays inside, she would recall what he had the power to demand from her. She'd remember all the things Raithe had done to her. And Mason wouldn't be at her back.

Taking the risk of unwelcome attention, he used vampire speed. Before she was halfway across the parking lot, he was beside her. He put his hand on the small of her back, just above the tiger's paw. Both of them a sign of protective possession he hoped would reassure her, even if it didn't do a damn thing for him but goad his own savage nature.

23

THE easing in her chest at his reappearance, the heat at her back, didn't entirely dispel her irritation with him, but it helped. To be honest, she'd wanted to jump him when she got out of the limo. As he'd shifted to hand her out of the vehicle, she'd noted the polished boots beneath the slacks had silver buckles at the ankle. He'd brushed his hair severely from his face and clasped the tail at his nape with a silver buckle as well, emphasizing the relentless sculpting of cheekbones and straight, aristocratic nose.

She assumed his choice of shirt was a nod to the environment, and while she was nervous about the club, she was willing to be thankful to it for this reason at least. The shirt was a black silk T-shirt that showed off his impressive biceps, the broadness of his shoulders. However, the fabric was a tight mesh, showing the tiger to good advantage in back, but providing a thin screen from touch. If she ran her fingers beneath it, she could imagine the mesh sliding over her knuckles as she explored the musculature of his pectorals, the flat nipples and sectioned stomach, down to the waistband of the slacks.

Yes, he was always a feast for the eyes. Unfortunately, he kept resisting her, throwing her own emotions and fears up to block her. As he reached Amara and Enrique, waiting at the door, he nodded to them, relaxed and in control. It made her want to choke him.

Mason wanted to laugh at the thought. If she only knew. Amara was admiring the decorative mask, but Enrique's intent gaze told him his servant was picking up his agitation. Mason forced his shoulders to ease, his fingers to open so they wouldn't threaten to smash into the faces of the nearest men openly gawking at her. They were still outside the club. Inside, rules were far more stringent about approaching claimed property. It made him glad he hadn't removed the collar. But it would be removed eventually, wouldn't it?

He knew his thought came through as a snarl, from the slight widening of Enrique's gaze. *Show her around and take her to the dance floor,* he ordered. *I won't be far.*

He was going to get a drink. While alcohol had no effect on vampires, the psychological benefit of downing a bottle of ninety-proof something might be distracting. At least give him something to grip other than the soft body he truly wanted to grasp.

Amara lifted her brow but slid her arm through Jess's without comment, shepherding her forward. Enrique followed them, Mason approving of his male servant's strategic flanking. It was more crowded tonight than Mason liked, but the few vampires who came were much younger and more provincial. They likely weren't apprised of Jessica's disappearance, let alone that she was now under his protection.

Inside the club it was crowded, noisy and dark. The pounding music made Jessica feel as though they'd stepped inside the body of a living animal, the bass line of the music its heartbeat, the people the rushing tide of blood cells. It was a familiar scene to her, and yet it wasn't. While some of the trappings were the same, there was a different tone she managed to identify, enough to latch on to it and use it to bolster her courage.

"Everything you are seeing is consensual." Amara's reminder, spoken loudly in her ear, was as if the woman had read her mind, and maybe she had.

Past the foyer, they stepped into a wide corridor, lined with St. Andrew's crosses. It reminded her of a life-sized paper doll chain, like the ones she'd cut in grade school, trying to remember where to make the snips so she didn't cut the chain apart. The crosses were in use, a place for Masters and Mistresses to restrain their slaves and display them for the touch of others if they chose. Amara's fingers stroked hers, soothing and anticipating.

Jessica did feel the fear rising, held by the thinnest of leashes. But Amara and Enrique were here with her, and somewhere in the crowd was Mason, his presence as much a thrum through her body as the pounding music.

She'd been the kind of child who hated to be afraid. She was the first to climb the too-tall tree, run her bike up the makeshift ramp to do the wheelie that could crack her skull. She'd take any schoolyard dare, not because the dare was issued, but because if it caused her a scrap of fear, she was determined to eradicate it. Facing the fear let her see past it, to what mattered.

Whenever too much of the animal in Mason came to the surface, he denied himself to bring it in check. While there was wisdom to that, because she did understand the savagery in his nature, she wanted to face his beast. She needed to know the unique nature of it. Otherwise, she was back in the schoolyard again, denying herself a wondrous mystery if she didn't stand before it, slay her fear and embrace that beast.

The thought gave her the courage to plant her feet and stare down her fear, hovering over this corridor. She held the word *consensual* in both hands, willing herself to believe what Mason and his servants had been telling her for over two months. After all, it was the primary rule of the club, posted clearly in each section, illuminated by black light. *Consensual play only. Guests who violate this rule, in the opinion of management, will be escorted from the premises and their membership revoked. No exceptions.*

So bolstered by internal and external reassurances, she gave herself permission to look. Really look. On the first St. Andrew's cross a woman had been stripped naked and spread wide, facing the crowd. Her Master was teasing her sex with fingers glistening with her juices while her head thrashed. Her mouth opened, releasing cries lost in the noise, but that didn't make them any less potent. Her fingers clutched against her bonds, and when he stepped onto the dais provided to reach her face, she sought his mouth eagerly, taking the kiss he awarded her, his hand cupping the back of her head.

On the next cross, a male slave was manacled and facing away from the crowd, his Mistress caning him with brisk strokes, leaving red stripes on his tight ass and upper thighs. But then she had water brought and gave it to him herself, stroking his throat as he swallowed. Her fingernails scraped over his erection, an impressive reflection of his pleasure in serving her.

Because she'd been conditioned to arouse and climax against her will, under extremes of humiliation and pain, Jessica knew the difference in what she was seeing. The next four were similar to the first two. One Master had chained his sub upside down and was having her deep-throat his cock, his thighs and testicles pressed flush against her face. He'd opened his trousers but not dropped them, so as a Master he was not on bare-assed display before observers, but his sizable organ, revealed when he withdrew and pushed back in, was slick with her saliva as she worked him. As his buttocks clenched rhythmically with his thrusting, her breasts quivered with her enthusiastic efforts. Jessica drew an unsteady breath, remembering the night she'd wanted to go on her knees, put her mouth on Mason there.

When she at last nodded, indicating she was ready to move on, Amara squeezed her hand, a flash of approval in her eyes. The next visual was a glass wall, behind which different scenes were played out in rooms where the Dominant wished the activity to be viewed. A Victorian maid being spanked by her irritated Master, a Roman gladiator taking control of his Christian slave, who was more than willing to do anything to save his life . . .

She was doing well. However, like the night on the beach when she'd tried the somersault before her body was ready, she realized her mind and body were giving her signs of overload. Her heart was pounding erratically and she was getting dizzy. She was becoming more aware of the attention of passing men, the crawl of their gazes over her flesh. It really was too crowded in this viewing corridor. A shudder, a need to move faster, swept through her.

Easy, habiba. *Amara and Enrique will take you to the dance floor now.*

He was here, and as usual, he spoke just when she needed to hear his voice. But damn it, she *could* handle this. She dug her heels in, determined to stare at the next brace of female submissives, tied to-

gether in elaborate Japanese rope bondage and suspended, blind-
folded and at the mercy of whatever their Masters inflicted upon
them. She would confront that overwhelming feeling, rooted in a
past she was determined to *make* the past. However, Amara and Enrique were implacable, their hands firm, Enrique's strong arm taking
her waist. They were too well linked with their Master, and she
couldn't stand against all three of them.

They emerged on the upper catwalk above the dance floor. As she
blinked at the wholly different environment, she lost her irritation.
"It's something, isn't it?" Amara shouted in her ear.

She realized the area through which she'd just passed had essentially been the foyer and entrance corridor of a much larger club. The
dance floor *was* astounding. The main floor was broken into lighted,
colored squares like a graduated stained-glass window. In those
lighted blocks beneath people's feet, bodies were moving on a lower
level, twisting beneath the thick glass. Naked and sometimes bound
slaves, a tinted mural of erotic undulations from pane to pane. The
dancers moved over them, looking down to enjoy, or giving the submissives pleasurable views in return, because Jessica was sure she
wasn't the only one without panties here.

The dance floor was flanked by scaffolding, a massive erector set
crisscrossing up to the fifty-foot-high domed ceiling, an impressive
feature of the club's architecture she'd seen from the parking area.
People danced along the wide scaffolds, some suspended on bars like
trapeze artists, only spread-eagled, bound in secure cuffs overlaid
with twisted ribbon. As they were pushed by the dancers across open
space, the ribbons flowed. One woman with red hair that fell to her
waist had her wrists and ankles bound on the top and bottom of one
ring of a sphere of interlocking rings. She was oscillating, the hair
and ribbons twining as the sphere drifted across space, up and down,
like a randomly floating bubble, only on wires. When she came close
enough to the scaffolding, the dancers reached over the railing and
touched her freely, giving her a push to send her on another flight.

At other places on the scaffolding, where metal bars crossed,
gagged and blindfolded submissives were crucified with manacles,
some with vibrators strapped into their bodies so that they trembled
and climaxed into the hygienic chastity belts they wore. Passing

dancers were allowed to tease and fondle them. However, in every case of a bound slave, she could search the nearest bystanders and find a carefully watching Master and Mistress, or an assigned security person, attractive and discreet, but obviously there to ensure the safety of the bound and helpless person in the dense crowd of aroused, dancing clientele.

Watching it all, Jessica realized she was wet, her thighs slick against each other as she walked, her body taut, eager for . . . something. Focusing so hard on how she'd handle the club without falling apart, she hadn't anticipated her own body's reaction to the stimulus. Trying to accept and understand that response was almost as harrowing as trying not to fall apart. Since she hadn't survived Raithe by rationality, she suspected it would be best to make it through tonight without it as well. Analyze later, she reminded herself.

"Want to go out and dance?" Amara had slipped her arm around Jessica's waist, holding her securely. Enrique pressed close behind them as well, a twofold reassurance of warm, protective bodies who meant her no harm. Who would allow no harm to befall her. And in her consciousness was one who'd sworn he'd tear apart anyone who tried. Who reinforced his presence with the collar on her neck, the bracelets on her wrists. But what if she was her own worst enemy? How did she fight herself?

Jessica looked up at Amara, the dark eyes shining with pleasure and anticipation. Amara wasn't afraid. She wore a collar, subjugated to two men. She was cherished, loved, strong. And she'd said she admired Jessica.

Jess swallowed. Nodded. "Let's dance," she called out.

Needing no further invitation, Amara took the lead, tugging her out into the disconcerting fray. However, with the grace and confidence of a professional dancer, she carved out a place for them in a matter of seconds. Enrique had stayed behind, but Jessica saw him take a position on the upper scaffolding where he could watch them both and secure a drink from a waitress. She wondered where Mason was in all of this. She wished the geographical locater mark was two-way, but for now she had to settle for knowing he was out there.

Amara had them dancing on a translucent blue square of glass.

Beneath it, Jessica saw a slave with a muscular build. His cock was in a harness, the organ so in need of release it was almost plum-colored. He stared up at them, held in a steel and nylon suspension system. Something was fucking him from behind, obvious from how he kept pressing himself against the glass in a rhythmic manner. His mouth was open, gasping, the eyes bright and fierce with lust. It stimulated her as well, as Amara fell casually into the pleasure of further goading him, straddling his face with her heels, shimmying her hips in those complicated belly-dancing moves that were so easy for her. She swept her hair across the square and then worked her way down into a lithe squat, swinging her hips low, giving him a close-up of her tightly encased ass and what was between her thighs.

"Amara." Jessica couldn't help laughing as the woman looked up at her impishly beneath her fall of dark tresses. Tugging at the hem of Jessica's short skirt, Amara eased forward on rocking knees, scattered a circle of kisses up Jessica's thigh before she was on her feet again, turning her in her arms, getting her to move out of her stiff, self-conscious sway into a more abandoned movement. As she moved around Jessica, keeping her in a protective circle, giving her space, Jess tried to relax and focused on the music, let it move into her.

She had loved to dance. High school dances, college parties, then the wide offering of clubs in Rome. As if answering her desires, the next song was a vintage heavy metal favorite, Quiet Riot's "Bang Your Head," sweeping her back to that time of her life. A smile spread over her face despite herself. Nothing said loss of inhibitions like hard rock.

Closing her eyes on instinct, she began to move her body with the vibration of that insistent opening drumbeat. When the lead singer belted out that opening scream, the dance floor screamed with him, and she was lost, remembering Mason's Berber yell in her ear as they sailed across the sand and surf on Coman's back.

She was rocking back and forth, her arms lifting as her upper body gyrated left, then right, hips swiveling, adopting some of the novice moves Amara had taught her into a couple turns, a light step or two. She was finally giving that gasping male slave a show, moving back and forth over his body as if walking on him, turning so he'd see the cleft of her bare ass and the slick lips between. Not as blatant as Amara, but she liked the power of it, the way it flowed over her. His desire was hot and potent beneath her while she remained untouchable, taunting him with what he couldn't have. Something that belonged to another Master.

As that power and unexpected thought filled her, she remembered her thought to Mason. *Maybe I want you off the chain . . . I've left the gate wide-open.* Her movements became even more provocative, a mating dance meant only for the strongest, most dangerous beast among this seething mass of humanity.

You are the bravest woman I've ever met . . .

She remembered his words, remembered she'd survived what few could. If she wanted him, damn his sense of honor, her fucked-up head, her fears. She could call him to her, make him break the chain himself. Letting her hands drop, she molded them over her breasts, her thumbs caressing bare flesh inside the low neckline. Sliding her palms down to her abdomen, then lower. Curling her fingers around the dress hem, she raked it high on her thighs, responding to the wild abandon of the song. She rocked down, bending low, tossed her head up and led with her hip to pivot and come back up straight. Her eyes still closed, she gave herself over to the music, her own raging desire. She would fear nothing here, not with the music beating through her like blood, like the pounding of sex, all its un-bridled, mindless rush of euphoria and dangerous need. The way it was supposed to be.

When her arms brushed something metal, she opened her eyes and realized she'd reached one edge of the dance floor. In between the scaffolding, they'd put panels of tall cage doors without the cages, the illusion of imprisonment. Some had slaves bound against them, and now she found herself brushing muscled flesh, a blond, blind-folded man of lean, tall physique who quivered under her touch. She curled her fingers around the bars beneath his spread arms and used them for leverage, pulling forward, then back, her rhythmic hip thrusts and circles far more insistent when she was straddling his thigh, brushing herself against his flesh. His cock was in a chastity cage, the organ bound in a condom inside, because, cage or not, he'd al-ready been goaded to climax.

She lifted on her toes, wondering how far she could push this, if she could put her mouth to his throat, tease his neck with her canines. Right before she made contact, a pair of familiar, strong hands closed on her hips. Triumph surged through her.

I would hate to ruin my membership by killing someone here, habiba. *There is a long waiting list.*

He spun her around. Thrillingly, he shoved her back against the man's body, using it as no more than a functional wall, underscoring who held control over her. His amber eyes were molten gold, taken straight out of the heated earth, and her eager hands slid up to grip that silk shirt over the thundering of his heart. She was so glad that vampires weren't dead and cold, as lore depicted. Right now she thought he could consume her in flame and she'd burn in joy.

He locked a hand over one of her wrists, but she wouldn't be denied this time. Sliding her free hand under his arm, along his waist, she gripped the muscular feast of him through that mesh shirt. When his mouth tightened, she twisted free with a quick move and ducked under his arm so she was pressed against his back, the curve of his taut ass. She began to work against him those same hip movements she'd offered the blindfolded and bound slave. Teasing her mound with the feel of the luscious male buttock inspired her to hook her leg over his hard thigh, her calf moving down the inside of his knee, her own knee brushing his arousal. She would twine around him like a vine, seduce him.

He was so tall, broad-shouldered. So much larger than her. She wanted to feel it, wanted that control to break, all the power unleashed.

She spun away and returned to his front. As she did, she closed her eyes, wanting everything about him conveyed through her fingers. It maximized his effect on all her other senses, for his body's perfect beauty was best experienced by touch. A vampire lost none of his impact in the dark, after all, because they were creatures of the night. Sliding a closed fist up his chest to the base of his neck, she spread her fingers like a starfish, caressing his throat, then began to slide down.

Abruptly her wrist was manacled by his again. Twisting her around, he maneuvered her to an unoccupied cage door and shoved her against it, face forward. The steel erection he brought against her buttocks was more unyielding than the metal. Clamping his hands on the bars on either side of her, he caged her there. Her breath caught in her throat.

Yes.

"I'm not them." She wasn't one of his damsels in distress. She wanted to be taken by him, and taken rough, because that was her desire, different from Raithe's, the rapes he forced on her. "And I'm not her," she added savagely, wanting to tease the beast to raging.

He bent, his breath caressing that sensitive juncture of her throat, the promise of his fangs so close. Possession. That was what made the bite of a vampire so scintillating, so overwhelming to a woman's imagination. That, and the knowledge that such a possession allowed her to give him what he needed to live. So many truths Raithe had buried beneath the brutality, but Mason had dug them out with his impact upon her senses, her very soul.

She turned her head to the right, giving him full access, closing her hands on the section of the bars beneath his. He released them to follow the line of her forearms, her elbows, the tender inside of the upper arm. She moaned as he swept her rib cage, molded her breasts, then settled on her hips, grip flexing, demanding.

The music had changed. No longer hard rock but the Latin strains of Marc Anthony's "I Need to Know." Mason swept her around again, away from the cage and firmly into his arms. When she looked up, his expression was pure predator, warming her skin. *I strongly suggest you let me lead*, habiba.

I've been waiting for you to do so.

A muscle twitched in his jaw. Surprising her, he took the lead literally, spinning her into a flawless Latin rumba, full of intimate twists and turns. She didn't know the dance, and so she had to rely solely on his command of the dance and her body to stay in step with him. While she trusted him to do just that, she teased him with a brush of bare skin, a length of slim thigh, giving herself any chance to touch him.

His hand rested on her lower back, one finger slipping under the scant back of the dress to nestle into the channel between her buttocks. Her breath shortened, her gaze fluttering up to his. She was tired of fear, of not understanding herself, of wanting him and not having him. Wanting him was the clearest thing, and though she knew he thought he was being a gentleman, giving her time to sort the rest out, it wasn't going to sort out. That part of her was going to be fucked up for a long, long time. That was a different person, a different Jessica.

This Jessica, the one at the club, was impatient. She knew what she wanted, and since she knew she couldn't consistently hold on to those moments of clarity, knew they could be fleeting, it ratcheted up her impatience that much more.

Still moving her in the steps of the dance, he lifted one hand to her face, touching her lashes, her needy mouth, all so sensitive since they were the only part of her face he could touch with the mask he'd put on her. Another turn, a dip, and she caught hold of his shoulder, though she didn't need to. He had her. As he lifted her in his arms, she slid her arms all the way around his neck, folding them over his broad shoulders.

It brought her body fully against his, and he adjusted his hold, continuing to turn her, though her feet were no longer on the floor. Music and lights, the sounds of other people, all of it became part of the rush of feeling inside of her, something beyond words or thought. Since she no longer believed in Heaven, she thought this might be as close to perfection as her slice of Purgatory could get, wrapped in the arms of a vampire she wanted beyond rational understanding, her heart and body vibrating in a near-perfect accord for once.

When the song at last ended, he lowered her back onto her ice-pick heels, retaining one hand as she stared up at him.

"Lord Mason." The shout had him glancing left, and she saw a male leaning over the nearby rail, giving him a wave, gesturing with his cocktail as if offering a drink. She recognized him as another vampire, as Amara had indicated might be here. He had a servant with him, a man decked out in a pair of tight black jeans and an impressively tattooed bare upper body. The man glanced at Jessica with typical interest. All servants were curious about other servants, as any guild of a specialized profession were. But the kind she'd experienced before Amara and Enrique had never been anyone she wanted to meet, let alone socialize with.

Things had been going well. Better than okay. But now, the music became a discordant blare, the notes ricocheting in her suddenly roiling stomach. She didn't want to go anywhere near this servant, or his vampire.

Mason's hand settled on her throat, squeezed lightly. It was a forceful reassurance that brought her attention back to him, captured her in his still-simmering gaze. *You're mine,* habiba. *You have nothing to fear. I share you with no one.*

She noticed he didn't qualify that as he'd always done before, indicating that it was specific to this night or any other circumstance. It made her fingers flex in the grasp of his, and in a brief motion, he'd caught the back of her neck in one hand and lifted her for a hard, quick kiss that seared her to her toes. *Nod to me, Jessica. Show me you understand.*

It was antithetical to what she knew of vampires. They always shared servants. It was part of their culture. Still, she gave him a nod anyway, needing to trust him.

Good. Keep dancing. I like to watch you. While I share a drink with my young friend Evan, I will enjoy your beauty.

Not an overlord, Region Master or born vampire, then, for he did not give the man a title. Which, hierarchy-wise, meant Mason owed him only the courtesies he chose. No expectation for interactive play with servants. Though she'd wanted to believe his words, that additional realization helped.

As he moved away from her, threading through the crowd, she noticed that more than one submissive, caught up in the music and their dancing, dared punishment to trail a hand over his shoulder, his back. He moved passed them, unconcerned, and of course they gave way before the path of an obvious Master. She couldn't fault their desire, but it was a reminder. When it came to vampires, they didn't belong to humans. Humans belonged to them. And the human that forgot that was asking for trouble.

Taking a deep breath and using the dampening thought to settle her sizzling nerves, she tuned back into the music. Amara was right about one thing. The club DJ was driven by what would keep bodies and feet moving, building the frenetic energy that made the environment addictive and all-absorbing. They'd switched to "Gimme! Gimme! Gimme!" by Abba, and Jessica couldn't help but see the irony of a song that demanded a man after midnight. A man coming out of the darkness to fulfill a woman's passion.

Beginning to move with that mysterious, almost exotic opening beat, Jessica tilted her head. Amara and Enrique were up in the scaffolding now, immersed in each other, their paired beauty and the one-step-short-of-illegal dance steps drawing appreciative attention. But when Amara did a lithe maneuver that dipped her over the railing, the harrowing move of a trapeze artist, she sent Jessica an upside-down wave. Enrique bent, nudged aside a gauze strip of her top and licked his way along the curve of an exposed breast, causing the woman's eyes to shift back to him as he swung her back over the bar.

Jessica honored the DJ's efforts, letting herself get swept away by the music again. She twisted and spun over a golden square now. There were two subs under the glass, a male and female moving in coitus. It was a mesmerizing display of muscles as they copulated in a sinuous rhythm far slower than the music, but yet still somehow fueled by it. Kneeling, she traced their profiles through the transparent floor. The man noticed, his gaze passing over her face. With a smile, he pressed his mouth to the glass as if kissing her fingers, while his partner met Jessica's hand palm to palm. She held that position, even as her body stiffened and the man's movements became frenetic and powerful, his climax rolling over him at the same moment, mouths opening against each other in cries of release.

Jessica straightened, watching them finish, then closed her eyes and began to sway. She imagined Mason taking her down on his bed, his body pressed to hers, sunk deep between her legs, giving her his seed, commanding her climax as his fangs took from her throat. No unbearable pain, just savage need. Was it wrong, imagining that she was cuffed, so he could move his mouth over her as he pleased? In her fantasies it was safe. She could get away, just by melting the restraints with her mind.

The music surprised her, changing to a soft rock ballad. She kept dancing, though, turning in a slow twirl, one, two, three. Step, plié, just like ballet class. Step ball change, just like jazz or soft shoe. She'd been a little girl when she took those classes, but she remembered the steps. Right now she was far from a little girl, and yet the child was there, a ghost in her consciousness. The present and the more distant past. Could she bring them both together and somehow leave the recent past in the cold, freeze it out?

When she reached the edge of the floor, gentle, nonintrusive hands eased her back toward the center. She spun slowly, executed an informal arabesque, remembering the lightness of the ballet moves that had supplemented the gymnastics. When she brushed another body, she heard a soft male laugh, nothing frightening, though, as again easy hands guided her back toward the center of the floor. It was like being in a dream. She had nothing to fear, for Mason was watching her.

Only when she realized she should be drifting into far more people did she reluctantly open her eyes. She was in the center of a circle of very aroused, attentive and attractive male submissives.

❦ 24 ❦

A glance around her showed that, while the dance floor was less populated during the slow ballad, the circle had been moving with her, keeping her from running into anyone, and providing her navigation when she reached the dance floor edges.

A lovely, sensual version of the horrid Marco Polo she remembered, such that the two layered together, black against white, and she wasn't afraid. The ringleader of the circle had to be the tall man directly in front of her now, Lord Evan's servant. When he gave her a slight bow, he drew close enough she could hear him over the music, leaning in so she got an eyeful of the expansive chest, the colorful tattoo of a male dragon molded over the flat of his abdomen, his pectoral. There was a smaller, female dragon wrapped around his biceps, roaring back at the male. "My Master offers you this circle to play with as you wish."

Holy God. She swept her gaze around the circle of six men, all of whom were gazing upon her with appreciation, but obvious reserve as well, awaiting her desires.

While the lust in their gaze was honest, clean and friendly, lust had a way of being too close to violence for her comfort, and she didn't know them. They were surrounding her, loosely or not. Being the center of attention like this was a little nerve-racking.

Lift your gaze to me, habiba.

She found him as if she did have a homing beacon to him, even among the heavy crowds. Though he was sitting with Evan, sharing drinks, he'd chosen a table on the second-tier level at the rail so he had a clear view of her and the dance floor. And she had a clear view of him.

Dance for me.

Do you want them to touch me?

Warmth flickered through her mind, a reassurance and more, something that stirred her already heated blood. *What if I do? What if that was my pleasure, to watch you be aroused, by my command, at the hands of others?*

She swallowed, staring up at him. *I'm not sure. But I'd be willing . . . to try. If I knew I could stop, if it was safe.*

You are always safe with me, Jessica. Always.

She'd told him safety was an illusion. But here, under his amber gaze, the club's flashing lights highlighting the hard beauty of his sculpted jaw and brow, she did feel as if she could dare to follow her curiosity, dare herself to face her desires, as well as her fears.

Let these men touch you with desire, habiba. *Passion. Reverence. Remember the difference.*

A communication must have passed between him and Evan, for Evan's servant had moved behind her during the exchange. His hands settled on her hips, a strong but easy touch. His jaw brushed her cheek as he placed his lips against her temple, took her into a sway, easing her back against his body so she was leaning her backside against the column of his thigh.

"I'm Niall," he murmured against her ear. "It's a pleasure to meet you."

Since she wasn't sure how Mason was introducing her, she chose silence as her response. She had enough to do anyhow, focusing on the way his hands felt, turning her in an easy two-step, into the hands of another man. Another strong, aroused body, a brush of hands on the bare skin of her back, then her fingers were clasped. Someone kissed them, she didn't know who, because she'd reflexively closed her eyes, and then she was leaning back into Niall again.

"You prefer keeping your eyes closed, little one?" he asked, seductive amusement in his tone. He had a faint Scottish accent, and it shivered up her spine in a pleasing way. She nodded.

"All right, then. Tell me if anything displeases you, so your Master doesn't rip my throat out, hear me? This is all for you. We'll do nothing you dislike." He dropped his touch lower on her hips, smoothing the stretch of the skirt, and the heat of his bare chest pressed against her naked, sensitive back, a reminder of her tattoo and scars there. Stroking a finger under the hem of the skirt, along the inside of her thigh, he made an idle circle.

"There's moisture here. Heat. I think your Master has aroused you well. But those stockings are far too pretty to ruin. Meet Lars."

Another hand slid up her leg from below, a large hand. Lars cupped the back of her thigh, inching up to tease the curve of buttock beneath the skirt as his lips touched her upper thigh, suckling off the moisture. He cleaned the quivering skin, playing in a maddening way around the hem of her skirt, never pushing it high enough to reveal her sex, though his mouth was close enough to make Mason's tiger mark on the inside of her thigh tingle.

She'd already seen nudity in the club, several couples fucking one another outright for the viewing pleasure of others in the public populace, so she knew it wasn't a club rule holding them back. Since only Niall could receive mental commands, she expected he was directing them. But she kept her eyes closed. Though this was a roller coaster she'd entered willingly, she was afraid she'd lose her nerve if she looked.

She'd been moved to another's hands, and the male holding her from behind now had long hair like Mason's, because it was brushing her cheek. Reaching back, she grasped the silk of it. Flicking her lashes up for only a brief moment, she saw it was gold, spun flaxen. When she twined her fingers in it, the blond smiled and bent to kiss her throat, placing his lips where Mason's had been. It reminded her of her lord's demanding bite. It stirred her to think of him watching. Was he perhaps instructing Niall what would arouse her most, through the intermediary of Evan's mind?

Hands moved up the curve of her waist and cupped her breasts, fingers stroking but not going as far as the nipples. It made them ache for contact. Her spiraling desire was being stoked higher and hotter by this teasing, circling the most intimate areas. That heated need drove away fear, but there was more to this.

You are clever even amidst your desire, habiba. *They act upon my command, and will only touch those areas when I allow it.*

The needy flesh between her legs contracted, her lips parting in a gasp. She was turned again, her brief peek showing she was in the arms of a handsome Latino with dark curling hair, whose eyes burned with passion.

"Cesar," Niall murmured, a hot breath passing near her ear.

Cesar gripped her with far more strength than the others. But by then she was ready for it, needy. When he rubbed his cock, tightly bound in his trousers, against her ass, she gasped and clung to the arm he'd slid across her chest. He clasped her upper arm to hold her there as he undulated his hips, teased the cleft of her buttocks with the impressive evidence of his arousal. Digging his fingers into her hair, under the lacings of the mask, he pulled her head back on his shoulder so her breasts jutted out beneath the bar of his arm. Niall knelt before her then, pulling the low neckline to the left so the one curve was exposed. His mouth settled on the ripe flesh, his tongue curling down into the fabric, almost brushing the nipple at last.

She cried out. Though it was lost in the club music and noise, their circle had attracted attention, and she knew her pleasure was being witnessed by a wider audience. Unlike the bloody gladiator she'd been with Raithe, now she felt like a virgin being willingly sacrificed to kick off a sensuous bacchanal. The idea that her desire might be driving other scenarios playing out around them—like Amara and Enrique's dance—made her shudder harder.

Her feet were no longer on the floor. Niall had risen and shifted to the left, though he kept his mouth on her breast. Lars had returned to take his place, kneeling to lift her legs onto his shoulders. Her heels slid down his back while Cesar continued to hold her upper body firmly. Lars kissed his way up the insides of her thighs, even as he reached up and gave Niall's cock, captured in the snug jeans over his head, a playful squeeze that had Niall uttering a growl against her flesh.

If she was suffering any trepidation, seeing the relaxed expression of their lust, their urgent enjoyment not a violent urgency, would have helped quell it. But after Mason's possession of her at the cage door, cut woefully short, followed by this, her mind was no longer hampering her. Mason had said he was here, watching, making sure she would be safe, controlling her pleasure.

Then thought disappeared as Lars at last spread her legs wider and put his mouth directly in between them. He had a tongue piercing, a barbell that vibrated, and he knew how to use it with a devil's skill against a woman's clit, and to tease her labia. Sensations crashed over her. She began to squirm against Cesar's hold.

"That's the way," Niall whispered, moving back to her ear. He took over from the Latino male, sliding in behind her, replacing his mouth at her breasts with his hands. Cleverly teasing the nipples, he gripped and squeezed them for the first time, causing her to whimper at the shock of sensation. "The masked beauties are always the most uninhibited ones, their pussies so sweet and wet . . ."

Mason . . .

If you wish to come, habiba, *you must ask first.*

And if I don't? She was surprised she had the coherence for rebellion. But when the sensual threat in his mind-voice sent a ripple through her that almost pushed her over by itself, she knew it wasn't the desire for rebellion that made her challenge him.

I will punish you. When I take you home, I will arouse you to three times the intensity you are aroused now, yet chain you to my bed so you cannot touch yourself. I will let you suffer the night that way. Then, right before dawn, I will come to you, ease my cock into you, make you mine. If you beg.

Was it like Raithe, or was it not? All she knew was that she was pure need, and need had migrated to a pulsing emotional ache in her chest which demanded a release as much as—if not more than—the release she needed between her legs.

What if I want you now? Not them.

Are you willing to have your pleasure now, or later?

Can I have . . . both?

His laughter in her mind had its own power, and as Lars cleverly stroked the vibrating ball over her clit, she screamed. *Mason . . . I can't . . .*

Lars withdrew so abruptly, she wondered if Niall had yanked

him away like a dog on a leash. She blinked, disoriented. The men were melting back into the crowd as a new dance tune started, the DJ having been astute enough to keep the ballads going until their impromptu floor show completed. Her knees were shaking, but Niall smoothly picked her up in his arms. Shouldering his way through the crowd, he left her attractive attendants behind as he made his way up to that second level where Mason waited.

She had a fleeting impression of Evan, emerald eyes and dark, closely cropped hair, a lean, tensile strength, his intrigued glance. But all she wanted was Mason. She was going to go insane, rend flesh like a rabid animal in about two seconds.

When Niall put her on her feet before Mason, she was still unsteady, so he stayed behind her, his chest a bulwark against her taut shoulder blades. Mason, his mind silent but gaze overpowering, took her hand. With an effortless movement, he pulled her away from Niall and lifted her to straddle his lap. He cradled her face as he adjusted her, his fingers brushing his collar on her throat. The touch of the crystal pendant was a featherlike movement against her cleavage, teasing that valley. With precision, Mason aligned her needy core against his cock, hard and straining beneath the soft fabric of his slacks.

"Ah . . ." Her breath clogged in her throat. When she would have touched him, Niall had both of her wrists, drawing them out and then back behind her, a human restraint that displayed her to her vampire Master, arching her back and throat to him while Niall stood behind her like a prison guard.

Mason.

When he gave a slight nod to Niall, the soft padding of a Velcro strap wrapped around both her wrists, holding her arms as Mason watched her face closely, delving into her confused, lust-starved mind, she was sure.

What . . . are you doing to me?

Showing you how it should have been for you, habiba. *How strong and amazing your desire is, so much so I am having difficulty not fucking you even now. But there is sweet pleasure in making a slave wait, in driving up her desire like this.*

Niall returned to his Master's side then. Through glazed eyes,

Jessica watched Evan fondle his tightly packaged cock, a tacit approval of his actions, before he brought him down for a long, demanding kiss that had Niall gripping his Master's shoulder. Then Evan bade him kneel at his side, teasing his hair like a favored pet.

Those were vague impressions, for all she knew was Mason. Balancing her on his lap, a steadying hand at her hip, he'd picked up his drink again. After he took a swallow, he removed a cherry from the glass and extended it to her lips. Greedy for the taste of his flesh, she nipped him hard as she took it, her muscles contracting on him. She wanted to rub, and he gave her that gift.

Bring yourself to climax against me, my love. Leave my clothes damp and my cock aching for you.

She was already twitching against him, an involuntary movement that could have made her come by itself. But now she began to undulate in earnest. She had enough brain cells left that she used the hip movements Amara had taught her, because she wanted to please him, this man who was more Arab sultan than British officer, a prince of his realm. She remembered the first time she'd watched Amara dance for him, enticing him. The dance was a message of desire, of need; an offering.

She had good musculature on her thighs and abdomen and could control her balance, but desire made her dizzy. She knew he wouldn't let her fall. He simply watched her, with an expectant stillness that only drove her desire higher, giving her little time to seduce him further. Her response shot up to a crescendo, her body shuddering.

Come now for me, habiba. *Give me your cream.*

She cried out, arching back into the strength of his hands, which slipped to her lower back, cradling those scars, the tiger she'd purposefully etched into them. The climax raced through her blood, firing it. From that night with Amara and Enrique, she knew that was when he most liked to bite, when that potent heat was surging, life force at its highest and yet closest to death point. But since their human surroundings prohibited that, the focus was on her performance for him, at his command, to please him. It made her feel a way Raithe never had, with his twisted public displays.

As if underscoring that, when it was at last over and she was quivering, making short, convulsive jerks from the aftershocks, Mason gathered her to him. Niall or some other helpful person had brought a cushioned ottoman, so Mason eased her out of her straddle, turning her onto her hip on the cushioned seat now positioned between his long legs. Letting her upper body lie against his chest, he pushed her head into a tuck beneath his chin. Her arms naturally fell low around his waist, curling to the back, fingers hooking into the waistband of his slacks, holding on as she caught her breath. He pressed his hand alongside her face, cradling there, holding her.

"Very good, *habiba*. That's my sweet love."

He was still hard as a rock beneath her, his heart thundering, but he asked nothing else of her, instead casually agreeing to another drink when Evan, expressing his pleasure at her display, offered to buy the next round. Niall's hand whispered over her calf, an approval of its own, before the man rose to go get his Master's order. Jessica closed her eyes, feeling the cool weight of the crystal tumble out of her cleavage and rest against the high rise of her right breast, mashed against Mason's chest.

There was no comprehension or logic to what she'd just done. But the noise of the club was gone for her, all the flashing lights. There was only the heat of his arm around her, the beat of his heart, his breath against his hair. This was where she was willing to stay forever, if time would stop and not force her to face future or past ever again. Perhaps that was why Farida had never regretted any of it. She'd had perfect moments like these.

His hand stilled on her hair. Tension swept the body beneath her, such that the planes and curves that had fitted perfectly with her limp torso a blink ago now felt awkward, unyielding. Though he brushed his lips across her hair, it was a perfunctory move as he lifted her and set her on her feet. "On second thought, I'll have to pass on that drink, Evan. I wasn't aware of the time, and there are some other errands I need to handle before dawn."

There was Evan's protest, Mason's response, lost in her confusion, but Mason wrapped it up smoothly, swiftly. "It's been a pleasure to see you. I'll plan on visiting next time I'm in Colombia."

Jessica's brow furrowed, but she remembered herself enough to bite back her questions. Regardless, he turned to her and spoke sharply, as if she'd openly defied him. "We're leaving." *Amara and*

Enrique will be staying in the city for a few days to gather some supplies for the estate. You should stay with them.

With that, he turned and left her standing there, her climax trickling down her leg, her skin chilled. Evan watched him with an odd glance, then shrugged as Niall returned.

Niall handed his Master his drink and then shifted casually so he blocked the view between him and Jessica. When she flinched back at his proximity, lifting startled eyes to him, he lifted both hands carefully. "Easy, girl." He dropped his voice. "I was going to say I hope we get the pleasure of seeing you again. And perhaps a name, next time. You might want to go. You know they get testy if you keep them waiting."

Giving her a nod and a reassuring wink, he moved back to Evan, who was watching the floor again. The human servant of another vampire was not worth his notice when she was not with her Master. Or performing like a licentious lap dancer.

Jessica swallowed, her hands curling into fists. She began to work her way through the crowd, the noise now seeming far too loud, far too close. Her peaceful interlude was gone. As if Mason had held her in a cocoon, the sultry languor she'd felt with him was now replaced with a simmering headache, egged on by the crashing music, too many strobe lights and the suffocating heat of too many bodies. Too many sexually stimulated bodies.

"Jess?"

She nearly clutched Amara in relief when she appeared at her side, Enrique behind her. "Lord Mason said he was departing and you would be staying with us. What happened?"

"I don't know. I didn't even know you were staying. Why didn't you tell me?" When Jessica stumbled, not yet steady on her feet, Amara guided her out of the press of traffic. The club was rife with small alcoves that could be shut off from view with a curtain for those desiring privacy. As they went into one, Enrique drew the velvet fabric closed, muting the noise a small amount. Amara pushed her down into a chair.

"Here, catch your breath. Lord Mason was going to tell you tonight. Only I thought he was planning—" She stopped, wincing. Enrique put his hand on her shoulder, brow creasing in concern.

"I'm fine," she said. Clearing her throat, she met Jess's gaze. "Lord Mason has just . . . reiterated you should stay with us for a few days. That would be preferable."

Jessica surged back up, gripping the back of her chair for balance. "I'm not an idiot. You wanted me to stay at the estate, the two of us, for a few days. What changed?"

Amara shook her head. "I—"

"I wasn't talking to you," Jessica snapped. Glaring into space, she balled her hands in fists. *Leave me standing there, like some . . . whore you paid for sex. You bastard.* "Never mind. We'll see you in a few days." Sweeping aside the privacy screen, she hesitated, then glanced back. "Thank you for tonight, both of you. And don't worry about me. Really. Have a good time and enjoy one another."

Then she disappeared in the crowd, leaving Enrique and Amara blinking at each other. Enrique sent Mason the message that Jessica was alone and headed toward the front entrance, but then he reached out and touched Amara's face. "Did he hurt you?"

She shook her head. "I think his emotions aren't under control right now. She might want to tread carefully."

"Hmm. She doesn't seem very calm herself." However, as he eased her to her feet, and she turned from his expression, it darkened. Enrique knew a vampire could express his displeasure with a servant in a manner comparable to having a migraine explode abruptly in a marked human's mind. Linked as closely to his wife as he was, it was clear Mason had come damn near to that.

My lord, that was not *necessary.* When Enrique met silence, he gritted his teeth, feeling a rare surge of anger. Perhaps it was good they were spending a couple days in the city. However, Amara was right. Mason rarely acted in this manner. Reluctantly, Enrique wondered if it was best for Jessica if they changed their plans.

If I wished to harm her, I could, Enrique, with or without your presence.

Enrique directed his wife through the crowds, a hand at her back, the other clasping the fingers of her free hand. *Yes, my lord. But it was my impression, as well as Jessica's, that you are not Raithe.*

A tiger does not stop being a tiger, Enrique, just because it knows how to sheathe his claws. Do not test me. Go and enjoy your time in town with Amara. I will see you in three days. I'm sure Jessica will be rejoining you after we speak together.

~

When she'd stepped into the club, she'd been terrified, but determined to face her fear. She'd found ways to overcome it, fragile methods for certain, but she'd done it. The mask had been part of that, and it had been his suggestion. In fact, all the things that had helped her get through tonight had rested on the foundation of his presence. For the first time, she'd acknowledged she'd begun to trust him as her protector.

In her pre-Raithe life, she remembered how her safe world glorified the label of victim, such that day-to-day crises were blown into melodramas, all to display the V proudly on chests. Those people in their safe worlds had no idea what truly being a victim meant, or how fiercely those who were true victims despised the branding of that label upon their souls.

Overwhelmed by uncontrollable, stronger forces, she'd been helpless, no options except base survival instincts, beyond the indulgences of morality or choice. She'd been hurt to the point she'd begged for death, been willing to do anything, suffer any humiliation, betray any part of herself—except her family—to simply make it stop hurting. Now that it might be in her past, she had no patience with being treated as if that part of her life was all she would ever be.

But as she pushed toward the club exit and the initial humiliation and stung feelings ebbed, she came to an astonishing realization. Something had overwhelmed Mason, and rather than thinking of her first, of her fragility, he'd acted to protect his own vulnerability. He'd considered her capable of pulling it back together, handling the aftermath of his mood swing herself. As angry as it had made her, it gave her a fierce sense of triumph—as well as renewed determination to get to the bottom of this, once and for all.

Jessica found the limo in the same place. The driver was leaning against it, smoking a cigarette, but she waved him away before he stirred himself to get the door. Circling to the opposite side, she yanked it open herself, ducking into the roomy interior. Mason was in the far corner, his face in shadows as he took a swallow from what appeared to be whiskey. One long leg was stretched out, the other bent, a tense hand on his knee.

She took the seat across from him. Since he seemed to be indulging one of his long, brooding silences, she took the time to sort out her own thoughts, not really sure now how to proceed. She'd intended to remove the mask, but she wasn't sure how he'd laced together the ties. In a way, though, she wasn't unhappy about that, for the mask did give her more courage.

Mason's gaze remained on the glass. "You need to go join Amara and Enrique."

"What if I prefer to go home?"

"While the Council has no plans to hunt your family, I wouldn't advise that yet."

Jessica bit her lip. "That's not what I meant."

"I know what you meant." He sighed. "Jessica, you know there's a hundred reasons why staying with me is only a temporary waypost for you. It's—"

"This isn't about me." She cut across him, ignoring his warning look. "This is about you. Why did you pull back from me, Mason?"

"That would be Lord Mason, or my lord. You of all people should be aware of vampire etiquette."

"How about my Royal Pain in the Ass?" she suggested sweetly. "Or—"

She didn't see him move, but in the next second he had her flat on her back on the seat, his hand gripping her throat, his body looming over hers. When his eyes flashed amber fire, the lip curled back, showing deadly fangs. The strength of his one hand was unshakable, and as he knelt over her, staring down at her with implacable eyes, waiting for her to come into line, she felt it close around her. The grip of the fear, always waiting, perhaps all the worse for being pushed back, like a wound that had closed over, only to have the scab pulled off fresh, a feeling that could be more painful than the initial strike.

But this time, she shoved it away with all her strength, the rage of a soul that refused to be bullied ever again.

I refuse to fear you. She snarled it inside, a female tiger taking on the wrath of a male, though the flames in his eyes could immolate her. "Treat me like he did if you wish, my lord. But you will have to kill me. I will not scrape like some cringing slave."

Her voice shook as she said it, but she reached up. He caught her by the wrist. She lifted the other hand. This time he didn't stop her as she touched his face. Instead, he whipped his head to the side, a striking snake, and sank his fangs into her wrist.

She cried out, but curled her bound hand in his grip, her fingers overlapping his knuckles. When his gaze closed, his head bowed, though he kept a firm grip on her, drinking, replenishing his body. A warm swirl of emotion penetrated the cold grip of her fear.

You are trying to push me away, my lord, and it won't work. You are not Raithe. You're something even more dangerous. But I want you anyway. "And"—she drew his gaze, speaking aloud—"I understand now, what you all have meant about a true vampire-servant bond. Amara and Enrique . . . they never capitulate because you order it. They capitulate to you, submit to you, because that's what they want."

The flash that went through his gaze was so fast she could hardly follow all the emotions in it. Desire, yearning, desperation. Rejection. She firmed her chin. "Don't say it. Don't say I don't know what I want. The problem is I do, but what I want doesn't make any sense. It doesn't make it wrong."

No. It doesn't. But my desire to take what you're offering may be.

He retracted his fangs, suckling on her wrist. It was to close the wound with the coagulants in his saliva, but it still had her lower body taut, willing to rouse to him again. When he lifted off her and moved back to his seat, her gaze drifted down his body. He'd untucked the shirt, the mesh disguising the evidence of her climax against the front of his slacks. Her scent would be there, on the fabric tight over his still-unappeased cock.

She eased off the seat onto her knees, feeling the limo's carpeted floor.

"Jessica, don't." It was a warning, but one she ignored as she moved toward him. As powerful as he was, he couldn't control his reaction, the naked hunger in his expression as she made the short trip in the subservient position, placing her hands on his thighs as she put herself between them.

"You have given me pleasure, my lord. Let me return the gift."

"If you think of him even once, of the unspeakable things he made you do like this, I won't . . ."

"Shhh. This is you and me." Fiercely, she willed her mind to believe that, as much as she wanted him to do so. Letting her hands glide up, she found the muscles beneath the translucent shirt. Impulsively, she leaned forward, mouthed the hard ridges of his abdomen, tongued him through the fabric as a shudder ran through him. While she did that, her hand found his belt, the fastening of the slacks, opened them, freed the hard shaft from his snug boxers. It pushed eagerly into her hands. Heat and power, the tip glistening in a way that demanded her mouth.

Mason dropped his head back on the seat, his body gravitating toward her, so that when she lifted the shirt and dipped her chin, it was easy to slide her mouth around the broad head, taste him for the second time, but in these circumstances, it was as incredible a sensation as if it were the first. He groaned, his hand gripping the back of the seat.

Touch me, my lord. Let me feel your need. Drive me down on you as you wish to do. Take control as you must.

She swallowed as his fingers convulsed in her hair. With one rough motion, he ripped the lacings free, pushed her head up and tore away the mask, making her gasp.

As he cradled her face, he stared down at her, his fingers on her mouth letting her know he didn't want her to speak. It had been easier to look at him, to act this way, with the mask. Maybe he knew that; maybe not. Maybe he just wanted to see her face. Thinking that eased something in her, giving a raw intimacy to this when so many things lay unresolved between them.

Then, thankfully, he directed her mouth back onto him. He was as impressive as she remembered, and stretching her mouth to take him, to work her way down the glistening length of him, stirred things between her legs anew. She wanted to feel him come in her throat, wanted to swallow his essence as he'd just swallowed hers.

She drew him deep, dragged upward again. It was something she'd been taught to do with consummate skill, but until this moment she'd never had any joy in her ability, never been glad for the punishments she'd suffered for not doing it well enough.

Jessica. Even his thought was a feral growl. *I am your only Master. Suck me.*

Her body shuddered at the demand, and she renewed her efforts. She remembered how he'd watched her, amber eyes burning as he commanded her to rub herself against him, bring herself to climax. And she'd loved it, felt no shame in the way he'd held her afterward, pleased with her. Until . . .

Deeper. Harder. As he increased his possessive grip on her, she let the thoughts go for now and obeyed, eyes tearing. She relaxed her throat to take him, for he was moving her on him urgently, now that he controlled the rhythm. With this lesson on the contrast between indifferent brutality and rough passion, he was turning everything inside her to liquid heat. Her thighs dampened again, her sex contracting on its too empty channel as her movements rubbed her labia against her calf, where she was on her knees.

His hand spasmed on her head. He was close. Encouraging, pleading noises came from her throat. Noises of desire and arousal, her body leaning against his leg, surrounded by his heat and power, his gathering need.

I want to taste you, my lord. I will swallow every drop.

With a snarl, he climaxed, the heated organ clutched in her fist pumping the fluids in waves beneath the pressure of her fingers, shooting seed into the back of her throat. The thick, viscous fluid almost choked her because, like the size of his cock, it was more than expected. Still, she swallowed him down, allowing only enough to escape to lubricate him further for her closed fist, so she could keep pumping him, working him in her mouth. Teasing him with her lips, she nipped at the curve of the broad head.

When she'd drained the last from him, he didn't give her time to put her temple against his knee, nuzzle his heavy testicles and semierect cock with her mouth and nose in languorous satisfaction as she might have wished. Instead, in those swift vampire movements a human was helpless to counter, he swept her up and put her on her back on the floor this time, his body stretched between her legs. His damp organ still had enough heat and hardness to press against her aching center, making her mewl and arch up against him. But he planted his hands on either side of her head, staring down at her with a harsh expression in his golden eyes.

All traces of honorable gentleman were gone, leaving the pure vampire, the one who would have what he wanted. She closed her eyes and tilted her head away, exposing her throat to him, a mute surrender of her body and blood, maybe even her heart and soul, for this precious moment.

He stilled. He stayed that way, his breath so close on her flesh, and God, she was trembling, wanting and afraid. *Please don't turn away from me. I need you so much, my lord.*

"Shhh . . . ," he said at last, but a quiver ran through that powerful body as he reined himself in. "I don't want to do this here. I want to take you home, Jess. I want to have you beneath me, in my bed."

She pressed her forehead into his shoulder, relief flooding her, because that was what she wanted as well. However, as intuitive and demanding as he was, she had her own lines in the sand. "Will you see me, or her, when you take me?"

Before he could answer, she stared up into his eyes. *"See me."*

The pain that flashed across his gaze was replaced by a tenderness that captivated her. He touched her face, his fingers caressing her short curls. "I always have."

"Then what happened?" she whispered. "Why did my thoughts about Farida change things? Why did you leave me standing there like that?" *Discarded.*

"Never discarded, *habiba*. Never. I was wrong to do that to you. I'm sorry." When he ran a thumb over her lips, she touched it with the tip of her tongue, causing his body to tighten against hers in a delicious way that made her want to writhe beneath him. His eyes glowed. "Do you wish to go with Amara and Enrique?"

"It depends." She rubbed her cheek against his hand. "Are you going to act like an ogre again?"

"Probably," he admitted, though there was a grudging smile in his eyes.

"Will you order me to go home with you, my lord?" She waited, sensing the struggle in him as his gaze coursed over her face, her throat, the nearly exposed breasts in the low neckline. When he pressed his lips together, she imagined the heat of his mouth there.

"No, Jessica," he said at last. "Not until you call me Master by your own choice." Rising on his knees, he tucked himself away and refastened the pants, then sat back on his heels. Because he stayed between her legs, she understood he wanted her to stay as she was, her legs open to him. He placed a hand on her leg, his fingers gliding up the inside of her thigh. Those vibrant eyes glowed in the semi-darkness.

If you were mine, I would make you sit across from me during our drive and keep the skirt pushed to your waist, your thighs spread. I would dip my fingers in my whiskey, paint your cunt lips with it, suck it off as I wished. Or simply watch you sit that way, obeying my plea-sure, trembling with your increasing desire. It is what we vampires enjoy.

"Not only vampires," she admitted in a low voice, stirred by it, stirred by all of it. She trembled because she wanted him so badly. Mouth, fingers, cock. Heart, soul . . .

His gaze rose to her. She wondered if it was possible to delve that deeply into Lord Mason. And if she'd lost her mind for wanting to do so. His gaze flickered.

"You are already in my heart and soul, Jessica. But there are things I need to tell you. Not merely the Council's decision. I do want you, on levels far deeper than my cock, and you're in the unique and terrible position of understanding, as few do, how deep those layers can go. It has been . . . a very long time, since I've wanted to claim a woman that way."

Their surroundings, a quiet limo, the noise of the club muted outside, were an odd backdrop for such momentous words, but everything else vanished for Jessica as he said them, as he wrapped her in the spell the import of those words offered.

"I wish to Allah that it were not so, because if I could have re-mained detached from you, I would not feel I've made your decisions far more complicated, obscured your future."

She was unsure if he'd just rejected her or brought them closer together, but he clasped her with unexpectedly gentle hands, helped her back onto the seat. He straightened her skirt, stroking her thighs, resting his hands on her knees as he stayed kneeling before her, eye to eye.

"Perhaps it will make things easier if I tell you that I will not claim you as mine until you call me Master, and mean it, to that deepest, darkest level of your soul." Though his hands were gentle, the look in his eye, the resolve in his voice, was implacable. "I will not take away your choices until you want me to do so. And"—that shadow crossed his gaze again—"the things I have to tell you may change things, how you view me and my world.

"For now, be still, *habiba*, and let me enjoy your beauty. We'll talk when we get home."

25

Trrue to his word, Mason had little else to say on the plane, or on the Jeep ride through the rain forest to return to the estate. When they got there, it was nearing dawn, and she knew it wasn't likely that she would get anything further from him. On the plane, she'd curled up, her head on his thigh while he'd stroked her hair absently. When she opened her eyes, he was gazing out the window, his thoughts far away. She curled both hands around his leg, holding on to him as if she could be an anchor line to keep him from getting too lost in his mind. As her eyes closed again, she felt his lips brush her temple.

In her dreamlike state, her thoughts wandered. She thought of Hasna and Coman, her room and the view of the ocean from it. In truth, she *was* anticipating it like a home. Was it because some part of her had been denied simple pleasures so long that she easily fixated on it that way, after only a couple months? After her night of discarded inhibitions, she was back to the same conflict, the one he refused to let her forget. What was real and illusion, but did she even care anymore? Yes, because it was important to Mason. Of course, she'd insisted he see her, not Farida, when he touched her, so some portion of the reality between them was important to her as well.

Since the sun was rising by the time they got to the estate, they drove into the underground parking garage. The Jeep was outfitted with tinted windows to protect him from sunlight, but she could tell he was instantly more comfortable when he parked the vehicle.

She hadn't even realized he could drive, but of course it would be absurd if he couldn't. On the way back, he explained all but a bare skeleton staff had been given several days off. Before she could assume that meant they had the estate pretty much to themselves, and the significance of that, he dispelled the mixed anxiety and pleasure of the thought with a much more harrowing revelation.

"I have some guests coming," he said quietly, as he took her hand to help her from the Jeep and opened the stairwell door to the upper quarters. "They'll be here in a couple days. They're vampires, Jessica."

She stopped on the stair above him. "I see," she managed.

"You handled yourself well tonight. You can handle yourself with them."

Amara and Enrique would be gone. She would be the only third-marked servant available.

"Jessica." His hands were on her shoulders, and she realized she'd backed up to the wall, was pushing at him. "You can go back to the city. You don't have to stay."

"If you meant that, you would have told me before we left."

"No. I didn't tell you then because my mind was elsewhere." His brow furrowed in a rare expression of frustration, catching her attention, because it made her notice something new and unexpected. He looked tired. Letting her go, he rubbed a hand behind his neck. "I didn't think of it. With these guests, servants aren't required to serve as entertainment."

"Vampires always share servants." She shook her head. "If you don't, you lose standing in their eyes."

He took one of her tense hands, so the clasped fingers hung between them, a link. He attempted a smile, but it didn't reach his eyes. "I don't give a damn what anyone thinks of me, and you know it."

"It doesn't matter. It's practically an unbreakable code for all of you. How do you get a free pass from that?"

He sighed, and began to lead her up the stairs, while Jessica tried to force down the butterflies. Vampires *always* shared servants. Always.

"Because when it boils down to it," he said, "what vampires respect more than anything else—no matter what they say or how they act—is strength and power. Control. I happen to have more of those three than any other vampire in the world, save one or two."

"You're lying," she decided. When he glanced at her, she shook her head. "No, I don't mean about the power and control thing. I don't know about that, but you do care what others think. Like me, or Amara and Enrique. You don't care what *vampires* think. It's what they did to you, growing up, that made you hate them, isn't it?"

"I should have burned that second journal." He bared his teeth in a feral smile. "Psychoanalysis is an amusing pastime, *habiba*, but vampires are what they are. Put any of us in a room with a human baby and no blood source, and eventually we will smell a basket of nachos with talcum powder seasoning."

"Crash an airplane in the Alps, and the survivors will eventually eat the wounded or dead," she retorted, unimpressed. "You yourself told me that the desire to survive is the strongest imperative, right?"

She could feel his irritation rising, but she pressed on anyway. He'd promised her answers here. She wanted them. She wanted a hell of a lot more than that, in fact.

"Occasionally trumped by love." His gaze flashed. "But that's appreciated only beyond the grave."

"Mason." She gritted her teeth. "I *hate* it when you bullshit me."

That startled him, not an easy feat. She would have smiled at his expression, if he wasn't frustrating the hell out of her. "I beg your pardon?"

"You want me to figure things out in my head, to know what I really want. Well, part of that is understanding you, why you've done the things you've done for me. Why you keep pulling away when you obviously want to fuck me ten ways to Sunday, and keep me as your third-marked servant. I can feel all of that, no matter what you say, but something keeps holding you back. Just tell me, goddamn it. I went through too much, for too long, to be patient over stupid bullshit."

She'd crossed her arms during her tirade, and when she finished, she realized she was shouting, the last words echoing off the walls of the stairwell. Reaching out with firm, not-to-be-refused fingers, he

cupped the side of her throat and drew her to him, until she was
pressed into his chest, her fingers resting on it, body canted into his.
The leg braced on the higher step pressed into her hip, the curve of
her buttock. "I would prefer it if you wouldn't use foul language
around me," he said softly. As she glanced up, the tips of his fangs
showed, reminding her it was well past dawn. "It doesn't suit you,
and it offends me."

She set her jaw. "Then answer my fucking questions."

His nostrils flared. Tension thrummed through his body, and
when she would have drawn back, a belated sense of self-preservation,
she found he could hold her immobilized with nothing more than
that one hand. "Jess, I mean it. You have nothing to fear from my
guests, for I do not force my servants to entertain them, vampire etiquette be damned. But I also do not brook active disobedience from
my servants. So if you want to get the spanking of your life, I'd keep
it up." His brow drew down, the sensual lips distractingly close. "I
will not cause you injury, but it will hurt, as every girl who's been
taken out behind a woodshed by her father knows."

She swallowed, made herself hold that gaze, knowing as well as
he did that most servants didn't lock gazes with their Masters in a
moment like this. "I've had skin stripped from my back, my lord. My
legs were broken in three places and cuffed in that position so the
healing could be delayed until I had been fucked by a quaint little
dinner party of five vampires. Do you *really* think I'm scared of having my ass paddled by Daddy?"

"Yes," he responded. In a quick shift, he had her against the wall,
his thigh pushing between her legs, causing her to suck in a breath. He
watched her bite down on her bottom lip. "Because 'Daddy' will not
only paddle your sweet buttocks; he'll do it until you're writhing
with pain and pleasure both. Then he will manacle you to the wall
next to his bed, put the most relentless little clit stimulator you've
ever felt between your legs, on just the right setting. Your waist and
hips will be anchored so you can't move, and you'll be painfully
aroused for hours, not allowed to climax until I wake. So you won't
disturb my sleep, I have a perfect ball gag for those clever lips of
yours." His thumb came up now to graze her exposed teeth where
they pressed into her lip, swollen with the compression. "The most

effective tortures are those of deprivation. You will be begging my forgiveness, promising never to curse again."

He was quite obviously getting aroused again, but she was being sucked along in the same tide. "Bring it on," she said, her mind torn between desire and apprehension. "When that's all done, you'll still have to tell me what you're wishing you hadn't brought up in the limo. And it's not the Council's decision. It's something even more important than that, at least to the two of us. The more we're together, the more it's eating at you."

Mason stared down at her. He had an overwhelming urge to do exactly as he'd threatened, but if he did, he wouldn't be able to keep from fucking her ten ways to Sunday, as she so inelegantly put it. With an oath he turned and left her, striding up the stairs. It wasn't easy, not with a hard-on like a tree trunk. He wanted her in his bed. He wanted to finally penetrate her deep, take her into him, make her his.

But because she was right, he left her behind. He had to tell her first.

~

He slept fitfully. Without Amara and Enrique here, she was fairly unsupervised. But she had the bracelets and collar still, and of course Jorge was on the premises, helping to cover any light maintenance needs as well as minding the horses. But he knew it wasn't that. He wasn't going to sleep well until he did take her to his bed. And if that never happened, well, he just wouldn't sleep well ever again.

He went to find her as soon as the afternoon sun slipped behind the horizon, while rose and gold still bathed the darkening sky. She was sitting on the upper verandah railing, her bare feet dangling over the steep drop to the gardens. As eager as he'd been to see her, Mason stopped in the shadows to study her at a distance, silent, not wanting her to see him yet, dreading what she'd shrewdly perceived he had to tell her.

She was beautiful, a slim waif sitting on a railing, a little too relaxed for his peace of mind. But as she'd pointed out earlier, what was worse—physically at least—than what she'd already endured? Falling off a stone wall and breaking a bone that would heal within minutes, with his blood, was trivial in comparison. But he hated her pain, her nightmares.

She was wearing a thin, flowing island dress. From the dampness of her curls as well as the idle drifting in her mind, he knew she'd been swimming. She loved the ocean, running in the damp sand. Playing with the horses. He wanted her here, always. He wanted to take her to the Sahara, to the families he knew who still raised Arabians, let her see the magnificent equine princes of the desert. Or to Montana, for the wild mustangs on the refuge he sponsored there. The first time he'd looked into a horse's gaze, he'd been drawn to them, to their complicated mix of strength and fragility, nobility and animal savagery. He saw it here, in the straight back and tilted head of the young woman sitting on the wall. When he'd had her flat on her back in the limo, making it clear he could tear her apart with as much effort as it would take her to rip up a sheet of paper, she'd practically bared her own fangs and snarled back at him.

"Are you staring at my ass?"

She changed the angle of her chin then, glancing over her shoulder directly at him, when she shouldn't have seen or even registered his presence.

"Here I was composing poetic analogies to your beauty, and you, with your vile American upbringing, assume only the most crass motives."

"We may be crass, but we do tend to endure. Us and the cockroaches." But there was a serious set to her sweet mouth as he joined her, leaning his hips against the rail so he was facing toward the house. "They want me executed, don't they?" she asked after a silent moment.

This, at least, was easy enough to discuss. As he slid an arm in front of her, loosely holding on to her waist, he was absurdly reassured when she curled gentle fingers over his forearm. He shook his head. "No, *habiba*. They agreed to spare your life. A moot point, considering I never would have allowed them to take it, but it certainly makes the rest easier."

She drew a deep breath, and he raised a brow at her shudder. When he drew her closer to his side, she rested her face on his shoulder, staring out at the ocean so he could see only the top of her head.

"Well, that relieved me more than I expected. I guess I thought I'd be hunted forever."

He brushed a kiss on the crown of her head. "You will not. But there are some conditions."

"Conditions? With vampires? You don't say." But she propped the point of her chin on his broad shoulder so she could look into his face. The proximity of her lips, the tempting line of her brow and nose, was distracting. He cleared his throat, shifted his gaze to the ocean.

"Their primary concern is that your success in killing your Master does not spread insurrection." At her incredulous look, he lifted a shoulder. "Yes, we both know it was amazing luck. Most human servants couldn't inflict a scratch on their Masters, let alone a death blow."

"Well," she said, a little defensively, "it wasn't *only* amazing luck. I am pretty tough, when all is said and done."

"You are tough as old shoe leather, *habiba*. You will get no argument from me." At her narrow look, he continued. "I pointed out that most human servants have no desire to leave their Master. They come willingly to that service. The relationship may not be everything they anticipate, for it is beyond human comprehension until it is truly lived. Still, human servants typically come with a disposition for the role, an instinctual desire for that bond."

Her fingers tightened on his arm, and he felt the press of every small tip, the light bite of her nails. She'd turned her head, looking toward the ocean again. "Their ruling is that you may live, *habiba*, as long as you stay under my protection, as my third-marked servant."

He stayed silent for a few moments, hearing the whirl of thoughts in her head, but before he was tempted to decipher them, he made himself continue. "Unless Lord Brian is successful, that is."

She raised her head. "Who is Lord Brian?"

"He's one of us, but he's a scientist as well. He explores the medical basis for our vulnerabilities. And how to make them easier to overcome." He hesitated, then resolutely plunged forward as her attention sharpened. "He has seen the aftermath, as you and I both have, of a human forced into servitude. There are vampires who are young, who cannot control themselves. They don't do it as Raithe did, with genuine twisted malevolence, but out of youthful mis-understanding of the consequences of power and control. Quite sim-ply, they don't realize there are any, when they see an attractive human they decide they want."

When she lifted her body from his, fixing her gaze on him as if realizing the import of what he was about to say, he looked toward the ocean himself. "Lord Brian has developed a treatment that can erase all of a vampire's marks. It would free you completely, Jess," he added quietly. "Once he has tested it and deemed it safe, then you could be transported wherever you wish, to start the life you want to lead. The treatment would be administered there. No vampire will ever cross your path again. I'll make sure of it."

Jessica shook her head. "How could the Council agree to this? What's to stop me from using my knowledge to help vampire hunt-ers, or expose your existence?"

Tracing her cheek, he wound a curl around his finger. Brushed a thumb over her lips and thought how her eyes could soften with de-sire or laughter when she looked at him. So simple and magnificent at once. Those gray eyes darkened, but he couldn't bear her to speak until he said it.

"Brian came up with a way to erase memories. When the serum is administered, a form of hypnosis will be performed, and you will remember none of it, *habiba*. Every horrible thing Raithe did . . . it will be gone. It shouldn't even linger in your nightmares."

She slid off the rail, standing on her own feet, her face pale. "Ev-erything?" she whispered. "I'd remember . . . nothing? Not even Jack?" Her voice trembled over the name.

Of course that would matter. Mason cursed the claws of jealousy that made him resent a man who'd loved her as she deserved to be loved, and died trying to help her. Pushing it away, he clasped her cold hand. "If I could leave you his memory, I would, but it's too closely linked."

She swallowed. "And Farida?"

Mason held her gaze. "She is even more closely connected to our world than Jack."

Jessica stepped back, withdrawing her hand. Her throat worked, her eyes darting around her as if she expected someone to leap out and administer the serum against her will. "But she was why I survived. You and her . . . the way she loved you."

"There will be nothing to have survived, *habiba*," he reminded her, remaining on the rail despite the fact he wanted to soothe her fears. "You'll remember nothing Raithe did to you. We will plant a suggestion to explain your scars, the tiger tattoo on your back. My third mark erased any other damage."

The tiger on her thigh would be gone, because all evidence of his marks would be gone. That tightness in her chest increased. "My . . . mortality would return to normal?"

"It appears so. His tests on the aging of cells showed an appropriate rate for a normal mortal." He cocked his head. "You will live to be an old woman of eighty or ninety, instead of three or four hundred."

Jess paced in a circle. "I can't get my mind around it." She lifted her hands, a helpless gesture. "Not having a memory of Raithe, but also Farida, and Jack? To live a lie?"

"To live the life you were meant to have lived. Not a lie."

"Who's to say what life I was meant to live?" Stress punched her voice up several octaves.

"Jessica." He came to her then, settling hands on her tense shoulders. "I know you are a fighter. Your first reaction is to resist having your mind manipulated. But remember what I told you about the bracelets and collar, versus Raithe's manacles. One was for your benefit. I have seen you chased by your nightmares into your waking hours, seen you want to hurt yourself rather than feel those memories. You will not lose Farida. You *are* her."

At Jess's startled look, he shook his head. "I don't mean that you are Farida come back to life. But there is something about you that reminds me a great deal of her, and I think you felt it when you first read of her. Perhaps there is a bond between all women of such strong character."

A faint smile touched his lips, but again it didn't reach his eyes. If anything, Jessica felt as though he was drawing more deeply into himself, the more he was telling her. Now she was the one who pressed forward against his grip, laying her hands on his chest.

"I can't think about it right now, okay? Let's just . . . leave that for the moment. Tell me the other thing, Mason."

Looking up into his face, she saw the pain flash through it again and softened her tone. "Why haven't you let her go, Mason? I understand about loving her and all, but this is more than honoring a woman's memory. What did you do to her that was so unforgivable you can't stop trying to make it up to her? Why do you keep using her memory to push me away?"

He shook his head, but Jessica curled her fingers into his white shirt. It was soft, but custom-tailored to his broad shoulders. While he'd looked edible at the fetish club, this attire was more the man she knew him to be. Though nothing fit him quite like desert robes. "Please."

"A vampire typically doesn't bare the darkest shadows of his soul to his human servant," Mason said at last. "I'm not sure of the wisdom of doing so now, no matter what I said earlier."

"Mason—"

"I don't want to bring you more pain, *habiba*." He couldn't keep the anguish out of his voice, his harsh expression startling her. "And I am afraid you will see me differently."

He removed her hands, albeit with a gentle squeeze, and went back to the railing. Jessica stared after him. Of all the things she'd expected him to say, that had not been one of them. A human servant, no matter how closely bonded to a vampire, was always below the line of equality with the Master. Reconciling that basic fact of vampire existence with his astounding words took a moment to digest, but then she rallied.

"Mason, I need to know what it is you won't tell me. More importantly, I think you need to tell me, too." She stepped forward, narrowing the space between them. "You've grieved for her three hundred years. She took you down with her, and I *know* she's the type of person who wouldn't have done that, who would have wanted you to live, and love."

Mason looked out toward the ocean. When he spoke, his voice was distant, monotone. "Do you know why Raithe wanted to third-mark you so much?"

"Because he was a sadistic bastard who never wanted me to escape him?"

Mason lifted a shoulder. "A given. But more than that, Jess, you've been second-marked. You know that gives me full access to your mind, and I can speak in your head, let you into my mind if I wish. So what's different about being third-marked?"

"Greater strength, agility, the extended life span. And the link to the mortality of the vampire."

"Deeper, Jess. Think deeper." He turned and looked at her then, holding her gaze.

Suddenly, it was as though she was immersed in the sea's warm waters and he was the current, carrying and surrounding her at once. He reached out to her. Not with his hands, not with his mind, but with the mark itself, so she felt its branding through her vital organs, in her bloodstream, in the circuitry of her nervous system, including her brain. His power flooded the darkest and lightest parts of her. When she physically tried to back away, it was as if he'd become an irresistible riptide in truth, holding her in the embrace of his will. Feelings, unconscious and subconscious, were stroked to life. Not only her nightmares and fears, but her deepest, most desperate yearnings as well.

Mason . . . stop.

She blinked, and it was gone. He was still sitting on the rail, she was still standing a few feet away. But she felt dizzy, as if she needed to sit down. With effort, she held her ground. "What was that?"

"That was a touch of what a vampire can do with the third mark. If I want to, I can feel everything you feel, Jessica. Everything. Not just what you *want* to think about and feel, but what you don't, unconsciously. I can drag every nightmare and fear to the forefront of your mind, lock it there so you would believe you were in Raithe's hands again. I can also stir the meadows of your best memories to make you smile, to give you eternal laughter. Or I can immerse myself there without your knowledge, when I need those good memories to supplement my own." He'd glanced back out at the ocean, giving her a moment to steady herself, and yet when he looked back, his eyes were far more expressive than she'd ever seen them before, full of something raw.

"If you close your eyes, Jess, you can feel me. You've begun to pick up on my moods, even my presence, before you can see me. You have an aptitude for it, because I've let the bond grow between us. If

I was being more honest with you than I should be, I'd say I don't think I did it consciously." When she took another step toward him, he shook his head, stilling her.

"If I keep letting that bond strengthen, it would become even deeper, until you would feel as if you rode inside the protection of my own soul. I've never allowed the bond with Amara and Enrique to progress to that stage. For one thing, it wouldn't be fair. I want them to enjoy their love with one another, and while what I demand of them is certainly unconventional for a marriage, there are certain lines I respect. Because I remember what it was to have that utter sense of bonding."

And because he couldn't bear to share that with another, ever again, she thought. The acknowledging flicker of his eyes was reflected in the pang that went through her heart.

"Now," he continued in a voice that became chilling, prickling gooseflesh on her arms, "imagine Raithe with that power over you. How he could intensify your tortures, your fears. He could have done it for the centuries of your life, because, short of steel driven through your heart, nothing would have killed you. Knowing that, it's a miracle he held off giving you the third mark as long as he did. But I suspect watching your terror grow over the anticipation of it was giving him a sadistic fix he wanted to milk as long as possible."

Jessica swallowed. "What does this have to do with Farida?" There was no moon tonight, she noted. As the night deepened, only the torchlight ringing the balcony gave light. The ocean had disappeared, only the rushing sound of it on the salt-laden breeze indicating its presence. But he could see it, she knew, because vampires could see many things humans didn't see.

"Let's go down to the garden," Mason said abruptly. "I'd prefer to be there." Rising, he gestured toward the stairs. When Jessica hesitated, his gaze flickered. "It doesn't have to be tonight, Jess. If you'd rather not . . ."

"No. I asked, and you're willing to tell me. If I don't do it now, you'll likely change your mind again and never tell me." She forced a smile. "And if I agree to Lord Brian's serum, I won't remember whatever awful thing you're about to tell me anyway, right?"

"Correct."

She hated that flat tone, the way his face could go so blank. But she preceded him down the stairs, noting he stayed close enough to provide her a steadying arm in the darkness, but otherwise didn't touch her. An ominous tension was gathering around him.

He took her to one of her favorite places, the fountain with the horse sculpture. After he seated her on the wall, inside a cloud of cooling mist, he moved to a bench, sitting alone. When he said nothing for several moments, Jessica warred between waiting him out and giving him a gentle prod. "I noticed you don't have any pictures of her."

Mason shook his head. "Images of living beings were a sin against her faith. I honored that, and I never needed them, anyway. She is in my mind, always." Abruptly, he stood, paced away and leaned against a tree, staring out into the darkness. "She was pure, delicate. I never should have been overwhelmed that way. I felt responsible, just for loving her, but I was helpless not to. I thought I could resist, until the day when she washed my feet." A muscle flexed in his jaw.

"I know you're still coming to terms with it in yourself and in others, Jess, but a vampire is irresistibly drawn to willing, loving submission. She was as innocent as a jasmine bloom, but some part of her knew the things that would lower my guard. When she knelt at my feet that night, I was tempted to spirit her away then and say to hell with any of it."

"You made her your servant, but you married her." Knowing vampires as she did, it still amazed Jessica to say it aloud, to see him acknowledge it.

"She wanted to be bound to me as closely as was possible, and once she found out about third servants, she pretty much demanded that." He lifted a shoulder. "As with most things concerning her, I capitulated. I was weak. But it never crossed my mind not to marry her."

He looked toward her. "In many different cultures, even yours historically, the bond between husband and wife was not so very different. The wife was asked to honor and obey, the man to honor and cherish. She belonged to him and served his needs, but she also could rely on him for care and protection of hers. And this was three hundred years ago, in a highly patriarchal culture, *habiba*. Marrying her was not necessarily antithetical to the relationship between vampire and servants."

His voice softened, his eyes distant. "I knew if I didn't marry her, it would fester in her mind, a wound suggesting she was what her father labeled her. I wouldn't tolerate that."

"You weren't weak. What the two of you had wasn't weak." Jessica drew his attention from what he was seeing in the dark. "Farida recorded your love in her journals. That endured, all these years. Whatever my life will become, whatever it is you're going to tell me, her writings, your love together, gave me the strength to reach this moment."

She felt it, fiercely. Mason studied her face, his jaw held in that tight set that told her she'd moved something within him. But then he took a seat on the bench again, leaning forward with hands loosely locked between his splayed knees. "If Allah is far more merciful than I deserve, you will feel the same way when I'm done, *habiba*."

The deadly stillness that settled over him skittered coldness up her spine. The unwavering focus of his preternatural eyes brought to the forefront of her mind the stories about Farida's village, her family. The decapitated first son, dragged back home behind his camel.

"Prince Haytham betrayed me," Mason began. "He alone knew where Farida and I were living in the desert. While he was forced by politics and his father to reveal our whereabouts, I could not forgive him, for surely he knew what would happen to her. In my kinder moments, I have thought, perhaps because he knew what I was, he thought that I could elude them. But that is hindsight."

"You never saw him again? Never spoke to him?"

He didn't shift. Not even a facial muscle twitched, reminding her forcibly that the male she faced was not human. "I killed him, *habiba*. I killed everyone involved with her death. Prince Haytham, his father. Farida's father, her brothers. I left no man in the camp alive. Even the women . . . those who spit on her, threw things at her, cursed her dishonor, I killed them as well."

Jessica's breath caught in her throat, her fingers closing into tense balls on her knees. There was no emotion in his voice. Just complete detachment. "But it was a male-dominated culture. Even if they didn't want her to die, they likely had to pretend—"

"I didn't care. Still don't. We all make our choices." His tone made it clear there would be no further discussion on that, cutting off whatever else she might have said. The man who'd held her with such gentle demand had used his hands, all that power, to take female life. Repeatedly, and without remorse. Rationally, she knew a human male was as fragile against a vampire. Yet the core morality of the Mason that Farida had described, that Jessica knew existed, would have been shattered by committing such an atrocity against a female.

Maybe it had shattered, she realized, staring at him. Like the Jessica who had risen from the ashes of Raithe's brutality, the Mason before her was a different man from the male who'd loved Farida. That core still existed, yet something had cracked it, never to be as strong and resolute in its faith again.

Mason rose and went back to the tree, so his words came over his shoulder, brought by the fitful breeze. "Farida's father was a smart man, even if he was a fanatical traditionalist. He'd sensed the same thing Farida had, that there was something different about me. He employed the talents of what you would call a shaman, or wizard. My life"—his lip curled in disdain—"was spared only because that wizard didn't exactly know what I was. He concluded I was some sort of djinn and as such, he assumed my essence couldn't be killed, only contained. He also decided I had some kind of mental bond with Farida."

Jessica studied the pale line of his shoulders, the way strands of his hair lifted and swept across them with the movement of the breeze. Other than that, he'd gone motionless again.

"He created a spell, a complex, impressive one. With it, they were able to ambush me in the desert at night, not far from home. The wizard wove the spell over me so I couldn't move, then they wrapped me in chains and dragged me, with ten horses and a fifty-foot length of chain between them and me, back to her father's village."

"Mason." She began to rise, but he made a sharp noise, stilling her.

"Stay where you are, *habiba*. Let me tell it here, to the dark, where tales like this should always be told. And it is not I who deserve your pity. Not even an ounce's worth." One arm lifted, his palm bracing against the tree's rough bark, fingers digging in. "She was at the cave.

I tried to reach out to her with my mind, but that damnable spell blocked the connection. I nearly lost my mind then. I didn't know it was just the beginning. Because though I couldn't reach her, I could still hear her every thought."

He glanced up at the bark, noted a nocturnal spider crawling down the trunk, moving over his fingers. Keeping them still, he watched the creature's progress. "She was making her dinner. Tuning into her thoughts was always like a lullaby, *habiba*. She was happier in that cave than she'd ever been in her whole life, and it was the truth for me as well. I felt such peace with her. Perhaps it made me stay longer than I should have there. I should have spirited her away to my family home right away, the night she came away with me, but I didn't want to take her from her desert too soon, hoping her father might eventually see reason, so she could have us both . . ."

He straightened, cleared his throat, though he stayed averted from her. "She sensed something was wrong. My horse escaped during my capture, and so when he arrived at the cave, her panic, and worry . . . I thought that was unbearable." He gave a harsh laugh, the laugh one heard in a graveyard in the darkest part of night. It made Jess shiver again. She was afraid her distress might stop his story, so she tried to quell it, but Mason's mind was elsewhere now.

"I expected them to track the horse to her, which is why I panicked when I couldn't warn her. But the wizard suspected I had enchantments on the cave that could destroy them all. He said, because of my hellish bond on her soul, she would come to me, and then they would have us both. On that part at least, he was correct." The bitter anger in his voice was undisguised.

"I taught her how to track. I thought it would enhance her ability to survive in the desert. Better I'd have left her innocent, defenseless. She realized I'd been taken to her father's camp, but she came anyway. You know the next part, how she rode into the camp disguised as a man and then declared herself, and her love for me."

Jessica couldn't tear her attention away as he squatted. Running his fingers over the soft, willowy branch of a jasmine bush, he disrupted the fragile flowers. "I wish I'd taken more time in that final moment to really look at her, to appreciate what she did. Farida never thought of herself as brave; did you know that? But everything she did, from the moment she met me, was an act of courage." He hesitated then, and Jessica's fingers scraped stone. "She said I made her feel so safe, she wasn't afraid of anything."

Oh, Mason. She closed her eyes. She'd been irritated with him for not telling her this story, and now she realized she'd been as immature as a child, thinking her parent was depriving her of a story simply to be mean. She was starting to understand the cost of his telling, but she knew she had to hear it. Opening her eyes again, she let him see he had her full attention.

"My horse, Bastion, was exceptionally large. Seventeen hands high and fractious. I'd always been cautious about her handling him. She rode in as confident as a Berber raider, back straight and hands firm on his mouth. No fear at all when her father came out to meet her. She got off the horse, prostrated herself at his feet and begged for the right to die with me. As my servant, she knew if I died, she would die, but she wanted to be close to me when we went."

He straightened again. "They had me chained and guarded in the middle of the camp, so dawn would have ended me. But it was midnight when she arrived. The lovely, idealistic little fool saved my life."

As he turned his head to look at her, Jessica met his gaze briefly, but then he swung away, paced the length of the garden, came back. When he put a booted foot on the edge of the bench, seeing the tension in his jaw, she thought he might smash it to bits, but he didn't.

"They'd gagged me, so I couldn't tell her they'd blocked our link. We were never allowed to touch. When they put a hood over my head and dragged me away, I heard her cries to me, but I could not answer her. Even on her way to the village, she was trying to talk to me in my mind. To her, it was as if we were thousands of miles away from one another. While to me, it was as if she was right before me, just beyond the grasp of my fingertips."

Dread was gathering in Jessica's stomach, an understanding of where this was leading. What Mason was intimating was worse than horrible. Thanks to his earlier, chilling demonstration of the third mark, she was in a position now to understand, more than she had been before.

"If they had ungagged me, I would have told them how to kill me. If I could have found a way to stake my heart, take off my own head, set my flesh on fire, I would have done it. But I was never given that chance. They took me out to a pit they'd prepared, threw me into it wrapped in the chains, and buried me under rock, reinforcing the spell over it. The irony was, they finished the task barely an hour before dawn broke and would have ended me."

Mason was on the move again, making a circle around the fountain, moving in and out of the shadows. Instead of following him, Jess closed her eyes, listened to his voice, the shift between helpless male rage and the raw sound of loss, and grief.

"The wizard told her father that, as a djinn, I was invulnerable, but I had placed my life essence in Farida. While they could not kill me, they could weaken me for many decades, so I couldn't escape the pit, if they tortured her as long as possible."

"Oh, my God." Jessica opened her eyes to meet his, glowing in the darkness.

"But the wizard, who should have known what a demon was, because the son of a whore looked at one every morning in the mirror, said that they must break Farida's will to protect me first. Sheikh Asim told her that they took me out in the desert and gave me a choice. I could have the spell removed and go my own way, as long as I never returned to the Sahara. Or I could come back and die with her. They told her I chose to cut my losses and run.

"She didn't believe it at first. But she cried out for me, over and over again, and I was silent." Mason swallowed, his face a rictus of pain. "As the hours went on, as the desert sun rose and dehydration and blood loss affected her mind, she began to believe their words. Steel through the heart is the only sure death for a servant, though sometimes blood loss can take a weaker one. She wasn't weak, *habiba*." His jaw clenched again and he moved back to the bench, sat. "When they saw her live through what no human could, they tried more lethal torments, like driving steel tent pins through her body. That was how it ended at last."

She died cursing my name. As she should have. She kept calling out for me, pleading with me to answer her . . . Not to save her. She begged me not to let her die alone.

His eyes were on her face, living, writhing fire burning him up inside. Jessica couldn't bear it. Sliding off the fountain wall, she went to him, sinking onto her knees only a foot away. As she moved toward him, though, he turned away, straddling the bench. The toe of his boot was so near, she covered it with her hand, the atmosphere too charged to dare touching a less protected part of his body.

"Things become very simple at such moments, *habiba*. I would have done anything. Sold my soul a hundred thousand times, destroyed the universe without a thought, for one second of connection between our minds, so she could know I was there, that I would have moved Heaven and Earth to get to her."

Jessica remembered his nightmare. The woman's screams. Her own, and how together they'd driven him to such madness. She reached up now, closed her hand on his calf under the snug riding breeches, drawing his attention there. His hair slid forward over his shoulder, the wind moving strands against his cheek, his hard mouth.

"But you believe in an afterlife, my lord. Even your words to me, in the tomb: 'Allah decides when we die.' Surely she knows—"

"I know He is there. But I don't know . . . It tears at my soul every day, every night . . . as if she suffers still, as if there is something I should have done that I have not."

His voice broke then and he looked away. Jessica sat for a moment, stunned. In her experience, even with Mason, vampires never showed great emotion, unless it was passion or anger. But then, not too long ago, she'd thought all vampires were monsters.

Jess moved onto her feet and slid her arms around his shoulders. When she guided his jaw toward her with a gentle hand, miraculously he turned and wound his arms around her hips, pressing his face into her bosom.

She'd learned *It's okay* was a balm on the most ludicrously disproportionate tragedies, but she used it now, a quiet murmur, because she understood what the words really meant. *It's not okay, but I'm here. I know. I understand.* Hadn't she realized, at some dark, instinctual level, that Mason knew what it was to be truly helpless to darkness and evil? After learning that, a person was never really whole or safe again. And maybe a vampire wasn't, either.

He didn't cry. She didn't expect him to. That one voice break was more than she'd expected from a male with his pride, his age. Vampires were so damned conscious of the consequences of perceived weakness. But his shoulders quivered with the effort of getting it all back under control, and she held him through those spasms, bending her head over his. When she thought it safe, she slid a hand to his jaw again and drew his attention up to her eyes. She locked him into her expression, the hope of her soul laid out before him.

"Before Jack was killed, before Raithe captured him, I was angry at him. Some irrational part of me thought he should find me, rescue me. I imagined he'd given up on me, that he wasn't as brave and strong and wonderful as he was supposed to have been." She took a deep breath. "When Raithe had him brought before me, he *did* fight, but he didn't stand a chance. I saw the hopeless fear in his eyes when he realized he was going to die. The very last words he spoke were 'I'm sorry.' That's what he said to me."

Now it was Mason who lifted his hands and cradled her face, his own expression reflecting her anguish, their shared pain. "It made me so ashamed of myself. He was a decent, brave, honorable man."

She was amazed when a painful smile crossed her face, one laced with regret and sorrow. "He wasn't superbly handsome, not exceptionally strong or gifted with invincible powers. He was just a wonderful, imperfect man who loved me. He deserved better than that. I'm not sure if I believe in God and all that anymore, but if there is a Heaven, my hope is that Jack forgave me for those terrible thoughts. Knowing him, I suspect he has.

"She loved you to the very end, Mason. Don't ever doubt it." Firming her chin, she straightened her shoulders, wrapped her fingers around his powerful wrists, held that amber gaze so close to hers. "From being sick and in pain for so long, I can tell you that I became a stranger to myself. My love turned to hate, my patience to fury and a longing for death. I only saw things as a very sick, damaged person sees them, not as the person I was. That wasn't me. And that wasn't Farida at the end. You understand?"

His expression flickered, doubt and pain reflected there, but she dug her nails into his wrists, willing him to see three centuries of entombed memories differently.

"She knows, Mason. She *knows*. If you believe there's any connection between her spirit and mine, know that I feel it so deeply nothing else is acceptable. She knows."

26

A quiet settled between them after that. Jessica, on an impulse, took his hand, drew him from the garden and down to the beach, so they could walk. He followed her without protest, his mind obviously heavy with the memories, and for this rare moment, willing to let her lead. In some ways, she thought it bound her heart even more fiercely to him.

As they walked, she risked sidelong glances at him. When his shoulders seem to be easing, his eyes less brooding, she decided it was best to try to draw his mind to other areas. "So is one of the reasons you studied wizardry so you couldn't be taken unawares like that again?"

"Part of it, yes." Mason's response was slow, but the even sound of it was a quiet relief. "The other part was what you saw, in the tomb. I wanted . . . I'm not a fool. I know there's nothing left after the life has left the body. I've stood over enough corpses to know."

That chilling tone again, but she refused to let him go back to that frightening part of himself. She tightened her hand on his. "You wanted to preserve her as you remembered her. Because you weren't ready to let her go."

He nodded, surprise crossing his gaze. Jessica raised a shoulder. "Raithe dragged Jack's body away. I never knew what became of it . . . whether he burned it or dumped it in the ocean. But I know if I could see him again, as he was, touch his face . . . I would have liked that." She'd looked away during the painful words, but when his hand brushed her face, she tilted into his palm, coming to a halt. "Oh, Mason. I just realized. Your fear of enclosed spaces, and then being buried under those rocks . . ."

"It didn't matter," he replied softly. "It's funny how all your fears for yourself will vanish when someone you love is being harmed. All I could think about and feel was her pain, her need for me, and how I couldn't get to her."

As they began to walk again, Jessica saw a cadre of sea birds fly over the dark water, silent silhouettes. "What happened afterward? Not . . . what you did to all of them. After that. What did you do? Where did you go?"

Mason gave a short laugh, a bitter sound. "To be honest, I'm not entirely sure. I know there were stories circulated in the desert for the next month about a djinn covered in blood, stinking of the dead, who might appear suddenly by your well or at your tent flap at night. Fortunately, this djinn only stared through the startled person and moved on. Thanks be to Allah and all that. I existed on pure instinct, apparently, going to ground during daylight and then drifting at night."

His hand loosened, as if he thought she might want to pull away, but instead Jess interlaced her fingers with his. His words painted a chilling image, though, reminding her of the violence that could exist in the bottom of any vampire's soul. But then, she'd discovered that darkness in herself as well, the night she killed Raithe.

He paused, looking down at their fingers, and something sad and tired passed over his features, aging him. "They even killed my horse, Jessica. Tortured and murdered the poor beast in front of Farida, in case more of my evil was trapped inside of him. That hurt her almost as much as her own torment, for she could not bear to see anything innocent harmed. Coman came from his bloodline, and I see him in the turn of his head at times, the flash of an eye. My vengeance was for him as well, for he had no way of understanding why humans, who had always treated him with such love and respect, would turn on him. At least humans understand evil."

"Or at least expect it," Jessica murmured. "I'm not sure I'll ever understand it. When did you finally recover yourself, my lord?"

"I didn't, not for a long time." He shook his head. "Somewhere along the way I reclaimed enough coherence to stop being a desert bedtime story to scare the children." That faint, humorless flash went through his eyes again. "But for many years after that, I wandered as aimlessly. Europe, Asia, the Americas, with no purpose, though I did find this place during that time. Alcohol doesn't impact vampires, not in terms of physical deterioration, but I'm happy to report if he drinks copious amounts of it, a vampire can wallow in a pungent swamp of self-pity for an indefinite period of time. I thought about dying, even tried it a couple times, but was always thwarted in my attempt. I'd pass out somewhere before I could walk into the sun, and then when I woke, it would be dusk again."

The return of his dry, self-deprecating wit loosened some of the tension in her stomach. "Fortunately, there was a vampire who did not give up on me. I've never gone out of my way to build friendships with my own kind. In fact, if asked, she would say I go out of my way to alienate them as much as possible."

"Because of what happened after your parents died?"

Mason slanted a glance at her, but nodded. "Farida's journal told you an unprotected vampire male adolescent's life is . . . difficult?" At her nod, a hard look came into his gaze. "If he can't figure out a way to fight them, he's exploited for the purposes of older vampires. A born vampire has value to them, though, even as they resent him for what's seen as purer blood. I've seen the ugly underbelly of the vampire nature, and no trappings of civilized behavior will ever make me forget it."

"But one vampire was different."

"Yes." That look went away, replaced by something different, though Jess wasn't sure if she preferred it. "When I was twenty-three, surly, hateful and violent, sure to meet a young demise, Lady Lyssa took me under her wing. She was only a century or so older, but she is our last queen, *habiba*, and she is royalty through and through. While she had the guidance of her parents only in her formative years herself, I don't doubt she emerged from the womb with a scepter in one hand. She is no one's victim. She would appreciate your courage greatly."

He turned her hand over, tracing the lines. "We are blood-linked, and her powers are stronger than most vampires', her range much further. She was the one who came and pulled me out of that pit."

∽

Time was a dark, painful haze beneath the punishing weight of the rocks, bringing a gnawing hunger that would not let him be. On this, the terrible fifth day, Farida had died at last, so the spell binding him in the chains had died with her. But he was too weak, and it didn't matter anyway. Even if he had been able to get his arms loose, he wouldn't have dug free. He would have torn out his own heart, shredded it so it would all end. When he sensed another vampire circling the rocks, he was past caring. Let the interloper free him, try to kill him. He'd take them both down to Hell. Then he sensed who it was.

She and her servant pulled the rocks off the pile with a speed that would have surprised the mortals who'd labored so hard to put them on him. His hateful body, refusing to die and ignoring his suicidal bent, got progressively more eager the closer she came. His bloodlust raged to life, focusing with malevolent intent on her and the human blood of her servant, so near. Finally, when the load lightened enough, he heard her firm rebuke to her servant. "Go to the top of the pit. I'm fine, Thomas. Move back. I won't let him hurt me, but you must be out of harm's way. He's more beast than vampire right now."

He'd loosened the chains enough that he shoved upward, erupting out of the rock. He stumbled on his feet, but she caught him. When he snarled and took her down beneath him, using the weight of the chains to help him, her arms and legs came around him, accepting. Her mind was in his mind, finding him in the dark red fury of his memories.

Tearing into her shoulder like an animal, he growled his hunger, his heart jackhammering, his punctured soul riddled by wounds that would never heal. The strength of Lyssa's arms increased, holding him. Holding him together.

She wouldn't stop screaming. I couldn't get to her, and she wouldn't stop screaming. She'll never stop screaming . . .

∽

He'd given Jessica the memory in his mind. From her strained expression, he'd probably given her too much. "After I fed from her, I ran, and those first few weeks you know about. But she came back after me when I was in my tenth year of mourning. Or maybe it was my twentieth. I lost track of so much time then. She told me that Farida would be ashamed of me, that she'd obviously chosen her Master poorly, if being a drunken, useless disgrace was how I intended to honor her memory."

Jessica winced. "She's not the nurturing type, is she?"

"Lady Lyssa, nurturing?" Now at last, she saw a glimmer of a true smile on his face, and it eased her own heart. "I'll let you ask that question of Jacob, her mate and servant, when they arrive. They're two of the vampires coming to visit me."

~

He was watching her closely. Despite the ground they had covered tonight, that familiar cold ball of fear flopped in her belly. But she pushed it down. "I don't understand. Jacob is a vampire, but he's also her servant, and her . . . mate?"

"It's complicated. Lyssa had to save Jacob's life by turning him, when he was her human servant. It violated Council law. Plus, after she turned him, she unintentionally transferred most of her vampire abilities to him. She's still part vampire by blood, but what power she has left is Fey. I'd tell you that made her less terrifying," he added dryly, "but I think she still terrifies almost everyone."

"What happened all those years ago, when she told you that you were a disgrace?"

"Oh, she nearly killed me." At Jessica's startled look, a wry look crossed his face. "Being drunk and angry, I challenged her. I got my ass kicked. Badly. Though I *was* drunk."

Jessica blinked. Yet again, she was learning that there was far more to vampires than she ever knew. "I would have liked to see that, my lord."

"I'm sure, *habiba*." His lips tugged. "Maybe you can ask her to challenge me to a rematch when she's here and I can attempt to regain my manly pride."

"Or lose it forever."

"Your confidence in me is overwhelming."

"Is that when you started helping . . . your harem?"

The brief flash of puzzlement in his eyes vanished, replaced by exasperation. "I am going to beat that woman. But yes. Again, that was Lyssa's doing. She got me started, giving me the name of one particular organization, and it went from there. She was right. It was a better way to honor Farida's memory, and still is."

When he turned toward her, she sensed the slightest of hesitations, as if he was uncertain of her reception of him, but then she lifted her chin and his hand cupped her face, a natural coming together. However, his eyes remained serious, watchful.

You worry needlessly, habiba. *I will not allow you to be afraid. You have seen me with Amara and Enrique, and learned to fear that less. This will show you how it is meant to be with vampires and their servants in a group.*

She didn't want to delve into that statement too deeply right now. "Have you and Lyssa . . . ?"

No, that question was equally fraught with peril, for her at least. Vampires being highly sexual creatures, she was certain that his relationship with Lyssa had been intimate, might still be. No matter how Mason viewed her, he would never see anything inappropriate about engaging in a relationship with a vampire female while maintaining a close bond with a human servant. After all, Amara and Enrique were married.

She bit her lip. He'd warned her about leaning on her fantasies of Farida, but now she wondered if Farida had sensed the danger of having to be part of his world as well. *He shows little interest in bringing me into that world. Though I wonder about it, right now all I want is to be with him, every waking breath.*

Was this really the life she wanted to live? Sharing him with others? Would Farida have wanted that life? Regardless of her feelings about him, whether true or distorted by her experiences, Jessica couldn't discount the importance of that serum, what it could offer her.

Mason's reaction didn't suggest otherwise. She could tell he'd tuned in to her thoughts, but he chose not to answer her charged, unspoken question, lifting her palm to his mouth again. He wouldn't lie to her, even now. And while she appreciated it, a stab of pain went through her. Still, her body didn't care, swaying inward to press against him, overriding her unease . . . for now, at least.

"Mason . . ." Her breath left her as he moved to her pulse, worked it between his lips, teasing her with his tongue, the brush of a fang. His other arm slipped around her waist, his hand sliding lower, cupping her buttock through the thin dress.

After the stark images of past pain and regret, violence and vengeance, not to mention the revelations of a future decision she needed to make, she should be putting on the brakes, taking a few moments. Until now, she'd relied on him to set those limitations. All the times she'd been eager to take it past this point, he'd been the one who walked away.

"I told you I want you beneath me, Jessica. In my bed." He spoke against her skin. When he lifted his head, it was only to take command of her mouth before she could reply. He moved his hand to her face, held it still as he traced her lips with his tongue, then delved between, teasing her some more. When he pulled back, his amber eyes remained close, holding her mesmerized as he spoke to her heart.

If you decide to go, you will have no memory of me. So I will tell you this. I do consider you mine. I will watch over you forever, make sure you are safe, even when you know nothing of me. And I will not eviscerate the men you choose to love. Unless they deserve it.

"And if I decide to stay?" The words came out breathless as he moved to her throat. Her fingers dug into his shoulders when he scraped her with his fangs. He lifted his head again and this time when he brought his lips onto hers, she kissed back, shyly trying to tangle with his tongue until he took over, plunging deep, penetrating, his hand on her buttock tightening, winning a mewl of desire that stoked the flame in his eyes.

Apparently wanting to move faster than her legs could manage, he swung her up in his arms. When she opened her eyes, after a rush of motion, they were at the base of the verandah steps.

"If you decide to stay, *habiba*," he responded, "then I will claim you as mine. My human servant, no longer in name only, not just for your protection." The torchlight flickered over the ruthlessly handsome features, his sensual mouth. "There are no half measures to that, Jessica. You know this. But if that is the decision you ultimately make, I will help you learn to trust, so that you do not fear to obey me, accept me as your Master, even when we are in the company of other vampires."

She stared up at his perfect face. "For tonight, I know I want to be yours, and believe in the fantasy that you're only mine. I want to trust you. Please don't stop this time."

He'd put her on a step two levels above him, so she trembled as his heated gaze passed over the rapid rise and fall of her breasts, the close hold of the gauze dress over her nipples, the transparency of the skirt with the torchlight behind her. He opened his mind, showing her how he wanted to peel it off her body, showing her the things he wanted to do to her.

He wanted to turn her onto her hands and knees on the stairs, take her there, her fingers digging into the marble, her cries rising above the ocean's distant murmur. He would turn her over after her climax, keep her stretched out on the stairs while he went to work on her with his mouth, rousing her again. He'd take her down to the shore, lie with her there. And then in the stables, in the fragrant hay, hearing Coman's sharp whinny at the scent of their arousal.

His gaze holding her in a sensual paralysis, Mason imagined her even in that frightening dungeon room, only he showed her in great detail how he would ensure she had climax after climax, devoid of fear. He would cuff her legs to the adjustable standing rod anchored in the floor. The top would be fitted with a phallus of impressive size, and he would slowly impale her on it. Her wrists would be anchored to her thighs, increasing her helplessness. When her arousal was flowing down her thighs, he'd apply a soft flogger to her breasts, teasing the nipples to hardness so she'd scream with pleasure when he kissed them. He would tease her cleft with his fingers, make her come when he turned on the phallus's vibration.

Her breath was short, caught between fear of the past, anticipation of the future, and frozen over what the present meant. But she couldn't deny his images stirred her. When his mind moved into the dining room, her lips curved, though it was an effort, her body shaking so hard already. "You're going to go room to room, my lord? You might exhaust me."

"Then I'll let you sleep in my arms whenever you tire, feed you from my throat to replenish you before I take you again. I will take you so often that your legs will open to me even in your sleep, knowing your Master and obeying him even in your dreams." He gazed at her intently, his body emanating that still power that vampires did so well, right before they attacked in some manner. "Come here, *habiba.*"

She cocked her head. "Catch me," she whispered, and bolted.

He could have caught her in a second, of course, but he let her run, indulge in the childish play that was anything but childlike. He cornered her on the verandah, then let her slip past, though he deftly snagged the thin strap of the dress so it tore, and she had to press her hand against the bodice to keep it in place as she sprinted onward. Back into the house, him in hot pursuit. The study. The solarium. Around the pillars in the breezeway, weaving in and out. He caught her against one, gave her another brain-numbing kiss, before she dropped under his arm and took off again.

She embraced the exertion, trying to outrun the fears that might try to spoil this moment, make her afraid of it. Like the trepidation she'd felt in the limo when she thought his savagery might overtake him and he'd ravish her there. Seeing his face as he chased her, she saw both sides of his nature. The male who would protect her, and the vampire who wanted her a little afraid. But it was the type of fear balanced with anticipation, a sweet drug to them both.

In the kitchen, she changed her strategy to projectiles, firing fruit from the bowl at him, and when she was out of fruit, going for a basket of hazelnuts. Mason dodged them easily, stalked her around the table. He lifted a banana. "I can think of a few uses for this."

Her eyes widened, but laughter was dancing in them. "So can I, my lord. They're good on sandwiches, with peanut butter." The other dress strap had fallen and as she tried to outmaneuver him, the bodice fell a little lower. Following his glance, she saw he was hungrily dwelling on the tempting swells of breast and hint of areola. In the next moment, he leaped. Despite her shriek and dodge, he caught her by the waist and lifted her onto the table, pushing her to her back as she swallowed, those dark pupils getting wider.

"Push the dress all the way down, Jessica. Show yourself to me." *I* can hear the racing of your heart, *habiba. Show me your beautiful breasts.*

With a slight tremor, her fingers loosened on the fabric, then edged it downward, the gauze bodice catching on the nipples before releasing them to jut upward, begging for his attention.

"Why would you eviscerate the men I choose to love?" she asked in a whisper. "Wouldn't you want me to find happiness? Someone I wouldn't have to share?"

Jessica waited, her breath held as his gaze lifted, very slowly, back to hers. "It doesn't have to make sense, my love. It is a vampire's nature to be sexual with whomever he pleases, but to be very territorial with what he considers his. I might share you with another, if I thought that would bring us both pleasure. But I suspect I would be quick to take you afterward, to ensure you understood to whom you belong." He lifted the banana, began to peel it, drawing the yellow skin away from the firm white fruit.

"You have no trouble with Amara having Enrique." Her fingers curled against the fabric she held at her waist.

"Because it was Enrique who was my servant, and who suggested the idea of third-marking the woman he loved, so they could serve me as a married couple." Putting his hand over hers, he pushed them gently but inexorably to the side, and then began to gather the short skirt. His gaze lowered, and air touched her exposed sex, for she'd worn no panties tonight. He'd moved closer, so her legs dangled on either side of his hips, spread for him. He studied her most private region with that casual ownership and fascination that made it almost impossible for her to remain still.

But you must do so, habiba, until I command you otherwise. Consider this practice, a safe way to determine if you do in fact have the willingness and desire to be my servant.

She pressed her lips together, and she thought she was going to hyperventilate soon, as hard as she was finding it to breathe. But she couldn't look away as she spoke in his mind.

Your hair. Will you take it down?

His gaze lifted again, and she saw a trace of surprise there. But he complied, loosening the tie holding it back so it fell loose on his shoulders, framing those strong features, the warrior's face.

He slid his fingers between her legs, finding her slick wetness. Jessica gasped and arched, and as she did, his fingers flexed to open her channel so it wouldn't break the fruit as he took the peeled banana into it. She caught her lip between her teeth at the sensation, the fruit's roughened texture and coolness. Easing what felt like more than half of it into her, he broke off the rest, tossed the peel aside and bent to place his mouth over her needy core. His fingers slid free and were replaced with his tongue. As he swirled it inside, he used it, then teeth and lips, to mash the banana into pieces and eat it out of her flesh.

Jessica was helpless not to respond, writhing on the table, crying out while he gripped her hips.

When he finished with that, he turned his head to his third mark, that silhouette of a tiger on the inside of her thigh, a reflection of what she'd put on her back. Though he only brushed it with his mouth, it might as well have been a hot brand, for the sensation that shot through her contracted her sex so she almost came then. He rose, his lips glistening from her juice and marked by the fruit, and peeled an orange next. After splitting the fruit over her breasts so the juice spattered there, he tasted. Licking the stickiness from her skin, he sucked on her flesh and then her nipple, drawing them deep into his mouth by turns, as she dug her fingers into his arms, her feet curling tensely around his calves.

He placed a slice in his mouth, then cupped the back of her neck, drawing her back up to his lips with swift strength as he rose over her.

Eat from my mouth, habiba. *Let me nourish you.*

She was eager to comply, but he held it in his mouth, on his tongue, so she had to go fishing for it, an erotic exercise that had her moaning as her hands fell to his waist, holding on to him there as she finally got hold of it, took it into her own mouth and chewed, the juice exploding in the back of her throat as he kept his mouth sealed over hers.

She curled her arms around his shoulders as his hands drifted down her back, making her shiver as he traced the scar, the tiger tattoo, while she traced his.

Your design pleased me very much, habiba. *Though it strikes me it could be mistaken for a caged tiger.*

Just perception, my lord. Can you think of a reason a tiger might like to be caged, tamed? She raised her gaze to his, shy and daring at once, moving her hand around to touch his mouth, while her other fingers tangled in his hair. She wanted his skin, and she tugged at the seam of his shirt, conveying her desire.

Giving her a look torn between sweet indulgence and simmering desire, Mason straightened, spreading his arms out. "See how far your tamed tiger will let you go, *habiba*. Do as you desire."

She didn't hesitate. Driven by the lust he'd roused in her to volcanic proportions with his clever mouth and hands, she curled her fingers in the front of the shirt and ripped, sending the buttons scattering. That amber flame jumped again, a curl of lip exposing a fang, but he remained still as she pushed the fabric aside, placed her palms upon his bare chest. Her fingers spread wide on his hard, muscled flesh. All that power, dangerous vitality, that immortal strength, fearsome and yet tempting beyond a woman's will to resist. She put her mouth on him, using teeth, knowing how the beast within responded to that. So many things she'd learned about vampires, things she'd never expected to be glad to know, she used now with ruthless pleasure, testing his resolve.

Scraping over a nipple, she followed the lines of his ribs, the ropes of muscle, then went to the fastening of his trousers, passing over that to palm him through the fabric, test the length of her hand against the shape and size of his arousal.

Sliding off the table, she was bemused when he took a step back, keeping his arms out to his sides, giving her that still, predator's look. Putting her hand back on his chest, she moved him farther, toward the stool at the island counter. When she got him there, indicating with her mind she wanted him to sit, he did so, and she stood between his knees. Putting her back to him, she straddled one of his legs and gripped his bootheel. Third-mark strength made it easy to slip both boots off. Then she turned back to him and, on impulse, slipped her arms around his neck, brought her mouth back to his for a kiss.

Not hard and demanding this time, not overt in hunger, but devastating in simple, sweet need, wanting to taste his lips, press her hands on either side of his face, on his brow, her fingers sweeping over his eyes, the sides of his nose, even trace his ears, the column of his throat.

She didn't have to voice the thought even to herself, because he was deep in her subconscious, as he'd said he could be. Before she even knew she wanted it, his arms lowered, his hands coming to rest on her hips, bringing her forward to lean into him, to be enveloped in his arms. He held her there for a kiss that went on and on while the wall clock ticked and nighttime insects buzzed outside, muted through the glass. The conflagration built from a flash burn to an enduring heat as the kiss spun out. The pressure of the erection against her abdomen, the tingling need in her breasts and the moisture between her legs gathering for him, wanting him, were all desires, but they were meant to be savored, drawn out.

The tiger was no longer in his cage, but he did not leap forward to savage and tear, which he was more than capable of doing. Instead he lifted her, guiding her to fold her legs around his hips. Rising from the stool, he carried her through the darkened kitchen, through the hallways, still kissing her. He let her stroke her hands through his hair, wind her fingers in it and tug as her desire grew to soft whimpers in her throat, particularly as his movements rubbed him against her. He could move as lightning striking the earth, but he could do this, too, a slow drift of wind through trees, no longer stalking his prey but absorbing the sounds and sensations the night brought to him.

She knew when they were in his bedroom, for that was where his pheromone-like scent was heaviest, such that even the night she'd come into his nightmare she'd wanted to stay there, wrapped in it. Wrapped around him. She wanted to look at his room, see all the things he kept closest to him when he went to dreams, but right now everything in the world was gone, even the terrible things they'd shared earlier, every terrible thing that had ever happened to her. Now, there was only this.

He laid her on her back on his large bed and she saw the open canopy above her, the contours of a stone ceiling. Instead of divesting himself of his trousers and her of the dress still rolled down on her hips, he lay down upon her, bare chest to breast, his hips cradled inside the grasp of her legs, one arm beneath her shoulders, the other propping his weight off her as he deepened the kiss, changed the angle. She caught hold of his biceps, her arousal spiraling higher, the deep, drugging strength of the kiss approaching euphoria, a mindless spinning. That spinning was starting to draw from lazy circles into a need to tangle, interlock, make the sense of connection even more complete.

As she had the thought, even though she loved his mouth on hers, she disengaged her head, turned her cheek to his pillow. Exposing her throat to him. Even more slowly, she released his shoulders, the trembling in her limbs increasing as she offered with conscious understanding the gift she could give him. Easing her hands up, up and up, her knuckles slid across his pillows until she grazed the iron rails of the headboard and curled her fingers around them, restraining herself. Offering herself to him fully.

Mason had lifted his head as she moved, the amber eyes getting more vibrant, glowing in the darkness. His age showed in those eyes, for never had she seen a vampire with such a supernatural gaze, something that said so clearly he was not human. He raised himself from the bed, his leg pressed against her calf, dangling off the edge of the mattress, for he'd laid her down at a diagonal angle. Now he unfastened his slacks, stripping off the remainder of his clothing with predatory grace.

His cock brushed his belly, a man's need, a vampire's drive to claim, all evident in its turgid state. He was beautiful, of course, and yet the butterflies in her stomach were like a flock startled in the darkest shadows of the rain forest by a tiger's passing. He was a threat, but there was such a tempting urge to flutter within reach of his lethal talons, brush against the lean flanks.

Reaching down, he took hold of the dress, slid it down and turned her body to her side, lifting it as needed to take off the garment. It left her bare to his gaze as well, except for the bracelets and collar, the pink-faceted pendant, all things he'd given her.

When he had her turned away from him, she could feel his heat. He sat on the edge of the bed, his palm curved over her hip. When his lips brushed the rounded curve of her buttock, she shuddered, her hands tightening on the rails. He worked his way up her spine, through her scars to her nape, and then he stretched out behind her and teased it with his lips as his hands clasped her wrists and he tied the dress around them, her restraint no longer a choice, but wholly his will.

Do not fear me, habiba.

He slipped his hand from her hip up her waist, then farther to cup a breast, idly playing with the nipple. His erection pressed against her bottom as he nipped her shoulder and then slowly, slowly penetrated her shoulder with his fangs, his tongue swirling against her flesh to taste her heated blood. She arched with a cry, pressing herself into him in involuntary reaction, but his touch remained maddeningly light, fingers brushing her nipple, his hand a gentle clasp around the curve. His hips moved against her now in a slow rhythm of copulation, rubbing up and down the cleft of her buttocks, stimulating himself while her sex clenched on emptiness.

Mason . . . my lord . . .

Shhh . . . be still, habiba. *I will give you pleasure when it is time. Accept my will.*

She wanted to twist, to press against him more insistently, but if she tried, he simply moved out of range, though he kept his mouth at her throat, taking idle sips from her, bringing his body back only when she stilled herself. His hand settled on her throat, above the collar, a reminder that she wanted to belong to him fully tonight.

By the time he was done with his meal, she was panting, her body quivering with the effort of not rubbing shamelessly against him or fighting her bond. He'd teased her neck, her ear, tipped her head back into his shoulder for another kiss where he held her chin, controlling the depth. Her thighs pressed together on aching, throbbing flesh. From the size of him against her, she knew he was also affected, and the increased strength of his grip at her throat, her breast, then back down to her hip, told her that his discipline had to have a limit as well. Though she was beginning to think it exceeded that of a marathon runner.

At last, he turned her to her back. She hadn't been certain how he'd do it. If he'd turn her to her stomach, bring her up to her knees and drive into her from behind, her face pressed into the pillows, or take her on her side, where he would raise her thigh and push into her as she bit into the coverlet. The intimacy of seeing his face was the answer to her own desires as well. She moaned at the press of him against her mound as he brought his weight back onto her. At the visible strain of withheld desire on his face, the raging fire in his tiger eyes.

Deliberately laying his hands on her wrists, digging his fingers into the soft cloth, compressing her pounding pulse, he seated the head of his cock against her sex. "You are dripping for me, *habiba*. Your cunt will pull me in like your hot mouth. As it does, I want you to come. You will come."

Without further explanation or an attempt for her to marshal her thoughts, he began to enter her, adjusting her for his size, taunting her with how deeply and fully he could fill her. Her body started to explode, a bomb that went off in tiny, explosive increments each time he moved forward, his strength and weight holding her down so she couldn't rush it, so that her cries became screams, short, staccato bursts, upper body arching up into his, legs quivering.

"Mason . . . oh . . . ah . . ." Coherence deserted her for pleading, whimpering, her eyes locked on his fierce expression, the concentration as she spasmed around him. "Move . . . please . . . I need . . . to feel . . . you . . . my lord."

But he didn't, not until he had stretched her all the way, seated himself so deep. She hadn't been sure if she could take him all. She knew, as a Master, he'd wanted her to feel that harrowing stretch, the border between discomfort and overwhelming need. Her muscles clenched spasmodically, milking him through an orgasm that continued to click upward like the buildup of a roller coaster, overpowering her, taking away her speech, for she realized the orgasm she was experiencing now was just the crest of a powerful wave.

But she wanted to hold on to that pinnacle for as long as she could. It seemed she'd waited forever for this sense of connection, total fulfillment. Poised here, no thoughts or doubts, she was totally his, and had no fears or regrets.

He closed his eyes, a shudder passing through the powerful body, and then he was moving, a withdrawal and a slam back in, fire licking across tissues already immersed in flame. Now she was free to move her hips and Jessica did so, surging up to meet his thrusts, feeling the heat and power of him drive home, withdraw, thrust back in, demanding everything from her. She needed every ounce of her third-mark strength, for though he held himself back, he knew she could take far more physical punishment than a mere mortal. He was apparently more than willing to test the limits of it. His grip on her wrists was bruising, the shove of his body in between her legs demanding enough to stretch tendons and overpower straining muscles. It was glorious . . . not the brutality of Raithe, but a violent passion that told her how much he wanted her. No, a feeling this strong was need. He needed her.

He went back to her throat, no gentle penetration this time. The tiger took her with fierce determination, biting into the shoulder, intending to give her pain amid his claiming, an understanding that his possession involved both, mindless pleasure and the possibility of pain, if it suited his needs. She could accept it, could accept him, at least in this moment of just the two of them.

At that moment of blood taking, he released inside of her, a flood of hot seed. Her body spasmed, toppling over that pinnacle with a shriek of raw desire that encapsulated the sound of his growl against her throat.

Once, she hadn't known the dark world of vampires existed, a world of nightmarish imaginings. Savagery such as this would have frightened the young girl she'd been, Mason's hunger far beyond what she could manage. For the first time, the lessons of instinct, pain and pleasure came together. She knew how to serve the needs of a tiger, stand within range of his desires, and not only survive them, but embrace him. Find a wholeness, a depth in the shadows of herself she never would have found otherwise.

Such clarity might elude her when she faced Mason's "guests" or again confronted the choice of whether she would leave or stay. But for this second in the darkness of his bedroom, totally his, her body and mind rocketed into the stars, and spiraling there without fear, she held on to the idea.

As they at last slowed, Mason licked her wound, helped the blood stop. He was still inside of her, and she held him with her muscles, wanting him to stay forever. He made a soft noise of approval. When he turned his head, nuzzled beneath her ear, his hand slid down to her hip to cup her buttock, his fingers gripping. As he began to tease the sensitive rim there, she realized, with shock, he wasn't done.

I don't intend to be done for a long time, habiba. *Before dawn comes, you will know what it means to be claimed, in all ways.*

27

Aʟʟ the things she'd imagined, he'd done. Pulling her up on her knees and elbows, driving into her with a rutting animal's pleasure. Taking her on her side, a slow, easy glide, hand on her belly to hold her as he moved in and out, in and out. Straddling her face and feeding her his cock, his buttocks pressing against her nipples as he shuttled rhythmically, his heavy testicles swinging against her working throat. Then moving down her body, licking and soothing her sore tissues but also bringing her back to climax again with that clever, relentless mouth. At times, she was so exhausted she thought she might need him to stop. But she couldn't deny him, and a stronger part of her didn't ever want it to end.

He freed her hands occasionally, turned her over to massage the shoulder muscles with blissful thoroughness. During those times, he forbade her to speak, and she realized, whatever his intent, it was a relief to simply be, nothing required of her but to serve his pleasure as he wished. Each time he finished the massage, he turned and bound her again, underscoring the point. When necessary, he'd carried her to his bathroom. He let her have her privacy for that, but then, when she opened the door, he carried her back to the bed and restrained her again.

The final time of the night, he took her as he had the first time. He lay full on her, hands cradled around her face, putting them eye to eye, so when she climaxed with slow, thorough pleasure, she had to gaze in his face, watch how intently he studied the frantic look in her eyes, the stretch of her mouth gasping for air, her breath on his face as she cried out again.

Dawn was approaching. She whimpered softly when he took her hands from the rail, but this time he left her wrists tied in the dress. Turning her on her side, he curved his body around hers. As he fitted his hips against her backside, he slid back into her once more, his hand low on her abdomen, holding her to him.

I would have you sleep, habiba. *Our guests will come tomorrow night, and I want you well rested.*

Her mind was as drained as her body, so fortunately his reminder only created a distant uneasy stirring. Her brain, drugged as it was, was absorbed by the feel of him inside her once more. God, he was still hard, though he had climaxed several times himself tonight. Of all the supernatural traits vampires possessed, sexual stamina was the most impressive. They could literally fuck a mortal to death.

His amusement flickered in her mind as he adjusted his hips against her, making her draw in an unsteady breath, a noise of soft pleasure. *You find this more impressive than my strength or speed? My immortality? My incredible beauty? My exceptional charm and patience?*

I'm ignoring all overly arrogant vampires in the room. I'm sleeping.

He chuckled, his breath at her cheek, chest against her back. Realizing he expected and intended her to stay locked in his arms, his cock deep in her while they both slept, made her lower belly flutter. A remarkable indication that her body might once again ready itself for him, long before he woke.

Then you shall simply have to wait, habiba. *I do need* some *sleep.*

Clumsily, she tried to kick his shin with her foot. He merely seated himself at a different angle, and she whimpered again. *Be still,* habiba, *or I shall make your torment much, much worse.*

~

He wasn't as cruel a Master as that. Or perhaps his control was not as unflappable as it appeared to be when it came to her. He roused twice during his daily sleep to sate them both again, and the last time, he unbound her hands, let her turn in his arms and held her close, one powerful leg draped over her, his hair a curtain brushing her cheek.

After brushing so close to this moment, and being denied so often by the demons that hounded both of them, she was caught between savoring every second, every touch and sensation, and wanting him to pound into her with insatiable urgency. He gave her both. He gave her everything, except she kept wanting more. Maybe vampire stamina could be matched only by a woman starved for love.

She woke in the afternoon. His breathing was even, but she knew his sleep was light. *I'm going topside, to run on the beach. Sleep, my lord.*

He cinched her in closer to him with a grunt that said what he thought of that. She pushed at him, though she couldn't resist a gentle stroke along his smooth forehead. *Don't be a bully. Let me go. Unlike some people, I don't believe in lying around in bed all day.*

Perhaps because you're not making optimal use of the activities that can occur there.

If we made any more optimal use of this bed, you'd need a new frame for it.

A light smile played on his mouth, but his hand loosened and he let her go. As his breath evened out, she wondered, amused, if he'd at last been depleted. Not that he'd ever admit it. Male pride was the great equalizer among species. Having far less of it, she knew she was sore and stiff. Though he'd been wondrously gentle as her tissues got more abraded, he hadn't given her a choice, treating her as his servant in truth. He'd taken her up to climax again and again, even when she thought it was impossible. Everything he'd demanded of her, she'd eagerly given. And craved more.

Staying carefully away from that thought, more difficult to examine in the light of day, she eased away and gathered up her wrinkled dress. As she slipped it on, she had her first opportunity to take a closer look at his room. From the tapestries and simple dark wood furniture, it was obvious the room belonged to a male who preferred desert tents. Or medieval castles. He had a few art pieces, most of them equestrian. His wardrobe was still open.

Seeing it, her cheeks warmed. He had mirrored doors, which had perplexed her, until he'd lifted her up and seated her on his cock at the end of the bed, leaving her wrists bound. She'd had the unique experience of seeing herself in coitus, being fucked hard and long by an invisible force, since he had no reflection. Her breasts bouncing, face strained with the approaching climax, the impression of his fingers in the soft flesh at her hips, even though she couldn't see the fingers themselves. The mouth of her sex gripping a thick organ that couldn't be seen, but was deliciously felt.

He didn't have much clothing, but what was there was custom-made. She could imagine him giving Amara his specifications and letting her coordinate with his tailors. Cocking her head, she looked down at five pairs of shoes, flanked by several pairs of boots.

It had bemused her, finding out that a monster like Raithe had trappings like these. A closet of clothes that might require laundering or ironing, shoes that needed polishing. Bedrooms that were dusted, linens washed. Vampires took showers. Read stock reports. As a child, she'd believed monsters lived in dank caves, their only possessions the bones of their victims. Their bodies would be ugly and filthy, foul smelling.

Raithe often made her do chores naked, except for heavy chains that made it impossible for her to move quickly. As such, he made sure she was assigned the tasks most difficult to perform with those chains in place. It left her exhausted at the end of daylight, his intent apparently to make her more malleable to his evening plans. When she demonstrated she still had the will to fight, it had impressed him, such that the next day would bring even more difficult chores.

One day he'd had a thousand cinder blocks delivered and scattered over the back field of his property. She'd been assigned to collect and restack them, fifty feet away. Her naked skin blistered and burned in the summer sun, and her feet were cut to shreds by sharp, spiny vegetation. He'd told her if she didn't finish them all in the course of the day, he'd have them scattered again. No one except a vampire could have completed the task. She did it for seven days. Because it was early in her captivity, she'd cried a lot while doing it. Eventually, the impossible task bored him and he simply had the blocks carted away.

Raithe had used the same brand of cologne Jack used. A macabre coincidence that had haunted her, for a long time after Jack's death. If she dreamed of her lost fiancé, for the first heartrending moment when she woke in Raithe's room, her mind would tell her they were in her flat and she'd been having a nightmare. Then she'd open her eyes to find Raithe, with that beloved and familiar male musk, studying her like a scientist contemplating what next torment to visit on his lab animal.

Jessica sank down on her knees in front of Mason's wardrobe. He'd hung the white shirt he'd worn earlier on a lower hook, so she tugged it free, threading her hands into the too-long sleeves to hug it around herself. Now she avoided looking into the mirror. How many decades would pass before random thoughts wouldn't resurrect memories of Raithe? If she decided to take Brian's serum, it could be a matter of days.

She liked Mason's cologne, she reminded herself. As well as his soap, and a shampoo that gave her the scent of the ocean, perhaps sea salts. Remembering where he'd first taken her, a faint smile played on her lips. Well, maybe *some* vampires lived in caves.

Closing her eyes, she put her temple against the wardrobe frame, conscious of his quiet breathing behind her on the bed. She tilted her head so she could see him. Had Farida watched him sleep? Of course she had. Did she marvel at the beauty of him? The creatures considered most beautiful in the wild were usually the fiercest predators. Occasionally people made the tragic mistake of taking them from their natural habitat, trying to make them a pet.

A predator was no one's pet. Stay too close to him, too long, and his nature changed. Or rather, it didn't, and you ended up the meal.

Oh, Jess. Shut it off for a while. Just be still. A tear was rolling down her cheek and she didn't care to look at the why of it. She had a few days. She didn't have to think about anything yet. Rising to her feet, she closed the wardrobe and slipped out of the room.

She didn't notice Mason watching her through half-closed eyes. Or experience the whorl of emotions going through him as well. When she'd put on his shirt, hugged it around her as if she needed the comfort of his arms, he'd wanted to go to her. Instead, he stayed where he was, because he was fighting a battle of his own—between his desire to overwhelm her, override the decision he was sure she was going to make, and love her enough to let her make the choice that would take her from him forever.

~

For the next day and a half, Mason didn't speak of choices, or the impending arrival of his vampire guests. Jess didn't, either. She thought of little else when she was away from him, but wisps of thoughts at the corners of her mind only. On some unspoken truce between them, she took the two days as a time to indulge in . . . well, just being with him.

During the day she was with the horses, running, or reading, but she found him more accessible to her thoughts than he'd ever been. When she discovered a computer in the office Enrique used, she surfed the Internet some, refamiliarizing herself with things that had been beyond her notice for so long. After thirty minutes of it, she wasn't sure if finding out the latest celebrity baby or marriage scandal, or catching up on the tedious hamster wheel of politics, had been worth the sacrifice of brain cells to read about them.

Try the library, my love.

She did, but she was in the mood for pleasure reading. While Mason was a well-read scholar, he was apparently not an escape reader. *You really need some paperbacks, my lord.*

I'm going to pretend you didn't desecrate my library by suggesting such a thing. But I will send a message to Amara that she might bring some back for you.

It didn't take long to realize the warm feeling she carried around with her during the day was contentment. She was happier in these two days than she'd been in a long time.

A sense of uneasiness came with the thought, for she knew it was a temporary lull. When Mason was with her at night, he was like a hot bath, immersing her in mind-numbing sensations of pleasure, stroking her emotions until she was purring, inside and out. He was willing to be her Master, but in an easy, light-handed way, cocooned in romantic gestures, as if they were young lovers.

Farida had been very happy in that cave, because there was nothing to make her unhappy.

On the second afternoon, she knew she couldn't put it off any longer. She asked him to leave her to her thoughts for a while. Whether that meant he withdrew from her mind or not, she didn't know, but so far he'd respected such requests by remaining silent, letting her think. She went outside, hoping the bright sunlight would prevent shadows from closing in on her mind as she finally gave serious consideration to what might be the most important decision of her life.

Stay or go.

In Mason's arms, as if Raithe feared him even beyond the grave, she'd not been troubled by a single nightmare. Nor had Mason, though she wasn't sure how often his nightmares occurred. If she wanted to return to a normal life, she would remember nothing of any of it. While she found it hard to believe that any combination of science and magic could eliminate the past six or seven years from her mind, she knew Mason was not the type to exaggerate.

He'd killed without remorse, his only regret that he'd not been able to save the woman he loved. When he spoke of what Farida had endured, it was as vivid to him as if it had happened yesterday, and she well knew how that kind of horror could eclipse issues of morality, right and wrong. Still, it underscored that the savage side of vampires was far more unfettered than that for humans. Their codes, etiquette and structure managed bloodlust and that savagery, but didn't prevent it. There were no vampire laws against what Raithe had done to her. A human servant was the property of her Master. End of story.

Yet through Amara and Enrique, even Mason, she'd seen a different side of that. He'd claimed the others she would meet tonight would not be the same as what she'd known, either. She understood all that, hoped it was true, but knew that there would always be vampires like Raithe. And Mason would be her one protection against them, in his world.

Leaving the verandah, she took the horses onto the beach, choosing to walk with them rather than ride. She remembered how he'd taken her riding, letting Coman run wild and free, as he would with no riders at all. Neither of the powerful creatures had ever known cruelty, malicious treatment of any kind. It was in the shine of their eyes, the carefree confidence and joy, as if everything around them was created for their pleasure.

She closed her eyes, pressing her face briefly into Hasna's neck. *Damn it, be honest with yourself.* Before she'd stepped into Farida's tomb, if she'd been given this choice, to forget all of it and reclaim her life, she would have jumped at it. Which meant the only thing making her hesitate now was Mason.

It was Farida, too. It was both. By picking up that journal, reading how much she'd loved him, Jessica had been pulled into their story and was loath to leave. As tormented as Mason was by his inability to let Farida know he hadn't abandoned her, she suspected— no matter the comforts of Heaven—Farida had been tormented by the inability to give him peace, to let him know all had been forgiven.

Was *she* Farida's voice? Was that her purpose? To give Mason that peace? *He is different with you*, was what Amara had said. But in reality, she knew Mason mostly through the pages of another woman's writings. How could she seriously contemplate binding her life to him? A vampire?

Did she doubt she'd find happiness if she remembered none of this? No. Without this darkness in her soul, she'd be the Jessica who embraced life, learning, travel. But she also wouldn't have Mason, Farida . . . or Jack.

Jessica sighed, squatted and scooped up some wet sand, letting it drip back into the water when it rolled back in, caressing her ankles. Coman snorted behind her. Perhaps it was more than that. She had changed. She was no longer that grad student. Yes, maybe she *could* get that version of herself back if those years were erased from her mind, but there were things this version of herself understood and appreciated that the other never would. Did she tamper with Fate, no matter what horrible path it had forced upon her? Or was Fate an illusion, and Chaos the only true arbiter of a life?

The setting sun startled her, the violet sky providing a backdrop as it cracked like an egg on the horizon to sizzle to its finale. She'd been out here for hours. The horses were trotting back to the paddock she'd left open for them, responding to Jorge's whistle for dinner.

Realizing Mason would be up soon, eagerness flooded her breast, along with relief to be done with her thinking for another day. Even though a lingering uneasiness told her she was twisting in the wind, perhaps trying to flutter in stasis forever. And vampires would be arriving later tonight.

Passing through the barn, she nodded to Jorge where he sat in his small office. He had his feet up, listening to a game on the radio, and gave her a friendly wave, his lined face creasing. Things here were familiar. She liked the people, the horses, the master of the estate. But she couldn't be a human servant.

Oh, God, that was the crux of it. If she could have it all, without that, she'd take it. But it didn't work that way. Not with vampires. Only in her fantasies, and she'd been suffused in a pitched battle between her fantasies and nightmares, instead of real life, for far too long. The serum would give her back a *real* life.

Her ebullience with the sunset faded. When she returned to the gardens, climbing the verandah steps overwhelmed her with weariness, intertwined as it was with an inexplicable sense of desolation.

"Excuse me?"

Starting out of her thoughts, her head snapped up. A male vampire stood ten feet away from her.

Instinct kicked in before thought. She scrambled over the balustrade, preparing her shins for the drop to the gardens below. When she was caught from behind, she screamed and kicked, twisting around to strike at the vampire's face, only to find herself in the center of the verandah, far away from the rail and steps. However, the vampire was now thirty feet away, positioned in front of the ballroom doors, both hands open and held up in a reassuring gesture. Vampires moved fast, but even for vampires, the speed had been exceptional. Her breath was short, heart thundering, legs unsteady. Rather than fear, she suspected it was the aftereffect of moving at the speed of sound.

"Didn't want you to fall that far, third-mark or no. We didn't intend to startle you." The vampire was tall, broad-shouldered, with startlingly beautiful blue eyes. His shoulder-length hair had traces of copper, but less than Mason's, mixed with appealing russet and sable strands. He also reeked of power so strongly she could feel the vibrations from here.

So much for her rationalizations. She was getting too damn used to impending darkness. She'd gotten careless, being caught outside. *Mason*. Even in her mind, the panic was akin to a scream.

"I'm here." When his hand settled on her shoulder, she sucked in another startled breath, so quickly she almost choked. He passed a reassuring hand over her hair, then stepped forward, taking the lead position, as was appropriate for a Master and servant. But her relief was short-lived, because when she returned her attention to the other vampire, two more had stepped out of the ballroom.

One was a lovely blonde with large blue eyes, wearing a disarming attire of slacks and blouse, accessorized with a flame opal necklace. She looked as if she should be teaching elementary school, inspiring a boy's first crush. The red-haired, green-eyed man who stepped out behind her appeared as if he'd be at home in the thick forest behind them, a rugged outdoor look to him. He brushed the blonde's arm with casual familiarity, telling Jessica he was her servant.

As she turned her focus to the remaining vampire, Jess realized there was something not quite vampirish about her. A marked servant could tell another vampire, but this one had a different power signature, hard to define. However, the brilliant jade eyes and miles of black hair that would diminish even Amara's sable tresses told Jess this had to be Lady Lyssa. Because Mason had it, she realized there was an exceptional stillness to the oldest vampires, honed to such perfection it seemed they could disappear from sight right where they stood.

Then she dropped her glance and got another shock, though less intimidating than their initial appearance. Lady Lyssa was holding a blue-eyed baby in her arms. The male infant looked like so many others, but regarded his surroundings, including Jessica, with a vampire's careful, eerie scrutiny. When he yawned, she glimpsed tiny fangs like a kitten's.

"It's silent as a grave around here, Mason," Lady Lyssa remarked. "Did your staff go on strike?"

"The staff has a couple days off. I'm pleased you're early. We weren't expecting you until later tonight." Mason lifted a brow, casual, but Jess felt the firm, steadying pressure of his mind touching hers, surrounding her.

"The four-wheel-drive with the tinted windows seemed very safe, especially since we were covered by the forest most of the way." Lyssa adjusted the baby, switching him to the other hip. "We decided not to wait until sundown. So, how are you planning to take care of us, without your staff?"

Before Jessica could tense, Mason chuckled. "Don't worry. I'm sure we can put together some peanut butter and jelly sandwiches to feed you, Jessica and Devlin. And there are plenty of clean bedrooms. Somewhere."

"Mason's method of handling guests," Lady Lyssa observed dryly to the other female vampire. "A foolproof plan to ensure he doesn't get them very often."

"Maybe we should try it." The red-haired servant glanced at his Mistress. He spoke in a lazy Australian accent. "Since you became Region Master, love, we need a bloody revolving door placed on the station."

Jessica, may I present Lady Lyssa, who you've already deduced, and her mate, Jacob. Their son is Kane. The blond vampire is Lady Daniela, who goes by Lady Danny, and the man is of course her servant, Devlin. Some type of greeting would be in order.

He didn't speak aloud, of course, for a human servant would never be accorded a formal introduction to vampires. She swallowed and nodded her head, the best she could do at the moment. Then her gaze inadvertently locked with Lady Lyssa's. The latent power in those jade depths, the coolly appraising look she knew too well, swept away whatever tenuous hold she'd had on herself. Fear sunk talons into her chest, yanking her back into places she couldn't go again, even with Mason's reassurance at her back.

I can't do this. I really can't. With a desperate look at him, she bolted. Taking the verandah steps at a run, Jess despised herself for acting like a cowardly child, but once she started moving, real panic took over, as if she had rocket fuel in her feet. When she reached the bottom, she didn't look to see if she was being followed, but ran toward the gardens.

Lady Lyssa arched a brow. "I suspect she isn't getting us a welcoming cup of wine?"

"We didn't intend to spook her," Jacob offered with a frown. "I'm sorry, Mason."

"I'd intended to spend some time with her before your arrival tonight." Mason pressed his lips together. "Excuse me. I'll be back shortly." He stopped in a turn toward the rail, and gestured. "If you'll make yourselves comfortable up here, there's wine and other things to drink in the cabinet behind the tiki bar."

Conscious of his visitors' speculative looks, the fact he hadn't properly welcomed the new infant, Mason hoped Lyssa understood his nature enough to forgive him. He had more important things to handle now. He took a shortcut over the rail, landing lithely on the grass. With a ripple of movement, he was gone from sight.

Jacob glanced at Lyssa, and Danny and Dev joined them in the exchange. "His abilities as host haven't changed since we saw him last," he observed.

"Hmm." Lyssa shifted the baby to her shoulder and Kane buried his face in her neck, gurgling. "But some things have changed."

"You know, I've suggested to Lord Brian that vampires are so cranky because of the lack of sunlight." This came from Devlin. "Every bloke feels better on a sunny day. Maybe you all need more vitamin D."

Jacob cocked his head at him. "What do you suggest? Helmets with plant lights mounted on them?"

Dev shrugged. "Or antidepressants. Your Yank doctors are pushing them like crack these days. Mason should be able to get himself a healthy dose by nipping from a blood bank."

"Devlin," Danny said, showing her fangs, "I think we need a bartender more than a psychoanalyst right now."

Dev gave her a short bow and a half smile. "I've always heard they're the same bloke with two different hats, my lady. But it's my pleasure to serve. What would everyone like?"

◊

Coward. She was a stupid, idiot coward. She could do this. Couldn't she? He said it wouldn't be worse than the club, and she'd enjoyed the club, despite her trepidations. But this wasn't like the club. Three vampires. *Three* of them. She'd close herself up in her room until after they left. Mason wouldn't make her spend time with the vampires. He'd said so.

"I did. And I meant it."

She looked up. Only then did she realize that she'd run blindly to the first refuge she could find, which was a garden shed. She was wedged in a corner, amid lawn implements knocked askew. *Oh, God.* She really *couldn't* do this. She couldn't see them, smell them, without thinking about Raithe, without being pulled into the darkness of her memories. The bracelets and collar wouldn't help, because she didn't want to hurt herself. She just wanted to get away.

"I know," he murmured. He was squatting on his heels before her, laying a hand on her bent knee. "It's too soon, Jessica. I'm sorry. But I had reasons for inviting them here now, things that have to do with your welfare. Lyssa and Jacob have many contacts in the States. They'll be important to setting up your new life for you, when you take Brian's treatment."

When, not if. Of course. It was clear she couldn't handle being his servant. Hell, she hadn't even been able to stand fast long enough to offer them a glass of wine after their journey. She looked up at him, at his serious eyes, the tightness around his mouth. Pain.

"Mason, I'm so sorry."

He leaned in and slid his arms around her, shifting her against his chest, her head tucked under his jaw. Her body curled, half fetal, between his knees in the dust of the shed. "*Habiba*, have I given you the impression there's anything for you to be sorry about? I am sorry. Vampires so rarely come here, I wasn't attuned to their arrival as I should have been. I don't want you to feel a moment of fear, ever again." He tipped up her chin, brushed her lips with his once, lightly, then more pressure. Soft, sweet and gentle, but with that erotic undercurrent that had her lips parting, letting him in, her body relaxing in his arms, remembering all he'd done for her and to her for the past two days.

When he raised his head, she was feeling a little more settled. "You could pass me off as stable help." She attempted a smile, because she didn't want to be the cause of the concern in his eyes, either. "I finished mucking out the horse stalls an hour or two ago. I smell like manure and probably have straw in my hair."

"You look lovely." He plucked out several straws and dropped them to the side, returning her smile when she narrowed her eyes at him. While nervous banter was a better choice than terror, she knew nothing felt better than his arms. She wasn't brave enough to say that, but of course, she'd already thought it.

Putting her head back down on his biceps, she closed her eyes. "I've fallen for a bloody vampire. But I can't stay. Mason, I am so fucked up."

"Shhh." He cupped the back of her head, his fingers gripping her hair with unexpected fierceness. "It's all right, *habiba*. You need time. It will take you more than a couple months to get past what Raithe did to you. We've both always known that. But you are young and strong, and you have that time." His voice lowered, his breath against her ear, his scent in her nose, his larger-than-life presence surrounding her. "Remember, whether you are here or somewhere else of your choosing, my protection will always be with you. I will keep you safe, if it takes my life to do it. If you trust in nothing else, trust in that."

She pressed her face deeper into his sleeve, into his heat and muscle, thinking her heart might break right there, and end any decision she had to make. Instead, he pried her off of him, held her shoulders so she had to look into his face. "Now, if you wish to spend the entire time they are here in the barn or your room, or anywhere that we are not, that is your choice. Though I will miss your company. That said, this would be a safe, controlled way to face this fear of yours, much like the club."

She swallowed, her trepidation rising again. Five years of social gatherings, everything she knew about vampires and their entertainments . . . But how could she refuse him?

"Because it might be what is best for *you*." His hand settled on her throat, stroking the tender flesh inside the collar, making her shiver. As he studied her involuntary response, the tightening of her fingers on his arm, the coil of warmth in her lower belly, a muscle flexed in his jaw. "A Master must be very careful about what he asks of a submissive like you, Jessica. Your compulsion to surrender is instinctive. You are too demanding of yourself. If you join us for a while, I will be glad to see you. If you do not, I will *not* allow you to castigate yourself. You suffered at the hands of a monster for five years." His grip commanded her attention. "You will *never* be a disappointment to me, you understand? Punishing yourself for not being able to conquer such a terrible, justified fear in a matter of two months is unacceptable to me."

She swallowed, caught between his tenderness and this protective, stern side, stirred by both. "Prefer to punish me yourself, do you?" she managed.

"It is a pleasure difficult to deny myself, my love. Particularly when you have been so responsive to my discipline." His eyes glinted and she almost smiled, but the butterfly wings in her belly were still iced with the lingering dread. "But do not test me. If you join us, while I will not compel you to participate in entertainments we vampires enjoy, it doesn't mean I might not have you straddle my lap, command you to curl your lovely little hands around my cock and guide it deep inside of you, right in front of them. I should have done that at the club."

His voice dropped to a husky seduction, his grip slipping to her nape to fondle. He drew her closer, trapped her between the muscled weight of his thighs. "I would order you to hold my gaze, forbid you to look away. You would know their presence is irrelevant, because it is only my pleasure you serve with the rise and fall of your body. I would push this T-shirt up, grip your breasts in my hands and suckle them. They would envy the lithe curve of your spine, arching back, the flex of your buttocks as they pressed down on my legs, your cries as you came for me."

Jessica stared up at him. He could take her to her back in the garden shed, and she would give him anything he wanted. "Does that arouse me because I truly want to be your servant, Mason, or because I can't be anything else?"

"Only you can answer that, *habiba*. But I do know that you are everything a vampire could want in a third-marked servant."

Riveted by the rare emotion he allowed in his tone, she reached up and touched his face. He caught her hand, squeezed it, not so gently. "You tempt me to damnation, Jessica," he added, low. "I know you want more time to make your choice. But I fear my own nature will eventually take over and deny you that choice. You must decide soon."

"I know." But she had no idea what decision to make.

His eyes shadowed then. "Go now, and get your shower. You'll know where to find me if you decide to join us. Be warned, though. If you do, I will request domestic services from you. That's to salvage my pride, so I don't look completely besotted." A light smile touched his lips. "Things like bringing me or our guests a glass of wine, or sitting at my feet, so I can stroke your hair."

Before she could respond to that, he'd lifted her and straightened to his feet, taking her with him. As he guided her out of the forest of gardening tools, she realized she was covered with cobwebs. He helped her brush them off once they reached the doorway, his hands lingering so that her body stirred, leaning automatically toward him. But when he was done, he stepped back from her. She might have felt hurt, except for the burning demand she saw in his eyes, the tight jaw that spoke of his restraint. And the devastating words he spoke before he left her there.

"I must see to my guests now. But if I only have a few days with you before I am out of your memory forever, I will not deny myself the pleasure I hold over your body. When dawn comes, wherever else you go tonight, I want you in my bed. Don't make me come look for you."

28

AFTER she showered, she looked through her closet. When she put on her choices and stared at herself in the mirror, she realized she'd subconsciously made her decision. She'd chosen a swimsuit and a matching wrap for it. Mason and his visitors had gone down to the beach.

They were at the large screened gazebo, which had swings and benches and a boardwalk to the beach sands. Since everyone in the group possessed enhanced senses, no torches had been lit, the ground illuminated only by moonlight. Jacob and Devlin were sparring with a variety of weapons borrowed from the arsenal Mason kept in the house. Danny and Lyssa were on one of the swings inside the gazebo, talking and playing with the baby.

She watched them all for a while, noting it truly was nothing like the usual vampire gatherings she'd witnessed, even the less volatile ones that Raithe staged. She wondered if Mason had taken them down to the beach because he knew she was most comfortable in the open spaces there.

The swimsuit she'd chosen was a reasonably modest one, a one-piece with a low scoop back and high French-cut legs. The vee bodice showed off her breasts in a pleasing way. It wasn't the string bikini with a thong bottom she'd found, which she absolutely would not be wearing among company like this. However, she knew certain aspects of her appearance were required to be attractively displayed if she was going to be joining them as his third-marked servant. Otherwise, it was a slap at his dominion over her. He'd given her something no vampire she'd ever known would have—a choice. She wouldn't insult him before his guests. Knotting the wrap low around her hips, she checked her appearance in the mirror and deemed herself ready.

She lost her courage halfway there, her breath starting to shorten, and detoured to the stables. Fortunately, Jorge had gone to bed. If only Mason had some drugs in the house. Valium, Prozac. Hell, she should have chugged some whiskey. Wincing, she pressed her forehead against Hasna's. That road was another form of helplessness. She could tell herself she didn't have to do this, but she did. Mason had known it. Not for him, but for her.

"Oh, Hasna."

The mare offered comfort in her way, pushing her nose against Jess for further petting until she won a smile. Straightening then, Jessica combed out Hasna's forelock with her fingers. "Wish me luck, beautiful girl," she murmured, and left the barn to go to the beach.

～

"The mystery guest has arrived." Danny nodded toward the boardwalk. Lyssa acknowledged it with a flick of her lashes, but she'd already sensed the girl coming on the breeze. Her interest was in Mason's reaction. He'd been the cordial host for the past few hours as the time moved past midnight, but Lyssa had picked up his waiting tension, a constant undercurrent, like the roar of the surf. He'd told them not to expect her, and they knew enough of Jessica Tyson's circumstances not to question it. Which only heightened Lyssa's interest and regard for her, as the young woman made her way toward them.

She was obviously frightened. She was pale, her movements stiff but determined, a soldier marching toward a battlefield in a lovely pale blue and lavender swimsuit and scarf wrapped low on her hips. Lyssa made note of the silver collar and bracelets, her Fey senses detecting the magic that hovered on them. A self-protection charm. *Interesting.*

The female vampire knew Jacob would have sensed Jessica's approach, and Dev, keen tracker that he was, would have caught her female scent of soaps and shampoos on the wind almost as quickly as the vampires had. But to their credit, the men did not turn, continuing their sparring. Mason was sitting on the edge of the boardwalk, outside the screened boundary of the gazebo, leaning back on a pillar and calling out his comments as they worked alternately with quarterstaff and sword, or hand-to-hand wrestling. Now, though, he twisted and held Jessica's gaze as she moved up the boardwalk. As he did, her steps became more confident, her focus locking on him, an obvious lifeline.

"It won't take much to make her bolt," Danny observed.

"Don't be too sure. She killed her own Master and avoided being caught for months. There's more to this one than a frightened deer. Mason's attention is not captured so easily."

Despite his casual stance, Lyssa could feel the tension in his mind. The protectiveness. When Danny cast her an intrigued glance, Lyssa gave her an arch one in return.

As Mason lifted a hand to her, Jessica took it, trying not to grip too obviously with her cold fingers. He closed his over them, bent his head to nuzzle her knuckles, warm them with his breath. "You look beautiful, *habiba*. There's wine in the gazebo. Why don't you top off my glass and get yourself one?"

He handed her his wineglass, his amber eyes glowing with bolstering approbation, but as Jessica nodded, turned, she realized she'd be walking into the enclosed space with the two vampire women. She stopped, her feet refusing to move forward.

He closed his hand on her ankle. She'd worn an anklet of beaten silver, so it appeared as if she'd stopped at his mental command, giving him the ability to tease her skin, play with the tiny bells. She'd put it on as a pretty enhancement, but now she remembered what the style was called, those silver jewels that alerted others to her approach, her whereabouts. Slave anklet.

You belong to me, habiba. *No one will harm you. No one will so much as touch you without my permission. That said, I can decide I am not so thirsty—if you come sit on my lap and gaze at me adoringly.*

Flicking him a startled glance, she saw the glint in his eyes. He almost surprised a smile out of her. Taking hold of herself, she shook her head, reached for the door latch. Her hand was numb on the wineglass. She was going to drop it by accident if she didn't focus. She could do this. Mason was right there. Resolutely, she turned the knob, stepped inside the screened gazebo. The small bar with its array of wine bottles, ice bucket and slices of lemon and lime, was in the corner near the door, so she didn't have to cross right in front of the vampire females on the swing.

Still, manners were manners. A servant's gaze didn't meet a vampire's eyes unless specifically permitted, and in this case, she was relieved not to do so. She kept her glance on the bar. "My ladies, may I get you something as well?"

The first part came out as an undignified squeak, but she got the rest out in her normal tone after an embarrassed cough.

"Certainly. More of the red for me. Here's my glass."

Jessica nodded and moved forward, focusing on the glass. As she reached out to take it from Lady Daniela, Lyssa shifted to recross her legs. Jess jerked back and the crystal dropped in the open space. Fortunately, Lyssa's hand flashed out and caught it, reminding Jess that broken glassware was a rare occurrence in any vampire household. Unless the vampire broke it deliberately.

She dropped to one knee on pure instinct, her head bent low. Not only as a sign of apology and respect. The convenient tuck was how she'd protected her face and fragile neck. A second-mark could heal better than most, but a broken spine would have been irreparable.

Mason was already on his feet, but Lyssa surprised Jessica.

"No. Mason, she's fine." The queen's voice was firm. Jessica quivered as her hand touched her shoulder. Even though Mason had said Lyssa's powers were Fey now, Jessica suspected the slim fingers closing around her collarbone could crush it. "It was only a dropped glass, Jessica. You've offended neither of us."

Was she mistaken, or was that a quiet compassion in the woman's voice? Before she could decide whether she'd imagined that, she felt another touch, one she'd forgotten in her focus on the two female vampires. From the bassinet between Danny and Lyssa's feet, a small set of fingers had emerged and passed haphazardly over the crown of her bowed head. Then they latched with remarkable strength in her curls.

"Oh no, you don't." Lyssa's hand withdrew. "Hold still a moment, or he'll leave you with a bald spot. Let *go*." She followed up the useless command by curling her hand over her son's, prying his fist open and letting Jessica sit back. "Kane does like hair, and yours is quite lovely. If he's been sucking on his fist as usual, he's likely left some drool on your scalp."

Jessica felt a sudden hysterical urge to laugh. She'd had far worse things on her head. Glass, blood, vomit, semen . . . She closed her eyes, her hands into fists. *Wine. Get them some goddamned wine and stop pulling yourself back to a place you're not anymore.*

Rising, she turned away, hoping they'd forgive the lack of response, because it was all she could do to perform the simple task. A glass of . . . what was it? Oh, hell.

She kept her eyes down. "My apologies, Lady Daniela. What did you say you wanted?"

"Red will be fine."

Of course. Very few vampires preferred white. The B-movieness of it was amusing, if anything could amuse her right now. But instead she clung to the one thing that seemed helpful. Kane's fist in her hair. When she filled the glass and handed it to Danny, she couldn't help but study the child.

She'd never seen a vampire infant. They were so rare, and this one appeared only a few months old. He was quite alert now, though, staring at her with those brilliant blue orbs. "He has his father's eyes."

She said it without thinking, not intending to address the ladies further, intending to get the hell out of that confined space into the open air of the beach. Perhaps decide she'd been plenty brave enough and escape to a beach walk, but the child fascinated her. No matter the species, all infants were innocent at this stage, inspiring an urge to protect, to hope that he would grow into something worth protecting. Raithe had been a made vampire. The idea that he'd once been a human child, loved by a mother, made her physically ill.

"He does indeed. As well as his stubbornness. Would you like to hold him?"

Startled by the offer, Jessica's gaze darted up to the queen. It was a full second before she recovered herself enough to realize she was meeting those jade eyes directly. Vampire infants were precious to their parents. She knew enough about vampires to know that. In fact, at Lyssa's offer, she saw Jacob come to a halt in his sparring with Danny's servant and wander over, with a casual interest that was anything but. She was a woman who had killed a vampire, after all. Which made the offer even more astounding to her.

"I . . . My lady honors me."

"Yes, I do." The queen's offhand arrogance was so like Mason's, Jess felt a wary stir of humor. "Would you like to hold him?" she repeated.

"I . . . Yes. Is there anything different about holding him?"

"No, he's like most babies." This came from Jacob, leaning on his quarterstaff outside the mesh screen. "Just cradle his head. His neck's not quite strong enough to support the overblown thing."

He gave Lyssa a smile, but from the intent expression in his eyes, Jessica suspected the two were having a far more serious conversation. She saw an almost imperceptible shift in his expression, a bare nod, and then Lyssa was lifting the child.

The last time Jessica had held a baby, it had been when her older cousin came home from the hospital after giving birth. She'd held the child on her shoulder while the mother hugged her welcoming party. The baby had been asleep. Several times during her captivity Jessica had recalled that memory. She hadn't appreciated the privilege, holding that tiny bundle of peace and innocence. Now she glanced toward Mason, who leaned against a supporting post. While he was still outside the screen, he seemed close as well, his gaze caressing her face.

If she left him, what would it be like, having a relationship with someone who couldn't be in her mind, know the yearnings of her heart and soul even before she knew them clearly herself? With Raithe, she'd hated it, longed to be free of it. In less than two months, Mason had made her see it, feel it, a different way entirely.

"Jessica?"

Jessica blinked back the unexpected moisture in her eyes, knowing the vampire queen hadn't missed it. However, to her credit, the woman let her maintain her dignity. She simply nodded at Jessica's arms, and Jessica lifted them to accept the child.

As she slid her arms beneath the small weight, it put her face close to Lyssa's, their arms brushing. Perhaps because she remembered the wineglass incident, Lyssa held on until Jessica nodded, confirming she had him. Slowly she straightened, holding the baby in her arms.

Kane gazed up at her, unconcerned by this new stranger in his life. While his eyes brightened when they went to her hair, fortunately he seemed more interested in waving his hand at her now. Jessica automatically closed her hand on his and he latched on to her finger, curling his own tiny ones around it. He smelled like baby. Powder and diaper, but not milk. Something more . . . metallic. Of course, a vampire baby would feed on blood. The thought didn't disturb her as much as it might have, not with the wide blue eyes examining her so closely.

"He's beautiful," she murmured. "He's going to be so handsome." He would be a replica of his father, the strong face and blue eyes, with his mother's dark, silky hair. Like all vampires, he would be irresistible.

"Thank you," Lyssa said, her attention on her child. There was an ease to her mouth that suggested pleasure, but she didn't appear to be a woman who smiled often. Of course, Jessica had seen things in five years that should have eradicated her ability to smile at all. What if she'd been around for a thousand years, like Lady Lyssa? Mason, too, was more reserved than most vampires she'd known.

She was used to not speaking in vampire company, doing nothing to draw attention, and so she almost thought better of the question, but then the female's attention lifted from her child to Jessica's face. There was no blood-link between them, but Lady Lyssa had apparently learned many things about reading body language. "What is it you wish to ask me?"

"Why did you grant me this honor?"

Lyssa cocked her head. "Look directly at me, Jessica Tyson, and I will tell you."

Jessica met those brilliant eyes. All vampires were beautiful, yes, but she wasn't sure she'd ever seen one like Lady Lyssa. Perhaps it was that sense of *other* coming from her, the undefined power that only enhanced the amazing allure of what was already there, in the dark hair waving around her features. There was a hint of Asian mystique in the almond shape of her eyes, her petite but formidable form.

"Because you have seen the very worst of us. This"—Lyssa's gaze went back to her son—"is the best."

She hadn't heard him come in, but now Mason was standing at her back, one hand on her shoulder. The other came forward and closed on her hand, clasping Kane's. The baby gurgled, fascinated by the two layers of fingers holding his own. Then he took his other hand, beat a small fist against Mason's.

"I think he's already challenging you for her affections," Jacob observed, lips curving. Glancing at Lyssa, he added, "Perhaps he wants to choose his servant early, my lady."

"If so, I expect I'm already defeated," Mason noted. "I'm not sure I could stand up to such a fierce vampire."

"Believe me, if he starts screaming, we'll all run for the hills," Devlin said dryly. "Try being trapped on a plane with him when he doesn't get what he wants. Or was that Jacob squalling? I forget . . ."

Jacob knocked out the base of his javelin, attempting to rap the other man's ankles. Dev moved nimbly out of range. "That was pathetic, Irish. I—" Then he dropped, a lithe roll, as the quarterstaff came whizzing back, with far more of a vampire's speed. "Well, then. That's more like it. Better not bruise my pretty face. My lady won't like it and she'll be forced to whip your skinny arse."

Danny snorted at that. "He heals quickly, Jacob. Do your worst."

"Would you like to join us, Jessica?"

"Hmm?" Jessica glanced up, startled. The vampire simmered in Jacob's blue eyes, but there was an open friendliness as well, reminding her that Jacob had recently been human.

"Mason says you're a pretty sharp fighter. Care to match a few moves with Devlin and myself, exchange techniques?"

"C'mon, love." Dev gestured toward the square of sand where

they'd been sparring. "Between the two of us, we can take him down. He's become unlivable since he grew fangs. Worse than a teenager discovering his bollocks have hair on them."

She blinked, but not at the crudity. Vampires and servants joking with one another. Of course, they appeared serious about the invitation, which caused her no little consternation. "I'm not really . . . dressed."

"Actually, last time they sparred, they had on far less." Danny gave Dev a thorough appraisal. "It was far more interesting."

"Well, never let it be said I want to bore you, my lady." Dev stripped off his shirt in an easy movement, revealing his third mark, an impressive outline of a raven, wings spread across his pectorals. When he shucked off the khakis he'd been wearing, he had on a swimsuit beneath, a pair of snug stretch shorts that emphasized the muscular haunches and a rather sizable—

Jessica caught herself staring and jerked her eyes away as Jacob chuckled, but before she could get embarrassed, he jabbed at the man's midriff with the quarterstaff, backing him a pace. "Last time you were naked, Aussie."

Devlin made a cocky come-closer motion as he maneuvered toward their sparring field. "Don't want you to get confused about which one's my weapon and whack the wrong thing." He twirled his javelin deftly, managing to block another forward lunge. "The other one's only a threat to the ladies."

"Jacob." Lyssa's voice was soft, but Jacob turned toward her immediately. At her unreadable look, Jacob gave her a slow, sexy smile. With a slight bow, he, too, stripped off his shirt, showing off a muscular, broad-shouldered body. Above his hip bone was a brand of a Christian cross. On his spine, Jessica was surprised to see his third mark had survived his transition, a serpentine-looking fossil. The male vampire then slid off his jeans, revealing he wore nothing under them at all. While Dev was obviously overly equipped, enough to cause a faint-hearted woman consternation, Jacob's blessings were nothing to be sneered at. Despite that, Dev snorted and rolled his eyes.

"Unless you're using a really short dagger, I won't have any problem telling your staff from that pitiful thing."

Jacob, though quite obviously quite comfortable with his un-clothed state, glanced over at Mason. "My lord, there are a pair of swimming trunks in the duffel there. Would you mind?"

Were they actually making an effort to help her feel more comfortable? She couldn't tell, because there were too many ways for these five to communicate without her having a clue as to what was happening. However, she had to admit the tension in her shoulders eased considerably when he put the trunks on. It wasn't that they weren't beautiful men. But this was how the "games" started, and they were inviting her to play . . .

She'd tightened her arms on the baby without realizing it, and Mason ran soothing hands down her arms, jolting her back to her current reality. He leaned down, pressing his jaw against her temple. When his hair fell forward over her shoulder, Kane latched on to it instantly with a triumphant coo and tried to stuff the ends in his mouth.

Jessica was taller than the vampire queen, but as Lyssa stepped in, the energy simmering in her luminous eyes suggested that, even if she was a pixie fairy, able to land on a daisy without disturbing a petal, she could still blast a giant onto his ass. "Here. I'll take him back now. At least if you're sparring with them, we won't have to suffer through a tedious stream of male genitalia insults."

Jessica didn't dare hold him with less than two arms, so there was a momentary delay as Lyssa extricated Mason's hair, with Jessica trapped between them. While the vampire queen held the little fist and pulled Mason's hair free, as she'd done for Jessica, she glanced up at him, gave him that half-smile look he returned with a similar warmth in his eyes. Lyssa pushed his hair back over his shoulder, a bit of a stretch for her shorter height. Though her forearm brushed Jessica's neck, she could have been a piece of furniture for as much notice as the queen paid her. When she drew back, she let her fingers linger in his silky hair, what any female with a hormone would be tempted to do. Still, the obviously intimate gesture pierced Jessica's lower abdomen like a small spiky ball.

But then Lyssa had taken her son back and Mason was squeezing her shoulders. "Go join them, *habiba.*"

Lifting his voice, he drew the other two males' attention. "Do not teach her anything that would make me uneasy in my bed at night."

Dev grinned wickedly. "I expect she already knows how to do that, my lord. We'll just teach her how to make it quick and painless."

"I'm not sure that's necessary," Jess muttered, stepping out of the gazebo. She didn't know if Mason had caught it or not. Likely not, because he was speaking to Lyssa. As he took a seat in a chair next to the swing, he picked up the wine she'd topped for him. Then he leaned forward in an attitude of full attention, one hand loose on his thigh as he sipped the libation and studied the child.

While he was doing that, Lyssa dropped the strap of her dress to bare a breast and feed. Jess's emotions warred with her curiosity as she stopped an extra second to watch. There were a pair of uneven scars on Lyssa's breast, just above her nipple. She couldn't help the sympathetic wince as baby Kane pierced her there, latching on to drink his mother's blood. The queen's breast was distended beyond the size of her frame, as any nursing mother's would be, only instead of swollen milk ducts, apparently she had swollen veins.

Of course, curiosity wasn't the only emotion Jess experienced as Lyssa so casually bared that plump breast before Mason's gaze and continued to talk to him, as if it were nothing. She laughed, a sultry sound, as Mason unpinned one part of her sable hair and drew the long lock forward, a silken veil to cover the breast and Kane's small skull. Jessica noted his hand lingered, gave the skeins a passing, soft stroke of affection before he withdrew, sat back and answered a question Danny posed. She had her arm stretched along the back of the swing behind Lyssa, her body turned in a relaxed pose to watch the mother nurse. Like Mason, but far different, to Jessica's way of thinking.

Turning on her heel, she moved toward the practice field. Of course they'd been intimate. She already knew that. Vampires were incapable of curtailing their libido around one another. She was just a human, after all. In his bed at dawn, her ass. She wasn't about to be part of some threesome he had in mind.

She was surprised to catch an expression on Jacob's face suggesting she wasn't the only one adversely affected. His mien as he studied the gazebo had become far less friendly, far more dangerous than he'd yet appeared, enough to bring her to a wary halt. But then Dev nudged him, murmured. Jacob's jaw flexed, his grip on the quarterstaff increasing. Though his face relaxed into a more ambivalent expression, she noted sparks of cobalt fire in those eyes.

A servant noticed everything, because that was key to survival around vampires, and Dev was no exception to that. "Choose your weapon, Jess," he said, giving her a steady look, an unspoken signal easy to decipher and intended to reassure, she expected. *This doesn't involve us.*

How she wished that was true, that it didn't matter to her at all. She wanted to be magnanimous. Lyssa had saved his life, helped him through some of his worst moments. He'd known her for hundreds of years. Their history was as natural a thing to them as breathing. But did they have to breathe so loudly? And of course, technically, vampires didn't have to breathe at all.

"Hand-to-hand. Whatever style works." She unknotted the hip scarf and let it fall, kicking off her sandals. She performed a few deep stretches, getting out the kinks. The overwrap bodice provided a generous amount of cleavage, and the spandex as she spread her legs to work her groin muscles would draw attention to the plump lips of her sex. The high French cut certainly offered a pleasurable view of her ass.

The last thing she'd expected to do tonight was deliberately flaunt her assets, but at the moment she received a certain satisfaction from being noticed by the two males. Coming to her feet, she rolled her head on the stem of her neck, shook out her hands like a boxer priming to fight.

Dev came to her side, his lips pressed against a smile, his sea green eyes telling her he was aware and perhaps familiar with her state of mind. "Now, my Mistress, she doesn't particularly care for me trying to improve my skills against a vampire opponent. She wants me to turn tail and run, thinking no human can hold his or her own against a vamp. You're living proof that's not quite the case."

"I got lucky. Very lucky." She didn't have any illusions of that, but Dev only nodded.

"That may be true, but the way I feel about it is this. If my lady is ever attacked by one and I can buy her a few seconds, well, then, that's what I'm going to do. In your case, you must have felt the same, for a different reason, else you wouldn't have taught yourself to fight."

She lifted a brow. "How much has Mason told you about me?"

"Enough to know to be on my guard. I don't want to have my arse kicked by a girl." He winked. Then his voice lowered. "And don't worry about Jacob. He's got his blood up about his lady and Lord Mason, but he won't be taking it out on you. Me, on the other hand, he'll beat on like a rug." He gave her a grin. "So you don't mind if I'm a bit unchivalrous and say 'ladies first'? You might coax him out of his foul mood."

She couldn't help it, his humor was too infectious. She managed a smile, but pounding on something for a few minutes sounded fine to her. Mason hadn't even noticed the stream of invective she'd sent his direction, and she'd thrown in some choice words. He was too wrapped up in his beloved queen and her maternal breasts that should be gracing a *Hustler* magazine centerfold. She could probably stake him where he sat, more oblivious than the wounded Raithe.

When she turned back to the makeshift field, Jacob nodded to her. Apparently reading her mood, he assumed an attack position without further conversation and began circling. Dev had obviously understood her feelings, but now she wondered about Jacob. He'd been a human servant. How often had he been forced to stand by while his lady took her pleasure with others? He was still with her, though, despite being a vampire, and male vampires were not known for sharing, unless it was their idea. She couldn't imagine what kind of power struggles the two of them had been forced to resolve as a result of Lyssa turning him. Obviously some of those struggles hadn't been entirely laid to rest.

When he lunged at her, she made herself focus. He could out-match her in an instant, she knew, but the purpose seemed to be analyzing potential strategies, not overwhelming his human opponents. She appreciated the value of testing skills against a vampire holding himself in check, but right now she was irritated, with herself mostly.

Avoiding the lunge, she moved in with a leg sweep, ducked past his attempt to seize her midbody, rolling away. He was on her again in a flash, and she went deadweight, bucking at the key moment to break his hold. Jamming an elbow hard into his thigh as she went down, she twisted beneath him, catching his ankle. It would have set another man on his ass, but he flipped out of it, lithe as a cat.

Dev whistled. "Nice."

Jacob nodded in agreement, backing off. "You could buy yourself a second or two with that, if you used seduction as an additional distraction. Males of all species are usually easy in that regard." His smile was faint, ironic. "Even if we know it's a distraction, we still have to look. Biological imperative and all."

They circled again. He taught her a few more maneuvers, had her break down a couple of hers. He worked her hard as Mason had, the night in the workout room. Then Dev came in, and the two of them worked out tandem strategies that kept Jacob on his toes. He increased the use of his speed and strength as they gained more confidence. Jess found herself concentrating so hard, everything else disappeared as she strained her mind and body to its limits to outsmart him, outflank him, acting in concert with Dev.

At some point, she realized she was having fun, in a way only competitive athletes could. Who couldn't enjoy the setting? Ocean in the backdrop, moonlight overhead, and two powerful, handsome men engaging her in a mock physical combat that brought her in close proximity to broad chests, a hip or buttock, a long length of thigh, flexing beneath her hands or against her body as they twined together, hit the sand or rolled off one another, like a particularly competitive game of Twister.

Despite her pique with Mason, it made her think of his body beneath her hands, her mouth. Then his body on top of her, flexing between her legs, challenging her to the utmost, in a different, far more erotic way than it was being challenged now, but there was a similar physical undercurrent to it that had her breath shortening from more than physical exertion.

Her guard slipped. Jacob deflected her punch and seized her body, flipping her through the air and over him. She braced herself for impact on the sand, but he slowed her descent, catching her under the small of her back as she came down. Still, she grabbed on to his shoulders automatically. When her soles hit the sand, her body was parallel to the ground, no more than a foot off it as he went to one knee so as not to dislodge her grip.

His hair was not as long as Mason's but she'd still caught some under her hands. Looking up at him, she couldn't help the instinct to wet her lips. Seen up close, his blue eyes and chiseled face were pretty mesmerizing. She had a feeling he'd been a woman's pinup, even as a human. So it seemed natural to reach up to his face, trace his lips, let that same hand trail down his chin and throat, to the expanse of bare chest, which of course drew his bemused gaze down to the upward tilt of her breasts and . . .

Devlin hit him like a battering ram as she rolled out of the way, somersaulting back to the balls of her feet as Dev knocked him flat on his back, his javelin pressed into his throat, knee on Jacob's chest.

As Jacob glanced over at her, she shrugged, gave him an innocent smile. "You're right. The seduction technique works very well, my lord."

He grinned then, tension dispelling, and shoved the javelin away, accepting Dev's hand up. "Aye, it does. And it's just Jacob. I'm not an overlord, or a Region Master." He nodded toward the gazebo, a shadow crossing his gaze. "I'm her servant."

"She's very fortunate to have you."

Jacob's expression warmed and it looked as if he might respond, then he stilled, his head cocking. As if he'd received a message of sorts, he shifted his attention briefly to the gazebo, then came back to Jessica. "That's kind of you, Jessica. And you fight very well."

He moved toward her, relaxed, the smooth muscles of arm, chest and abdomen moving in that ripple of male power hard to ignore. She started when Dev's hands ran down her upper arms, though not to grip and hold. Simply to caress her skin, energize nerve endings.

"You have a choice, Jess," Dev murmured. "According to our ladies, you may spar with us a different way, if you like."

As Jacob moved forward another few steps, those vibrant blue eyes holding hers, she backed farther into Dev, but her reaction wasn't fear, not exactly. The Australian man's powerful, compact body pressed into every curve of hers, but his hands remained as gentle as if he were holding Kane.

She couldn't deny the grappling had gotten her blood up. Truth, since over the past two days there was barely a room where Mason hadn't taken her body, she seemed to arouse at mere suggestion now. Maybe that was why she didn't feel afraid. That, and Jacob was obviously being very careful not to spook her. They were giving her the choice.

Mason had told her they were different and they were. Jacob was a vampire . . . but acting like a servant, at the command of his lady? It was confusing, but she didn't say stop when Jacob drew closer. Or when Devlin put clever lips to the juncture of her throat, a capable hand easing the strap of the suit down, giving Jacob the ability to simply lean forward and put his mouth over the bared breast.

Her body was loose and warm, receptive. They'd tested her abilities, built up gradually to a workout that had pushed her to the limit of her abilities, enough to tell her where her weaknesses were, where she needed improvement. This felt like more of the same, testing the waters, seeing how far she wanted to go, how much she wanted to stretch herself. But still, something was moving through her uneasily, a sense of absence. Was this her Master's will?

I am here, habiba. The words came after a long silence in her mind. *Give yourself pleasure. It's making me desire you all the more. You only have to say stop.*

She gasped as Jacob's skillful lips suckled her nipple, his hands taking possession of her hips just over Dev's. The Aussie was still working on her nape, the juncture of shoulder, the hard pressure of his intimidating organ pressing into the cleft of her backside.

I want you. I like this . . . but I want you.

Then you know where I am, habiba. *Come to me.*

As if the message was passed and received, Jacob straightened and Dev lifted his head. They knew how to keep a woman's senses tingling, for they let their hands linger as she left them, and the appreciation in their eyes filled her with a sense of her own sensual powers. Her fingers slipped with some reluctance off Jacob's broad shoulder. Dev brushed a fond kiss over her knuckles before he let her go.

Moving back across the sand, she saw Mason was back on the steps to the gazebo, watching her approach with those amber tiger eyes. She'd left the strap of the bathing suit down, knowing he'd want to see her walk toward him like that, her breast bare to his gaze.

What I want to see is all of you.

Her mind seemed to have clicked into a languid stasis, not questioning or fearing his commands, simply obeying. With only the hesitation necessary to remove the suit, she walked naked across the beach to him. While in some peripheral way she was aware she'd bared herself to the others, his eyes were what mattered.

When she reached him, he tilted his head the amount needed to meet her gaze. His expression wasn't dispassionate in the least. An underlying strong emotion made his usually velvet-smooth voice rough. "On your knees, my love."

When she sank down before him, he cupped her face with his large hand in that way that was part gentling, part demand. "What is it my servant desires?"

She stared at him and swallowed. Slowly, she lowered her gaze, turned her face into his palm, touched her lips to it. "I want what will serve you, my lord. What will pleasure you." Though if it was something that involved the Lady Lyssa, she knew it might break her heart.

His fingers dug into her scalp in a way that brought her eyes up to him again. "I want you never to touch another man, unless it's at my express command."

"An interesting sentiment, Lord Mason. One we share."

Jessica looked up to see Jacob, now standing only several feet away. Danny had come out of the gazebo to meet Dev on the sand of their practice field, but Jessica saw her turn, picking up the undercurrent of trouble. Lyssa rose, still inside the gazebo. "Jacob."

Jacob lifted a hand, a quelling, commanding gesture that startled Jess, particularly when Lyssa heeded it, though her gaze sparked. "Whatever once was, is no more," he said, locking gazes with Mason, and the heat built with that connection. "Circumstances made me vampire, and I see things through the eyes of both now. The vampire who claims her, and the servant who serves her. Your friendship and love are valued beyond measure, but there is a line. You cross it again, and things will become far less friendly between us."

Mason rose then, pressing his hand on Jess's shoulder briefly, an unspoken command of his own, indicating he wanted her to stay on her knees. She glanced toward Lyssa, saw the vampire queen watching the scenario with a now unreadable expression. But Mason was nine hundred years old. Jacob had only recently become vampire, by Mason's telling, though Jacob emanated a power that was oddly a match for the vampire who stood over her, so close his thigh brushed the back of her shoulder.

"You are right," Mason said at last, his voice cool but even, releasing some of the tension holding them in the tight triangle. "My apologies, Jacob. It was not my intention to take uninvited liberties with your lady."

Jacob nodded. His jaw eased fractionally. "Good." Then his glance moved down over Jessica, a swift, easy passage that she felt shiver over her skin, remembering his sensual treatment on the shore. "You're fortunate in your choice of servant, Lord Mason. She's beautiful and strong. I hope your usual winning personality doesn't drive her away. She brings out better things in you."

Then he turned, the moment broken. As Jessica drew in a breath, Jacob moved past them, onto the gazebo. Lyssa stood silently, watching him. Jessica couldn't tell what passed between them, but Jacob first bent to his son, passing a gentle hand over his brow, and then straightened. Putting his hand on her nape, beneath her hair, he drew her to him and captured her lips, a slow but thorough, heated gesture, one that had Lyssa reaching up toward his face, but Jacob captured one wrist, held it in a grip that suggested a less than mild rebuke, a reminder of their bond. Lyssa's answering growl, in the back of her throat, sent chills up Jess's spine. It was clear the creatures with whom she kept company tonight could be as primal as Hasna and Coman, quick to lay back their ears, bite and savagely kick if cornered, or if they felt something that belonged to them was being threatened.

Trouble now past, though, Danny and Dev were walking closer to shore. She watched, bemused, as they gravitated to each other,

Danny reaching out a hand and Dev taking it, so they walked hand in hand in the moonlight.

Mason was sitting behind her again. She leaned against the inside of his thigh and he stroked her hair as she watched the two, yet her head tilted into his touch. Her lips grazed his palm.

You are all right, habiba? *You are not frightened?*

Not much.

Good. Putting his hand beneath her chin, he tipped her head straight back, holding it at that awkward angle for his kiss. With the lazy and typically unexpected moves of a tiger, he turned her, strong hands coming under her armpits to lift her up to straddle his lap, cinching her in hard on his cock with two possessive hands on her bare ass. Remembering his earlier words, she recalled how she had desired the fantasy, but feared the reality. Now, with the warm touch of the tropical breeze, and the moon's light on the planes of his handsome face, she wanted him, and she didn't care how. Or who was watching.

When she moved her hands between them to open his shirt, he caught her wrists. "Please," she said softly.

He nodded then, let her open the shirt all the way, find the fastening of his trousers. She had to scoot off to get them out of her way, with his shoes, and when she did, she sank to her knees on the sand and took him into her mouth.

Mason saw her intention right before she did it. The flash of overwhelming lust took him over as the wet heat of her mouth enclosed him, sliding down his shaft, all the way to the root, her throat relaxing with devil-blessed skill to take all of him. Ten feet away, Jacob and Lyssa's turbulent kiss had become something more. Though he didn't look in their direction, he could hear the rock of the swing. Lyssa was straddling Jacob's lap with that catlike grace of hers, Jacob's response muffled as he brought his mouth to her sternum. Even as pleasure would suffuse Lyssa's body under Jacob's skillful touch, and his beneath hers, the message was blatant. *Mine.*

Could he say he felt any different about the woman on her knees before him now? Jess was making it hard as hell to think of it any other way, servicing him with her mouth, her slim body naked as her Master had every right to demand she be, even in the presence of his guests. If this had been a normal vampire gathering, he might have commanded her to let Dev and Jacob take her even higher, all the way to climax, get her good and slippery for his final claiming. If he were a normal vampire. But merely seeing their hands and mouths on her, knowing Lyssa and Danny had been teasing him, seeing what his limits on Jessica were, hadn't altered the burn of jealousy. Or the need to pull her away from them, make it clear to her, as soon as she gave him an appropriate opening, what he expected of her.

As they'd stimulated her, she'd thought of him, as if they were no more than sexual toys he'd given her to use while she fantasized about him. That had helped manage that burn, saved him from embarrassing himself. Allah, what an egotistical, insecure son of a bitch he was.

Did it matter? She could be his for now and forever, but he still had to let her go. In some part her bravery tonight, her indulgence of her own sexuality, was because subconsciously she'd already made the choice. He was certain of it. He was just too much of a damned coward to dig down and look for it in her mind.

He wished it wasn't Raithe who'd made her so good at this. But then he realized that tightening of her hand on his base, stroking his testicles with her fingertips, might be technique and skill, but the hungry noises she was making in the back of her throat were for him. She licked him, suckled, even bit him now and again, her hips moving restlessly on her calves, telling him what she wanted.

Thank Allah she'd removed his slacks entirely, otherwise he would have stood up, tripped and fallen right on his damn face. Lyssa would certainly never have let him live that one down. Instead he rose, guiding Jess's mouth from him, and put her arm around his neck so he could lift her. When she tilted her face back, he took her mouth, tasting himself and her own need.

Moving swiftly, he left behind the beach, their guests, following the shortest route back to his room. He'd meant it, wanting her in his bed by dawn. But he didn't want to wait for dawn. He wanted time to ravish her beautiful body, several times, before sleep would capture him. He wanted her exhausted enough she'd sleep by him throughout the day, not leaving his side. He'd tether her there if he had to do so.

When they reached his room and he stretched her out on the bed, Jessica saw something stark in his face, drawn with need. Despite the small amount of time she'd truly spent with him, this side of him made her yearn to say the hell with all of it and stay. This was Mason without charm or seductive power, just sheer need and loneliness, seeking her to fill him, to help him find himself. In those moments she desired nothing else in the entire world but to do just that, as if by making him whole, she'd help heal herself as well. The answers would become clearer.

Thoughts of Lyssa, of every woman he'd ever had, disappeared. She lifted her hands to him and wasn't surprised when he grasped her wrists again, but instead of drawing them up, he held them there between them. In that hovering space of time, she mouthed it. *Let me touch you. Let me love you.*

Slowly, he released her. Weaving her fingers into his beautiful mane, she slid her thumbs along the slope of his jaw on either side, down to his strong throat as he curved his powerful arms beneath her bare body, tilted her up and slid into her with no further preamble, making her breath clog and throat arch to him, offer. He nuzzled it, but his hungers lay elsewhere. He closed his mouth on the breast Jacob had suckled and laved her there, then bit. Not a nip, not a scoring. He sank fangs into the breast on either side of the nipple. Jessica cried out at the pain, her hands gripping his shoulders, digging in, startled and yet holding still for him, understanding in some primitive way this was part of being vampire, too. Her punishment and his promise at once. She was his. And in this suspended space, there was no fear of that in her. No matter what else came.

He began to stroke her inside as he drank, drawing from her breast. His hips moved rhythmically, a clench and withdraw. She let her fingers drift down his back and then over his buttocks, feeling that delicious pump of male movement, the friction of his stomach against hers, the brush of his hair over her face.

Releasing her breast, he licked the abraded skin, then shifted position. He put his elbows on the pillow above her shoulders to make the thrusts vigorous, slapping into her core so hard she could only hold on to him. The climax was no gentle build, but an explosive, tearing agony of pleasure she couldn't escape, even as she twisted and writhed, screamed and called his name.

He whispered hers in return, holding her down until she'd given out completely, her body quivering. When his release came, flooding her, his seed was so rich and hot she couldn't help but think what it would have been to have him do it in her mouth, swallowing every drop.

Your thoughts are going to destroy me, habiba. *But you will be on your knees, taking me in your mouth before dawn comes.*

"I wasn't going to come to your bed," she admitted after a while, when it was quiet between them. "You made me angry, with Lyssa."

"It would not have been wise to defy me. Not as much as I have wanted you all day. I would have found you, taken you wherever I found you."

"I thought you were going to do that anyway." She'd seen Jacob and Lyssa in the shadows of the gazebo. Despite their earlier power struggle, what she'd seen on the swing had been a perfect synchronization of desire, Lyssa's lovely bare back arching as Jacob brought both her breasts together in his hands and teased them with his mouth. She'd been straddled on his lap as Jessica had been on Mason's earlier, only in this case, it was obvious Jacob was fully penetrating her, the way she rose and fell, her gasps and sighs a match for his groans. Sounds of demand and need while Kane slept peacefully nearby. It had stoked Jessica's own desire such that when Mason had lifted her she'd been wild to be the same, impaled on that thick shaft, having it filling her deep and hard.

But she liked it best like this, pressed into the pillows with him above her. Despite it all, maybe she was a traditional girl, for she preferred the male she loved surrounding her, holding her down and deep inside of her, so when he at last released, he'd collapse upon her, keeping her pinned yet letting her wind her arms around him, press her cheek against his jaw. Even if he was so heavy she couldn't breathe. That was when she felt the most needed. Maybe even loved.

Ah, God, Jess. You're a fool.

He didn't chastise her for her self-deprecation, though she was certain his mind was linked as closely to hers as their bodies. Maybe because they were both fools, he didn't say a word, merely held her closer, and began the welcome process of arousing her again.

29

H<small>E</small> took her twice more. Before that, as he'd promised, he put her on her knees and made her work him in her mouth until he came. Binding her hands behind her back for that, he held her steady, guiding her with his hand on her head, making her dependent on him for balance. It left her wild with need for him again.

When he lifted her back to the bed, he made her take an egg-shaped position, knees folded beneath her, breasts pressed to her thighs, face to the mattress. Her arms stretched forward, fingertips touching. He explored her anus and sex at the edge of the bed with mouth and fingers as she shuddered in the position that allowed no real movement except for involuntary quivering. Then he eased his cock into her wetness, slow, long strokes that built until the climax came the same way, long rolling tide lines that never seemed to end.

The last time was when she came out of the bathroom. She'd taken one step across the threshold before he had her pinned against the wall. He simply hiked her up and took her there, rough and needy, as if he hadn't already had her twice before. She clung to him, swept away by his rough urgency and yet still as well. A quiet place inside of her wanted to reach into his heart, tell him it was all right. She was here, it was okay. But she wasn't sure why she thought he needed the reassurance, so she just held him.

When at last he drew her down next to him, right before dawn, she was worn out, but she had a question lingering in her mind.

"Mason?"

He was idly stroking her brow, his arms holding her close in the curve of a very relaxed, obviously sated male body. His grunt almost made her smile.

"They love each other, don't they?"

His fingers stilled. "Who?"

She tilted her head up to look at his face. "You can read my mind, my lord. You know who. Both of them. I don't understand Jacob and Lyssa's relationship, because it's not very clear-cut, but it's there. With Danny and Devlin, it's obvious. They really do love each other."

His chest rose and fell, a sigh. "Yes, they do, *habiba*. But what you have seen here, you can never reveal anywhere else, for Danny and Devlin particularly."

"Why?" She propped herself on an elbow, looked down into his face as he dropped his caressing touch to her upper arm. "I mean, of course, I wouldn't, but why does it matter?"

"It is a complex world we live in, *habiba*. Danny's nature is vampire, so she does exercise a dominant control over Devlin. Though she never truly tames him, because they do love one another. While it is not his nature to submit, it is to protect, and for a male, one can often dovetail into the other. It is a give-and-take, depending on how much you love someone."

He fingered a curl of her hair again. "With Farida, I considered myself her Master, and I was. She also considered me that. But I would have walked on my knees over glass to prevent her from having so much as a tear. Power is a fluid, unclear thing, my love, when you are dealing with hearts and souls. Unfortunately, the minds of our world are somewhat rigid. It is impossible for our current society to believe Danny can hold the authority of a Region Master and love a human the way she loves Dev. True love, the kind that is a circle, with no clear up or down, beginning or end."

Jessica swallowed, looking at him, and of a sudden, she thought she understood his disturbing urgency outside the bathroom, what lay unspoken between them. But before she could say anything else, he cupped his hand over her temple and pressed her head down on his chest, so his voice rumbled beneath her ear. "This is a safe environment for them, to be as they are to one another. However, if the vampire overlords or Region Masters thought Devlin had any type of emotional control on Lady Danny, and they convinced the Council of it, they would kill him. Strip her of her Region Master title, probably marry her off to a more powerful vampire who could dominate her, teach her the error of her ways."

Jessica raised her head and stared at him, horrified. "That's . . . medieval. You would . . . Would no one help her?"

"You have seen the friends she has, *habiba*." He gave her an admonishing look. "And do not be deceived by her disarming appearance. Lady Daniela is relatively young, but a formidable vampire. She did some amazing and rather brutal things to become Region Master.

"Our civility is a mantle we choose to wear," he added at her surprised look. "You yourself have pointed it out. Under threat or anger, our instincts can rise up and take over. The same as for any species who deceives itself into thinking they have outgrown their primal roots." He lifted a shoulder. "You saw it earlier tonight. For male vampires in particular, issues of territory are basic to who we are. And if the territory in question is female, it is worse."

"But you're not like that. What I saw tonight . . ."

"There is a right way and a wrong way to exercise it. Jacob's actions were appropriate tonight, and he earned a greater measure of my respect for it, though we shall let that be our secret as well." He pinched her arm lightly.

Maybe it wasn't in a human to completely understand a vampire, or vice versa. Though Mason was different, she'd sensed an implacability to him from the beginning, a line he wouldn't allow her to cross. He would protect her, and yet he would not allow her to defy him, beyond a point. However, some part of her *did* understand that, and God help her, it was a component of what made her crave him.

Mason had helped her see that not all vampires were monsters, no more than humans, but both species were fully capable of producing them. In some odd way, she did understand what he was saying. Mason and Jacob's behavior had been a necessary step to avoid bloodshed, by drawing boundaries regarding the very beautiful vampire they both loved. Perhaps because they acknowledged those bloodlust instincts, rather than pretend they could rise above them, they fell prey less often to their own savagery.

"I understand about Danny and Devlin. But Lyssa and Jacob?" she asked.

He yawned, showing his fangs, like a big, sleepy cat. "Why females have so much energy after sex, and males have so little, is one of Allah's personal jokes. Perhaps we need to redefine the meaning of vampirism."

She poked him, but propped both elbows inside the curve of his arm as he wrapped it around her back, letting his hand lie loosely on her hip. "Who holds control there? Officially, I mean. I understand the rest."

"Mmmm. For them, it is a difficult question to answer. Because of her turning Jacob, and her embrace of her Fey ancestry, they exist outside the range of Council ruling now. From one perspective, Jacob holds mastery, since his transition took her vampire strengths. He had a devil of a time learning to control them," he added, amused remembrance crossing his face. "I had the pleasure of shepherding him through that process. It's a good thing for you I am a vampire, otherwise I would have been so scarred and ugly when it was done, you would not have looked at me twice."

She suppressed a smile. "What makes you think I look at you at all, my lord? I find you quite plain and unappealing."

He squeezed her bottom, making her squirm closer so he could nuzzle her brow, brush his lips over it. "Jacob took the upper hand by necessity after his turning. She was pregnant, with only Fey abilities she'd never really explored. So for a while she was weak and greatly needed his protection. He third-marked her as he would a servant for that reason. She still has the blood of a vampire, but she's no longer bound to the night, nor does she live on blood. Her Fey blood allows Jacob to feed on her, nourishing him as a servant would. But Jacob told me earlier she's embracing more of her Fey heritage these days, and her powers are growing exponentially."

Seeing her bright-eyed curiosity, Mason sighed. "Perhaps letting you hear it directly from my head, rather than repeating it, will satisfy your curiosity, and let me get to sleep faster."

Raithe had so rarely opened his mind to her, it was still a novelty, the strength of Mason's will drawing her mind into his. It was as if he took her by the hand and stepped over the threshold of a world that looked much like hers, only she was seeing it through his perspective. His thoughts and memories opened up images that engaged her senses, so it felt as if she had been there when it happened, his conversation with Jacob . . .

∼

He and Jacob had been sitting in the dining room, sharing a drink while Danny took her feeding from Devlin and Lyssa got Kane settled in the nursery. "Lyssa seems far more sure of herself now than she was in those first months," Mason observed. "More like herself."

Jacob inclined his head, tipped his whiskey glass in Mason's direction. "We owe much of that to your continuing help to Mr. Ingram, managing her estates. We've been able to spend more time with the Fey."

Mason shook his head with a half smile. "They haven't been seen for centuries as you are seeing them. I'm envious."

Jacob snorted. "I thought vampires were insufferably arrogant. They're humble as monks in comparison to the Fey. Still, it's been worthwhile. All those years, because of the way the Fey tried to kill her mother before she was born, Lyssa embraced the vampire side, except when the Fey filtered in subconsciously. Now she's getting to explore more of that side of herself."

When Jacob set his glass down, swirled the contents, Mason noted the whiskey had a deeper hue to it. That, and the scent, told him it was mixed with Lyssa's blood. It was still odd to him, to see that reversal in their circumstances, and when a shadow passed through Jacob's gaze, he realized that he was not the only one that might find it unsettling.

"But they have accepted her," he pressed.

"It's hard to tell what the Fey accept. From one day to the next, it's as likely they'll disappear without a trace or threaten to annihilate you with a flash of heat lightning. But yes, for now they've been willing to teach her, guide her." Jacob's glance flicked up to the other vampire. "It doesn't matter how she changes, Mason. She's always a queen, and only a fool would underestimate it. It's in her heart and brain, her very soul. The powers she may or may not have are only secondary."

The Irishman stretched out his long legs, crossed his ankles. Despite the fact he carried the mantle of Lyssa's power, and Mason knew him quite capable of wielding it, he still chose to dress as the Faire player and drifter he'd been for some years before he met Lyssa. Well-worn jeans, a black T-shirt imprinted with an alehouse logo that featured a green and gold dragon. However, the simmering tension to his lean, muscular body, and the intelligence of his blue eyes warned against underestimating *him*.

"I remember Lord Brian telling me once that the Fey could kick a vampire's ass any day of the week," Jacob mused. "And he's right. Those powers she has, her grasp of them, are growing exponentially. Her vulnerability during her pregnancy, and her transition from full vampire, were only a short-term thing. She doesn't require my strength and protection anymore. Not in that manner, at least. And she's shrugging on the mantle of Fey arrogance quite easily. After all, being a vampire gave her a millennium of training for wearing that."

Mason gave him a sharp look. "She'll always need you, Jacob."

Jacob waved a dismissive hand. "You mistake me. I'm not worried, Mason. I love her, she loves me, and that's always a balancing act." He sobered then and met Mason's gaze directly. "I *am* her servant, Mason. I never stopped, and I never will stop, even if the nature of that has gotten more complicated. As if it wasn't complicated enough to begin with." A smile tugged briefly at his lips.

"I was the port in the storm, and I'll continue to be that, or whatever else she needs me to be. While I wish the future was more certain, particularly for Kane's sake, it never is, is it?"

Mason lifted a shoulder, his head filling with memories. "No, it never is."

Jacob inclined his head. "So I can give her one certainty. I will want her forever, love her forever, until the stars fall out of the universe, and we all blow away to dust. No matter what either of us has to become to accomplish that."

~

True love, the kind that is a circle, with no clear up or down, beginning or end . . .

Jessica put her head down in the crook of Mason's shoulder, her arms still folded beneath her like a prone bat. "It seems there are no simple choices."

His hand traced her back, the line of her bare hip. "No, *habiba*. There aren't. Sleep now. Or at least have mercy on your poor Master and be silent. Before I gag you."

She smiled. *Can't gag my mind, my lord.* Then she shrieked, giggling as he rolled her over and began to tickle her, until she promised to be quiet and let him sleep. As she settled, she wondered if he'd done it to keep her from descending into darker areas, but regardless, it worked. She dropped off to sleep as well, curved into his body, his arms crossed protectively over her.

~

She didn't rise until around noon, and she did so with an unexpected sense of guilt. Amara would have put effort into making sure their guests were more comfortable, their domestic needs attended. While she realized the irony of taking on a role she would have scorned a couple months ago, as she moved around the lower level of the house she discovered the vampires had found the best bedrooms for their needs. Mason had been right—many of the chambers had been ready for guests. Amara had apparently set up a nursery while Mason was still in Berlin.

While Jess understood Mason had not given Amara leave to tell her about the vampires' arrival until he returned, it still rankled some. Was it a sign of improvement that she felt as cranky as Mason about being handled? Of course, being a terrible patient didn't mean the patient wasn't sick.

Pushing that irritating possibility aside, she stopped at her room to change into jeans and a T-shirt. At least she could check the kitchen to see what breakfast arrangements were possible for Devlin or Lyssa. Then she'd go to the stables to help a short-staffed Jorge feed the horses.

Instead, she found Dev already in the kitchen, scrambling eggs and listening to a country station on the radio. His deep timbre was humming along with a George Strait song that declared everyone had a desire to go to Heaven—but no one wanted to go now.

She was almost certain the amazing aroma that met her at the door was pancakes, and he was pulling out some biscuits from the oven. A bowl of cut fresh fruit was already on the counter. Without turning, he slanted an affable smile over his broad shoulder. "Eggs, love?"

The Aussie was fully clothed this morning, in the khaki trousers he seemed to favor, a white T-shirt and hiking boots.

"How did you know it was me?" She shook her head. "Of course, the third mark."

"Well, it does enhance things a bit. But that jasmine soap you wear teases a man's senses. And you carry Mason's scent as well. 'Course I knew it wasn't him, this time of day. Have a seat and I'll feed you."

She wasn't sure what to think about the curl of warmth in her belly at the idea Mason's scent was upon her, so she focused on more practical matters. "I feel like I should be feeding you. I'm sorry you're having to do for yourself."

The surprise in his gaze was reassuring. He swept his attention over his surroundings. "This is nowhere near doing for myself, love. There've been mornings a few moths and a snake were the best I could do for breakfast, after a night on the hard ground with no warm and generous arse, like my lady's, to snuggle up to."

Considering she'd experienced five years where feeling safe and warm were as remote possibilities as a heavenly welcome for Raithe, she had to agree with him. The smile she gave him was genuine. "You're absolutely right."

"That I am. Really, this is a holiday of sorts for us. No one to impress or pretend for. No chance my Mistress can put me into unlikely situations to feed her insatiable needs." He winked and then winced. "Ah, she heard that. Light sleeper, that one."

"Where are Lady Lyssa and Kane?"

"Poor bloke." Dev grimaced. "They'll have a time of it when that one's running about on his pins. He has the vampire aversion to the sun, so he's sleeping with Jacob until Lyssa gets back from her morning flight. She'll be back"—he glanced toward the window—"right about now."

Flight? Jessica looked out the bay of windows, only to suck in an astounded breath. A creature was flying above the shore, circling down toward the sand of the beach. Blinking several times, she wondered if she was distorting a pelican into a much larger size.

She doubted it, because what she was looking at reminded her of an effeminate but still powerful gargoyle, one who'd somehow managed to free herself from the edge of a French cathedral. Sleek silver-gray skin, the small skull devoid of hair. Pointed, elongated ears, with fangs pronounced and curving out over her bottom lip. The flying creature had a long tail with a sharp spike end and lethal-looking talons for fingers. It gave the creature a deadly appearance despite a thinness that showed every rib. While Jessica could detect the mounds of her breasts, they were integrated into lean musculature. Large, round eyes, spaced wide like an animal's, no whites, just pure darkness, riveted on the house as she chose her landing area. Leatherlike wings came to a half fold as she met the ground, exposing another wicked-looking claw on the elbow joint. Jess estimated the wings were about ten feet, tip to tip.

As Jess continued to stare, the being drew herself upright and began to move forward, such that what had been an animal crouch and stride melted into a woman's graceful movement. The wings folded down and vanished, the gray fading into creamy skin, the talons retracting. In a blink, she was looking at a naked Lady Lyssa, who bent to retrieve the silk wrapper she'd left on the sand. Shrugging into it, she freed her yards of silken dark hair from the collar before twisting it up in a clip.

"It's quite something, first time you see it, isn't it?" Dev slid a plate of pancakes and eggs next to Jess at the kitchen island, nodded to it and began to fry a couple more for himself.

"She's . . . Is that what a Fey looks like?"

"Hard to say. She's the only one I know. Jacob says the Fey come in all shapes and sizes. Since she's the first ever that's a mix of vampire and Fey parentage, she's the only one of her kind that anyone knows about. Might want to eat that before it gets cold."

"She's amazing." Jessica swallowed a bite of egg that didn't go down as smoothly as she expected, watching the breathtaking woman make her way back up toward the house. She remembered the elegant bare body, no marks on it, sheer perfection.

"Mmm. You're nothing to scoff at, love. Lord Mason may have a past with her, but you're his present."

Jessica glanced at the Australian who, despite the comment, had his back to her at the stove. "Am I that pathetically transparent?"

He chuckled. "Only to another servant." But then he raised a serious gaze to her. "We all deal with it, figuring out what we mean to our Master or Mistress. It's hard to explain or classify, based on what we knew of relationships before, so the first decade or two, we all have some confusing, bad times."

"Like Jacob, last night?"

"Yes and no." Dev shrugged. "That wasn't too bad, all in all. Jacob has it figured out pretty well, better than I'd expect for as short a time as he's been with her. But when you see those two together, it makes sense. It's like they've been together since before time began. Of course, as he said, he couldn't let that pass last night. Not only because of how he felt about it personally. He's with a very strong woman. She won't respect anything less from him. And no matter how things stand"—he sent a meaningful glance out the window—"don't make the fatal mistake of thinking she's like us servants, just because he's marked her as one."

"No chance of that, unless I was a complete idiot," she observed dryly, and earned another grin. "How about you? And Lady Danny?"

At his arched brow, she bit her lip. "I'm sorry. I know I seem to be nosy, but it's not personal curiosity. Not completely. It's—"

He waved a hand, dismissing the apology. Grabbing a pot holder, he dumped the biscuits into a bread basket and put them on the table. "We've all been through the Q and A period, love. In the beginning, with this lot, you have far more of the Q than the A. Lady Danny is my Mistress," he said bluntly. "I serve her, however she needs me. That's unconditional, though I'm not saying she and I don't have the occasional blue on what her needs truly are."

When he flinched again, he tempered it with a grin. "Serves you right, for eavesdropping instead of sleeping," he said to the air in front of him, then winked at Jessica. "You know, you women don't always know what's best for you."

"Oh, really?" Jessica fired a biscuit at him, which he countered with a block by his spatula, and caught the spinning bread deftly in the air.

"Crikey, it's a flank attack. I'm buggered now." Taking a bite, he winked at her, leaning back on the sink. Even as she shook her head at him, she didn't stop smiling. While vampires were all beautiful, she was beginning to appreciate their choices in servants as well. A man who looked like that, who could cook like this . . .

I can cook too, habiba.

She laughed out loud then. Dev gave her an amused look, but didn't ask her what she was laughing at. Another intuitive sense of servants, apparently, knowing when these dual conversations were occurring.

Then Lady Lyssa came in the kitchen door. Without conscious thought, tension returned to Jessica's shoulders. She stopped short of standing, but it was a near thing. Lyssa had gone through the outdoor shower, because she was toweling her hair and mopping at some of the beads of water running down her throat. She swept her glance over Jessica, but then found Dev.

"Eggs, my lady?" he queried. "A pancake?"

"No, I found food. A boar."

"The whole thing?" Dev cleared his throat at her searing look. "Which is entirely appropriate, of course, because you're eating for three. Left the hooves?"

Lyssa gave him a gimlet eye. "Danny really should have you whipped daily. I'm going to suggest it to her."

"I promise, my lady, she chides me well and often on my many faults."

"Hmm. I've never been in a temperate rain forest." Lyssa changed subjects so easily, Jess realized the sardonic banter was a familiar ritual. The tight coil in her belly eased a wary fraction. "I'll have to take Jacob through it tonight. Beautiful, really. Dev?"

"'Course, my lady." Setting his frying pan off the burner, he came to the table where she'd found a seat. Taking up the towel, he helped dry the thick ribbons of her hair. When he nodded to the comb on the counter next to Jessica, she handed it to him, watching the big man's hands move with ease over Lady Lyssa's scalp, working out tangles.

So it seemed Lyssa and Danny visited each other often enough that Lyssa felt comfortable borrowing her servant. It made sense, since the four were obviously bound by a unique set of vampire–human servant relationships. Unfortunately, that was not enough to calm her suddenly reactivated nerves when Lyssa glanced at her. Before Jess could look away, avoiding the appearance of insult, Lyssa pointed in front of her. "Come here."

Though Dev had said her vampire powers were gone, it was obvious to Jessica that Lyssa expected to be obeyed, whether as Fey or vampire. It reminded her of the memory Mason had shared. *She's always a queen, and only a fool would underestimate it.*

While Dev sent her a reassuring glance, Jessica still had to force herself off the stool to stand before Lyssa. Before she could wonder if Lyssa wanted her to kneel, the female made a motion for her to turn around.

As Jess did, she felt Lyssa's eyes boring through the light cloth on her back. "Remove your shirt. I want a closer look at that work."

She swallowed. "May I ask why, my lady?"

"Because I commanded you to do so. I will not do so twice."

Her lower abdomen roiled, eggs rising uneasily as her heartbeat started to do a birdlike, panicked flutter. Of course, Raithe would have already knocked her to her knees with a fist to her temple for daring to open her mouth rather than instantly comply.

Then she recalled the way Mason had touched this woman, smiling intimately at her. Vampire queen, Fey-bird . . . *thing*, Jessica was *not* going to fall apart in front of her. Pride, that ridiculous thing she'd discarded for so long, had somehow gotten a tenuous grasp on her. Even though she suspected Lyssa could shatter her pride as effectively as Raithe.

Taking the edges of the shirt, Jessica raised it. While she could have taken her arms out of the sleeves and yoked it around her neck, she didn't. Straightening her spine, she removed the garment, laying it over the stool in front of her. She felt Lyssa's regard on her flesh like a burn, and when the woman's fingers grazed the scars, she jerked. She couldn't help that, but she was surprised when Lyssa made a soothing noise, and she realized the touch was gentle.

"Easy, child. Mason has shown me some of your experiences."

Her tone became hard. "A vampire like Raithe will not be missed. Unfortunately, not missed isn't the same as forgotten."

"No, my lady." Jessica worked the words past the ache of her throat.

"The tattoo is lovely work, though. An intriguing choice. Yours or Mason's?"

"Mine, my lady." She wanted to ask the queen to stop, else she would crack like one of Dev's eggs, what was barely held together inside running out before she could stop it.

"Where is your third mark? I wish to see it."

She'd always thought of pants as a more substantial covering than a skirt, but in a situation like this, the quick ability of a skirt to be lifted and then dropped to reconceal was much more comforting. Jessica cleared her throat. "I'd be willing to let you see it, my lady, if I could go put on more suitable garments to reveal it."

"You mistake me, Jessica. I didn't ask if you were willing. Turn toward me."

The words fired through her mind like a shot flushing out a flock of vultures, feeding on the carrion of her memories. The room began to tilt, her palms to sweat.

No. Jessica forced the world to steady with the one word. Had Mason drifted back off, or was he seeing how this played out? She wasn't sure how she felt about that, but he'd said he wouldn't let anyone harm her. Perhaps he was listening, and seeing if she would trust in those words without his physical or mental presence to reinforce it. Or perhaps she was giving a vampire more credit than he deserved and he was snoring, oblivious in his bed.

There was only one way to find out.

She pivoted to face the seated woman. "Lady Lyssa," she said, though her voice shook like a child's, "as a third-marked servant, you know I obey the wishes of my Master. If he commands me to show it to you, I will do so. But until then, I don't feel it's appropriate for me to submit to your desires."

Dev was still behind Lyssa, working on her hair, though Jess could sense his attention. His earlier friendliness had vanished from her mind. Now all she could remember were the servants who, at best, would only look at her pityingly when she resisted her fate. Then there were the worst, those who'd helped Raithe find Jack, who'd hauled away his body afterward. His lesson to remind her how alone she was, how she couldn't count on anyone to protect her.

Her hands closed into tight fists, a tremor sweeping the taut scars embedded forever in that tattoo. She couldn't run this time. Bolting yesterday when Mason was present had been accepted as a one-time thing. Lady Lyssa would have her down on the tile floor in an instant if she moved a foot. The dangerous vibrations from her said so.

"Dev, please leave us."

The queen spoke with quiet firmness. The Australian moved away from Lady Lyssa to turn off the stove, then brushed Jess's shoulder as he passed behind her. Perhaps he meant it as further reassurance, but he was still abandoning her to her fate without a look back. She expected nothing more of a human servant.

"Jessica, you may put your shirt back on."

As Jess did so, she was surprised when Lyssa sat back, and began to plait her hair, a thoughtful look on her face. The silk wrapper was loose, showing Jess the curve of ample breasts. A nursing mother's breasts, at odds with the sleek and lean predator she'd seen only a few minutes before. Lord Mason had snorted over the idea of Lyssa as nurturing. Yet, remembering her protectiveness with her son, Jess recalled this was the female who'd rescued Mason from the rock pit, who'd led him away from self-destruction, not once, but twice.

She wasn't sure if Lyssa was waiting, or deciding how to react to her stubbornness, like a spider contemplating how best to subdue the dinner caught in her web, but Jessica spoke before she could find out.

"If I may revise my position, my lady"—she focused hard on the slim hands, braiding the dark hair—"though I am commanded only by Lord Mason, I would honor the request of the one who saved his life."

Lyssa's hands stilled, but Jess did not raise her gaze. She unfastened the jeans, and then, trying not to think too much about what she was doing, she slid them off, balancing to remove them entirely because she couldn't bear to feel hobbled. Then she straightened, her lower body exposed to the lady's gaze.

Lyssa's jade eyes slid down the front of her T-shirt, to her exposed mons, and lower, to her thighs. Willing the shaky tremor of her limbs to cease, Jessica spread her stance, knowing the tiger mark slid too far inward to be clearly viewed without spreading the legs. It was said that vampires had no control on how a mark manifested itself, but in this case, she wouldn't be surprised if that feature of her mark was a reflection of Mason's appetites. At a quiet movement at the kitchen entrance, she saw Devlin deposit a folded skirt on the counter, within Jess's reach, his gaze briefly sliding over her before he took his leave again.

"Definitely a daily flogging." Lyssa's voice reflected acidic amusement. But when Jessica turned her attention to the other female again, she didn't see any of it in the queen's face. Lyssa touched the tiger mark, impersonally enough that Jessica didn't feel it was sexual, but the physical intimacy was there, enough to keep her from relaxing her guard. Lyssa raised her gaze to her face.

"You understand the significance of this. And yet you still intend to leave him. You may dress."

Jessica immediately turned, pulling the skirt across the counter, and stepped into it. Yanking it over her hips, she backed away from Lyssa, behind the deceptive safety of the counter. She wondered how Devlin had found her room and the skirt in it so quickly. And how he'd been that damned intuitive. "I don't know, my lady. This life was not my choice. He is giving me a choice."

"I understand that," Lyssa responded, impatience in her voice. "Mason has had many human servants in his lifetime. Only two have ever born the mark of his own totem."

"I'm not her."

"No, you're not. You're stronger, smarter, more ruthless." Lyssa rose, a quick snap of movement that suggested she might not have vampire speed, but it still exceeded mortal abilities. "If it had been you in that situation three hundred years ago, you would have found a way to contact me, to bring me and what other few friends he has to his aid. You wouldn't have died in a futile act of nobility, plunging his soul into darkness for three hundred years."

Jessica was too stunned by the words to remember not to meet her eyes. Lyssa's expression was flat, but the fierceness in her gaze had all but swallowed the jade color, leaving Jess a forceful impression of darkness.

"She didn't know about you."

"Yes, she did. He'd told her. As much as she defied convention to be with him, she had her people's inherent distrust of outsiders, and way too much faith in her God. Nomadic peoples like Farida's are intensely community dependent. In the end, that was what brought tragedy upon them. When she rode into the camp and faced the hatred of her family, she believed her death, and Mason's, was meant to be."

Startled, Jess's brow furrowed. "I don't understand."

"While she knew her love with Mason was sacred, honor to one's family was sacred as well. She'd committed a grave sin against them, and she realized the price must be paid." Lyssa tightened her slim jaw. "She understood by that time that the vampire world would never accept the idea that Mason loved her the way he did. So no community would have either her or Mason. If she gave herself willingly to Allah's judgment, perhaps she and Mason might then be together in another world, a Heaven where such love would be treasured and not scorned, if she suffered enough."

"This wasn't . . . She didn't write any of that down."

Lyssa's delicate nostrils flared, her lips thinning. "While he was still in mourning, he told me a great deal about her final thoughts, when the torture that went on for five days broke her mind entirely. All her preconceived notions were torn away, leaving her nothing but desolation, utter hopelessness. I wish her body had been as weak as her mind, and she had died much sooner, before those thoughts could torment him as they have, all these centuries."

"She loved him, Lady Lyssa." Galvanized by all that Farida had given her, meant to her, Jessica defended her. "She loved him to the utmost of her ability. But she was a young woman in a sheltered environment. She could only go to the limits of what she could conceive. She can't be blamed for that."

"No, she can't. But I lived hidden from sunlight for over a thousand years, Jessica. The first time I felt it on my skin, I wasn't sure how to react to it, but I adapted. I learned what its dangers and pleasures were. I pity the fact she didn't have time to do that. But I ache for his pain, his loneliness all these years, the blame he's put on his shoulders."

Lyssa turned away toward the window, her lips pressed together. The sunlight limned her petite oval features, bringing the jade glimmer back. One hand lay gracefully on the back of a chair, the other resting on the doorjamb. The silk wrapper molded her curves, revealed the line of one smooth leg.

She was a painting, a creature who, on first glance, wouldn't understand limits and boundaries such as Farida and Jess had experienced, for everything about her shattered preconceived notions. But then Jessica recalled that she'd risked her life, given up her authority and exalted position in the vampire world, to save Jacob. When Mason came out of the rocks half mad with bloodlust, she'd let him tear into her flesh, held him in her arms.

Jessica swallowed. "Raithe forced me past all boundaries, my lady, into a world that haunts my dreams, as well as my waking moments. Even now, I fear being in your presence. Devlin seems a good man, but I could never trust him, for I have seen what a servant will do against others if it is his Mistress or Master's will."

Lyssa glanced at her. "Time will ease those wounds."

"They will become manageable," Jessica responded. "They will never heal. They will never be gone. I've lived in the ugliest, darkest side of this world, and I know exactly how close it is to the light. It's no further than the shadows in the corners, and in a heartbeat it can close in and shut out the light entirely, whether or not you're vigilant against it, because too often it comes disguised as good intentions, or wishful thinking."

She saw something in Lyssa's face, a flicker she didn't understand, but she pressed on. "You know what the vampire world requires. Eventually, despite how reclusive he is, he will need me to be a true servant, and what happens when I can't? By vampire standards, I was handled like fragile glass last night. You think I don't realize that?"

She shook her head. "He can't avoid more formal circumstances forever, because I know what he's become among the Council and others since your absence. What happens if he demands something of me I can't give in those circumstances? He'll have to punish me, force me to obey against my will to maintain the appearance of strength. He knows that as well as I do. I would end up hating him, fearing him, for my mind will never be able to accept that. It will break, and I'll be lost in Raithe's dark world forever. It's best if he lets me go."

Lyssa leaned her hip against the table, cocked her head. "Come here, child."

Jessica's brow furrowed, but she obeyed. When she stopped a couple steps away, Lyssa gestured her forward again. Though the butterflies came back in force, she did it, and was nonplussed when Lyssa simply plucked a loose string off the collar of the T-shirt, snapping it with a quick flick of her wrist. Her knuckles brushed Mason's silver collar.

"You are assuming you know best what he wants and needs. A common problem with human servants, when they think they can read their Master or Mistress's thoughts. Regardless, that is not the true question that troubles you." Her gaze pinned on Jess's face, holding her there.

"Mason was the equivalent of your human street child among vampires after his parents died. Except a human child would have had the slim luxury of occasionally finding a friend, a soup kitchen haven for a night, or an adult who isn't a complete monster. A teen vampire is in the company of killers, all more experienced than himself. To survive that, he had to cultivate his darkness and play terrifying games of chance beyond your comprehension, perhaps even beyond mine, at an age where he was prepared to do none of that. But he did it. He lost his soul doing it, several times, which is why I think he did what he did to Farida's family. When he loses his moral compass, there is no more deadly and dangerous vampire than Lord Mason. And I include myself in that evaluation."

Remembering the coldness she'd seen in his eyes when he spoke of Farida's village, Jessica couldn't think of a response to that. But Lyssa was not finished. "It took some doing, but that savage wisdom became part of his strengths, honed ruthlessly with finer, nobler attributes. I'm not ashamed to say I was almost as brutal with him as those others, in order to see that happen." She inclined her head. "But in the many years I've known him since then, I've only seen him lower his guard twice. Once with Farida, and now, with you. The question isn't whether or not you can be the proper servant to him, Jessica Tyson. The question is whether you love him enough to risk everything you are to stand at his side. Give him your love, your heart and your trust, no matter how illogical and senseless it seems. Because that is what love does."

Jessica pressed her lips together, her mind in confusion. Fortunately, Lyssa didn't appear to be seeking a response. She sighed instead. "No matter how noble or foolish her actions, Farida loved him," the queen acknowledged. "I do not disagree with that. She loved him completely and senselessly, but she lacked the necessary understanding of darkness to love him wholly. The woman who can be his moral compass and hold his heart, that is the woman he needs."

Leaving the towel and comb behind, Lyssa moved to the kitchen doorway, paused. "What goes on between two hearts is far, far apart from the matter of whether you stand at his side as his wife, or three paces behind as a servant. That was something Farida *did* understand. Loving him was everything."

30

W HEN sundown came that night, Jacob joined Lyssa at the boundaries of the temperate rain forest, the two intending to spend some time exploring the lush jungle of exotic plants and animals, and each other. Jessica sat on the verandah, watching them go, her bare feet through the railings, the gauzy skirt Dev had brought her hiked up to her knees. She'd showered and changed after the horses and put it back on, though instead of the T-shirt, she wore a light halter, one she knew Mason liked.

As they stopped at the forest's edge, Jacob drew Lyssa to him, caressed her face. He spoke and she smiled, then his hands were on her shoulders, pushing her light dress off her shoulders. It pooled around her feet. As he bent to touch her neck with his lips, a flash of fang catching the dying sun, she twisted away. In that blink, she'd transformed, her amazing winged self performing a teasing loop above his head and then disappearing into the trees. Jacob picked up the dress, tucked it into the duffel he was carrying and vanished into the shadows of the trees as swiftly as the hunter he'd become, the beginning of an obvious game of cat and mouse. Though Jessica couldn't imagine Lyssa as something as gentle as a mouse.

Danny and Dev had volunteered for babysitting and, last she'd seen them, they were tucked away in the library, playing games with baby Kane, surrounded with a variety of his toys. She'd leaned in the doorway there for a bit, watching Danny on the floor, laughing, those deceptively Disney-like blue eyes dancing as she held him above her on straightened arms and swung him back and forth as if he was a tiny superhero. Dev had been stretched out on a lounger near her, so her bare feet twined with his as he read, her toes caressing his ankles under the cuffs of his pants, a casually intimate pose.

She might have been looking at a domestic scene in any human home, like her cousin with her baby and husband. But it was a lie. Wasn't it? Leaning her forehead against the rail, she sighed. Regardless of what Lyssa said, or her own heart, she wasn't sure of any of it.

"You know I cannot bear your sadness, *habiba*." Mason touched her shoulders as he sat down behind her, sliding his legs through the railings on either side of hers, wrapping his arms around her chest. She hooked her hands over them, feeling his solid strength all around her, even as he had her effectively trapped in this one position. "You were not there when I woke. I was displeased."

She smiled despite herself as he nipped her shoulder. Tilting her head to the left, she dropped it on his shoulder as he marked her skin. He was shirtless and wearing a pair of jeans, apparently having decided to match the casual garb of his male guests. It was a far too appealing look for him, the rough denim and hard muscle squeezing her hips, his groin pressed up against her lower back and upper rise of her buttocks. When she leaned back into his grasp, she lifted her arms to link around his neck, automatically giving him access to slide under her brief halter and fondle her breasts, stroke her nipples to aching hardness with little effort. Did a servant ever tire of wanting a Master? Did the third mark come with a compensatory elevation in sexual drive to keep her from being exhausted by her vampire's carnal appetites?

"I would say yes, but I much prefer the ego-boosting idea that I keep you in a state of wanting me."

His hand descended now, gathering the skirt, and the breeze touched her bare skin as he found his way under it, found her. Jessica arched, when, with little preliminaries, he simply eased his fingers into her, slow, finding her gathering wetness. "Mason . . ."

"This is what I want right now, my servant. I want to make you come, helpless in my arms. Drive your worries away." Caressing her clit with devilish knowledge, he used his other hand to knead one breast and then the other. His mouth burned a path down her throat again, tongue flicking the pounding artery, the cord at her neck. She bucked and writhed as he took her up swiftly, more swiftly than he ever had before, making her wonder if his ego-boosting idea was right on target. All the things she'd been mulling in her head were gone, wiped away by his demand that she surrender to him.

This is what I desire, above everything, habiba. *Not your willingness to play games with others at my pleasure, but that at my very touch you surrender your will, trusting me to carry you to ecstasy, letting me satisfy my need to own you, body, heart and soul.*

Her breath sobbed in her throat as his words and the climax pitched her into abandon. Her cry was as wild as any that might come from the thick, dark forest where mysterious creatures such as Lyssa roamed, connecting to instinct and need, not thought and intellect.

She spasmed against his fingers, and his fangs scraped her neck, not biting, just a reminder of another way she served him, as the waves of the orgasm rose and fell in her. She couldn't fight his strength, and the diabolical vampire knew exactly where to hold her still, where to let her move so that she strained, whimpered and capitulated all at once. When at last she was limp in his arms, another part of her still ached to be filled by him in other ways.

However, after that heated greeting, he seemed content to hold her cradled against him for a while, his lips brushing her brow. Occasionally, he murmured to her in Arabic, and though she didn't know what he was saying, it didn't matter. He was thick and hard against her back, but when she thought to concern herself with that, he simply bid her to be still with a flex of his arms.

Turning her cheek to his chest as the night darkened, she gave him pictures of her day, her favorite things about it. Sometimes he liked her to speak the words, but now she let the thoughts drift between them like clouds. Lights flickered on the ocean, local fishermen she'd seen out there before. Tonight they appeared to be casting in closer, though they had a bit of a struggle, since the wind was blowing them off the shore.

"Do you have a boat?" she asked, her fingers intertwined with his on her thigh. His thumb stroked her knuckles with idle gentleness.

"I do. I can take you out in it. There's a nice cove not too far from here. At low tide, there are caves you can explore while I watch."

She smiled. "I forgot. Vampires don't like to swim."

"No, we can't swim. We sink. Most don't even like boats, but I like the water." He nodded to the view. "Obviously."

"It reminds you of the desert," she guessed, shivering as he stroked the damp lines he'd created between her thighs. Her fingers convulsed under his nape. "The waves and vastness."

"So it does, *habiba*. You know me well."

His head lifted then, and she sensed him studying the darkness. "Mason?"

"Shhh. I heard . . . something."

She straightened in his arms, searching the night with him, listening to the lap of the waves on the shore. "Maybe Lyssa and Jacob?"

"No." His hands opened, an easy caress, at odds with the sharp thoughts that abruptly flooded her mind.

Jessica, I want you to obey everything I tell you to do. Without hesitation or thought. Do you understand? Do not speak aloud. And do not be afraid.

"Good evening, Lord Mason."

She expected him to leap to his feet, but instead Mason brushed his cheek over her temple, gave an irritated sigh. "You're forfeiting your life, Trenton, coming to my home uninvited. There is no welcome for you here. What do you want?"

"It is who we want, and I think you know the answer to that."

She stiffened, but Mason's grip reminded her to stay relaxed. Only then did he slip from around her and rise, taking a spread-legged stance that covered her in front while the railings provided some protection behind her. Glancing through the slats, however, Jessica saw a cadre of male vampires, seven of them, come from beneath the shadows of the verandah. They formed a semicircle below. Despite the ball of ice that formed in her chest and stomach, she showed them to Mason in her mind, felt a flicker of acknowledgment. Then she slid her legs out of the rails and turned on her backside to see the threat before Mason, while keeping at enough of an angle to maintain the others in her peripheral vision.

She'd recognized Trenton's voice right off. Now she saw him, with a dry-mouthed surge of panic she tried to push down. She also knew most of the eight vampires who stood behind him. Raithe's progeny and hangers-on. Her heart stopped as she realized two had crossbows notched with wooden arrows aimed at Mason. They were accompanied by well-armed servants.

"What foolishness is this, Trenton?" Mason asked coldly.

"We intend to kill her. Slowly, as she deserves. You can find another servant. Raithe's death must have justice."

"Raithe's death *was* justice. And while Raithe sired most of this litter"—his gaze coursed over them contemptuously—"I don't think their motives for being here are devotion to their sire's memory. You think you can take my home, live off of my earnings?"

Trenton's face tightened. "Everyone knows you spend most of your time in the desert or isolated in this palace of yours. If you disappear, no one will even think to ask about it. But I can be merciful, Lord Mason. Start walking away, toward the forest now, and don't look back. We'll have your estate and your servant, but you'll have your life."

God, he doesn't know you at all, does he? What an insufferable little prick.

That desperate, wry humor she used so unexpectedly would have eased the tension in his chest, if Mason wasn't preoccupied with the odds, her safety, and the fact that beneath the grim bravado, Mason could feel her terror. She was holding together so far, but her mind was too fragile. It wouldn't take much to snap her. Darkness was already swirling in her mind, taking away her ability to think and act. It infuriated him that they'd entered his property, given his servant even a moment of fear. A darkness of his own surged up in his chest, only it would compel him past thought, into pure, murderous action.

He cursed himself for being off guard. Having three other vampires already in his home had covered their approach well. Thanks to the shift in loyalties of Gideon, Jacob's vampire-hunting brother, Mason's estate was off-limits to all but isolated rogue hunters, and vampires didn't typically attack this way. He'd never expected vampires to approach from the water. Obviously he hadn't reckoned on the impetuous stupidity of youth, or how destructive it could be. Or Trenton's soon-to-be fatal audacity, in the face of Council ruling.

Pushing aside the self-flagellation for later, he focused on the vibrations of bloodlust around him. Most of it seemed directed at him, not Jessica, which told him, regardless of Trenton's feelings, his companions wanted this property more than anything else. Of course, that didn't make Jessica any safer from them, unless he was, in fact, killed.

He wasn't making that mistake again. If he couldn't take them down, he would make damn sure they took him out, and she would be safe.

"If I intended to let you survive this day, Trenton, I'd haul your ass before the Council and let you explain your actions to them." He swept his gaze over the others. "Even if you managed by some miracle to kill me, they'll still hunt all of you down."

"Doubtful." Trenton sneered, an unattractive look for his otherwise attractive features. "The Council doesn't like you all that much. And for all your fierce reputation, we figured a way to reach your property without detection, my lord. You're outnumbered and cornered, and I think you're nowhere near as dangerous as Council thinks." He jutted his chin out, glancing at Jessica. "Why protect her? Why is she worth that?"

"This has nothing to do with my human servant," Mason retorted. "You've forfeited your life for attempting to take what's mine. As far as being outnumbered and cornered, hunting a crippled rabbit on open ground would be harder than ripping your hearts from your chests."

He narrowed his focus on Trenton and could imagine doing it, enough that his fangs started lengthening. There was some nervous shifting, but he already knew intimidation wasn't going to do the full job. They were too committed, too bolstered by their numbers to back down.

"You've gone stupid over a human cunt, the same way it's rumored you did three hundred years ago," Trenton snarled. "Once we chain you down and punish her for her crime against Raithe, maybe you'd do well with some pain yourself, to remember what being a vampire is about. Maybe you'll beg for *my* mercy."

"This is ending only one way, Trenton. With your death."

"Not if we get you first," the vampire to Trenton's right snapped. Yanking the crossbow to his shoulder, he fired, despite Trenton's angry shout of protest.

During the exchange, Jessica had been struggling to hold on to her composure, to remain as outwardly dispassionate as Mason. As the tension built, she'd realized this was going to escalate quickly beyond a war of words. She'd warred between growing terror, anger, and an overwhelming need to escape, to run.

When the crossbow fired, that desire disappeared. She leaped up. At the same moment, Mason's voice resonated in her mind. Not the rebuking tone he'd used in the past, but pure command, the voice of a Master who would be obeyed, or there would be Hell to pay.

Get down.

She dropped without thought, but he was already on her, yanking her down and spinning as several arrows shot over the railing, singing past the arrow that had fired at his chest. It spun off into the gardens, but one of the others went into his side, above his hip bone. Fleetingly, she realized it was where her unprotected back had been a blink before. He shoved her back down, putting her against one of the wider support posts, and then turned to confront the vampires. Snatching the arrow out of his flesh, Mason tossed it aside, ignoring the spurt of blood that stained the waistband of the jeans, though Jessica gasped as some of it splattered her skirt.

"You've already lost, Trenton," he hissed, his voice roughening, traces of civility disappearing. "She is beyond your reach, and in truth, far above your worth."

Jessica's gaze rebounded to his face in time to see amber burst into flame, his face transforming into the rictus of a desert djinn about to unleash Hell. The voice that resonated in her head was raw with fury. *They won't get to you. I swear it.*

"Your fight is with me," Mason stated, now ignoring Trenton, instead moving his gaze over all the rest. "Take me down, *children*, and all the opulence you see is yours. Enough to bloat parasites like you." He bared his fangs. "But you have to kill me to get to it."

"Actually, your fight is with all of us."

Trenton spun around. Danny stepped out of the shadows from

the open ballroom doors. She held a saber in either hand, the blades catching the flash of the outdoor sconces. Dev was at her side, wearing a brace of pistols, as well as an impressive array of daggers and wooden stakes. He had a shotgun leveled on his shoulder, the green eyes that had smiled at Jessica at breakfast now cold and steady.

"And he's right, Mason," she added. "The Council *doesn't* like you. You really need to work on those people skills."

"This isn't your fight." Mason kept his unsettling gaze on the vampires holding crossbows, the menace in his voice unmistakable.

"Damn right it isn't. Doesn't mean I'm not a part of it now." She flicked her attention at Trenton, catching him in a glance toward the upper level. "Took care of those crossbow snipers behind the widow's peaks. Dev's very handy with a knife. Not to mention your servants are slow."

Jessica noticed several of Dev's blades were bloodstained, as Danny offered a chilling smile. "You shouldn't ever use first-marked servants for an attack." Her blue eyes glinted with a tinge of red, revealing a hint of the formidable Region Master that Mason suggested she was. "No way for them to tell you they're dead, or under attack. If you want Mason's land, have the balls to fight him like a vampire, not a fucking human hunter."

Trenton tightened his lips in fury. As the invaders shifted, muttered, Danny looked toward Mason, saluted him with the right blade. Then she was in motion.

Go into the house. As Danny charged and the shotgun roared its first report, Jess heard the uncompromising command in her mind. Mason sprang forward with the blond vampire, both faster than she could follow. The two crossbow holders fired, but Jessica saw instantly that the weapons were only effective if the vampire was immobile or caught unawares in the sights. Both arrows went wide, and in that blink of time, Mason and Danny were among them.

The first crossbow holder, the one who'd taken the shot at Jessica, was Silas, Trenton's closest crony. He attempted to meet Mason's charge and was knocked down like a sapling, Mason taking him to the stone tile. Her brain locked up, everything in her freezing as Mason plunged his fist through the chest cavity and came back with the heart, flinging it away and snapping Silas's neck in almost the same motion. Springing up, he left him in his death throes to meet the rush of two more.

The crossbow of the second vampire skidded across the tiles as Danny knocked his arm up with her guard and then skewered him, bringing up her booted foot to shove him off her blade. She smoothly sidestepped as Dev's knife sliced through the air above her shoulder and lodged in the throat of one of the human servants. By good fortune it was the servant of Mason's next opponent. The vampire stumbled, gripped by the brief paralysis that afflicted younger vampires when their servants were killed. That moment sealed his fate, and another heart hit the tiles with a sickening splat.

Jessica screamed, startled out of her shock, when the seven from below scaled up the walls and joined the fight, but none paid any attention to Jessica. As Mason had accurately stated, they wanted the property more than they wanted Trenton's vengeance. If they took him down, they got them both, and he was far more of a threat to them than a girl cowering against the railings.

Despite their greater experience, Danny and Mason were now vastly outnumbered. Jessica jerked herself out of her stupor. Seizing the abandoned crossbow, she scrambled away from the fight.

Mason, locked in combat with another vampire, caught the flash of a stake coming down and swung to the side, knocking his vampire opponent into the human servant who'd made the attempt. Dev was suddenly there, sweeping the man's legs as he brought the butt of his shotgun down on the skull, crushing it and ducking aside as Danny swept by with her dual swords, a spinning, graceful dance Mason knew even Amara would have envied.

Mason yanked one of Dev's stakes out of his improvised baldric as he passed, and jammed it into the chest cavity of his third victim. As he bent to yank it free, reuse it, an arrow whizzed over his head. He spun in time to see one of two vampires rushing his back fall to the ground, the arrow lodged in the heart cavity.

He ducked the rush of the second one, seized him about the waist and brought him down on his knee, breaking his spine like kindling. He flipped the stake and used it again, then sprang to his feet, backtracking the path of the arrow.

Jessica had made it to the opening to the ballroom, but not to hide, as he'd ordered her. As he watched, she reloaded the crossbow with remarkable speed, but he wasn't interested in her impressive weapons training or marksmanship.

Jessica, get under cover. Now.

Trenton had vanished, and Mason didn't like not knowing where he was. Plus, while the vampires were focused on him, if she kept firing at them, they would decide she needed to be handled on her own merit. *Damn it, Jessica—*

As she shouldered it to take aim again, he swore. "They never listen."

"Tell me about it," Danny grunted, lunging past him. Her blade slashed, spraying them both with blood as she disemboweled the screaming vampire. Close behind them, he heard the report of one of Dev's pistols.

Mason flung himself at two more coming at him, a vampire with a mallet, his human with a mace. When he knocked the mallet loose, he caught the mace's chain, swinging the servant toward the ballroom. Jessica's next arrow went through his back, so Mason could spin around and crack the vampire's neck.

Danny and Dev had been fighting in a rotating, loose back-to-back triangle with him, so Danny finished off the vamp with a decapitation strike. Mason pivoted around, seeking Jessica again. In that moment, everything slowed and stopped, for he found Trenton. And Trenton found Jessica.

The vampire leaped from the recesses of the ballroom when her head was down to reload. She cried out when he seized her about the waist, knocked the bow from her hands and threw her up against the outside wall with bone-crushing force.

If rage alone could have killed Trenton, he would have been dead. But it wouldn't, and she was a human going toe-to-toe with a vampire. She made a futile attempt to bring up the arrow she still had clutched in her hand. Mason moved faster than he'd ever moved before, but Trenton plunged the steel spike into her chest just as his hand reached the vampire's shoulder.

A hoarse scream erupted from her throat. It wrenched in Mason's vitals, the threat of an impending severed connection between him and his servant. A mortal blow. He stumbled into Trenton, but still managed to slam him forward, take him through the outer brick and inner Sheetrock of the ballroom wall. It was enough to knock his opponent insensible, but Mason wasted no time beyond putting him down to scramble to her side.

It was fortunate no one was in his path, for he couldn't tell friend from foe. Everything was an obstacle between him and Jess.

Danny and Dev fell back to flank him then, putting the ballroom at their backs as he went to one knee by her. Allah, be merciful, she was soaked in blood, her body jerking, her eyes unfocused. Death throes. He could feel it in his own marrow, in the strangled pounding of his heart. The remaining vampires and humans were closing in, decimated but still greater in number than their small force, particularly now that only Danny and Dev were able to engage.

Run . . . Jessica's eyes focused on him, struggling to hold his gaze. Her voice in his head was faint. *It's senseless for us to both die. Meant to be. Can't go back to my world. Can't . . . stay in yours. Proof . . . should have died . . . in tomb.*

Habiba, *you go nowhere without my permission. We go together or not at all.* Picking up the pike that had gone through her chest, he drove the sharpened end into his own. She gasped, strangling on a cough. His lips curled back at the agonizing pain, the sudden gush of heart's blood, the richest blood a vampire could offer to a servant. Urgency taking precedence over care, he gripped the back of her neck and brought her mouth there, flooding her mind with his voice, his demand.

Drink, habiba. *We will argue about this later, but you* must *live.*

He repeated it, holding her close against his chest as her mouth moved awkwardly against him. Inserting his fingers between them to guide the flow of blood, he brought her lips to the place the blood was flowing most strongly. Her hand gripped his arm, a silent answer to his strong emotion. Dizziness took him. He knew he should be helping Danny and Dev, that if they lost ground, they were all lost. But if he left her now, she would die.

I refuse to live without her. She is my third-marked servant. A servant follows her Master into eternity. She is afraid of the dark, and I won't let her be alone in the dark.

He was lost in such thoughts, pleas, prayers or threats, he didn't know which. It took a battle cry, thunderously deeper than the rest of the battle noises, to return him to the present. Lifting his head, he blinked hazily to see two vampires spinning away from the back of the attacking group, their clothes and flesh on fire. It was an Irish war cry that had heralded Jacob, brandishing two torches. He staked another vampire with one of them in a swift move that exploded fire out the vampire's back. Then he was darting forward, cutting a swath through the now confused group.

He was shouting. "Fall back! Duck down and—"

Abandoning gestures or words, he dropped the remaining torch, caught Danny and Dev's arms and plowed forward, bringing them down over Mason and Jessica, their three bodies shielding the two wounded as the world erupted behind Jacob's broad shoulders.

Mason, with his back to the wall, holding Jessica fast against him, saw the remaining vampires spin around, warned by Jacob's yell, only to confront a puzzling nothingness. A nothingness that exploded with a lethal percussion. Abruptly, seven remaining vampires and a handful of human servants were jerking, convulsing like dolls being shaken violently. Only their feet remained rooted to the ground, an appropriate choice of words, Mason realized, given what erupted from their bodies.

Branches speared out of their arms, the main leader shooting out from their wrists, obliterating hands in horrifying expulsions of flesh and blood. Vegetation bloomed, fresh and green from the branches, spattered with blood as smaller branches erupted from the soft tissue orifices of the eyes, noses and ears. Skin sprouted bark, and heads disappeared in the enclosure of thick trunks that shot up from the ground. Limbs broke and shattered as flowers and fruit bloomed. The feet expanded into fully mature root systems, cracking the marble tile like sharp gunshots. The verandah rumbled ominously.

Jacob cursed and pressed them back into the ballroom. The three helped shift Mason, since he could not move without releasing Jess, and blood loss was leaving him weak, so weak he felt disoriented. If not for the reaction of the others, he would have been unsure if the fantastic scenario occurring before him was happening or if he was slipping into a blood-drained hallucination. Half of the wide verandah area gave way under the weight of the new forest, still thickening and expanding. As tile, plaster, wood and brick crashed with a deafening cacophony to the lawn below, the trees held their position along the slope of concrete and marble. The rubble evolved into a hill as lush grass and runners of white morning glories overran it. Expansive jasmine bushes filled in the spaces, perfuming the air, mixing with the scent of blood in Mason's nose.

Jessica had lost consciousness against him. He didn't know if she'd drunk enough. But her heart still beat, faintly, and her wound was closing under his hand, pressed against her sternum and curve of small breast. *Please, Allah, let it mean she'll be all right.*

He was aware of someone trying to lift Jessica from him. He growled, not sure who the blond woman was.

"We need to help, Lord Mason. Jacob, help me. He's lost too much blood. I can't get him to let her go—"

Mason hissed at the male vampire, who had blue eyes that seemed familiar, but he was male, and he wasn't touching her. He was tired. If they'd let him alone, let him lie down with her in this cool marble place. A tomb. He'd wanted to die in someone's tomb . . . her tomb? The woman he was holding. Jessica.

"Look, Mason. Lyssa. Lyssa's coming. Jacob, hold on a minute. If he fights you, we'll lose him . . ."

Vague impressions. He wasn't lost. This was a garden. His garden. There was a new garden in his backyard. No verandah, though. Damn it, if he was facing construction again, he was obviously dead and in Hell.

No, he couldn't be in Hell. This was Eden. There were even two large trees in the middle, leading down to a grove of quite a few more. The biblical story, the tree of life and the tree of the knowledge of good and evil. One permitted ignorant bliss, the other gave sorrow and pain. By Allah's mercy, he knew what choice Jessica needed to make. No one who had a heart like hers, permeated with love and goodness, deserved the curse of knowledge, all its agony.

Out of that garden, a naked woman came, as if she were Eve herself. Only instead of walking with shame, she walked as if she should be nibbling the forbidden apple, the serpent twined intimately around her.

The haze cleared, for he knew her. Lyssa. Her jade eyes flamed in the aftermath of their battle, the power she'd commanded still arcing off her like stray bursts of lightning.

The blue-eyed vampire—Jacob, Mason remembered now—straightened from his tense crouch near Mason. Danny called out urgently. "Lyssa, he needs your help." Somehow, her fingers were on him, pressing on his heart, stopping the flow of blood completely. He tried to shrug away, because that was for Jessica, if Jessica needed more, but he could barely move. He felt cold and sluggish. When they eased him down to the ground, they let him keep the slight body in his arms, so he allowed it. He couldn't let his guard down, though, couldn't slip away. He tightened his grip on Jessica further.

Lyssa crouched over him, her attention on the wound, but she glanced at Danny. "Our son?"

"Safe. In the barn, with Mason's head groom. When this all started, I took Kane to him. Jorge was ready to slip out unnoticed into the forest if things had gone badly. I'll go check on him now."

The blond vampire rose. She'd held on to one of her sabers, but Mason remembered now that she'd pinned one vampire to the ground with the other. He saw her gingerly tug the weapon from the clutches of a new bush dotted with red flowers, giving it a bemused look. Lyssa's fingers probed his wound, and it hurt.

"Oh, Mason," she murmured. "What did you do to yourself? You may have killed both of you, trying to save her."

"The weapon was steel," Jacob said, his blue eyes concerned.

"Thank the heavens it wasn't wood. *Mason.*" Lyssa's tone became firm, unyielding, and her hand cradled his face, making him focus on her relentless gaze. "If you want to save Jessica, you must let her go. Right now."

Yes, she was right. He knew that. But he'd also thought something else . . . What was it? That he didn't want to be left alone again. He couldn't bear it.

But she needed him to let go. It was best for her. So he did, despite the fact it made his heart hurt even worse, and not from blood loss. When Jacob and Dev eased Jessica back, he turned his head and watched Lyssa kneel between them. Using one of Dev's knives, Lyssa opened the artery at her own throat and brought it to Mason's mouth, cupping her hand behind his head. Jacob steadied her, holding her shoulders as she brought the rich taste of her blood to his lips.

With that first swallow, her hair fell forward, brushing his jaw. He was glad for it, because as he looked at Jessica's pale, unconscious face through the curtain of it, he didn't want to shame himself with the tears that were trying to fall. Perhaps it was all right. Jessica would take Brian's serum and the third mark would be erased. Then he could die without harming her. He could go to Farida's tomb. It wasn't Jessica who was supposed to die there. It was him. His time had been over for a long while. Allah, he didn't even know how to use a cell phone or computer, couldn't care less about learning. He'd thought a remote location, a forest and an ocean would keep interlopers out of his home, in a world of fast powerboats and GPS.

You will not die. Lyssa's voice. *Jessica needs you. Will you let her go so easily? Will you leave her unprotected in the world, no matter what she chooses?*

No. He would never leave her unprotected. He'd promised. It didn't matter whether Jessica took the serum or not, knew of his existence or not. He would always be near to protect her. Make sure she found the happiness she deserved.

And you can *learn to use a damn computer.*

31

DEV looked down the slope of the lush, tangled, wild ravine, to the untamed garden that had spilled out below it, bumping up against the more manicured landscaping. He cocked a brow at Jacob, sitting next to him on a pile of rock they'd adapted into a rudimentary bench outside the ballroom. "I'm thinking this verandah was never meant to be. Second time in recent history it's been blasted."

The corner of Jacob's mouth tugged up as he took a swallow of his beer. "As Lord Brian said—once they find their power, the Fey can kick vampire ass any day of the week."

"Hmm." Dev sobered, gave him a thoughtful look. "You know, Mason's still pissed at us for leaving Kane with Jorge like that. Told us we should have run off, gotten him to safety. You and Lyssa haven't said that, but still, I'm sorry if we made the wrong decision."

"No." Jacob lowered his beer and put a hand on his friend's shoulder. "I trust your instincts, Dev. You wouldn't have left him there if it wasn't the best decision. Without you and Danny, Mason would have been overwhelmed before we returned. Even though Trenton didn't know you were here, how long do you think it would have taken them to discover the scent of a vampire infant and track you? What you did was the best choice for risky odds, for all of us. And Kane."

"Well, truth is, Danny tried to get me to leave with Jorge. Got

pretty ugly, except we ran out of time to fight about it." Dev pressed
his lips together. "And yeah, I can say I did it because it was the best
decision, but—"

Jacob finished it for him, locking with his gaze in perfect accord.
"You wouldn't leave her. Just because you can't leave her side doesn't
make it any less the right decision. No worries, mate." Imitating Dev's
broad accent, he tapped his bottle against the human servant's.

The Aussie nodded, his shoulders easing. When he glanced down,
he saw a small female figure appear on the left corner of the old garden area, near the horse sculpture. She sank down on the fountain's
edge, reaching out to the spray. "Do you think she feels that way
about Mason?"

"I don't know." Jacob frowned. "But I have a feeling we'll soon
find out. He received the third-mark removal treatment from Brian
two days ago."

~

The return of the full staff several days earlier had been a relief, because it was the first time she and Lyssa were able to convince Mason
to retire to his rooms and seek a truly deep, restful sleep, one he desperately needed. While technically he couldn't have died from a
metal stake, the wound had been serious enough that he was still
paler than Jess would expect even a vampire to be. Her chest had
healed as it should, thanks to him, but that too had been a near
thing. She was better off than Mason, but she still had unsteady moments if she worked out too hard or spent too long in the stables,
pushing herself in an attempt to manage her worry about Mason.

It was an unpleasant echo of the many months she'd fought off
that near-death feeling in her search for Farida's tomb. She'd lived
on the edge of uncertainty, or certain tragedy, for far too long.

When he'd finally agreed to take that full day's rest, she'd gone
with him. After his tense grip on her waist at last eased, she studied
his face for a long time, tracing his straight nose, firm lips, the eye-
brows and soft strands of hair over his forehead. When she finally
slipped away, it wasn't because she wanted to leave his embrace, the
reassurance of his very much alive, powerful frame. She needed to
think.

Before he'd slept, his silence, the long, steady looks where he'd gazed on her face as if he was preparing never to see her again, had disturbed her. But he would speak of nothing, and gently shushed her if she tried to voice her own thoughts. He told her he was simply weary. But she knew it was bullshit. She longed to hear the endearment in her mind, *habiba*. Or some encouraging or even infuriating comment, a seductive suggestion or romantic observation that would melt her insides.

But there'd been only one moment he'd been open to her since the fight on his property, and that moment had been neither seductive nor romantic.

~

They'd chained Trenton up in the dungeon she'd feared, Jacob and Lyssa wrapping him in chains and suspending him, ensuring he'd be in nearly unbearable discomfort for the two days that passed before Mason was recovered enough to decide his fate.

He'd brought Jessica with him down the spiral staircase. Jacob came as well, a silent, dangerous presence at their backs. She suspected they'd all wanted to come, all worried about Mason's paleness, but his pride would brook only Jacob coming along, and only because Lyssa pointed out it was additional protection for Jess if anything went awry.

They had Trenton gagged. Lyssa had definitely not been kind, Jess saw with a wince. The gag she'd used was the spiked ball of a small mace, the sharpened steel prongs piercing his cheeks and lips so they poked out of his blood-encrusted face. Jessica had swayed at the sight of him, and Mason's arm went around her.

I don't want to be here, my lord.

I know. We won't be here long. He released the lever that kept Trenton suspended and the vampire hit the stone floor with a muffled cry, his frightened, pain-filled eyes rolling. Mason shoved him to his back with his foot, held his boot on Trenton's throat to keep him from thrashing. When he extended a hand, Jacob put a wooden stake in it. Then, meeting Jessica's eyes, Mason put the stake in her palm, closing her fingers on it.

Jess stared at it, curled her fingers around the wood. When she lifted her gaze to Mason's face, she saw something dark and deadly lay there. She couldn't deny something that matched it stirred in her own breast, when she looked back down at the creature who had stood by and laughed at her pain and fear. Trenton's attention darted back and forth between them. Jessica swallowed. What Mason was offering her was an act that violated Council law.

"He is yours, *habiba*."

She swallowed, felt Mason's arm come around her, the gentle hand passing down her back at odds with the violent situation, the stench of fear and death that hung over them all. *What if I want to let him go?*

Mason tipped her chin, studied her eyes. He understood, she knew he did, for he could see everything in her mind. She also saw the restless violence in him, his rage at what Trenton had done to her.

Without his moral compass, there is no deadlier vampire than Lord Mason . . .

His thumb touched her lip. *We cannot do it, Jessica. He knows too much about Lyssa, and perhaps even Danny and Dev.*

She considered that, ignoring the fearful, strangled whimpers under Mason's foot, Jacob's tactical shift to be in a better position if needed.

All right, then. Giving him a nod, and gripping the stake, she squatted next to Trenton, aware of the other two males tensing, despite the fact Trenton was trussed so securely. Mason's low voice was sibilant in the shrouded gloom of the dungeon, running a chill even up her spine. If Trenton wasn't a vampire, she was sure he would have pissed himself.

"You have a choice. She will stake you as you lie, and you can meet your fate, but if you so much as twitch, try to harm her in any way, I will put you through everything you did to her, twice."

Trenton's pain-crazed eyes went from Mason back to her. There was pleading there, of course, a mindless fear, but she saw the contemptuous savagery behind it as well. No, it wasn't the nature of every vampire. But some natures didn't change. Nor had hers, not as much as she'd thought. And she loved the vampire next to her too well to unbalance his.

Rising, she handed Mason the stake, closing his fingers on it.

This time she spoke aloud. "Show him what he never showed me. Let his end be merciful and quick, and let's have it done. Please. We have enough ghosts haunting us."

After a long moment, he nodded, those deadly shadows replaced by something else. A soul-deep yearning, as if he might want to clasp her hand on the stake tighter, tight enough to fuse them together. Then, his gaze becoming unreadable again, he released her and turned to do her will.

~

Men weren't supposed to be this bloody complicated. Sitting on the fountain's edge, Jessica scowled up the hill at one of the new fruit trees. She preferred not to think of their origins, and in truth, they were one of the loveliest groves of trees, with their graceful shapes and mature forms, than any she'd ever seen. Like a grove straight from a fairy world, she thought ironically, even as she wondered how the delicate pear tree would do here, exposed to salt-laden winds. It seemed to be thriving for now.

Lyssa's efforts on their behalf fairly pulsed with Fey power. Jacob had indicated when they returned to their mountain home in the States, they would consult the Fey there, to determine if the forest needed to be dissolved or could stand as it was, a beacon of powerful protection for the estate, built on the blood and bones of vampires and their human minions.

She shivered at that thought. If Mason had been overwhelmed, she would have been at their mercy for God knew how long before they killed her. Or, since most hadn't cared for Trenton's cause, but Mason's wealth, she might have ended up servant to one of them, even while her mind and body were still possessed by Mason. They would have chained him in his own dungeon, where her torment would have driven him mad, same as with Farida.

Lyssa and Mason thought this was the end of it, though. Trenton and his friends, all now fertilizer or vegetation, had been Raithe's most active supporters. The other hard-core dissenters disagreed with pardoning a human servant who had killed her Master. They had no personal issue worth coming after her, particularly if it was clear she was contained by Mason's third mark and protection.

If she took Brian's potion and had no memory of any of it, it was even less likely to become an issue. The medical supply case containing the three vials now sat on her nightstand, the physical evidence of the decision to be made. She recalled Enrique's words when he brought it to her.

Lord Mason reminds you that it is your decision to make. While he does not wish to hasten you, he thinks it would be wise to choose within the next week or so. We will need to move you to your new location before you take the serum, of course.

Jessica had nodded, but she remembered Amara's face, as the woman stood at her door. She'd had a light sheen of tears, but when she went to her, Amara shook her head. "You know my mind, Jessica. But Enrique and Mason, they've always been right. What's best is what will make you happy. If you go, I will miss you, though. We all will."

She'd studied those three vials of emerald green liquid, held them in her hands and felt the heat from them, portents of the magical as well as scientific miracle they contained. Three vials, to remove three marks. The ultimate soul cleaner for a human servant.

As she rose from the fountain and walked between Mason's garden and Lyssa's, she didn't think about that, though. She listened to the song of the ocean, and wondered why he wouldn't talk to her.

~

Near dusk, Mason stood at the window, but not in his study. There was a little-used room on the top level of the estate, in one of the turrets. The small room was big enough for ocean viewing, furnished with only two chairs. He rarely came up here, for sometimes the sight of all the vastness of the ocean and sky, while sequestered in the silent room, made him feel oddly isolated. But he wanted to see her, without her knowing she was being watched. She'd spent most of the day in the garden, according to Enrique, pacing back and forth as she was doing now in the evening light. Her arms were wrapped across her midriff, a feminine sign of defensive uncertainty and deep thought at once.

He loved her. He'd known he cared deeply about her, but in that key moment, when he'd seen Trenton attack her, he had felt her panic give way to a rush of fury, he'd heard the curse go through her mind—*never again, you worthless son of a bitch*—and he'd known he loved her.

It was so fast, but a universe could be blinked into existence, couldn't it? And in that blink, he knew he loved her as much as Farida, perhaps more in some ways. Not because Farida had been lacking, but because of who he'd become since then. He knew how to love more deeply, more painfully, because of what he'd learned since.

When she was dying, he'd felt it in every part of himself. At this age, a servant's death was more of an emotional impact than a physical one, but perhaps he had given her all that he was, matter as well as spirit.

If he was ever lucky enough to win Jessica's love, her absolute trust, that courageous heart of hers would never doubt him. He'd dedicate himself to it. Even if their minds were separated, as his and Farida's had been, even if all the forces of Hell severed the connections between heart, body and soul, she would know his heart was hers, and that he would never abandon her. Some things were beyond the reaches of Hell.

He realized he was no longer alone. "You've left a formidable challenge for my gardening staff," he observed. "It looks like a prehistoric forest down there."

"Since Gideon's attack, your incessant whining about your destroyed rosebushes had become annoying. I was merely trying to help." Lyssa sat down, crossed her legs. "If I were you, I'd stop worrying about your hedges and work harder on your security. A dozen fledglings crept up in your backyard and practically staked you. It would have been mortifying if they'd succeeded."

"At one time, the rain forest and ocean served as very effective deterrents." He frowned out the window. "But you're right. It's a different world now. It's time for me to return to the desert, let Amara and Enrique move into a safer location. Perhaps Cairo."

"Hmm. What's that?" Lyssa glanced at the book he'd left in the seat of one of the chairs.

"One of Farida's journals. I was looking for something in it."

"Oh." Lyssa was as capable of reading his thoughts as he was hers, since a blood exchange had happened several times in their history. But she entered his mind with a courteous warning touch, making sure he preferred that she read it there rather than wait for it from his lips. He gave her both.

"I didn't find it. It wasn't there. Not in either one of them."

That first night he'd taken Jessica's body, he remembered what he'd told her. *I kiss your mouth, your breasts, worship every inch of you even as I declare you mine, the way my heart and soul and breath are mine . . .*

But it was her reply that had stuck in his mind. *I am yours, my lord. In all ways. I have no fear of it.*

Because of the circumstances, he'd been certain she'd adopted words from Farida's journal, her broken mind meshing with the dead woman's writings. He'd been wrong.

"So the words were Farida's, and yet hers as well. The same words, from her own heart." Lyssa was quiet a moment. "It's problematic, feeling so much for your servant, isn't it?"

He glanced at the vampire queen, pulled himself reluctantly out of his thoughts. "I certainly hope you're not going to lecture *me* about giving inappropriate weight to our relationship, considering all you did to keep Jacob at your side."

"No. I'm simply reminding you of our reality. You're absolutely right. The best thing is for her to no longer be here, no longer be part of you. Though vampires tend to be a little more concerned about what's best for ourselves, particularly when it concerns our human servants."

"Your opinion of our kind is almost as high as mine, my lady." Leaning an arm against the glass, he stared down at the slim woman who'd now been joined by Amara. His servant's wife slid an arm around the younger woman, support and encouragement. Fondness.

He could feel her struggle, her confusion with her choice. Some part of him wanted to jump in, urge her to delay. Take more than a week. Take a month, a year . . . a hundred years to decide. The serum had no shelf life, after all. But how much more would he feel for her in a week, a month, those hundred years? He could barely contemplate her leaving now, her memory being erased. He knew he would stay close for however many years her mortality gave her, but if he passed her one night on the street, she might glance at him as she would any handsome stranger, but that was all. He'd no longer hear her thoughts, or be able to speak into hers.

He'd had that connection with Amara and Enrique for so many years. It was a comfort when he availed himself of it, but he'd forgotten what it was like when the human servant was a true bond, a link pierced into the soul, binding them together.

"Of course, it's only the right decision if no other factors outweigh it."

"What?" Irritated, he looked over his shoulder at her.

Lyssa raised a brow. "I'm sorry. I didn't mean to interrupt your brooding. Goddess, are you so determined to be miserable, Mason? Why not go after what you want? You want her to stay. Tell her."

"But it's best for her—"

"Is it? I've seen the way she reacts to you. Yes, she was treated horribly by Raithe. What if she'd never been part of our world? What if, instead, she'd been kidnapped and brutalized by one of her own kind, her fiancé killed by human savagery? Would you say the best thing for her was to be cloistered away like a nun?"

"You know it's different, Lyssa. How can she ever be safe in this world, with her past?"

"Because you will be her Master."

"I was Farida's Master."

"And there, at last, is the crux of it." Lyssa rose then, moving to the window to face him. "You think I don't wake from nightmares, trembling in fear for what could happen to Kane? You think I don't know how my many enemies would love to get their hands on him?"

Mason immediately straightened, a dangerous scowl on his face. "Let them try. Whoever you and Jacob don't tear from limb to limb, I would finish off."

"Exactly. You are willing to fight for my son's right to live safely, embracing his full potential. Why are you not willing to fight for your right to Jessica? We are different from humans, Mason. When we possess a servant, truly, rightly, *not* like Raithe, we know, deep down, they belong to us."

Her eyes glowed with sudden fierceness. "A vampire and servant's relationship is never going to be on the same footing as two humans or two vampires. It is different, because the species are different. But in certain circumstances, those differences mesh in an undeniable way. There are plenty of servant relationships like yours with Amara and Enrique. Love, pleasure, service. Appropriate, clearly defined. An accepted sense of place. But there are some, like yours and Jessica's, that go beyond that. It is the unspoken thing all of us know.

"Think of it this way as well. If you let her go as a purportedly selfless act, then you are denying not only yourself." She nodded toward the gardens. "That woman survived the unthinkable with indomitable courage, an unmatched will to live. I suspect she is prepared to love the man who wins her heart just as courageously." Her eyes softened on him, her hand going to his face. "Honor that courage."

"But what if she chooses me, and regrets it?"

Lyssa stroked a finger down his jawline, then scraped him, none too gently, with one of her sharp nails, earning a narrow look from him. "Make sure she doesn't have a reason to regret it. Idiot."

Brushing a brief kiss over his mouth, she nodded to him, once, and then left him alone. Mason watched her go, nonplussed, then looked out the window again. The garden was empty. Searching his mind, he found her location, but even as he did, her mind reached for his.

My lord, I need you. Please come to me?

~

She was in his upper-level study. Interestingly, she was engaged in mundane work, stacking up some of his scattered files, setting them on the credenza, arranging a tiny spray of new Fey-conjured flowers beside his pen set. "You know, if you'd keep these things in some kind of order, you'd actually know what bills need to be paid."

"I have my own system," he defended, caught off guard when she glanced up with a soft smile. His throat thickened with an ache he couldn't swallow.

"You, my lord, have no system at all. When it comes to paperwork, you are a master of chaos."

He wanted to kiss that smile, but instead he moved into the room, taking a seat behind the desk. Purposefully, he kept himself out of her mind now. He knew her request wasn't idle, as much as he realized with dread why she'd called him. "You've made your decision."

"I have, my lord. I'm waiting for yours."

Brow furrowing, he studied her. "I don't understand your meaning."

"What do *you* want, my lord? You've barely spoken to me, barely touched my mind since Trenton nearly killed us both." She drew a breath. "And I find I need the intimate touch of your thoughts in my mind, even more than I need your hands on my body. Though I would prefer both," she added crossly.

Her words stirred him on every level, but he struggled to hold the reins. "A servant can't make demands on her Master, Jessica. You know that. There are times a servant cannot know her Master's mind. That's the way of it." He would not cave. He wouldn't try to coax or cajole, seduce or romance. Even though he knew how to make her knees weak, her heart pound. Knew what romantic gestures would soften her.

Damn it, she'd made her decision. As a matter of honor, he wouldn't sway it.

"I see." She pursed her lips, nodded and moved to the French doors. Pushing them open to get the night breeze, she drew in a deep, steadying breath. "You, my lord, are being . . ." Her voice drifted off, as if she were seeking the right words. Spreading her fingers, she laid them on the side table, on top of a bronze horse.

The rush of her temper was a blast of heat that alerted him. He leaped into her mind in instinctive self-preservation as she picked up the sculpture and hurled it at his head with all the strength her muscles possessed. Since she was a third-mark, that meant she could put it through the wall. Or his skull.

He caught it in time to keep it from breaking, only to discover that had simply been a ruse, as she launched a much more replaceable but still rather costly vase on the same path. Despite his speed, he barely ducked it, and it hit the wall with a resounding shatter.

She was going for a torpedo sequence now, with pillar candles snatched out of the candelabra on the wall. He wouldn't put it past her to rip the metal holder from the wall and try to pin him to the wall with the five sharp prongs. Fortunately, by that time, he'd put down the horse and flashed across the room, seizing her by the waist. Pinning her up against the wall with himself, he was immediately conquered by the lean strength and soft curves, the immediacy of her perfume, the softness of her snarling lips.

She bit him. He slammed her wrists to the wall on either side as he kept kissing her, forcing his way into her mouth until she yielded with a soft sigh, coiling her legs around him.

Jessica felt his desire surge over hers, like a dam swollen by storm, cooling the burning ache of her fears. She strained against him, rubbing his body in blatant invitation, but she wasn't yet forgiven, her mouth still being plundered, her Master seeking her surrender.

Promise me forever, my lord, and I will be yours. I am *yours.*

He broke away then, pressing his forehead on hers. "Jessica, damn it, this isn't the life you want. It doesn't matter . . . I *want* you to feel the way you feel about me, but it serves no purpose. I want you," he repeated and closed his eyes, unable to bear looking into her gray eyes, see what he couldn't have. "If that is the torture you have devised for me to be left with, I accept it. I've never wanted anything more."

She slid one hand free, threaded it through his hair, cupped the back of his skull, her thumb teasing the artery in his neck. "My lord, you didn't admire the flowers I brought for your desk."

Mason shook his head. "They're lovely. But—"

Jessica snapped her teeth perilously close to his ear and he jerked back. *Look at them.*

Mason, impatient, shot a look across the room, then took another, closer look.

"I made my decision, my lord. That is my answer."

She'd taken the rack of three vials containing the bright green liquid of Brian's serum and poured it out. Filled them with clear water instead, to hydrate the flowers she'd cut from Lyssa's garden.

Slowly, he let her down. Her hand stayed on his arm, though, as he turned in that direction. Jessica watched his usually so unreadable face. The emotions struggling there were so harsh, her heart ached. She'd thought he'd closed himself off to her, but she realized now it was only to shield her from the turmoil that was going on in his own mind, trying not to sway her decision. In this unguarded moment, all she had to do was look at his face to know the deepest shadows of his mind.

But perhaps she'd known them all along. The heart's blood with which he'd nourished her, demanding that both live or neither, had fused them even more closely together. The possible need to separate herself from his world was nothing next to the pain of leaving him alone. Of hurting him. It was something she couldn't bear, even if staying at his side was ultimately what destroyed her. Until it did, it would also be her salvation.

He turned toward her then, and she saw he heard her thoughts. She could also tell he was trying to determine if he could honorably accept her decision. Her old-fashioned vampire. Tears threatened, but for the first time in a long time, they were the good kind.

"You've shushed me for the past few days," she said quietly. "But hear my words now, my lord. Please."

When at last he nodded, she moved into him, folded her hands on his chest. A faint tremor ran through his body, and she saw his hands close into fists as he struggled not to touch her. She raised her attention to his face. "I fought for so long, Mason, so hard. At a certain point, I knew it was hopeless. Training myself to fight, continuing to resist him, it all meant nothing. I gave up on God then, because Raithe even took away the choice of death.

"But I kept resisting, because it became about me, who I am. So after he was gone, there was this void of nothingness. I'd made it all about that fight, and I'd cannibalized every last bit of myself to keep one last spark. But you . . . you stepped into that void. Maybe in some perfect world, or according to nine out of ten therapists"—a soft smile touched her face—"it would make sense for me to go out into the big wide world and reclaim myself. But I'm not that Jessica anymore. She's gone. And despite all these horrible things that happened to me, I look at you, and I don't regret what I endured. Nothing but Jack. It's in the past."

She held his gaze, let him see it, go as deep as he wished to be sure. "I don't need to reclaim the Jessica I was, because the Jessica I am now wants you. And she worked too hard, fought too long, sacrificed too much of herself, for me to deny her that prize because of regrets and wishes, for what could have been."

She drew a breath. "You told me there is a difference between forced servitude and willing submission. I willingly submit to you. I want to belong to you."

In the fateful, weighted seconds that ticked between them then, she remembered watching him cross the courtyard to come to the study, responding to her call. Everything, from the way the light shirt blew against his body, to the stretch of his riding breeches on his thighs, and the long boots, the severe line of his aristocratic face, the perfect silk of his tied-back hair, had stirred her. But what held her mesmerized was more than the beautiful body and face.

As she'd watched him from the shield of the window's curtain, she'd spoken the words aloud. "I'll take care of him," she whispered. A message to the woman who'd loved him so well, so long ago, as if they were touching hands over the centuries, a tactile oath. "I'll make sure he has that home."

Whether she'd been sent by Farida or it was all her own desire, it didn't matter. A soul could be many different individuals, as she'd become many different versions of herself to be the Jessica Tyson she was now. She loved him. That love was so new, with so many things to learn and discover. There'd be so many challenges to face in their conflicting worlds, she was sure she would be afraid and anxious, often. But she'd also feel eagerness, passion and love. Those emotions would grow and deepen, and help supplant the others. The roots were already anchored.

As his handsome, beloved face continued to reflect his internal war between honor and trust, love and need, she curled her hand around his forearm and dropped to her knees, pressing her forehead against his thigh. "I am yours, my lord. Your third-marked servant, by choice and desire."

Mason, overcome, turned his gaze away to those vials of flowers. Fey flowers, enchanted so they likely wouldn't die, not as long as Lyssa lived. A reminder of this moment, of what Jessica had chosen for herself. For him.

He raised her to her feet, tipping up her chin with a hand that had an unmanly tremor, but seeing the love in her face, the curve of her lips, he knew she wouldn't point it out. "I don't know if I should accept." He cleared his throat. "An obedient servant wouldn't pelt her Master with expensive statuary."

"I will stay whether or not you accept, my lord. Just to teach you that I am more stubborn than your will." Jessica's eyes sparkled, her lips parting as his grip on her body tightened, belying his words. "Admit it, my lord. If you made me leave, you'd end up going back to the desert to brood. And without someone to defy you, your arrogance would grow as rapidly as Lady Lyssa's forest."

"Hmm. I can see that I will need to spend a great deal of time training you. Perhaps even resign my advisory position on Council."

Her eyes darkened. "When you must serve the Council, I will go with you. I belong at your side, and I'll learn to be the servant you need." Before he could speak, she shook her head. "I trust you to take care of me. You were right. It's not serving your pleasure, in whatever manner you demand, that created terror inside of me. It was how Raithe twisted my desire to serve a Master. I'll learn to trust you, my lord, if you help me."

By Allah, what have I done to deserve her? "Jessica." Mason realized he was incapable of more than her name, but that encapsulated everything he was feeling. He repeated it, a murmur, and her lips parted, though her eyes remained determined, her chin firm.

"If someone like you had been on Council, maybe Raithe couldn't have gotten away with what he did. Excesses must be controlled, my lord, and you have a fairly heavy and intimidating hand." That sparkle again, the hint of a taunt that stirred his heart as much as his groin. Particularly when, her patience with words at an end, she slipped one hand down and boldly cupped him, teasing him, though her lashes fanned her cheeks, his sweet submissive.

"*Some* excesses must be controlled," he amended with a wicked smile, catching her wrist and squeezing it, a sensual warning. Then he sighed. "It doesn't matter, anyhow. As one of the conditions for your pardon, I agreed to serve as a full Council member for the next twenty-five years. If Trenton *had* managed to kill me, Belizar would have been sure I forced his hand, merely to escape the horror of it."

Her gaze snapped up to him, face suffusing in shock. Then, her fair brow lifted, her face captured by a full, mischievous grin, more unguarded than any he'd ever seen on her face. "You should have told me that a long time ago, my lord. It would have saved me a great deal of soul-searching. How could I doubt such an enormous sacrifice? Raithe's torments were *nothing* next to that."

He was after her in a thrice, she dodging him. Snatching a pair of nunchakus from the wall, she tried to fend him off, but she was laughing too hard. He ducked under her swing, caught her arm and spun her back against him. When he divested her of the weapon and held it against her throat, the chain pressing above the silver collar he'd given her, she turned the tables on him, rotating her hips across his groin, bringing her hands back to scrape her nails up his thighs. While it appeared as if she was his prisoner, he felt like a wild beast in a cage. He'd take her on her stomach, bent over his desk, all those unprocessed bills crackling beneath her, so the vendors would wonder why their invoice stubs were so wrinkled.

The vixen. Those had been her imaginings, her thoughts.

Even as his blood stirred at her teasing, he let the nunchakus drop to the floor, his heart swelling with a different emotion. While her own heart pounded under his palm, he nudged her neck until she'd tilted her head fully, put it on his shoulder. He pierced her slow, deep, and the shuddering breath that left her was akin to a climax. Only it went from mind to heart, and even deeper.

He'd had the grace to be loved by two remarkable women, somehow combined in Jessica. She would survive Raithe's aftermath, or whatever the world threw at them. He'd make sure of it, while he had breath to protect and love her. Serve her in all ways.

Give her no regrets about her decision. She was his servant, but as he saw the love glowing in her eyes, he accepted what Lyssa had said, and what he'd always known. Some vampire-servant relationships were far more complicated.

He shifted to her mouth, covering her lips. They parted, accepting him, surrendering to his desires, his needs. So overwhelming, he anticipated that they might lead to great, pleasurable excess indeed, because he had a feeling they would never ebb.

Her arms held him closer. *Let me be your home, as you are mine.* Jessica knew her thought echoed inside of him, from the way his kiss intensified, his grip on her body growing even tighter. Her greatest fear for the future would be his loss, her only lasting regret not having more time with him, no matter how many years she was granted to live.

He lifted his head then, locked with her gaze, even as his fingers caressed her mouth, a promise.

Then, like the Sahara, may we live forever, habiba.

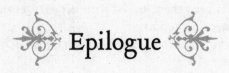

Epilogue

THE sands whispered over the desert dunes as the sky lightened, anticipating dawn. A camel made a comfortable grunt, settling herself. Mason stood at the entrance to his cave, sensing the sunrise coming. He'd laid her body down on a bed of flower petals and palm fronds, fifty feet away from the cave entrance. Fresh flowers also lay upon her, and she wore her wedding dress.

"Do you want me to go out and be with her?"

Jessica's soft question. He glanced down at her. She was growing her hair out, and it was already a silky mass past her shoulders. It waved around her petite features, as she lifted her face to meet his gaze.

He nodded. "I do . . ." His throat felt tight. "Jessica."

She squeezed his arm, shook her head. "You don't have to ex-plain, my lord. You don't want her to be alone. It would be my honor. After all," she added softly, "it was her love for you that brought us together."

With that simple statement, his servant, his love, his soul, walked out of the cave, down the slope. She wore a full robe, though she'd pushed off the head wrap. He knew every curve of the body beneath the garment, all of her scars as well as the tiger mark and tattoo, both evidence that she belonged to him. When she turned at the bottom of the slope, she sent a thought to him.

I would like to say something to Farida, my lord, but I would like it to be private.

He nodded, winning that soft smile again. She had become so much more comfortable, her confidence growing every day with their love. It thickened his throat anew, made the ache in his chest increase.

Turning away, she proceeded until she knelt by Farida's enchanted body, laying her hand on the woman's shoulder. He saw her lips move, but respected her privacy, feeling that coil in his heart tilt as she touched her lips to Farida's brow.

Right after sunset in the desert had always been his favorite time, for the heat of the sun lingered for a short time in the sand. And of course sunset heralded the freedom of the night, a new beginning.

Sunrise brought the need to sleep, endings. But now he was reminded an ending had its own peace and value. As the first ray of dawn speared over the horizon, he murmured the words that would lift the charm, that would allow Farida to become part of her beloved desert. He made himself watch, though it was difficult to see the flesh gray and wither, turn to ash, slowly disintegrating. But then she began to float away, on a wind that rose as if called by the release of the magic that had kept her preserved for three hundred years. His heart. His love. His soul. She'd sent them all back to him, in the form of the woman who lifted her face, closing her eyes and letting that ash swirl around her like a desert spirit. She spread her hands and lifted them, a devotion, and he almost imagined Farida there, caressing this woman, giving her a blessing before she became part of the desert world in the way that nature had intended.

Once it was done, Jessica rose with a look of quiet reflection and came back to him. Willingly she stepped out of the sun's embrace and into his, her arms circling his waist and back, cheek pressed to his chest as if she thought his heart was there, rather than beating inside of hers.

He didn't need to worry about sunrises or sunsets. His endings and beginnings were a circle.

This circle; her arms.